MURDER IN THE MERCHANT'S HALL

MURDER IN THE MERCHANT'S HALL

A Mistress Jaffrey Mystery

Kathy Lynn Emerson

severn
House

This first world edition published 2015
in Great Britain and the USA by
SEVERN HOUSE PUBLISHERS LTD of
19 Cedar Road, Sutton, Surrey, England, SM2 5DA.
Trade paperback edition first published 2016
in Great Britain and the USA by
SEVERN HOUSE PUBLISHERS LTD.

British Library Cataloguing in Publication Data

Emerson, Kathy Lynn author.
  Murder in the Merchant's Hall.
  1. Murder–Investigation–Fiction. 2. Walsingham,
  Francis, Sir, 1530?-1590–Fiction. 3. Great Britain–
  History–Elizabeth, 1558-1603–Fiction. 4. Detective and
  mystery stories.
  I. Title
  813.6-dc23

ISBN-13: 978-0-7278-8538-8 (cased)
ISBN-13: 978-1-84751-641-1 (trade paper)
ISBN-13: 978-1-78010-176-7 (e-book)

All Severn House titles are printed on acid-free paper.

Severn House Publishers support the Forest Stewardship Council™ [FSC™],
the leading international forest certification organisation. All our titles that
are printed on FSC certified paper carry the FSC logo.

Typeset by Palimpsest Book Production Ltd.,
Falkirk, Stirlingshire, Scotland.
Printed and bound in Great Britain by
TJ International, Padstow, Cornwall.

ONE

The quiet of London's Soper Lane on a mid-October evening in the year of our Lord fifteen hundred and eighty-three was shattered by the sound of raised voices. They came from an upper room in a tall, handsome building, the house of a mercer who sold velvets, satins, and damasks from his shop on the ground floor.

'I will not go through with the wedding!' Godlina Walkenden shrieked at her sister's husband. 'You cannot force me into the church or into his bed!'

'Lower your voice!' Hugo Hackett bellowed in return. 'Do you want the entire neighborhood to hear you?'

Although heated from the start, their quarrel had not begun with shouting. It had built in volume as tempers rose until Lina no longer cared if the whole world knew that Hugo had schemed to marry her to a monster.

'You knew all along that Alessandro Portinari was steeped in vice!'

Growling like a baited bear, Hugo sent her a look that promised retribution, but at the same time he took a step away from her. His nostrils flared as he drew in deep breaths to calm himself. The fury in his narrowed eyes would have frightened Lina had she not felt so certain that he would never dare beat her. To do so might damage her value as trade goods.

Hugo managed to lower his voice, but there was no less venom behind his words. 'Who told you these things?' he demanded. 'What wicked person put such notions into your head?'

'Someone who thought I should be warned of my danger.'

'If you mean that young jackanapes, Portinari's nephew, he—'

'I do not!' The hectic color in Hugo's face made Lina fear for Tommaso's safety. In haste, she blurted out the truth. 'It was Goody Kendall.'

This revelation further inflamed Hugo's anger. His hands clenched into fists. 'That mad old woman? What can she know? How can she say anything to Portinari's detriment?'

'She is his near neighbor in Lime Street and she has eyes in her head.' And servants who fraternized with those who worked for the rich, elderly Italian silk merchant Hugo had picked to be Lina's husband.

'Even if what she told you is true, what does it matter? This is a good match. You will reap many benefits.'

'As will you. I will not go through with the wedding,' Lina repeated, this time with less heat but just as much conviction. What did it matter that Hugo controlled her marriage portion? She would sooner starve than couple with that foul old man.

'You will do as you are told.' Hugo's voice had gone ice cold. 'If you do not, I will lock you up without food or water until you are more amenable.'

She yelped when he seized her by the upper arm. His grip tightened painfully as he hauled her up the stairs. Her howls of outrage rose in pitch, but she was powerless against his greater strength. He shoved her into her bedchamber with such force that she fell to her knees.

By the time Lina scrambled to her feet, she was locked in. She beat on the solid wooden door until her fists were bruised and swollen but to no avail. At length, she flung herself onto her bed and wept, spending half the night in tears. Only when there were no more left to fall and she was too exhausted to feel either rage or despair did the glimmer of an idea pierce her muddled thoughts.

She lay still, pondering the risks. Then she considered the alternatives and came to a decision. When she had secreted the few pieces of jewelry she owned on her person, she tied the bed sheets together to make a rope and escaped through her window.

The moment her feet touched the ground, her nerve failed. It was dark and cold in the garden behind the house. An unpleasant smell drifted toward her from the kennel where garbage was tossed. A rustle in the shrubbery reminded her that rats were everywhere in London, even wealthy neighborhoods an arrow's shot from Goldsmith's Row.

The idea of stepping out into the street terrified her. How did she think she could survive alone in the city? She'd had some vague notion of pawning the brooches and pendants and rings but whatever money she received from such a sale would not last long. She would need help to survive.

She thought of Tommaso, but he was Alessandro Portinari's nephew and lived in his uncle's house. That was the first place Hugo would look for her. And if Alessandro caught her there—

Shuddering, she shied away from what that would mean.

She could not go to any of her acquaintances in the city, either, not that she had many. Her half sister, Isolde, knew them all and would be as determined as her husband to find Lina and force her to go through with the marriage he had arranged. Isolde always did what Hugo wanted. The wishes of a much younger sibling mattered not at all.

Rosamond, Lina thought. She could ask Rosamond for help. She would know what to do. Rosamond *always* knew what to do. Sometimes it was the *wrong* thing, but she was never at a loss when it came to making plans.

Lina wondered what Rosamond would do if she were the one standing alone in a dark garden at the back of a London mercery? Rosamond would go back inside, Lina decided, not to surrender to Hugo's plans for her but to better prepare herself for an escape from the city.

The lock on the garden door yielded to the pin on the back of one of Lina's brooches, a trick Rosamond had taught her when they were no more than thirteen. Moving silently through the dark house, Lina found her way back to her own bedchamber door. Since Hugo had not bothered to take away the key, she had no trouble gaining entry.

Once inside the room, by the light of the candle she had left burning when she fled, Lina added a second layer of clothing to what she already wore and tossed her warmest cloak over the whole. She had been shivering in the garden for want of one. Then it was down to the larder to stuff bread and cheese into a cloth bag.

It was the middle of the night and no one else was stirring. Hugo and Isolde, Hugo's apprentices, and the servants were all asleep in their beds. The girls Isolde was training to be

silkwomen, all but Lina herself, went home to their parents
at night. Lina hesitated, then turned her steps in the direction
of the chamber above the kitchen that Hugo used as his
counting house.

Greatly daring, she intended to help herself to whatever was
in the cash box. She told herself it would not be stealing. She
was reclaiming what was rightfully hers. Besides, she would
be long gone before anyone discovered that both she and the
money were missing.

She stepped over the threshold, candle held high . . . and
froze. The room was not empty, as she had expected it to be.
In the flickering light of her candle, the only illumination in
the chamber, she recognized her brother-in-law seated at
his writing table. He appeared to have fallen asleep over his
ledgers.

Then she saw the knife and the blood.

Her screams woke the rest of the household.

TWO

A gentlewoman traveling from London to Leigh Abbey
in Kent customarily took two days to reach her destination. She might travel in a coach, or perch on a
pillion behind a male servant, clinging to his waist, or ride
her own horse using a saddle that required her to hook one
knee over the pommel in order to remain in place.

When Rosamond Jaffrey was summoned to her childhood
home by an urgent, if rather enigmatic, message from Susanna,
Lady Appleton, she at once dismissed any thought of coach
or pillion or sidesaddle. Instead, she donned the boy's garments
she had acquired earlier in the year and rode astride. The moon
was just past the full. That and Rosamond's excellent night
vision allowed her to push on through the hours of darkness.
She arrived just before dawn on the twenty-second day of
October.

Despite the early hour, the servants were up and about. So,

to judge from the light showing in Lady Appleton's study window, was the mistress of the manor. Rosamond reined in just short of the gatehouse. Of a sudden, her heart raced and her hands, encased in gloves of the finest leather, dampened the lining. Although she despised herself for cowardice, she wanted nothing more than to flee straight back to her own house in Bermondsey. If she left before anyone caught sight of her, who would ever know she had been here?

'I would know,' Rosamond said aloud.

At the sound of her voice, loud in the early morning quiet, her mount's ears twitched. Just behind her, Rosamond heard the creak of leather as her manservant, Charles, shifted in his saddle. He had made the journey at her side without complaint. That he was a mute and could not vocalize an opinion did not signify. He had other ways to express himself.

What plagued Rosamond as much as anything was how to address the woman who had sent for her. For years, she had called her 'Mama,' reserving the more formal 'Mother' for the woman who had given birth to her.

Rosamond was the daughter of Lady Appleton's late, un-lamented husband, Sir Robert, by one of his many mistresses. She was therefore illegitimate, a bastard, a merrybegot. Despite the circumstances of Rosamond's birth, Susanna Appleton had taken her in, raised her, educated her, and loved her as if she was her own. She had even taken legal steps to make certain Rosamond would one day inherit her father's fortune.

Had she come to regret that generosity? Rosamond often wondered. In seizing control of her inheritance at her first opportunity, Rosamond had become estranged from all her kin, both her blood relations and her foster family.

She had no one but herself to blame for that and she had, of late, been pondering how to make the first overture toward reconciliation. Her fingers tightened on the reins. She had considered writing an abject letter of apology. She would most assuredly have sent New Year's gifts to Leigh Abbey when Yuletide came. Before she could do any of that, the message from Leigh Abbey had arrived at Willow House, Rosamond's home in Bermondsey, a village located just across the Thames from the Tower of London.

A sigh escaped Rosamond as she used her knees to urge her mount into motion. She had been overcome by panic when she first read Lady Appleton's note, convinced that her foster mother was at death's door. Nothing less seemed sufficient to explain the urgent request that Rosamond come at once. She'd set out knowing it was too late for regrets and praying that she would arrive in time to make amends.

During the long hours on the road, she'd had time to ponder other possible interpretations. Something was amiss. She had no doubt of that. But in retrospect 'a matter of life and death' might have many meanings, especially when those words came from the pen of a woman who was an expert on poisonous herbs.

Leigh Abbey's gatehouse, a square, solid tower built of local sandstone, guarded the entrance to the house. Hearing horses approach, the porter stepped out of his lodging to block their way into the courtyard. He was an old man, Jasper Marsh by name, so feeble he had to use a stick for balance. Despite his age and infirmity, he'd been known to use that same stick, when provoked, to defend the house against unwanted intruders.

'Hold, good sirs,' he called in a quavering voice. 'Identify yourselves.'

Sending him a wide smile, Rosamond swept off her cap and the wig she wore beneath it, revealing her face and her own dark brown hair, tightly-contained by pins and netting. 'Do you not know me, Goodman Marsh?'

'Mistress Rosamond! You have come home again!' He hobbled closer, until he stood at her stirrup, squinting up at her to make certain his failing eyes had not deceived him. ''Tis glad I am to see you back where you belong.'

His effusive greeting brought Rosamond close to tears, an uncomfortable sensation when she already felt vulnerable. Strong emotions made a woman weak. When she'd been younger, she'd been arrogant enough to think this meant she must use every means at her disposal to assure she was beholden to no one. Winning her freedom, as she now knew to her sorrow, had cost her dearly.

Back straight, head up, chin stuck defiantly forward,

Rosamond rode into the courtyard to dismount. A young groom of the stable appeared to take the horses. She did not recognize him, another reminder of how many years had passed since her last visit.

She saw no one else as she made her way up the winding stair to the gallery that ran around three sides of the courtyard. Like a dagger aimed at the heart, she flew straight to the door of Lady Appleton's study.

At first everything seemed unchanged, from the small carpet-draped table holding Venetian glass goblets and fine Rhenish wine in a crystal flagon to the enormous *mappa mundi* displayed on one wall. Behind it was the secret compartment where Lady Appleton kept small valuables and important papers. A hearth with a marble chimney piece took up most of the space on another wall. The linenfold panels on either side caught the early morning light flooding in through the east-facing window that looked out over Leigh Abbey's fields and orchards.

Lady Appleton, seated at her desk, appeared to be so engrossed in writing a letter that she could not be troubled to look up and see who had entered. Rosamond's forehead wrinkled as she frowned. A second window, hard by the silent woman, boasted an excellent view of the approach to the gatehouse.

'Unless you have lost both hearing and sight since the last time we met, I warrant you heard hooves approaching and saw me arrive. Do you mean to ignore me indefinitely?'

The older woman shifted position until she could meet Rosamond's eyes. A tentative smile hovered about her lips. 'Mayhap I wished to give you a moment to remember that this is your home.'

'It was so once upon a time.' As soon as the words were out, Rosamond wished them back. She had always been too quick to speak her mind.

An awkward silence settled between them as each waited for the other to say more. Rosamond studied her foster mother, noting the subtle changes in her appearance. Hair that had once been dark brown was now shot through with gray. Her face was more deeply lined, especially around the eyes and mouth. When she rose from her chair, Rosamond could not help but notice that she no longer stood as tall as she once had.

Lady Appleton's sharp-sighted blue eyes surveyed Rosamond in return, missing nothing. Age had not diminished her powers of observation. 'There was no need for you to ride all night,' she said, 'but since you did, I am glad to see that you were sensible enough not to attempt it in skirts.'

'Were it not against the law, I would dress this way all the time. Men's clothing is marvelous comfortable.'

'And passing scandalous.' There was no censure in the words.

'But practical, as you have just admitted, and there was a certain urgency in your summons. You said my presence was required in a matter of life and death.' Rosamond's voice hitched when she added, 'I feared you were dying.'

'My dearest girl! I never meant to give that impression but if that belief spurred you on, then I can only be glad of it.'

When she opened her arms, Rosamond stepped into the embrace, clinging to the older woman while emotions threatened to drown her. Waves of relief and gratitude and love swept over her.

'I was wrong to push you away, Mama,' she whispered. 'I know you only wanted what was best for me.'

'You were not the only one who handled things badly.' Stepping back, Lady Appleton put one strong, square hand on each of Rosamond's shoulders, holding her in place until their gazes locked. 'We will speak no more of the past. That you are here now is all that matters.'

'You are certain you are well? And no one else is at death's door?'

'If you mean Jennet, you must say so.'

Rosamond felt her lips curl into a rueful smile. 'Yes, I mean Jennet. To hear Rob tell it, his mother's health has been passing precarious ever since we married.'

Jennet Jaffrey had never cared for Sir Robert Appleton's by-blow, even before Rosamond persuaded Jennet's only son to marry her as the means to claim her inheritance. That was another fence that needed mending, but just at the moment Rosamond had a more pressing concern.

'Why *did* you send for me, and why in such a vague and alarming way?'

'I feared someone might intercept my letter. I preferred to take no chances.'

Taking Rosamond's arm, Lady Appleton drew her out of the study and along the gallery to the door of the chamber that had once been Rosamond's schoolroom. In company with Rob's sisters, Susan and Kate, and two other girls, Godlina Walkenden, daughter of a wealthy London merchant, and Dionysia Tallboys, a Derbyshire heiress, Rosamond had spent many happy hours at her lessons. Mama had seen to it that they received an education equal to that of any gentleman's son.

The furnishings of a bedchamber had replaced those suited to the study of mathematics, geography, logic, and languages. Rosamond's eyes narrowed. The bed was occupied. At the sound of the door opening, the lump under the covers rolled over and sat up, blinking in confusion. For a moment, Rosamond did not recognize this bedraggled creature as her old friend Lina. When at last she did, she was even more perplexed.

'A matter of life and death?'

'A matter,' said Lady Appleton, 'of murder.'

THREE

Lina Walkenden at twelve, the age at which she and Rosamond had first met, had been a plump girl who loved sweets of any kind, giggled at the least provocation, and had never hesitated to follow Rosamond's lead. As their friendship grew, Rosamond had inspired Lina to bursts of bravery, some of which they both afterward regretted.

The woman who emerged from beneath the bedcovers wearing naught but a shift had lost flesh everywhere but her bosom in the years since then. Always plain-featured, she still had hair best described as the color of mud on a spring morning. Her eyes, when not puffy and tear-reddened, were her best feature. Their hue was an exact match for the shell of a hazelnut.

Before Rosamond could brace herself for the impact, Lina flung herself across the room. Engulfed in an embrace that knocked the air out of her lungs, Rosamond instinctively tried to free herself. Taking this as a sign of rejection, Lina sagged and burst into tears but, at the same time, clung to Rosamond ever more fiercely.

Unaccustomed to giving comfort, Rosamond administered a series of awkward pats to her friend's back. Over Lina's head she sent Susanna Appleton a mute appeal for help.

'Dry your eyes, Lina,' Lady Appleton said in a voice that brooked no argument. 'Rosamond will help you to dress. While she does, you can explain how you came to be here.'

With a final sniffle, Lina released her hold and backed away, swabbing her face with her sleeve. Still mopping up moisture, she began to gather her clothing. It had been carelessly discarded when she undressed. A petticoat was draped across the seat of a chair while her kirtle had come to rest half on and half off a chest with a curved top. Other items of dress were scattered throughout the bedchamber.

'After you two have talked, you will find me in the small parlor.'

'But Mama—'

The closing door cut off Rosamond's protest.

Resigned, she regarded Lina with critical eyes. The other woman had managed to assume her petticoat but her fingers were tangled in the laces, and another bout of crying appeared to be imminent.

'Let go of that.' Rosamond's voice was sharp with impatience.

Lina jumped and looked cowed. The petticoat pooled around her ankles.

'Who,' Rosamond asked as she took on the role of tiring maid, 'has been murdered?'

In a choked voice, Lina managed to speak a name, but it was one that meant nothing to Rosamond.

'Who is Hugo Hackett?' Having dealt with the petticoat and

fastened both kirtle and bodice in place, Rosamond searched for Lina's sleeves and finally spotted them lying on the floor beneath the small table that held a wash basin and ewer.

'He was my sister Isolde's husband.'

Finger-shaped bruises marred Lina's upper arms, plainly visible through the thin lawn of her shift. 'Did he do this?'

Lina nodded. 'But I did not kill him, Ros. I swear it on my mother's soul!'

Rosamond frowned as she tied the points that fastened the sleeves to the bodice. Lina's mother, who had died when Lina was ten, had been the second wife of a wealthy London merchant. Lina was their only child, so Isolde had to be a half sister. It seemed likely she was much older than Lina.

'Who thinks you did kill him?' She suspected she already knew the answer.

'Isolde.' Lina stuttered trying to get the name out and choked back a sob.

Rosamond smoothed a lace collar into place. The clothes were of good quality but plain. Lina had dressed in much finer garments when they were girls. 'Why would Isolde accuse you of such a thing? And if you start crying again,' she warned, 'I will slap you.'

Lina bit her lip, swallowed hard, and regained enough control to answer Rosamond's question. 'S-she s-saw me s-standing over Hugo's body. I was the one who found him.'

'Did you have reason to kill him, aside from the bruises?' Her task complete, Rosamond stepped back so that she could watch Lina's face as her friend answered.

'S-she thinks I did.'

'Explain.'

After taking a few deep breaths, Lina did her best. Her voice was steadier, but she still looked as if she might be about to flood the room with tears.

'It's because of Father's will. When he died three years ago, he left me a generous marriage portion but no money to live on till I wed. He charged Hugo with my keeping and added a provision to say that if Hugo did not approve of the man I married, he could withhold my dowry.'

'He intended that Hugo choose your husband for you.' Rosamond's voice was flat. Such arrangements were not unusual, but they often led to unhappy marriages. 'I take it you had some objection to the man he selected?'

Her expression bleak, Lina nodded.

That was unfortunate, Rosamond thought. If Lina had reason to see Hugo as an obstacle to her happiness, that made her an obvious suspect in his murder. Still, she had said that she did not kill him and Rosamond believed her.

'Come and sit, Lina.' Rosamond climbed up on the bed and chose a spot at the foot, folding her legs beneath her in tailor-fashion and patting the coverlet beside her. 'You must go back to the beginning and tell me everything that happened.'

'The beginning?' Rosamond heard a touch of asperity in her friend's voice as Lina settled herself at the opposite end of the bed, her back against a bolster and a pillow held in front of her like a shield. 'That was when you wed Rob Jaffrey. The moment Father heard you'd made a runaway marriage, he ordered me to leave Leigh Abbey and return to London, lest I be corrupted by your wicked example.'

Rosamond had intended her to begin with the period imme-diately prior to the murder but she held her peace, determined to let Lina tell the story in her own way.

Setting aside the pillow, Lina drew her knees close to her chest, wrapped her arms around them and rested her chin on her hands. A faraway look came into her eyes. 'Father was furious. He'd sent me to be trained as a gentlewoman only to have the household tarnished by scandal. As a result, he gave up his plan to marry me into the gentry and instead sent me to Isolde to learn a trade.'

'He apprenticed you?' Startled, Rosamond sat up straighter.

'Not in the way that boys are bound by contract for a term of years. The silkwomen of London are not so strictly regulated. It is the only profession I know of in which a woman is permitted to keep all the money she earns. Her husband has no claim on her income but she must *have* a husband in order to set up as a silkwoman in the first place. Then she can work as a throwster or a weaver or deal generally in silk goods. The way Father arranged matters, I was to remain with Isolde until

I married.' Her voice bitter, she added, 'After he died, I became little more than an unpaid servant in Isolde's household.'

'Why did your father make Isolde's husband your guardian?' Rosamond asked. 'I seem to remember that you also have a half brother.'

'Yes. Lawrence. He is fourteen years older than I am. He has never been unkind to me, but he has always been too busy with his own concerns to take much notice of his little sister. I suppose Father thought to spare him the trouble of dealing with me.'

Abruptly, Lina stopped speaking and sniffled. Fearing another spate of weeping, hoping to stem the flow, Rosamond asked, 'When did Hugo announce that he'd found you a husband?'

'Two months ago.' Lina's involuntary shudder spoke volumes.

Rosamond unfolded herself and scooted forward until she could grasp her friend's hands. They were icy to the touch. 'What manner of man did he seek to inflict upon you?'

'A wealthy one. His name is Alessandro Portinari.'

'An Italian?' Rosamond did not share the inherent distrust of strangers – anyone foreign-born – common among the English, but she could not quite keep the surprise out of her voice.

Lina drew herself up as if affronted and sent Rosamond an annoyed look. 'He is a silk merchant here in London. He was born in Florence but became an English citizen years ago.'

Eyebrows lifting, Rosamond moderated her tone. 'I meant no offense.' She hesitated, then added, 'I thought you disliked him.'

'I did not object to him at first. He made much of me, showering me with gifts. He is always courteous.' She heaved a deep sigh.

'What, then, is wrong with him?'

'He is old, nearly three score years, and fat, and ugly. He wears an over-strong scent and too many rings. One of them is a large cameo of a death's head.'

Rosamond waited. If he was wealthy enough, most young women in Lina's situation would be willing to wed a man who was old and fat and ugly, even if he did have poor taste in jewelry. There had to be some other count against him.

'He is diseased.' Lina's cheeks flamed as the words burst
out of her. 'It is the French pox.'

Rosamond thought herself worldly, but she could not suppress
a gasp. The ailment had many names – learned men called it
syphilis – but all of them were spoken in whispers. Persons
known to have contracted the disease were shunned long before
they succumbed to the inevitable painful, lingering death.

'When I found out,' Lina continued, 'I confronted Hugo
and told him I would not go through with the marriage. We
quarreled, loud enough to be overheard by my sister and half
the neighborhood. Hugo did not believe me, or else he did not
care. He seized hold of me and locked me in my chamber and
threatened to starve me until I relented.'

That, Rosamond realized, must have been when Lina
acquired those bruises.

The remainder of Lina's story spilled out in a rush. Her
escape. Her return. Her discovery of Hugo, dead in his counting
house.

'My screams woke the household. Isolde was the first to
reach me. She took one look at Hugo and then turned and
slapped me across the face. By then the apprentices and servants were all standing around, mouths agape. Isolde ordered
one of them to run and find the watch and told two more to
take hold of me. She said I had killed Hugo and would suffer
for it. That is when I fled.'

'Wise of you,' Rosamond said. Had Lina hesitated before
taking flight, she might well have been imprisoned, tried, and
executed by now. 'Did you come straight here?'

'First I had to elude Hugo's apprentices, although I do not
think they pursued me as diligently as they might have. I had
already thought to ask you for help, Ros, but I did not know
where to find you. Then I remembered the stories you used
to tell us about Lady Appleton and how she helped people
wrongly accused of crimes, so I pawned the jewelry I'd carried
away with me and hired a horse and came here.'

'And what did Lady Appleton suggest?' Rosamond asked.

The ghost of a smile flitted across Lina's wan features. 'That
we lose no time sending for you.'

FOUR

Susanna Appleton prayed for patience. 'You cannot avoid speaking to her, Jennet.'

'And why not?' Jennet Jaffrey worried her lower lip with her teeth, a sure sign that she was upset.

That was only to be expected, given the way she felt about Rosamond, but after all this time, Susanna's tolerance had worn thin. 'This feud between you has to end.'

'She—'

'I do not want to hear it.' Susanna held up one hand, palm out.

She was well aware of the complaints Jennet had against her son's wife. They had begun to accumulate long before Rob and Rosamond married. She'd been against Susanna's decision to foster her husband's bastard daughter and had never approved of Rosamond's high spirits or her tendency to lead the other children, Rob and his sisters among them, into trouble. As for the marriage itself, that never should have happened.

Rob Jaffrey's father, Mark, was Lady Appleton's steward. His mother, Jennet, had once been her tiring maid and now served as Leigh Abbey's housekeeper. It was not unheard of for the gentry to marry beneath them, but both families had envisioned other futures for their children. Rob had already matriculated at Cambridge. Rosamond's mother, Eleanor, had dreams of matching her with a nobleman's son. That Rosamond appeared to have married Rob solely as a ploy to gain control of her inheritance had been the final straw where Jennet was concerned.

Susanna's own feelings toward Rosamond had always been complex. Barren herself, she'd been deeply hurt by her first sight of this child who was, unmistakably, her husband's get. Even as an infant, Rosamond had shared Sir Robert Appleton's most prominent features, especially his deep brown eyes. In

Rosamond, his wavy dark brown hair, his narrow face, and his high forehead combined to create a pretty creature who had never been above using her attractive appearance to get her own way. Susanna had long accepted responsibility for that character flaw. She'd spoiled the child.

Even that first day, when she had seen Rosamond in her mother's arms and realized that Robert had betrayed his marriage vows, Susanna had not blamed the baby. Susanna had done her best for Robert's illegitimate daughter after his death, taking an interest in her upbringing and welcoming the little girl into her own home when Rosamond's mother, Eleanor, married Sir Walter Pendennis and went abroad with her new husband on a diplomatic mission for the queen. As Rosamond's foster mother, Susanna had felt it her duty to make the child's future secure. Morally, if not legally, she was her father's heir. Susanna had made it so in law, as well, setting aside a small fortune to come to Rosamond when she reached the age of twenty-one, or when she wed, whichever came first.

That was what had led to her misalliance with Rob Jaffrey. To put an end to Eleanor's constant pressure to marry some young sprig of the nobility, a sixteen-year-old Rosamond had talked Rob Jaffrey into a clandestine marriage. She had always been able to twist the boy around her little finger. She even persuaded him to sign away his rights, acquired the moment their vows were exchanged, to all the goods, chattels, and land she brought to the marriage. Rosamond had been furious when she learned she'd miscalculated. Only sixteen himself, Rob had not been of legal age to enter into any contract other than a matrimonial one. Rob's father, not Rob himself, gained control of Rosamond's fortune, and Mark Jaffrey was not inclined to be as generous as Susanna had been.

In the tempestuous weeks and months that followed, with threats of a legal battle on the horizon, the household at Leigh Abbey had been torn asunder. Rob had sided with his bride. Jennet, who had always been quick to criticize Rosamond, calling her prideful and a troublemaker, had suffered a seizure and taken to her bed. She had been gravely ill for weeks afterward and had been subject to dizzy spells ever since that episode.

Studying the other woman as they waited for Rosamond and Lina to join them in the small parlor near the ground floor hall, Susanna noted ominous signs. Jennet's cheeks were flushed, her breath came a little too fast and her steps, when she moved from one side of the room to the other, were a trifle unsteady. Low of stature all her life, Jennet had never lost the weight she had gained with her first child. She'd increased in girth from year to year until she was nearly as round as she was tall. Along with the weight had come the tendency toward heightened color and a chronic shortness of breath.

'Have you taken your tonic this morning?' Susanna prepared it herself – a distillation of horehound, sage, mullein, and raspberry leaves. Imbibed daily, it strengthened the heart.

Sending her a mutinous look, Jennet shook her head.

'Now, of all times, you must not skip a dose.' Susanna had also advised her old friend to avoid nuts, milk, cheese, meat, and fruits, but she knew full well that Jennet ate what she pleased. As a countermeasure, Susanna was wont to surreptitiously mix a little feverfew into Jennet's wine.

About to launch into a lecture on taking better care of herself, Susanna maintained her silence when she heard footsteps approaching. A moment later, Rosamond entered the small parlor. She had taken the time to change into more suitable clothing, garments she'd apparently brought with her in her saddlebags. Eyes bright, she opened her mouth to speak. She closed it again with an audible smack when she caught sight of Jennet.

Every trace of Rosamond's animation vanished as if a shutter had swung closed. She stood stock still, hands clenched in front of her, staring with a blank expression at her husband's mother.

Jennet took a step toward the younger woman, her eyes ablaze with years of pent-up animosity.

Susanna moved swiftly to step between them. 'Enough! You will declare a truce here and now, if for no other reason than that you both care for Rob.'

For a time, Rosamond had also been estranged from her husband. They still lived apart, with Rob pursuing his studies at Cambridge and Rosamond established in Bermondsey, but Susanna had been assured that they were once again on friendly terms with one another. She dared hope that, before long, they would be fully reconciled. What choice did they have? There was no undoing a marriage, not in Elizabeth Tudor's England. Once the matrimonial knot was tied, only death could sever it.

Rosamond drew in a deep breath and addressed Jennet. 'I know I have not behaved well in the past, and I am most heartily sorry for it. I never meant to hurt you. I was thoughtless and selfish. A brat.'

'And therein I bear some responsibility,' Susanna interrupted. 'I was never good at discipline.'

Eyes wide, Rosamond turned to her. 'No, Mama, you must not blame yourself. I should have hated it, hated you, if you had been strict with me. No doubt I would have rebelled all the sooner. *Mother*'s machinations were what drove me to act so impulsively, not yours.'

'Whatever happened in the past, it is the present that is important now. And the future.' She leveled a stern look at Jennet. 'Must I remind you that Rosamond will one day be the mother of your grandchildren?'

Rosamond winced. Jennet cast a speculative glance at her daughter-in-law's midsection. 'I see no sign that you are increasing. Are you certain you understand the duties of a wife?'

'I even *enjoy* some of them,' Rosamond shot back, 'but if you ever expect to dandle my baby on your knees—'

'Rob will have his degree soon,' Susanna interrupted, 'and then you two will be able to live as man and wife.' It was not Rosamond keeping them apart, she assured herself, but only the rule at Cambridge that did not permit wives to share undergraduates' lodgings. 'Meanwhile, there is the matter of Godlina Walkenden to occupy us. I expected her to come down with you, Rosamond.'

'I left her resting. It seemed to exhaust her to relate her tale. She would not even let me help her undress, but sprawled fully clothed on the bed and fell at once into a doze.'

'It is no wonder she is still recovering. She showed remarkable fortitude in making her way to Leigh Abbey on her own.

She was close to collapse by the time she arrived. Since then she has had to endure the strain of wondering if her sister will remember this place and send searchers here to look for her.'

'I do not understand how you can be so certain she is innocent,' Jennet grumbled. 'As a girl, she did not always tell the truth. There was that matter in Derbyshire—'

'Lina is the victim in this.' Rosamond's defense of her friend was immediate and fierce.

Quietly pleased, Susanna drew her aside. 'Anyone can kill, given enough provocation, but I cannot see Lina stabbing Hugo Hackett to death.'

'Lina did not seem to know where the knife came from or who it belonged to or even what kind of knife it was.'

'It may well have been Hackett's own blade. It is not surprising that Lina was too upset at the time to take note of details.'

'She said she thought at once of me,' Rosamond said with the hint of a smile.

'You are in an excellent position to help her.'

'I do not see how. No one has any reason to talk to me, let alone answer intrusive questions about Hugo Hackett's death. I warrant you are better suited to make such inquiries than I am.'

Susanna shook her head. 'I have not the excuse of long friendship for meddling in this matter. Moreover, if I were to go to London and approach Isolde Hackett, it would not be long before she guessed that I had seen Lina. I can be of more use if I stay here and keep Lina hidden. You, on the other hand, may with impunity go anywhere in the city and talk to people who knew Hugo Hackett, even his widow.'

Jennet, who had been listening to every word that passed between them, gave a disdainful sniff. 'She cannot compel anyone to answer her. And if she gives as the reason for her interest that she was Lina's childhood friend, it was at Leigh Abbey that they knew each other, the authorities will come here searching for the fugitive, you mark my words.'

'I have been reliably informed,' said Susanna, not without pride, 'that our Rosamond is skilled in the art of disguise and also most adept at uncovering secrets. No less a person than Sir Francis Walsingham, the queen's spy master, was moved to employ her of late on a mission of some delicacy.'

Rosamond's look of astonishment had Susanna stifling an urge to laugh aloud.

'No one was supposed to know anything about that!'

'You forget, dearest girl, who drew you into the affair in the first place.'

Susanna had not been pleased to learn what danger Rosamond had been in, and Rob, too, but by the time her neighbor, friend, and occasional lover, Nick Baldwin, had shared the details, everyone was safe.

'I will do all I can to help Lina,' Rosamond said. 'Never doubt that. But I am uncertain where to begin.' Susanna could almost hear the wheels turn and the gears grind as Rosamond mulled over the problem.

'I am confident you will be able to discover the murderer's identity. As for beginning, you must talk to Lina again. Ask her what persons profit from the death of her sister's husband. They are the individuals you must contrive to meet. Observe them closely and you should be able to whittle down your list of names. When only one remains, that will be your killer.'

Rosamond laughed. 'Not *my* killer, I hope. I should like to survive the discovery.'

'I feel certain you will be as cautious as you are diligent,' Susanna said. 'Now go you and rest for a few hours while you can. You have had a long and arduous journey yourself. We will speak of this more anon.'

Rosamond resisted at first, but a jaw-popping yawn gave the lie to her claim that she was not tired.

When Rosamond had gone from the small parlor, Susanna turned to Jennet. 'If what Nick Baldwin has told me is true, Rosamond is not only clever and resourceful but also knows how to defend herself. And yet, I will worry about her. Someone who has killed once will not hesitate to kill again rather than be caught and punished.'

Jennet sent her a sour look. 'Too late now to think of that. You have set her on her course. Tell her not to go on with it and she'll do just the opposite.'

'She had a rebellious, impulsive streak in her nature when she was younger, but surely she has outgrown that.'

Jennet sneered at that notion. 'No doubt,' she said, 'that is why she donned male garments and rode through the night to arrive here the sooner.'

FIVE

Rob Jaffrey was on his way from morning prayers to the first lecture of the day when he noticed the stranger. Like everyone else in sight, the man wore a hooded, ankle-length academic gown. The wool was London brown in color. Although black was more usual, this was an acceptable hue, but its wearer was far too old to be an undergraduate at Christ's College. In passing, his pale blue eyes fixed on Rob in a hard stare. His thin lips pursed with disapproval.

Such rude behavior was not unheard of at Cambridge but neither was it common. As Rob kept walking, he looked back over his shoulder, squinting in the sun for a better look. He was just in time to see the stranger scuttle away, head down, as if he did not wish to call attention to himself.

His curiosity aroused, Rob wondered who the man was. A tutor? A fellow of the college? No one Rob had seen before, of that he felt certain. He'd have remembered those ice-colored eyes. There had been something wrong with the way the stranger wore his hair, too. It was over-long, even for someone who was no longer a student.

Then again, those who matriculated at Cambridge did not always follow the rule that required them to keep their locks polled, knotted, or rounded. There were many who willingly paid a fourpenny fine rather than be shorn and could afford to, just as more than one gentleman's son habitually left off his gown, an eightpenny fine. The only other penalty suffered for one such recent offense, wearing a cut taffeta doublet in the buttery, had been to be hauled before the provost and lectured.

To Rob's mind, such scholars were vain as peacocks, strutting about, desirous of calling attention to themselves by their defiance of authority. The man he'd seen was just the opposite. He had not wanted to be noticed. Rob wondered if he belonged at Cambridge at all, but if he'd come in disguise, he'd have done better to try to pass himself off as a servant.

Rob continued on his way to the lecture and forgot all about the incident until mid-afternoon when he kept the appointment he'd made with a prospective tutor. Interrupting his university studies for more than a year had left him scrambling to catch up. He'd returned to Cambridge just before the start of Michaelmas term and if he meant to be among those awarded a bachelor's degree on Palm Sunday, only six months hence, he had need of the best teachers. And thanks to his wife's wealth, he had the wherewithal to hire them.

This tutor, whose specialty was philosophy, had been described to Rob as short, round, and bearded. The man standing at the window of a small room in a Cambridge lodging house, his back to the door, was a scrawny beanpole, spindle-shanked and knob-kneed. All these flaws were emphasized by the dark clothing he wore. He had tossed a London-brown academic gown over the back of the chamber's only chair.

Seeing that garment gave Rob a start, but it prepared him for what was to come when the man turned to face him. This time the pale blue eyes glittered with contempt.

'Sit,' the stranger commanded in a preemptory tone, jerking his head toward a three-legged stool. 'I would have a few words with you.' He settled himself in the uncomfortable-looking wooden chair without troubling to move the gown out of his way.

Sensible, Rob thought, since the fabric provided a layer of padding between the man's bony bum and that rock-hard seat.

He glanced at the stool, then ignored it to let his gaze roam over the rest of the cramped chamber. It was simply furnished with a camp bed, a table holding a brace of candles, and a chest with a flat top. The place had the appearance typical of any poor scholar's lodgings . . . except for the absence of books and the bog myrtle burning in the fireplace, scenting the air with its sweet fragrance. A fire of any kind was an extravagance on a sunny, late October day. A tutor without a pupil three weeks into the term was more likely to put on an extra layer of clothing than deplete his winter's supply of fuel.

'I believe there has been some mistake,' Rob said. 'You are not the gentleman I came to see.'

The stranger's face turned an ugly red. He had a prominent Adam's apple that bobbled when he barked an order: 'Sit down, Jaffrey. It is your own best interest to hear what I have to say.'

Rob continued to stand and stayed well within bolting distance of the exit, but he was intrigued enough to remain in the room. Was that the trace of a Welsh accent he heard? 'Who are you and what do you want of me?'

'You have been out of the country.' It was not a question.

'I have.' Rob leaned back against the paneled wall beside the door, arms crossed, curious to hear what the stranger would remark upon next.

'In your travels, did you encounter heretics?'

'I met men whose religious practices are different from my own.' Rob worded his reply with care. They had just ventured into dangerous territory.

'Papists?'

'No. The church in Muscovy is not ruled from Rome.'

The stranger sat forward, shoulders hunched, putting Rob in mind of a hunting bird as it loomed over its kill. He gave himself a mental shake to dispel the image, but when he had spent another quarter of an hour subjected to additional questions that touched upon the orthodoxy of his own beliefs and his tolerance of the faith of others, he could not help but picture himself as playing mouse to the other man's raptor. Finally, he lost patience, interrupting the interrogation with a question of his own.

'I am required to swear to the Act of Supremacy before I can take my degree. Is that not sufficient proof of both my loyalty to the queen and my adherence to tenets of the Church of England?'

Lips pursed, eyes narrowed, the stranger, who had declined

to give Rob his name, spat out his reply. 'It will prove you are not a recusant, but not what beliefs lie hidden in your heart.'

Rob understood the distinction. Those called recusants, because they recused themselves from attending church services and from taking the oath of loyalty to the queen, did so because these things had been forbidden by the Pope after he excommunicated Queen Elizabeth, the nominal head of the Church of England. Recusants believed in the Catholic faith of their ancestors and paid ruinous fines for each absence from their parish church. They were persecuted by officials seeking proof they harbored priests in their homes or owned forbidden Catholic books. Many had fled abroad to Catholic countries where they could worship as they wished . . . and where Protestants were the ones persecuted by Catholic rulers and their clergy.

The other sort of Catholic attended Church of England services and pretended to conform to the religion founded by the queen's father, King Henry the Eighth, when he dissolved all the monasteries and divorced his first wife to marry Elizabeth's mother, Anne Boleyn. All that had taken place well before Rob was born. In his own lifetime he had known only one faith, but at the same time, he had been raised to feel sympathy for anyone who was oppressed. His earliest lessons, at Leigh Abbey, had taught him to see all sides of an issue and to show respect for views that were not his own. In this he was out of step with most of his contemporaries. Had he been foolish enough to express such a radical belief to the wrong person, he'd be chastised, mayhap even imprisoned, for indulging in 'dangerous talk.'

One such 'wrong' person was currently staring at him with disconcerting intensity. The stranger's officious manner had convinced Rob that he had the authority to ask his questions, but whether he was interrogating a scholar at the behest of the university, on the authority of the church or as a representative of the queen, Rob could not tell.

'What of your friend Needham? Will he take the oath?'

'Andrew Needham?' Startled, Rob came away from the wall. 'You do much mistake him, sirrah, if you think Needham is a recusant.' He had been Rob's closest companion from the moment he'd taken up his studies at Christ's College and these days they shared lodgings. Rob spoke with complete confidence.

'A recusant? No. But he is suspected of being a Catholic sympathizer.'

Rob kept his mouth shut. Needham despised intolerance, just as Rob did. Unfortunately, there was a surfeit of closed-mindedness at Cambridge. The Godly, as they called themselves, wanted to reform the Church of England to make it even more unlike the Catholic roots from which it had evolved. Because these men sought to purify religion, their detractors had coined the derisive name 'Puritan' to describe them. As a movement, it had been growing in both numbers and influence and one of its goals was to suppress all dissenting opinions. Christ's was the most Puritan of all Cambridge's colleges, saved from extreme radicalism only because the current master, Edmund Barwell, was more open to reason than most of his ilk.

'Your friend Needham was overheard expressing his desire to be "a turd in the teeth of all Dutchmen." What say you to that?'

'I say he was cup shot at the time.' Rob forced a smile. 'Or, mayhap, that he has taken the men of the Low Countries in dislike.'

The stranger's smile was as cold as the frost in his eyes. They both knew that 'Dutchman' was just another name for Puritan. 'You vouch for his loyalty, then?'

'I do.'

Rob could think of no reason why his interrogator should take his word for anything. It occurred to him that his defense of his friend was as likely to send them both to gaol as spare Needham that indignity. He wondered if it was too late to flee and decided any such effort would be futile. Whoever this man was, he was aware of Rob's history and associates and no doubt knew where he lodged.

'Invisible Catholics, those who outwardly conform but secretly corrupt youth, are dangerous to queen and country. Such men prey on passionate, impressionable young scholars. Some they recruit to study at Rheims.' Distaste twisted the stranger's thin lips into a grotesque shape.

There was a seminary at Rheims, Rob recalled. Priests were

trained there. After they were ordained, they were sent back
to England to minister to the faithful. The Papists they served
had to hide them and all evidence of their religious practices
or risk arrest.

At last, the stranger came to the point. 'The Crown has need
of intelligencers to root out such vermin at Cambridge.'

'I wish you well in finding someone to help you,' Rob said,
'but I have no talent for such things. Moreover, I have a lecture
to attend at three of the clock. I must leave now or I will be
late.' He turned his back on the other man and reached for
the latch.

'Your wife did not hesitate when she was asked to serve
her queen.'

The statement stopped Rob in mid-movement, one hand
extended. He thought about pleading ignorance. When a
married couple lived apart for nearly the entire time they'd
been wed, it was not unreasonable to think they might be
unaware of each other's activities. In truth, however, he understood the reference all too well.

The previous year, Rosamond had been recruited by the
queen's principal secretary and chief spy master, Sir Francis
Walsingham, to follow in her late father's footsteps as an
intelligence gatherer. She had been cozened into accepting the
assignment, believing that her cooperation was necessary to
keep Rob safe. She'd been lied to, exploited, and nearly killed
and had vowed she would never do such work again.

Everything Rob had heard about Sir Francis Walsingham
indicated that the spy master was a Puritan. It was said that
he looked for Catholic plots under every rock and that if he
did not at once discover proof of his suspicions, he had
minions in his pay who were adept at providing it, even if
they had to conjure it out of thin air. Rob wanted nothing
to do with such a man. He wanted no part of conspiracies,
real or imagined, and he had no intention of reporting on
the activities of other scholars, especially one who was his
friend.

'Circumstances change,' he said as he opened the door
and stepped through without looking back. 'Neither my wife
nor I can henceforth be of any assistance to your employer.'

As he walked away, he heard footsteps cross the room to the doorway. He felt the other man's eyes bore into his back. Sweat beaded on Rob's brow. It was dangerous to refuse a man like Walsingham, but in good conscience, what else could he have done? He breathed a little easier when he was beyond the range of a thrown dagger.

Rob told himself that the queen's principal secretary had better things to do than persecute a humble Cambridge scholar, especially one who had done nothing wrong. And Rosamond, surely, was safe from Walsingham's machinations. She'd done him good service, even if she had, more than once, challenged his authority. Rob resolved to forget all about his encounter with the stranger. It was not as if he did not have more important matters to occupy his thoughts. For one thing, he still had to find someone to tutor him in philosophy.

SIX

'Who wanted Hugo Hackett dead?' Rosamond asked. Her blunt question made Lina scowl. 'How should I know? I had little to do with him.'

'You lived in his house for several years. Your sister was his wife. You must have some notion of what the man was like. Was he quarrelsome? Was he litigious? Did he gamble excessively? Was he in debt?'

'I tell you, I do not know!' Lina's hands curled into fists, but she was closer to tears than to violence. Installed on the cushioned window seat in Lady Appleton's study, her face was the very picture of misery.

Rosamond made an exasperated sound. She lacked the patience to coax information out of her friend. They had already wasted most of the day while Lina dithered. First she'd pled exhaustion. Then it was a headache. Then she'd needed feeding, since she'd slept through dinner. If Rosamond was to find the real killer, she must depart for London on the morrow. As it

was, she doubted there would be anything left to see at the
scene of the crime. The murder had taken place nearly a week
earlier. Then, too, the more time that passed, the less reliable
memories became. If anyone had seen or heard something
untoward that night, such recollections would by now have
been influenced by Isolde's insistence that Lina had killed
Hugo Hackett.

'Sit here.' Lady Appleton indicated the chair drawn up to
her coffin desk, so called because of all the long, narrow
compartments, or 'coffins', used to store pens, inkpots, paper,
and various other writing supplies. 'Write down a list of
suspects as Lina gives you their names.'

Rosamond obliged and took up the sharpened quill. She
slanted a glance at Lina as she dipped it in thick black ink.
'If she has no suggestions, I can make a few of my own.
Isolde Hackett is the most logical person to have killed her
husband.'

Lina came to life, sputtering in protest. 'My sister would
never do such a thing!'

'The victim's spouse must always be considered. Who else
benefits more?'

'Ask rather who loses more?'

'That depends upon the marriage.'

'She was there in the house,' Lady Appleton pointed out
from her perch atop the trunk that held her collection of books
on herbs, medicines, gardens, and poisons.

'So were others,' Lina objected. 'Servants. Apprentices.
And someone could have broken in. Or Hugo might have
invited his killer to visit. I do not know how long he had been
dead when I found him.'

'All true, but we cannot rule out your sister. For all you
know, she may have spent years nursing a grudge against her
husband.'

Twisting her hands together in her lap, Lina hunched forward
but she did not meet Rosamond's eyes. 'Everything I saw
between Isolde and Hugo spoke of their affection for one
another. They never quarreled.' She made an odd, choking
sound. 'Sometimes I hated Isolde for that because I knew it
would do me no good to appeal to her for help. She always

deferred to Hugo, certain he knew best, even when it came to what man I must marry.'

'But Isolde has profited by his death by at least her widow's third. Had they children?'

'No.' Lina looked pained as she added, 'Isolde inherits all Hugo had.'

Rosamond held the pen poised over the paper. 'What of other kin? Or a business partner?'

'There is no one.'

Rosamond drew a double line beneath Isolde's name. Isolde was now free to marry again if she chose. If she'd had her eye on someone else while Hackett was still alive, there was motive aplenty. Lina had said that silkwomen ran their own businesses. Mayhap she'd wanted control of his, as well. For the most part, Rosamond's own situation being an even more rare exception, widows were the only women who could enjoy such legal rights as managing their own money and property and making a will, free of interference from any man. In the ordinary way of things, a woman became her husband's property when they wed, no better than a slave under the law.

'Hugo Hackett tried to coerce you into marriage. How did he treat his apprentices and servants? Was he the sort of man to beat or threaten them into obedience?'

'He did not tolerate laziness,' Lina admitted, 'but I never saw him beat either of his apprentices.'

'Names?'

Rosamond wrote as Lina ticked off each member of the household. As a mercer, Hackett had taken two apprentices. As a man of wealth, he'd employed three maidservants – a tiring maid for his wife, a scullery maid, and a maid of all work – as well as a cook and a cook's boy.

'What about his business associates? Other mercers? His suppliers?'

Head in hands, Lina made a low sound of distress. 'I never paid any attention. I had my own trade to learn.'

Rosamond wrote 'business rival,' but that was nearly as useless as adding 'unknown thief' to her list. 'Does Isolde have her own shop?'

'A workshop.'

'So what her women produce goes to Hugo to sell.' Most mercers dealt in luxury goods. 'Mayhap she discovered he was cheating her.'

'To cheat her would be to cheat himself,' Lina countered. 'He had no claim on her income but she nevertheless gave him all she earned. She said men were better at managing money.'

Rosamond busied herself sharpening the pen and made no comment.

That Hugo had surprised a thief seemed unlikely, especially when Lina herself had been obliged to pick the lock on the garden door before she could get back into the house. He might have let someone in, but how was she to discover that person's identity if he had? She set aside her penknife and drew a line down the middle of the page, starting a second column. Isolde was at the top of that list, too.

'I need names of people to talk to, Lina. The Italian merchant you were intended to wed – what was his name again?'

'Alessandro Portinari.'

'And the person who told you of Portinari's . . . illness?'

'Cecily Kendall. She is his neighbor in Lime Street, an elderly woman but a good customer. Isolde was wont to send me to her to deliver goods. I . . . I think that is how Alessandro first came to notice me.'

Rosamond wrote down the name and underlined it, then glanced at Lady Appleton, wondering at her silence. She had not spoken for some time.

A thoughtful frown on her face, the older woman's gaze rested on Lina. 'I do not pretend to know much about the mercery of London, but it seems to me that there has always been rivalry between English merchants and strangers. Is it not somewhat unusual for an English girl to be wed to an Italian?' She did not mention the age difference. That was *not* uncommon.

'It is not unheard of,' Lina said in a whisper.

'Is there some special reason Hugo Hackett promoted the match, mayhap a business advantage? Did you not say this Portinari is in the silk trade?'

Lina nodded but did not speak. The dull red color seeping

into her cheeks betrayed her embarrassment but did not entirely explain it. Rosamond could not fathom why she would hold anything back, but it was obvious she was not telling them all she knew.

When Rosamond would have spoken sharply to her friend, demanding the whole story, Lady Appleton signaled for her to remain silent. She addressed Lina in a gentle, unthreatening voice. 'Dear girl, we cannot help you if you do not trust us.'

'I may be wrong.' Lina mumbled the words.

'If it concerns Hugo Hackett,' Rosamond said, 'you must tell us. It could be important.'

'I think . . . I think the reason he would not relent when I repeated what Widow Kendall told me was that he owed Alessandro a great deal of money.'

'He arranged your marriage to pay off a debt?' Rosamond knew that men bartered their female relatives all the time, but that did not make it right.

'It is possible that he did, yes. But I cannot see that it matters. Alessandro was not at the mercery that night.'

'Are you certain? What if Hugo sent for Portinari while you were locked in your bedchamber? What if he confronted him with Goodwife Kendall's accusations? What if Hugo tried to renege on their bargain? Perhaps the Italian lost his temper and killed him.' In her enthusiasm for this theory, Rosamond gestured so vigorously with one hand that she nearly overturned the inkpot.

'He might have struck Hugo in anger,' Lina conceded, 'but I doubt he would stab him to death. How could he expect to collect a debt once Hugo was dead?'

'From his widow.' A thought struck Rosamond and she grinned. 'Then again, if neither of them killed Hugo, mayhap Alessandro will decide he'd prefer to marry Isolde to settle Hugo's account.'

Lina shuddered. 'I'd not wish a man with the pox on anyone. Despite her accusations against me, Isolde is still kin.'

'But such a solution would leave you free to marry elsewhere,' Lady Appleton murmured.

At those words, the expression on Lina's face turned wistful.

Lady Appleton's eyes narrowed. Her voice had an edge to it when she asked the next question. 'Who else objected to this marriage?'

'No one.' Lina's reply came much too quickly to be believed. She began to toy with one of her rings. It was of the type known as a gimmal, with double hoops and bezels joined together at the base. Such rings were customarily given by a man to his beloved.

'Whose name is inscribed next to yours?' Of a sudden, it occurred to Rosamond that if there was someone else Lina would prefer to wed, the revelation of Portinari's affliction provided her with a convenient excuse to refuse the match.

'Tommaso has naught to do with this.'

Rosamond exchanged a skeptical glance with her foster mother. 'Tommaso? Another Italian?'

Abandoning the coffin desk, Rosamond crossed the room to give Lina her handkerchief. Once again, tears appeared to be imminent.

Sniffling, dabbing at her eyes, Lina blurted out her answer. 'Tommaso Sassetti is Alessandro's nephew, his sister's son.'

'His heir?'

'Only if he does not displease his uncle. He has no money of his own. If we were to wed, we would be penniless without my dowry. At best, Tommaso might find employment as a translator, and I would have to work in some other silkwoman's shop.'

'How long have you known this Tommaso?' Rosamond asked.

'I met him when Isolde and Hugo and I dined with Alessandro.'

'So he must have been aware of his uncle's plans for you.'

Underscored by pitiful sobs, Lina provided a disjointed account of her courtship by Tommaso. To Rosamond it sounded as if that young man might have believed that Hugo Hackett was the only obstacle between him and Lina's dowry.

She returned to the desk and added Tommaso Sassetti's name to her list of suspects.

SEVEN

The next morning, when Rosamond would have resumed her male attire and ridden astride to London, even though doing so put her at risk of arrest for pretending to be a man, Lady Appleton offered her an alternative. 'Take my coach and keep it until you are able to return here with it and the news that the murderer has been apprehended.'

'You own a coach?' Rosamond could not hide her surprise.

The sight of these cumbersome vehicles had become more common in recent years, especially in London, but the usual state of England's roads made coaches slow and unreliable for long distances. While old age or frailty might persuade some wealthy persons to purchase one, Rosamond would have expected her foster mother to prefer a litter when she could no longer keep her seat on a horse.

'It is convenient for trips to Canterbury or Dover. You may find it useful to convey the impression that you are the sort to spend freely. Arrive in a coach, richly dressed, and every door will open for you.'

'That could be an advantage,' Rosamond conceded.

The decision made, she set aside the disguise and put on the clothes she had worn the previous day. They were simple garments, easy to slip into and unadorned. She looked more like a servant than a wealthy gentlewoman, but that would scarce matter on the journey from Leigh Abbey to London. Rosamond adjusted the looking glass and began to comb her long, thick hair.

Behind her she could see Lady Appleton neatly folding the parts of her discarded disguise and packing them in Rosamond's saddle bag. In addition to her wig, there was a shirt of fine Holland cloth, knitted stocks to cover her lower limbs and breeches for the upper, a blue doublet with matching sleeves and turned-back cuffs and, last of all, the warm black wool coat and a black cap with a silver badge. She had another cap at home, of the sort all males who had not sufficient income to be deemed gentlemen were required by law to wear on Sundays and holidays. It was an undistinguished item, flat and made from closely knitted and felted dark brown wool. Rosamond much preferred the black one.

'I have been thinking about how to best get answers. I could go as myself, as Lina's friend, but if Isolde truly believes her sister is the killer, she will not welcome my questions.' Rosamond's comb caught a snarl and she winced. Working with great care, she untangled it. 'Worse than that, as Jennet suggested, my very presence might make Isolde remember Leigh Abbey and lead her to suspect where Lina is hiding.'

'If you are as clever with disguises as I have been led to believe, you could visit her shop using several different identities without anyone being the wiser. Has Lina's sister ever met you?'

'No, but she might recognize my name.'

'If Lina has spoken of you, it would be from her time here, *before* you wed. Anything to do with your marriage would have been a forbidden topic in that household. Isolde might be suspicious of a Mistress Appleton, but she'll not know the well-to-do Mistress Jaffrey.'

Rosamond wished she could feel certain of that. 'A disguise is likely safer.'

'Just remember to tell as few lies as possible, whether you are there as yourself or another. That way it is easier to keep them straight.'

It was good advice. Rosamond took it into account during the two long days she spent making plans while the coach transported her over the bone-jarring ruts and bumps of the old Roman road to London. It was in better repair than most, but cushions on bare wood offered little in the way of padding, and Charles was an inexperienced driver. Rosamond clung to the leather strap beside her head and prayed they would not end up in a ditch.

By the time she arrived home, her body was a landscape of colorful bruises.

Willow House in Bermondsey was a goodly messuage complete with gardens and outbuildings. Moments after the coach rattled into the courtyard, the entire household turned out to welcome the mistress. Even the gray and white cat, Watling, bestirred himself.

He was picking his way across the cobblestones when Rosamond scooped him up in her arms and hugged him tightly to her breast. When he grunted in protest, she scratched him behind his ragged ear, damaged in a long-ago battle for dominance with another feline, and cooed at him until he obliged her with a rumbling purr.

Slinging the cat over one shoulder, Rosamond greeted her servants while Charles saw to the horses and the coach. Formalities complete, she entered the house and made straight for the stairs that led to the upper floor and her private quarters. Within a quarter hour, her tiring maid, a short, stocky woman with small, wide-spaced eyes, entered the privy chamber between the gallery and Rosamond's bedchamber bearing a tray heavy with the cook's idea of a light supper.

Like a good servant, she stood by in silence while her mistress assuaged her hunger. Only after Rosamond had eaten her fill did the maid speak. Her comment was pithy, verging on rude. It was also in Polish.

Rosamond laughed and replied in the same tongue before switching to English, a language that Melka, for all that she had been born in Poland, understood perfectly well. She gave her maid an abridged account of the visit to Leigh Abbey.

Shortly after Rosamond and Rob had married, Rosamond's mother, Eleanor Pendennis, had sent Melka, her own tiring maid, to wait upon her daughter and to send detailed reports back to Cornwall. It had taken many months, but gradually Melka's loyalty had shifted from mother to daughter. Rosamond no longer hesitated to confide in her and had no qualms about trusting Melka with the secret of Lina's hiding place.

As Rosamond outlined her plans for the coming days she could tell that Melka did not approve. The clucking sound she made and the way she was shaking her head as she departed with the tray gave further proof of the Polish woman's opinion, but Rosamond knew that Melka would not attempt to talk her out of her quest. Rather, she would do all she could to help her mistress prove Lina innocent and discover the identity of the real culprit. On the morrow, although she would still grumble about it, she would accompany Rosamond on her first visit to the scene of the crime.

Melka was already inside the coach when Rosamond climbed in for the ride across London Bridge and into the city. It would have looked odd for a wealthy woman to travel without a female servant but it belatedly occurred to Rosamond that Melka's distinctly foreign appearance made her far too recognizable. The Polish woman would have to remain in the vehicle when Rosamond went into Hugo Hackett's mercery.

Rosamond's appearance was also distinctive, but it was not her own. She had altered her looks by wearing a coarse black wig, gluing a large, hairy mole to her chin, artfully applying cosmetics and adding several inches of padding to her figure. Her own mother would not recognize her, although she suspected that Lady Appleton might.

Once in London, the coach moved up Gracious Street at a ponderous pace. Rosamond had too much time for second thoughts. Long before she reached her destination, she regretted her decision to present herself as an older woman of wealth and prestige. Her disguise, the same one she wore to attend plays in the inn yard of the Horse's Head in Southwark, was heavy, cumbersome, and over-warm on this mild October morning. To add to her discomfort, the coach slowed to a crawl in the Stocks Market.

Built around the stocks where lawbreakers were pilloried, the Stocks Market was home to at least a dozen fishmongers and nearly that many butchers. Wood and canvas offered shelter from the elements, but they were no protection at all against the putrid odors of London's streets. In the Stocks Market, fish and flesh combined with the rest to give off a mighty stench. Rosamond felt a deep sympathy for the wrongdoers sentenced to penance. She was herself trapped in what amounted to a great lumbering cage.

'I should have told Charles to drive through Bucklersbury instead of taking Lombard Street to the Poultry,' she muttered, pressing one hand to her unsettled stomach. There would still have been foulness in the air, but it would have been mitigated by the heady aroma of imported spices from the many groceries and apothecary shops in the area.

The noise of the streets was filtered by canvas curtains. Rosamond pushed one aside once she felt the coach bear left into the Poultry and head toward West Cheap. Just past the Great Conduit another left turn brought them into the much more narrow Soper Lane. The sound of wheels rumbling over cobblestones failed to drown out the curses of a pedestrian forced to press himself into a doorway or suffer severe damage to his toes.

Charles brought the horses to a halt in front of a tall, timber-framed house in the north half of the street. A sign bearing the image of a maiden's head, the symbol used by members of the Mercers' Company, was prominently displayed above the door to Hugh Hackett's shop.

'Time to begin,' Rosamond said aloud. As soon as she spoke the words, her doubts vanished, as did the queasiness that had troubled her in the Stocks Market.

Once the coach's wooden steps had been unfolded, Rosamond emerged, bewigged and padded and confident she could carry off her deception. She was a wealthy matron of indeterminate age seeking the finest silk goods and the latest tittle-tattle.

Nine days had passed since Lina's discovery of the body. Hugo had been safely buried, most likely in the nearby church of St Pancras. Rosamond expected that the widow, no matter how sincere her mourning, would be deeply involved in the day-to-day running of her late husband's business. She should be, since her own livelihood depended upon it.

Before leaving Leigh Abbey, Rosamond had questioned Lina further about life in her sister's household. Her answers gave Rosamond some understanding of how husband and wife had worked together to make and market luxury goods. Hugo had acquired the silk yarn used for weaving, some imported and some prepared by Dutch silk workers living in London. Isolde Hackett and the silkwomen she trained wove the thrown silk to make laces, ribbons, bands, tassels, fringe, points, and buttons. Isolde traded on her own behalf and was therefore responsible for her own debts, but by selling everything her workshop produced in her husband's mercery, she enjoyed the best of both worlds. *Clever woman, Isolde*, Rosamond thought as she went in, *save for that bad habit of always deferring to her husband.*

'I am Lady Noone,' she announced in a carrying voice. She waved the stout walking stick she carried in the general direction of a display of caps, cauls, and coifs embroidered in silk. It had a solid knob at one end, useful for clearing a path when rude persons refused to give way. 'Is this the best you have to offer?'

She addressed her question to a pale-faced, slightly-built girl of no more than fifteen but before this waif could answer, an exceeding thin figure all in black appeared from the back of the shop. The widow's eyes lit up at the sight of the impressive vehicle standing just outside. Rosamond hid her amusement. It had been to produce just such a reaction that she had left the door to the street standing open. With luck Isolde Hackett, eager to please a potential customer wealthy enough to afford her own coach, would be willing to answer even blunt and insensitive questions.

Rosamond pretended to examine some silk buttons while she covertly watched Isolde's face. 'I heard you lost your husband, madam. A pity, that. Will his death affect your ability to obtain raw materials?'

The shopkeeper's smile did not waver. 'The Mercers' Company looks after its widows and orphans.'

Rosamond thumped her walking stick on the floor. 'A woman should know how to look after herself. I hear the Florentines import the best silks.' She chose that nationality deliberately, since Portinari had come to England from Florence.

'They dominated the trade in the past, it is true, and there are a number of Italian silk merchants still living in London. There are also several Flemish merchants here who specialize in silk production and the silk trade.'

Isolde's voice was steady but she held her hands tightly clasped together at waist level. To keep them from trembling? Rosamond wondered how much the other woman would tolerate in order to make a profitable sale. After examining points and laces and Bruges stockings, Rosamond moved on to pincushions and embroidered purses. She selected one of the latter to buy and handed it to Isolde to set aside for her.

'You should pick the wealthiest one and marry him,' Rosamond said in Lady Noone's most strident tone of voice. 'That would be the practical thing to do.'

Isolde's face drained of color. 'W-what?'

'Someone told me your sister was to marry Alessandro Portinari. Rich as old King Midas, he is.'

Tight-lipped, Isolde said, 'It is doubtful that there will be a marriage between them.'

'No? Well, then, I say marry him yourself.'

'I am newly widowed, Lady Noone. Aside from anything else, it is too early to think of such things.'

'Nonsense. Plan ahead, I always say.' Rosamond inspected the workmanship on a linen shift and added it to the pile of small but expensive items she intended to buy.

The pale-faced girl had already begun to tally the cost.

Rosamond moved closer to Isolde, lowering her voice. 'I heard something else, too. I heard that your husband did not just die. I heard he was *murdered*.' She gave a theatrical shudder as she whispered the last word.

Isolde swallowed convulsively. Rosamond hoped she was not about to be sick. Lady Noone was such a horrible old beldam that Rosamond almost felt sorry for anyone who had to deal with her. Almost. Isolde had brought this inquisition down upon herself by being so quick to accuse an innocent woman.

'Well?' The walking stick struck the floorboards with a resounding thump. 'Is it true?'

'It is.' Isolde squared her shoulders. 'He was most foully slain.'

Rosamond opened her eyes as wide as they would go, but she did not have to feign her avid interest in Isolde's answers. 'Who did it? When will he hang?'

'That very sister you spoke of stabbed him to death. Ungrateful, unnatural creature! Then she fled. No one knows where to find her.'

In her best Lady Noone manner, Rosamond scoffed at the idea of Lina's guilt. 'A young woman kill a strong man?

Nonsense.' She wagged a gloved finger under Isolde's nose. 'You mark my words, if he was slain with a knife, it was a man killed him. A woman would have had sense enough to use poison.'

Isolde gaped at her.

'What man got in and did foul murder?' Rosamond asked as she reached into her purse for the money to pay for her purchases. 'You ask yourself that and you'll find the real villain!'

EIGHT

Back in the coach, Rosamond told Melka everything that had transpired in Hugo Hackett's mercery.

'Girl?' Melka asked.

Rosamond frowned. She had been concentrating on Isolde and nearly forgotten there was anyone else in the shop. Did the girl know anything useful? Rosamond supposed she was one of Isolde's silkwomen-in-training, although now that she thought about it, the girl had been sewing some small linen item all the while Rosamond had been questioning Isolde. One of the servants, then. Lina had said there were three maids, but that didn't seem right, either. Would a maidservant be trusted to mind a shop full of valuable merchandise for her mistress? To wait on customers? Rosamond trusted Melka with her life, but Melka was no ordinary servant.

The coach swayed as it made the turn from Aldgate Street, and she forgot all about the nameless female in the mercer's shop. There were many fine, fair houses along the gentle curve that was Lime Street. One belonged to Alessandro Portinari. Cecily Kendall dwelt in another.

There was no trade sign to guide Rosamond this time, but Lina had told her to look for a house that had boxes filled with flowers beneath its windows. Widow Kendall lodged with a family of Walloons, refugees from the Low Countries where those who had broken away from the Catholic Church feared execution as heretics if they stayed in their homeland. They were Dutch, or mayhap Flemings. The queen had welcomed such immigrants for what they could teach English workers about weaving, but ordinary folk, especially in London, treated all strangers with suspicion. Rosamond had been a trifle surprised to hear that an English woman was willing to rent rooms from them.

'There!' she called out, and the coach rolled to a stop.

Once again Rosamond told Melka to remain where she was. She descended the folding steps, black wig and padding in place and walking stick in hand. She took the time to look both left and right, wondering which house belonged to Portinari, and nearly stumbled when she recognized the young man just leaving the house on the left. He was a portrait painter, Marcus Gheeraerts the Younger. She started to call out a greeting but remembered in the nick of time that he would not know who she was in this disguise.

A servant took her up to Cecily Kendall, whose rooms were at the top of the house. Although Rosamond had not changed her clothing, she now called herself Mistress Flackley rather than Lady Noone. She presented herself as a comfortably well-to-do widow from Kent who was seeking to purchase a house in the city. By this ploy, Rosamond hoped to persuade Cecily Kendall to talk about everyone who lived nearby. Later, if necessary, Rosamond would question more of Portinari's neighbors in search of intelligence about the Italian silk merchant and his habits.

The old woman sat beside a window that overlooked the house to the right. One leg rested on a stool and a pair of crutches lay near at hand. Seeing no bandages, Rosamond assumed her difficulties in walking stemmed from age and infirmity rather than from some recent injury. After she thumped her way across the room, Rosamond repeated the story that had satisfied the servant.

Cecily Kendall was not so easily deceived. She reminded Rosamond of a hawk and not only because of her beak-like nose. She peered into Rosamond's face with beady little eyes and a penetrating gaze, studying her intently. When she was satisfied, she made a snorting sound that could mean anything from 'despite all that face paint I can see how young you are' to 'that is a very ugly mole on your chin.' Rosamond had attached this last bit of her disguise with the help of her glue pot and was uncommon proud of the way it looked.

Whatever Widow Kendall concluded, she did not send her visitor away. Her desire to enliven what appeared to be a passing dull existence worked in Rosamond's favor. 'Pull that stool over here next to me, Mistress Flackley, and sit down. Otherwise you will give me a crick in my neck looking up at you.'

She did not offer refreshments, not even a drink of barley water, but she proved more than willing to answer questions about her neighbors. After warning Rosamond that many of them were foreign-born, she expressed admiration for immigrants from the Low Countries.

'Hard workers, they are.'

'And those from elsewhere?' Rosamond inquired. 'Spain? France? The Italian states?'

'I do not trust any Spaniard or Italian and I am wary of the French, as every good Englishwoman should be. More southerly climes produce even more dangerous men. I came upon a visitor from Morocco once. In Rye, it was. Strange clothes. Strange manners. And his skin was as black as the devil's own heart.'

Rye, a coastal town, attracted many foreign visitors. 'I wonder what he thought of you?' Rosamond mused.

'I've no doubt he wanted to make a slave of me. He was a Barbary pirate. I feel certain of it.' Head nodding so vigorous that a few gray strands escaped her close-fitting linen cap emphasized her conviction that this was so. She leaned closer to Rosamond and placed one hand on her arm. Her voice dropped an octave. 'They attack English ships, those Barbary pirates do, and take everyone on board prisoner. They sell the poor souls in the slave markets and their new masters make them turn Turk. If they do not, the pirates kill them outright in most horrible ways.'

To turn Turk meant to forsake Christianity for Islam. 'I have heard that,' Rosamond replied. 'You had a lucky escape. If you had been alone with him for even a moment, he would most assuredly have tried to carry you off.'

Widow Kendall chuckled. 'I was much younger then, and

pleasing to look at. I'd have brought a good price from a wealthy Turk in search of a concubine.'

Rosamond found the old woman's words disturbing and the hand still resting against the rich brocade of her sleeve even more so. Every finger joint was swollen. Across the back, blue veins bulged in parchment-thin, deeply-lined skin. She was glad she had remembered to disguise the youthful appearance of her own hands by wearing gloves and plagued by the thought that one day she would not need a disguise to look old.

She cleared her throat. She must not let herself become distracted. She had come here for a reason. 'Have you lived in Lime Street a long time?' she asked.

'More than forty years. This house belonged to my husband until he sold it to the Flemings who live here now. Sick, he was. Dying. And I was none too well myself. They bought it with the provision that I hold life interest in these rooms.'

'They are most excellent lodgings.' Rosamond glanced through the window and caught her breath. Cecily Kendall released her arm as she, too, leaned closer to the opening.

From this vantage point, they could see straight inside the house next door. When she looked into the first floor room, Rosamond saw no signs of occupation but on the second floor two maidservants stood in plain sight. They appeared to be quarreling. As Rosamond and Widow Kendall watched, one flounced off. The other stamped her foot, then flung herself down on a narrow bed and burst into tears.

'How amusing for you,' Rosamond said to her hostess. 'Do you observe many such dramas?'

'Hah! This is nothing. Some days what goes on in Portinari's house is better than anything you'd see in a play.'

Rosamond's heart beat a little faster in anticipation. It seemed her luck was in. The widow herself had brought the Florentine into the conversation. 'Tragedy?' she asked. 'Or is it comedy? Or mayhap farce?'

'All three. After all, an *Italian* lives there.' Goody Kendall's sage nod spoke volumes, but Rosamond needed specific details.

'This Portinari – is he wealthy? I hear some Italian strangers are so rich that they even make loans to the queen.'

'That may be so but I would not trust any of them to deal fairly with me, and this one, Alessandro Portinari, is an exceeding vile creature.'

'In what way?'

'He visits whores.'

'How can you possibly know that?' The widow appeared to be too infirm to leave her rooms.

'His servants talk to mine.' She hesitated, but the desire to impress overcame any scruples she might have had about sharing confidences with a new acquaintance. 'I set someone to follow him, so I know whereof I speak.'

'Why would you do such a thing?' Rosamond's astonishment was genuine. Most nosy neighbors contented themselves with watching through the windows.

A sigh escaped her. 'I felt responsible.' Her gaze shifted away from Rosamond's keen-eyed stare. 'There is a young woman who was wont to deliver silk goods to me. Alessandro Portinari would never have known she existed had he not glimpsed her on one of those visits. When I saw her go into that house to dine with the ugsome old devil, she and her family with her – a sister and the sister's husband – and then I heard talk of a betrothal, I felt compelled to discover if what my maid had told me was true.'

'But surely such a marriage is respectable. It is not as if most men do not make use of prostitutes before they wed.'

Tears welled up in the widow's beady black eyes. 'I warrant her kin were happy to sell her to him for their own profit. All of them are in the silk trade, you see, the Hacketts and Portinari. Pots of money to be made there.'

Rosamond waited, sure her informant would provide more details without prompting. Once again a gnarled hand crept out to clutch at her sleeve. With a quaver in her voice, the old woman resumed her story.

'When I heard all that betrothal talk, it fair made me sick. To find proof of Portinari's wickedness, I devised a plan. Young Roeloff is a good lad. The oldest son. His mother is in the habit of sending him up here to make sure I have everything I need. She does not speak much English, for all the years she's been in this country, but he was born here.'

Rosamond nodded encouragement. Widow Kendall had recruited a boy from the family she lodged with. 'You set him to spy on Portinari?'

'I did. I told him to follow the merchant when he went out, especially at night.' Her grip tightened on Rosamond's arm. 'Roeloff discovered that he frequents a notorious brothel in Clerkenwell. He followed Portinari to the bawdy house and there he saw them *both*.'

'Both? Portinari and a bawd?'

'Portinari and Hugo Hackett, my young friend's guardian. They went together to the brothel run by a woman they call Black Luce.' With an abrupt movement, Widow Kendall removed her hand. A stricken expression came over her features.

'What is it?' Rosamond asked, alarmed by the old woman's sudden pallor.

Cecily Kendall spoke more to herself than to Rosamond. 'Mercer Hackett was most horribly murdered not three weeks afterward.'

'Because he visited a bawdy house?'

The widow toyed with the lace at her wrist. 'Mayhap I should not have told her what Roeloff saw.'

So that was it – the old woman felt responsible for Hugo's death because she had told Lina what Roeloff discovered. Rosamond frowned, wondering why it had not occurred to Cecily Kendall until now to blame herself. She did not suppose it mattered. Her misery was plain, and it was obvious that she held herself accountable because she believed Lina guilty of stabbing Hugo. Rosamond wished she could assure her that Lina was innocent but that was not possible without revealing that Mistress Flackley was an imposter.

Rosamond's frown deepened as she considered the widow's story. The old woman's behavior had been exceeding odd. She had sent a lad to spy on Portinari, but, assuming that the sequence of events Lina had sketched out for Rosamond was correct, she did not tell Lina what Roeloff had discovered until some time after that visit to Clerkenwell. The dinner at Portinari's house had to be the one at which Lina and Tommaso had first met, and that placed it weeks, mayhap months before the murder.

There was something else bothering Rosamond, too. Lina had refused to marry Portinari because Cecily Kendall had told her he was afflicted with the French pox, yet the widow had made no mention of that condition to Rosamond. Indeed, now that she thought about it, she had to wonder how even the nosiest of neighbors could know such an intimate detail. As far as she could see, Widow Kendall had observed Portinari only from a distance.

'I do not condone immoral behavior,' she said, choosing her words with care, 'but if every bride demanded virginity in a husband, few couples would ever marry.'

'It is not just that he went with whores, but that he was with unclean women.' Cecily Kendall lowered her voice. 'He caught the French welcome.'

'How—?'

'His manservant bore witness to the sores on his member.' For emphasis, Goody Kendall nodded again, this time with so much vigor that she nearly toppled out of her chair.

'And the manservant told *you* this?'

'As good as. He revealed the ugly truth to one of Portinari's maidservants, as a warning not to let the master have his way with her. Then she told my maid and my maid repeated the story to me. I'd have her tell you so herself if I had not sent her out to buy food for my supper.'

Rosamond made a tsking sound and leaned closer. 'This is a most serious accusation. It is true that sores are a symptom of the pox but might there not be some other cause?'

'He has thinning hair, another sure sign of the disease. And the young woman, Godlina her name is, when I told her what I knew, confirmed that Portinari speaks in a raspy voice and that he douses himself in strong scent, no doubt to hide the stench of his illness. Altered voice, bad breath, loss of hair, and the figs – all signs.' She gave another vigorous nod.

'Figs?'

'Figs – the sores. Venomous pustules with a certain hardness that stick out in the head, the forehead, the brow, the face, the beard, at the corners of the lips, and in a man's secret parts.'

The widow's eyes gleamed with satisfaction as she reeled off the catalog of symptoms, making Rosamond wonder what

Portinari had ever done to offend her. Surely just being Italian was not enough to provoke such venom. The old beldame seemed fit for Bedlam when she made such wild claims, or else she had first-hand experience with someone else afflicted with the French pox. Her late husband, mayhap? Rosamond was not about to inquire. Instead she ventured the question Mistress Flackley might be expected to ask.

'Are you not afraid to speak so freely of this? If your young friend goes to Master Portinari with your story and he can prove it is not true, he will be most wroth with you. Why, I have heard of many a lawsuit filed and damages collected when similar charges have been made without foundation.' She had also heard of a husband suing a barber-surgeon when he'd failed to cure his wife of this foul disease.

'I considered long and hard before I spoke,' Widow Kendall assured her, 'but I know my duty as a good Christian. That young woman had to be apprised of the situation. I had no choice but to warn her.'

She had passed on her conclusion, convincing Lina it was the truth. Rosamond had her doubts. Young Roeloff might well have told the old woman what he thought she wanted to hear. As for the stories spread by servants, she did not put much faith in such tales. Employees dissatisfied with the way their employer treated them were not above taking petty revenge. And a manservant warning one of the maids about the master? Rosamond would not be surprised to learn that the manservant wanted the maid for himself.

A little silence had fallen between the two women. With a sense of alarm, Rosamond realized that Widow Kendall was staring at her with a speculative look in her eyes. Rosamond did not think she had said or done anything to make the other woman suspicious, but the widow's next words came as a relief all the same.

'If you are looking for a house in Lime Street, Mistress Flackley,' Cecily Kendall said, 'mayhap you can persuade Alessandro Portinari to sell you his and move elsewhere. You would acquire a fine, fair dwelling and everyone who lives hereabout would be rid of a blight on the neighborhood.'

'Has he family here in England?'

'There is only a nephew – Tommaso.'

Rosamond detected a new note of disapproval in the widow's voice. 'Does this Tommaso also live next door?'

'He *did*. He moved out a few days ago . . . after a great noisy row with his uncle.'

That would have been right after the news of Hackett's murder reached them. Rosamond's interest quickened. 'What did they quarrel about? Where did he go?'

'No one knows the answer to either of those questions.'

'You must have a theory.' Busybodies like Cecily Kendall always did.

With an absent motion, the old woman rubbed her knee through the thick layers of skirt and petticoat and shift. It pained her, Rosamond supposed, her gaze sliding to the crutches and back again.

'No doubt they argued over the lad's spendthrift ways. As to where he went, some few months back, when he had need of money, Tommaso found employment as a translator for the French ambassador. It is possible he returned there after his uncle threw him out.'

To give credence to her story about looking for a house to buy, Rosamond extended her visit for another quarter of an hour to discuss other property in the vicinity. There was little available but she did learn that the Gheeraerts family, portrait painters all, lived in the house from which she'd seen young Marcus emerge. Widow Kendall revealed nothing more about Portinari, Tommaso, or Hugo Hackett and when she began to ask questions about Mistress Flackley's family, friends, and current abode, Rosamond made haste to take her leave.

At the door, she paused to look back. When her gaze fell upon the crutches, she was moved to pity for an old woman confined to these few small rooms. She spoke on impulse. 'When I was a child, my mother was crippled in an accident. During the many years she struggled to regain the use of her legs, she got about by means of a wheeled chair. I am certain you could find someone here in London who has the skill to make such a thing for you.'

Embarrassed at having shared something so personal,

Rosamond hurried away without waiting for Widow Kendall to respond. She did not often speak of that period of her life. Her mother had taken her away from Leigh Abbey, insisting that Rosamond belonged with her and her husband in distant Cornwall. Confined to bed and chair, Eleanor Pendennis had been a tyrant to deal with on her best days. In hindsight, Rosamond regretted that she had not shown more compassion for her mother's suffering, but at the time she'd been consumed by her own misery.

She jerked open the door to the coach and heaved herself inside without waiting for Charles to pull down the steps. Coming face-to-face with Melka, who had nursed Eleanor throughout those difficult years, did not improve Rosamond's mood. She brooded all the way back to Willow House.

NINE

Rosamond set out at mid-morning the next day. Once again she was accompanied by Melka but this time they walked from Bermondsey to Pepper Alley Stairs in Southwark, the first landing place west of London Bridge. There Rosamond hired a wherry to take them upriver to the French embassy. Lady Appleton had meant well, but a coach was more hindrance than help in London's crowded streets. Wearing a disguise had also proven cumbersome. For this day's outing, Rosamond was dressed as what she was, a young married woman with the means to indulge whatever whim struck her fancy. Her plan was to pretend that she had developed an interest in learning to speak foreign languages.

Salisbury Court, the house that had been home to French ambassadors in England for the last fifteen years, was situated between Fleet Street and the Thames, a short distance to the west of the ancient London wall but still within the boundaries of the city. Lord Buckhurst's house was on one side of the embassy with the buildings that comprised the Temple, one of the Inns of Court, on the other. All three properties were hard by Bridewell, the infamous house of correction where bawds were imprisoned and set to work picking oakum.

Rosamond and Melka disembarked at Water Lane, a narrow street that led north from the river. A second path that was even more narrow veered off to their right and climbed steeply as it followed the garden wall on the east side of Salisbury Court. Rosamond reasoned that there must be a door in that wall, if only for the convenience of the gardeners. It did not take her long to locate it. She was pleased to find that the heavy wooden gate was unlocked. It swung silently open at the merest touch.

Although the gardens appeared to be empty, Rosamond hesitated before entering them. What did it signify that she could gain access so easily by way of a back entrance? Some of the ambassador's visitors, she concluded, did not wish anyone to be aware of their comings and goings. Finding a reason for this did not require much thought. An embassy inhabited by the representative of a Catholic country was one of the few places in England where papist rites were permitted. Some English men and women who secretly clung to the tenets of the old church must come to Salisbury Court to hear mass. Perhaps they were married here, too, or brought their children to be christened.

Religion did not much interest Rosamond. She complied with the law by attending church every Sunday at St Olave's and made certain that all the members of her household did likewise. She avoided meat on fish days. But she had far more interesting books to read than her Bible and never paid the slightest attention to sermons. If the Church of England had kept confession as one of its requirements, she'd have been inclined to invent sins just to shock the priest.

She had passed through the gardens and was approaching a door when it was flung open to allow a man to exit the embassy. Rosamond stopped short. So did the man. Melka took a protective step closer to her mistress.

Rosamond did not have to pretend confusion. Uncertain whether to go forward or retreat, she presented a convincing picture of a damsel in distress. The stranger's eyes roved over the jewels sewn into her gown, lingering first on her wedding

ring and then on the long rope of pearls looped around her
neck. Seeing by these trappings that she was no Puritan, he
smiled and spoke to her in English.

'You need have no fear of betrayal here, madam. Enter in
the assurance of God's grace and man's charity.'

He took her for a fellow papist. Rosamond collected her
wits and whispered, 'Is there a priest?'

The man's smile widened. He was older than she, no youth
but not yet far advanced into middle age. By his dress, he was
a gentleman. 'Aye. He is a good man and will give you comfort,
except that he is not here at the embassy this morning. If you
would hear mass, you must return on the morrow and some
hours earlier than this.'

Rosamond endeavored to sound meek. 'If I come then,
where should I go? Is there a chapel in this place?' As far as
she could see, no separate building existed for that purpose.

He offered her his arm. 'Let me show you the way.'

Rosamond drew back, feigning caution. 'I-I do not know
you.' When he seemed reluctant to reveal his name, she pushed
harder, although she was not sure why. She never expected to
encounter this gentleman again. 'You say it is safe here, but
if you will not even tell me who you are—'

'Throckmorton. Francis Throckmorton. There. You see?
There is trust among co-religionists.' He looked expectant.

Head down, voice low, Rosamond grasped the proffered
arm and mumbled the word Mistress followed by a few
nonsense syllables. Whether from courtesy or simple lack of
curiosity, he accepted that she'd given him her name and did
not ask her to repeat it.

With Melka trailing after them, Francis Throckmorton
escorted Rosamond into the embassy. Like the door into the
garden, the one into the house was unlocked and swung open
on well-oiled hinges. As he'd promised, he showed her the
way to the chapel and then, in haste, took his leave of her,
remarking that he was late for an appointment.

The chapel, fortuitously, was empty. Rosamond was spared
the awkward pretense of kneeling and crossing herself, actions
she supposed any good Catholic would take upon entering a
church. In truth, she was uncertain how papists worshipped.

There was a great deal of praying to saints, or so she'd heard. And their clergy wore rich vestments instead of plain black.

Rosamond left the chapel as soon as Throckmorton's footsteps faded away.

'We must locate one of the ambassador's servants,' she whispered to Melka, 'someone who will know where to find Tommaso Sassetti.'

She turned a corner and found herself in a gallery. The windows faced the river and offered an excellent view all the way across the Thames to Paris Garden, the place where the bull and bear baitings were held.

A woman sat reading in an alcove. She looked up at the sound of Rosamond's entrance and quickly rose to her feet. She wore plain clothing without ornamentation, indicating that she was a servant of some sort – a privileged one, if she had time for books, but not so grand as to risk offending a gentlewoman as finely dressed as Rosamond was.

Rosamond addressed her in French, saying that she had come to the embassy because she wished to further her knowledge of languages both by improving her command of the French tongue and by learning others. Was it true, she asked, that the French ambassador had an Italian translator in his employ? Was it possible that this man might be willing to tutor her in that language?

Like any well-trained domestic, the woman showed no surprise at this admittedly odd request, only asked that they follow her out of the gallery. After passing through a maze of rooms and passages, they came at length to a spacious chamber. It was occupied by a girl of four or five years, seated at a small table littered with papers and books, and a man who was too old by at least a decade to be Lina's Tommaso.

'Monsieur Florio,' their guide announced, adding by way of explanation that he was the Italian tutor to the French ambassador's young daughter.

Florio looked puzzled by their arrival but inclined his head in courteous greeting, first to Rosamond and then to the Frenchwoman. He spoke to the little girl in a language Rosamond supposed was his native tongue. The child replied in kind and took the time to curtsey to Rosamond before she grasped the hand of the plainly dressed woman – her nursemaid, it would seem – and the two of them left together.

'I did not mean to interrupt your lesson.' Rosamond spoke in English.

Master Florio replied in the same language and with only the slightest trace of an accent. 'It was almost time to end our session for the day. It does not do to overtax young minds.'

Once again, Rosamond explained that she wished to improve her command of French and learn to speak Italian. As she talked, she wandered about the schoolroom, idly touching this object and that, the perfect picture of a bored gentlewoman. Master Florio was not the Italian she had been looking for but surely he knew where she could find the elusive Tommaso.

'I am told you are the best of language teachers,' she said, seeking to flatter him before she started asking questions.

'That is my humble distinction.'

No modesty there, Rosamond thought. 'You speak excellent English.'

He smiled. 'My mother was English and before I came here I was at Magdalen tutoring young Emmanuel Barnes, eldest son of the bishop of Durham, in both Italian and French.'

'Magdalen?'

'A college at Oxford.'

'Ah.' Rosamond knew something of Cambridge but nothing at all about England's other great university.

'I teach with the help of a manual of my own composing.' Florio plucked a slender volume from the table where the girl had been sitting and offered it to Rosamond.

In silence, she read the title, *Florio, His Firste Fruites*, then opened it to see that he had dedicated the book to the Earl of Leicester, Queen Elizabeth's favorite. It was also addressed to 'Gentilhoumini Inglesi' and to 'Gentilhoumini e Mercanti Italiani.' The text ran for forty-four chapters, much of it arranged in two columns of phrases, Italian and English. There was an Italian grammar at the end. A very sensible arrangement, Rosamond thought.

She could not help but notice that some of the Italian words were similar to their French counterparts. That should make it simpler to master the new language. Rosamond was already

fluent in Latin, Greek, Polish and Russian, as well as in
French. Learning to speak in other tongues had always been
easy for her.

'Do you live at the embassy?' she asked aloud.

'I do, but I am permitted to give private lessons in my
lodgings.' His gesture encompassed both the schoolroom and
whatever lay beyond the closed door opposite the one through
which Rosamond had entered.

He named his fee, to which she readily agreed, adding, 'I
wish to begin daily lessons as soon as may be.'

'You have not yet given me your name, madam.'

'Have I not? How careless of me.' Lie or tell the truth? Her
real name, she decided. What harm could it do? 'I am Mistress
Jaffrey. My husband and I have an interest in the world beyond
these shores and plan to travel to both France and the Italian
states one day.'

This had the advantage of being true. Rosamond had an
aunt who lived in Padua. There was a small English conclave
in that city, predominantly made up of gentlemen studying
medicine at the university.

Belatedly, she remembered that she had not come to find
someone to teach her Italian but rather to locate Lina's beloved.

'Tell me, Master Florio, are you the only gentleman of
Italian descent employed by the French ambassador?'

Florio's hand clenched on his book but he gave no other
sign that her question disturbed him. 'There is the ambassador's
gentleman, Giordano Bruno. We both joined this household
at the same time in late summer, just after the ambassador's
wife returned from France with their daughters.'

Rosamond frowned. It appeared she would have to be blunt.
'I had heard that Tommaso Sassetti was also in residence.'

She knew at once that she had made a mistake. Master
Florio's scowl was fierce. 'That young man is nothing but
trouble. And you, as a married woman, should know better
than to show an interest in such a fellow.'

Behind her, Rosamond heard fabric rustle as Melka reacted
to a perceived threat to her mistress. Rosamond moved between
her maidservant and the tutor, head bowed in an attempt to
look chastened. 'He seemed pleasant enough.'

'Is he the real reason you wish to learn Italian?' Florio asked. 'Do you think to impress young Sassetti?'

'You misjudge me, Master Florio,' Rosamond said with as much dignity as she could muster. 'I have told you I have plans to travel on the Continent.'

Florio made a small sound she took as a sign of disbelief. Stalking past her into the passage, he called for one of the ambassador's servants. When a man in livery appeared, Florio ordered him, in French, to find Tommaso Sassetti and bring him to the schoolroom. Then he turned a stern look on Rosamond. 'You may speak with him in my presence but then you must leave.'

A tense quarter of an hour passed. Although Rosamond spent the time staring at the pages of Florio's Italian grammar, her mind was filled with questions about the man she'd come to meet. Was he a lover or a murderer? He had given Lina a ring, but that did not mean he cared for her. It was more likely he was after her dowry. Master Florio clearly thought he was an unscrupulous scoundrel who took advantage of women.

Should she try to cozen Tommaso? Or catch him off guard with a direct accusation? And what would Master Florio make of it if she revealed her true reason for coming here?

She was both disappointed and relieved when the servant returned with the news that Tommaso had left the embassy an hour earlier. He was not expected to return until evening.

Rosamond closed the little book and rose from the table. Her time at Salisbury Court had not been wasted. She had confirmed that Tommaso was part of the household and she had an excuse to return. She fully intended to pursue her study of the Italian language.

TEN

By water and then afoot, Rosamond traveled from Salisbury Court to Soper Lane. En route, she bought two meat pies from a street vendor, offering one to Melka. Muttering in Polish, the actual words inaudible, the

maid sent her mistress a look that said she'd rather eat a live
rat. Since the morning's activities and the long walk had made
her hungry, Rosamond ate both pies, popping the last morsel
into her mouth just as they reached the Hackett mercery. A
small crowd had gathered outside to eavesdrop on the loud
argument already in progress within.

'That Goodwife Hackett is most intemperate,' one man said,
shaking his head.

'Always did have a sharp tongue,' said a woman in a dove
gray gown.

'A virago,' another man pronounced.

'A shrew,' agreed a third.

'Who is she berating?' Rosamond asked, pushing through
Isolde's nosy neighbors to reach the shop door.

Before anyone could answer her, Isolde's voice rose to a
shriek. 'Only her death will satisfy me!'

Rosamond sucked in a startled breath.

'She speaks of her sister,' said the woman in gray.

Rosamond opened the door and stepped into the shop,
closely followed by Melka. Neither combatant took any notice
of them.

'She must pay with her life for killing my husband!'

Isolde shouted the words into the face of a toothsome young
man. Dark hair curled over his forehead. Dark, soulful eyes
beseeched Isolde's mercy as he seized one of her flailing hands
in both of his and drew it toward his mouth as if he meant to
kiss it.

'Will nothing else satisfy you, *madonna*?' His voice was
deep and carried with it the sultry flavors of Italy.

Rosamond's eyes narrowed. Tommaso Sassetti – he could
be no one else.

Isolde used her free hand to slap the impudent fellow.
Tommaso released her and stepped away. The look on his face
put Rosamond in mind of a puppy kicked by its master, but
it provoked neither sympathy nor remorse from Lina's sister.

'I will be satisfied when I have proof that Lina is dead. I
want to see her burn.'

'My turtledove would not kill. She is all that is gentle and
sweet.' Tommaso's hands moved when he spoke, as if to

emphasize his agitation, but his voice lacked conviction. He had no doubt begun to question the wisdom of wanting to marry a woman accused of murder.

Isolde leaned in, one finger jabbing the embroidery at the front of Tommaso's dusky orange doublet. 'If you know where she is hiding, sirrah, you are as guilty as she is and must pay the price.' Then her lips twisted into a terrible mockery of a smile. 'If you *do* know, tell her I will settle for seeing her bloated corpse pulled out of the Thames. If she regrets what she did, let her fling herself into the river out of remorse and so drown.'

Rosamond cleared her throat. 'How do you know she killed him?'

Isolde turned on her, a wild light in her eyes. 'How do I know? How do I know? I will tell you how I know. She was standing over Hugo's body when I found him, the bloodstained knife still in her hand. And then she flung it away from her and ran. What further proof does anyone need of her guilt?'

Holding the knife? Lina had not mentioned that detail, but Rosamond thought she could explain away the omission. 'What more natural, though foolish, than to attempt to save a man who has been stabbed by pulling out the blade?'

'She will not listen to reason!' Tommaso flung his arms wide to express his exasperation with Isolde. 'It is no use talking to her.'

Rosamond gave him a wide berth as she moved closer to Isolde. Lina's sister ignored her to snarl at the Italian. 'Get out of my shop or I will send for the constable and have you thrown in gaol.'

Tommaso made a sound of disgust, accompanied by an emphatic hand gesture in Isolde's direction.

'Go!' she shrieked.

He went.

Rosamond watched him stalk out of the mercery. Follow him? Or stay and question Isolde?

She wanted to ask Tommaso where he had been on the night of the murder and if he knew that Hugo Hackett had been determined to marry Lina to his uncle. Did he know of Alessandro's visit to the house of a bawd named Black Luce?

Yet all those questions could wait. She knew where to find the fellow.

Hugo Hackett's widow struggled to rein in her temper. Her hands, curled into fists, rested on fashionably padded hips, and she stood with her feet braced, staring at the exit as if she expected Tommaso to return at any moment to assault her. She'd be no match for him if he did, Rosamond thought. Isolde Hackett was an exceeding scrawny woman. On the other hand, fury could lend strength to even the weakest child. She stayed out of the widow's way, biding her time.

When Isolde finally turned and noticed Rosamond, she sent a baleful look in the other woman's direction. 'Who are you and what do you want?'

'Shall I take my custom elsewhere?' Rosamond inquired.

'Alys will help you.' Isolde snapped out the words. 'Alys? Where are you, girl? Assist Mistress . . .?'

'Jaffrey,' Rosamond answered. She had convinced herself that Lady Appleton was correct in her assumption that Isolde would not recognize the surname.

The same pale-faced girl Rosamond had seen on her first visit to the shop scurried out from behind a tall stack of merchandise, where she had been doing her best to avoid Isolde's notice. Her voice shook when she addressed Rosamond. 'How may I serve you, madam?'

Best to ignore Isolde for the nonce, Rosamond decided, and give her time to settle. She smiled at the girl. 'Silk. I have come for silk. Are you by chance an apprentice silkwoman?'

'Oh, no, madam. I am only a shepster. I sew shirts and sheets and linen underwear and other small linen items.'

In other words, she earned her living by doing piecework. She had likely had a hand in making the shift Rosamond had purchased on her last visit, when she'd been pretending to be Lady Noone. Of a certainty, the girl was poorly paid and beholden to Isolde Hackett for her livelihood. A complexion that pasty was proof enough that young Alys rarely saw the sun.

'Do you live here?' Rosamond inquired.

'Yes, madam. What may I show you?' Alys was so nervous she squeaked. 'We carry all manner of silk goods, all of them very fine.'

'Let us begin with tassels.'

Following Alys to that display, Rosamond pondered the girl's answer. Lina had not mentioned the shepster when she'd provided the list of servants and apprentices. Rosamond wondered if the oversight had been deliberate or if her old friend had simply forgotten about this quiet mouse of a girl.

Rosamond lowered her voice. 'Who is this woman your mistress believes killed her husband?'

'Her own sister!' Alys blurted out the answer before she could stop herself. Then she shrank back as Isolde, overhearing, bore down on them.

Rosamond turned to face the silkwoman, trying her best to look solicitous. 'What a tragedy! How brave you are to keep the shop open.'

Having regained control of her temper, Isolde sounded more bitter than angry. 'I have little choice. My livelihood depends upon it.' She grimaced. 'Many new customers have come into the mercery these last few days. How can I object so long as they buy?'

She put only the slightest extra emphasis on the word 'buy' but Rosamond took her meaning. Hackett's murder had been good for business. If a gawker wished to visit the scene of the crime, Isolde meant to make certain he left with a lighter purse. No doubt that was why she had been so amenable to answering questions when Rosamond had presented herself in the guise of Lady Noone.

'You must forgive my curiosity,' Rosamond apologized, 'but I do not understand why your sister would have killed your husband.'

'Because she is a wicked, ungrateful young woman!' Isolde pulled out a handkerchief and dabbed at eyes that showed no obvious sign of tears.

'There must be more to the story than that.' Rosamond selected two overpriced silk tassels, handed them to Melka to carry, and moved on to a display of embroidered ribbons. 'Did he offend her in some way?'

'He did naught but carry out my father's wishes.' Isolde had a mulish look on her face and sounded defensive.

'What wishes were those, if I may be so bold as to ask?'

Rosamond chose the most expensive ribbons the shop had to offer. Silent, as always, Melka took charge of them.

'My father asked my husband to arrange a good marriage for her, and he did so. He knew what was best for her.'

Rosamond nodded, as if she agreed that men always made the best decisions on behalf of their female relations. Inside she was writhing with indignation on Lina's behalf. 'Did he match Lina with a worthy man?'

'He found her a wealthy one, Mistress Jaffrey.'

Rosamond forced herself to laugh. 'Not that young man who just left, then?'

'Indeed not.'

Rosamond was about to ask another question about Tommaso when she noticed the odd expression that had come over Isolde's face. Had she said something to arouse the other woman's suspicion? She could not think what it could have been. To distract the shopkeeper, she turned her attention to an array of silk buttons. 'I must have some of these.'

'Alys, help Mistress Jaffrey.'

Leaving her customer to the shepster, Isolde bolted toward the rear of the shop and disappeared behind the curtain hung across a doorway. Was she in need of more time to compose herself? Or was she ill? Rosamond wondered if Isolde might be with child. She'd heard that the early months of pregnancy made some women sick to their stomachs.

'What is back there?' she asked of Alys in a whisper.

'That is the workshop. She's likely gone to make sure the apprentices are not dallying with the girls she's training to be silkwomen. She is harder on those two boys than her husband ever was.'

Rosamond would have pursued this point had Isolde not returned as abruptly as she'd departed. Her lips were set in a grim line and she had a determined look in her eyes. Following close at her heels was one of the apprentices.

'I have remembered who you are, Mistress Jaffrey,' Isolde said. 'You are Rosamond Appleton, Lina's friend, the one who was such a bad influence on her. I have sent the other lad for the constable.'

'If you know who I am, then you also know I am a respectable married woman with a considerable fortune at my disposal. Your constable can have no interest in me.'

'He will if I tell him you are hiding my sister.'

'But I am not. I am merely curious as to why you think her capable of murder.'

Behind her, Rosamond heard the shop door open and close. She glanced over her shoulder to see who had come in and realized that Melka had left the mercery. She did not understand why her maidservant would abandon her but she had no time to ponder Melka's uncharacteristic behavior.

Lina's sister seized hold of Rosamond's forearm. 'You know where she is. You have talked to her. How else would you have learned of Hugo's death?'

'I heard of it the way everyone else did. Your husband's death is a nine-day's wonder here in London. You said yourself that your business has increased since he died. Has there been a ballad written yet about the crime? Mayhap you should commission one.'

Isolde's fingers dug deeply into the fabric of Rosamond's sleeve. 'Where is she? Tell me what you know!'

'I know that Lina is a sweet-tempered girl, just as that young man said. To kill someone, especially with a knife, would be most out of character for her. Why is it that you will not even consider the possibility that she came upon your husband after he was already dead?'

'She ran away!'

'Not at first. At first, she screamed, waking the entire household. Why would a murderer do that?'

Isolde tightened her already vise-like grip. For a scrawny woman, she was surprisingly strong. 'How do you know she screamed? You *have* seen her. I knew it. You *are* hiding her.'

'I am not!'

Now nearly as infuriated as the woman grasping her arm, Rosamond attempted to wrench free. Tenacious as a terrier with its teeth clamped tight on its prey, Isolde refused to let go.

Rosamond gave her a push. Isolde shrieked as if she'd been skewered with a hot poker and tried to claw Rosamond's face with her free hand.

She is a madwoman, Rosamond thought, ducking her head to evade the attack. She caught Isolde's wrist to prevent a second attempt, forcing the arm back.

In the tussle that followed, Isolde never released her bruising hold on Rosamond's forearm. Rosamond's struggle to defend herself knocked Isolde's cap askew but did no other damage. The two women were locked in a stalemate when the door banged open and a big, rawboned, red-faced fellow charged into the shop.

'Here, what's all this?' He stepped between them and pried them apart.

'Arrest this woman, Clem,' Isolde demanded. 'Take her to the Compter and lock her in with the thieves and strumpets.'

Clem looked from Isolde to Rosamond and back again to Isolde. Then he stuck one finger beneath his cap and scratched his head.

The lad Isolde had sent for the constable slipped inside the mercery and went to stand beside his fellow apprentice. Both took care to stay well away from their mistress. Alys remained where she was, cowering behind the display of buttons.

'Did you not hear me?' Isolde shouted. 'Arrest her, I say!' A tiny line of spittle ran out of her open mouth and down her chin.

'This woman has run mad from grief.' Rosamond was relieved to hear that her own voice sounded calm and reasonable. 'I do much pity her, but I do not intend to stay here and be insulted.' Head high, she turned her back on Isolde and the constable and started for the door. Her hope of making a dignified exit was shattered an instant later.

'Noooo!' Isolde flung herself after Rosamond and would have attacked her again had the constable not caught hold of her as she flew past him.

'Here now!' With a lack of effort Rosamond envied, he hauled Isolde away before she could inflict any more harm on her intended victim. 'Stand here,' he ordered, setting her down beside the display of tassels.

Rosamond was trying to slip away when he hailed her. 'You, mistress – what is your name?'

Haughtiness seemed called for. 'I am Mistress Jaffrey,'

Rosamond said, head held high and jaw thrust slightly forward. 'I will have you know that I am a respectable married woman who came here only to shop for silks.'

Keeping one eye on Isolde, as if she was a powder keg about to explode, the constable whipped off his cap. 'Clement Dodge, madam, one of the constables of Cheapside Ward. If you are what you say, then what was all this to-do about?'

'She helped Lina escape.' Isolde glared at Rosamond. 'No doubt she is hiding the wretched girl. You must go and search her lodgings!'

'Where do you dwell, madam?' the constable asked.

Rosamond hesitated. Although she'd given him her real name – what choice had she had when Isolde already knew it? – she saw no need to reveal the precise location of her house. 'I reside in Surrey.'

At this, Clem Dodge's shoulders slumped. He sent Isolde an apologetic look. 'She does not live in London, Goodwife Hackett. That means there is little I can do.'

The scowl Isolde bestowed on him was formidable. 'Do you mean to tell me that you cannot search outside the city for an outlaw?'

Dodge shifted his weight from foot to foot, looking everywhere but at the silkwoman. 'In truth, I cannot even pursue a cutpurse into the lower end of Soper Lane, not once it crosses into Cordwainer Street Ward. Constables from one jurisdiction to the next guard their territory like jealous lovers.'

'I will complain of this to the Lord Mayor. Surely London's sheriffs have sufficient authority to bring wrongdoers to justice.'

The constable shook his head. 'Even if they do, they will scarce bestir themselves if it means upsetting a member of the gentry.'

Rosamond could not suppress a small smile at this good news. If the constable was reluctant to venture beyond the parishes that made up his own ward and would not cross the Thames into Surrey, then he most assuredly would not go hunting for Lina in Kent. As long as she remained at Leigh Abbey, she was safe from arrest.

Dodge stopped shuffling his feet to address Isolde. 'You might offer a reward.'

The widow's eyes lit up. 'Is it money you want? I will give you a gold sovereign if you take Mistress Jaffrey into custody and ten times that much if you capture my sister.'

Dodge looked sorely tempted.

'I can afford to pay you far more to keep my freedom than she can to deny it,' Rosamond countered. The constable had only to look at the way she was dressed to see that she was telling the truth.

'I have no charge to bring against Mistress Jaffrey.' Dodge's voice was rife with disappointment. 'But the promise of a reward could lead to someone finding your sister.'

'Mistress Jaffrey is harboring a murderess! Is that not a crime?'

'Indeed, I am not,' Rosamond said, annoyed all over again. 'I have broken no law, not even the most minor.'

Clem Dodge began to edge toward the door, but Isolde was not about to let him go until he did as she wanted. She scooped up a silken coif from a nearby table and waved it in his face. 'She tried to steal this from me!'

'It is not in her possession now.'

'I made her put it back. Ask Alys. She will tell you this is true.'

Everyone turned to stare at the girl and Rosamond felt the first stirrings of fear. If Alys supported her mistress's lie, the constable might well arrest her and lock her up in one of London's notoriously unpleasant gaols. A charge of theft was nothing to be taken lightly. Conviction for stealing any item valued at more than a shilling was punishable by hanging.

'I pay for what I desire. I am a wealthy woman, constable.' She hoped he would interpret this reminder as the thinly veiled offer of a bribe.

Since Alys appeared to be too frightened to speak in support of Isolde's claim, the widow threw a new accusation at Rosamond. 'She has broken the sumptuary laws. My late father knew her history. He told me she is the bastard of a knight and she married a man with no claim at all to gentility. She has no right—'

'What fabrics one is allowed to wear is determined by income, constable.' Rosamond had to raise her voice to be heard above Isolde's raving. 'I assure you, my husband's income is greater than the required hundred pounds per annum.'

She held her breath, knowing that she *was* in violation of the law. Only the wives of barons, knights of the order, councilors' ladies and women who waited on the queen were permitted to wear petticoats of tufted taffeta. Fortunately, no one in the mercery could see what she had on beneath her kirtle.

Trapped between two strong-willed, angry women, Constable Dodge appealed to the third and addressed young Alys. 'Speak up, girl. Did Mistress Jaffrey try to take merchandise without paying for it?'

Alys swallowed hard. She kept her eyes lowered and her head down. Her voice was so soft that Rosamond had to lean forward to catch her words. 'She did not, sir.'

Isolde's glare promised retribution.

'Does that satisfy you?' Rosamond asked the constable.

At his nod, she lost no time heading for the door. She had almost reached it when it occurred to her that her quarrel with Isolde Hackett had placed young Alys in an untenable position. She addressed the shepster over her shoulder. 'Are you bound by apprenticeship or any other legal contract to Goodwife Hackett?'

The girl's head jerked up. Her wide-eyed gaze skittered toward Isolde before fixing on Rosamond's face. The look in her eyes was full of hope. 'I am not, Mistress Jaffrey. I do piecework and mind the shop in return for my room and board.'

'Well, then,' said Rosamond, 'you are free to come away with me now. What say you, Alys? Would you like to have a permanent place in my household?'

The desire to escape from Isolde Hackett outweighed any qualms Alys might have had about accepting such an offer from a total stranger. In so much haste that she stumbled twice before she reached her new mistress, Alys abandoned all that was familiar to her and seized the opportunity Rosamond offered.

Isolde's howl of outrage followed them into the street.

ELEVEN

Rosamond regretted that she was on foot, but there was no help for it. She marched young Alys south along Soper Lane until it intersected with Budge Row. That placed them in Cordwainer Street Ward and greater safety but she kept up the rapid pace into Candlewick Street and through Great East Cheap, not to be confused with West Cheap from which they were fleeing. Once they reached Gracious Street, leading directly south to London Bridge, she breathed a little easier, although she did not doubt that Isolde Hackett would send men in pursuit if she could marshal her forces with sufficient speed. Every few feet, she cast a wary glance over her shoulder. She saw no one she recognized, not even Melka.

Although it had been premature of her maidservant to panic at the mere mention of a constable, Rosamond presumed that Melka had left the mercery to seek help for her mistress. She was acquainted, through Rosamond and others in her family, with a number of respectable individuals who had lodgings in London. None of them, however, lived anywhere near Soper Lane.

Crossing London Bridge, Rosamond's progress slowed to a snail's pace. The towering houses that lined both sides of the roadway did not leave much room for traffic on the best of days, and on this one the thoroughfare was thronged with travelers. Fearful of losing Alys in the crush, Rosamond took hold of the girl's arm and kept a firm grip on it until they reached Southwark.

The moment she let go, Alys stopped and dug in her heels, refusing to go any farther.

'Whatever is the matter with you?' Rosamond was impatient to reach Willow House. Although she did not believe they had been followed, she could not be certain.

'Where are you taking me?' Alys's voice trembled.

'To my home.'

'Are you . . . are you . . .?' She stuttered to a stop, unable to complete her question, but the frightened glances she cast toward the businesses that lined the south bank of the Thames told Rosamond what she feared.

'By the stars, girl, do you think I am a bawd?' Rosamond did not know whether to be amused or insulted. 'I promise you I will not sell your maidenhead to the highest bidder. What I will do is pay you well to sew for me.'

Alys said nothing more until they reached Willow House. Then her eyes went wide at the sight of so much opulence. She goggled her way through every room as Rosamond led her to the upper floor where the servants slept.

'Will this suit you?' Rosamond opened the door to a small bedchamber furnished with a simple bedstead, a stool, pegs on which to hang clothing and a table large enough to hold both a wash basin and a candle.

The girl seemed incapable of speech, and it was not until Rosamond nodded and made a shooing motion that she scurried inside. With one hesitant hand she touched the blanket, then the pillow.

'All this for me? I do not have to share?'

'This chamber is for you alone.'

Rosamond entered the room and seated herself on the edge of the bed. She indicated that Alys should take the stool, noting as she did so that the girl's eyes were luminous with unshed tears.

'Come now,' she said in brusque tones. 'We have practical matters to discuss. First and foremost are the terms of your employment. They are simple enough. You will make and repair garments for me. I have no skill with a needle and my tiring maid, Melka, will be happy to be relieved of such chores. In return, you will be paid six shillings eightpence a year, the same as a maid of all work.'

'Oh, madam!'

'No tears, I beg you! Now, then, if I am pleased with a particular piece of sewing, you will receive a reward in addition to your wages. Do you accept these terms?'

'Oh, yes, madam. God bless and keep you.'

'God has more important things to do than worry about me. Did you leave belongings behind?'

'Naught but a spare apron and an extra shift, madam.'

'Let Isolde Hackett keep them, then. I will provide you with new ones and more besides.'

Rosamond shifted into a more comfortable position on the thin mattress. She had removed her cloak upon returning to the house but was still wearing the rest of her wealthy gentlewoman's finery. The bum roll that held her skirts away from her body was bothersome when she was seated but far easier to manage than a farthingale.

'Have you a surname, Alys?'

'Greene, madam.'

'Family?'

'They are all dead, madam, my father five summers ago and my mother and younger brothers when the plague broke out last year.'

'I am sorry for your losses.' Although Bermondsey had not been as badly affected by the epidemic as London, where some seven thousand people had died, even in this small village the plague had taken its toll. 'Is that when you entered Isolde Hackett's employ?'

Alys nodded.

'You heard the accusations your former employer made against me, Alys. Not the one that I was a thief but that I am harboring her half sister, Godlina Walkenden. Lina is not here but I do want to help her. I think it most unlikely that she could kill anyone. To that end, I wish to ask you questions about the Hackett household. Answer me honestly, even if you think I will not wish to hear what you have to say. Will you do that?'

Again, Alys nodded. The timid mouse was back. *No*, Rosamond corrected herself. *Not a mouse.* Alys looked more like a frightened rabbit. To avoid sending the girl into a panic, Rosamond kept her voice level and unthreatening.

'Isolde Hackett would like me to believe that her husband was a paragon of virtue who never beat his servants or apprentices and had not an enemy in the world. How did he behave toward you, Alys?'

'*He* never beat me.'

'But she did?'

Alys nodded. 'She keeps a switch for that purpose – to discourage sloth.'

'And how did Hugo convince his apprentices to work harder?'

'He whipped them with words,' Alys said. 'And most cruel they were, too. He had a gift for picking out the most tender place to strike.'

'Could one of them have been driven to strike back?'

Alys's eyes widened. 'Never, madam! They'd be too afraid. A servant who kills a master is burnt at the stake. Hanging may leave you just as dead, but burning's worse.'

That same penalty would be Lina's fate if she were found guilty of killing Hugo Hackett. He had been the head of the household. For any of his dependents to kill him, whether wife or cook's boy, made the crime petty treason rather than mere murder. Picturing Lina tied to a stake, the flames rising to consume her, Rosamond could not suppress a shudder.

'Tell me about Hugo Hackett's dealings with his equals. Other merchants. Neighbors. Did he quarrel with any of them?'

'He was always threatening to take this one or that one to law for some petty offense. And after he was dead, his creditors were quick to come to the shop to press their claims to the widow.'

'Hugo was in debt when he died?'

'He was. And his wife had no idea how much he owed. I'll swear to that, madam.'

It seemed doubtful that one of Hugo's creditors would murder him over an unpaid debt. As Lina had pointed out with regard to Portinari, it was passing difficult to collect money from a dead man. All the same, she asked Alys for names and committed them to memory.

'Alessandro Portinari,' she repeated, unsurprised when Alys named him along with the others. 'You know he is the same man Hugo Hackett wanted Lina to marry?'

'The very same, madam.'

'And he came to speak with Isolde after Hugo was dead?' She wanted to make certain of her facts.

'Oh, yes, madam. Right quick, too.'

'What can you tell me about him?'

Sensing that her new mistress was pleased with the information she'd so far supplied, Alys's face began to lose its pinched look. 'He is old and ugsome but he must be very wealthy. He wears rings on nearly every finger and all of them are gold.'

'And you are certain Hugo Hackett borrowed money from Portinari?'

'Either that or he took delivery of silk from the Florentine and had not yet paid for it,' Alys said.

'So Hugo was unquestionably indebted to him.' Had Lina had the right of it? Was that why Hugo had been so determined to marry her off to Portinari? Had Hugo, as Rosamond had theorized at Leigh Abbey, sent word to Portinari after his quarrel with Lina, warning him that his intended bride had changed her mind about the marriage? In Alessandro Portinari's place, Rosamond would have been furious. Had he been angry enough to go to Soper Lane, argue with Hugo, and kill him in a fit of rage?

That might well be what had happened. The difficulty lay in proving it.

Rosamond leaned forward, her gaze fixed on the girl she was interrogating. 'Tell me about the night Hugo Hackett was murdered.'

Alys sprang up from the stool so quickly that it toppled over. She backed away, arms wrapped around herself as if she wished to appear smaller . . . or mayhap disappear altogether. Her face, pale to begin with, lost every trace of color.

'Calm yourself, Alys!' Rosamond snapped at her, as angered by her own impatience as at the girl's timidity. She left the bed and busied herself righting the stool. 'I am not about to accuse you of the crime. I need your help to discover what really happened that night.'

'I was asleep. I do not know what happened.'

'Come now, Alys. Seat yourself and answer my questions. We will not speak of this again once you have told me everything you recall. Servants always know more than their masters suspect. I feel certain you overheard Hugo Hackett's quarrel with Lina and that you know he locked her in her chamber afterward.'

The look of surprise on Alys's face made Rosamond forget what she'd meant to say next.

'What is it? What have you remembered?'

'I did not know she was locked in. How could she have been when she was there in the counting house, dressed to go out, only a few hours later?'

Rosamond let the question go unanswered. There was no reason for Alys to know that Rosamond had heard Lina's side of the story from Lina herself. Instead, she approached the girl and placed her arm around her thin shoulders, giving them a comforting squeeze. 'Did anyone come to the house after Hugo's quarrel with Lina?'

'I do not think so, madam, but it was already late and I was abed soon after.'

'Where did you sleep?' Rosamond guided Alys to the bed, where they both sat.

'Under the eaves. The mistress's sister had her own chamber but the rest of us, the three maidservants and myself, shared a bed at the top of the house, where it is coldest in winter and too hot in summer.'

'What of Isolde's apprentices? Where were they?'

Alys kept her eyes downcast. Her hands, clasped in her lap, showed white at the knuckles. 'They are not apprentices in the usual sense, madam, just girls being trained to do silkwork. They go home to their families at night.'

Rosamond nodded. That agreed with what Lina had told her. 'And Hugo's apprentices? I warrant they are bound to him for the traditional seven years. Where do they sleep?'

'On pallets in the warehouse.' With one arm still draped over the girl's shoulders, Rosamond could feel her anxiety lessen.

'What about the counting house where Hackett was killed? Is that adjacent to the shop as well?'

Tension returned in a rush. 'No, madam,' Alys mumbled. 'The shop and the workshop and the warehouse beyond, they are on the ground floor. The counting house is located on the floor above, at the back.'

'How is it reached?'

'Through the hall.'

As in most houses, one room would run into another. If it had not been the middle of the night, Rosamond felt certain Hugo's murderer would have been seen both coming and going.

In a small voice, Alys added, 'There is another entrance. A stair leads up to it from the yard that lies between the warehouse and the kitchen.'

'That means someone could have come in from outside the house.'

'We might all have been murdered in our beds,' Alys said in a terrified whisper.

Rosamond felt only excitement. 'Would it have been possible for Hugo Hackett to admit his killer without anyone else in the household knowing that he had done so?'

Alys nodded in mute agreement.

'Excellent! Now tell me what happened when you were awakened.'

'Oh, madam, I was ever so frightened! I was jerked out of sleep by the most horrible loud screaming. At first I thought the house must be on fire. Then the mistress called for help and we all ran downstairs and there he was in his counting house, stabbed to death.'

'What sort of knife was used to kill him?'

'I-I do not know.'

'Kitchen knife?' Rosamond prompted her. 'Eating knife? Dagger? What kind of handle had it? Was it ivory or bone or wood? Carved? Plain?'

'I do not know!' Alys wailed.

'Isolde said her sister was *holding* the knife. Is that true?'

'It was on the floor when I saw it, madam. I did not look at it long. It was stained with blood. And then your friend ran and the mistress sent the apprentices after her.' With a shudder, Alys squeezed her eyes tightly shut.

Rosamond fought the urge to give the girl a shake, knowing that would only terrify her. Alys was already doing a splendid job of frightening herself. 'Alys! Attend me! Isolde Hackett sent for the watch. *Who* did she send?'

'It was the cook's boy, Nate.'

Rosamond gave Alys a little time to compose herself, then asked, 'Did you believe Isolde's claim that Lina had done this?'

Alys's eyes flew open. 'She was *there*, madam. She *ran*.'

'And so would you have done, had you been the one accused of such a heinous crime.'

After a moment, showing a glimmer of common sense, Alys murmured, 'None of us *wanted* her to be caught, madam, except for her sister.'

'Do you know what happened to the knife?'

Alys shook her head. 'I did not want to know.'

There had been eleven people in the house that night, Rosamond mused. Alys, Hugo, Isolde, Lina, three maids, two apprentices, the cook and the cook's boy. Was one of them guilty, or had someone else entered the counting house from the outside? Had it been Alessandro Portinari? His nephew? A neighbor or fellow merchant?

Rosamond wondered if she could eliminate Alys from her list of suspects. She reminded herself that Lina had never mentioned the girl, although she had given Rosamond the names of everyone else in the household. Had she been trying to protect Alys? Or had she simply forgotten about her? Alys *was* the sort who sought safety in the shadows, hoping to be overlooked.

In the distance, church bells pealed the hour. Rosamond realized she'd been questioning her newest servant for some considerable time and had given no thought to the girl's comfort beyond installing her in this chamber. She slid off the bed and strode toward the door.

'Come along, Alys. It is almost time to sup. I will take you down to the kitchen and present you to the rest of my household. I must warn you that some of them are a bit unusual. Melka, my tiring maid, does not speak much English, and my manservant, Charles, does not speak at all. He is a mute, but there is nothing wrong with his hearing and I will not tolerate unkindness toward him.'

'Yes, madam.' Alys scurried after her, clearly relieved to be done with the inquisition.

'If you wish to remain in my employ,' Rosamond continued as they descended one narrow flight of stairs and then another, 'you will repeat nothing you hear in this house. Is that agreeable to you?'

'It is, madam.'

Rosamond stopped short at the entrance to the gallery, nearly causing Alys to run into her. Melka had returned. Hiding her relief, Rosamond scowled at her tiring maid. 'Where have you been all this while?' she demanded.

Instead of answering, Melka sent Alys a suspicious look.

'You remember young Alys here from the mercery. I have hired her to sew for me. Take her down to the kitchen, if you will, so she can meet the others. Then return to me here. I am most curious to learn of your whereabouts for the last few hours.'

Once the two women had left the gallery, Rosamond crossed to her favorite window seat. It was already occupied by Watling. The large gray and white cat ignored his mistress, even after she lifted him onto her lap and began to stroke him.

Melka reappeared a short time later bearing a tray that held a wedge of cheese and a cup of wine.

'Is Alys settled?' Rosamond sipped the sweet white wine Melka had selected, silently approving the choice.

'*Tak.*' Melka, a woman of few words, used the Polish affirmative.

'You went to Billingsgate, I suppose?'

'*Tak.*'

'I am surprised Master Baldwin did not return with you.' Nick Baldwin was an old friend, a prosperous merchant in his own right, someone who might be expected to have some influence with a constable, even if that constable served a different parish.

'Gone.'

Rosamond blinked in surprise. 'He was not at home? Excellent! That is, it is excellent news so long as you did not foolishly confide in Baldwin's servants.'

Melka looked offended by the very suggestion but Rosamond saw the question in her eyes.

'We must not bring Master Baldwin into this matter, Melka. He is a Justice of the Peace in Kent. If he discovers that Lady Appleton is hiding a fugitive, a suspected murderess, it would be his duty to take Lina into custody and escort her back to London. Worse, he might feel obligated to arrest Lady Appleton as an accomplice.'

Such an outcome would make everyone miserable. Although Rosamond's foster mother had repeatedly refused Nick Baldwin's offers of marriage, preferring not to cede control of her person or her property to a husband, the two had been lovers for many years.

'Where did Master Baldwin go?' Rosamond asked.

'Candlethorpe,' said Melka.

The tension in Rosamond's body eased at this news. Baldwin's second country house, Candlethorpe, was located in Northamptonshire near Rockingham Forest . . . a goodly distance away from both Leigh Abbey and London.

TWELVE

When an aged crone demanded entry to Willow House that evening, Rosamond's servants let her in without argument. One maidservant, thinking no one was looking, made the sign of the cross to ward off evil.

Rosamond, interrupted while reading in her privy chamber, was not in the best of moods when she entered the parlor on the ground floor. Located between the chapel and the hall, it was one of the rooms she had turned to a new purpose when she first bought the property. It had a flat ceiling with painted panels between the massive timbers and retained some of its original paneling, a mixture of linenfold and medallion heads, but the bed that had once been a permanent fixture had been removed. On occasion, Rosamond dined in solitary splendor in this chamber, which was why the largest piece of furniture it contained was a heavy oak table. For the most part, she used the parlor to receive visitors she did not wish to admit to the upper regions of the house.

A fire had been lit but there had not yet been time for it to banish the chill in the air. The old woman stood beside the hearth. Her stooped back with its prominent widow's hump was the first thing Rosamond saw from the door. The visitor held bare, sun-darkened hands stretched in front of her in an attempt to capture what little warmth radiated from the small blaze.

Rosamond started to address her unexpected guest as Mother Malyn but something in the old woman's manner kept her silent. Although she had never dealt directly with the local herb woman, Rosamond had seen her out and about in Bermondsey. Some called her a cunning woman, others a blessing witch. She cured the sick and had an uncanny ability to find things that had been lost. The figure before the fire was dressed in much the same manner, engulfed in layer upon layer of woolen garments. She carried a walking stick that looked like the one Malyn used, but when Rosamond stepped closer and squinted in the candlelight, a host of differences leapt out at her. The person by the fire was too tall, too muscular and, most of all, too young to be old Mother Malyn, despite an attempt to counterfeit great age.

'Who are you?' Rosamond was prepared to scream for help. One hand flexed, ready to reach for the knife she kept in a purpose-sewn leather sheath in her right boot. 'What do you want with me?'

The figure straightened as it turned and at the same time reached up to remove its hat. A ratty gray wig came off at the same time. Beneath layers of face paint, a familiar mouth curved into a grin.

Rosamond reached behind her to close the door, then sagged against it. 'Henry Leveson! What are you playing at?'

'I could scarce approach you as myself.' The 'old woman's' voice, unmistakably masculine, sounded amused.

'True enough,' she conceded.

By profession, Leveson was a player with Lord Leicester's Men. Clean-shaven, with youthful good looks, he was accustomed to taking the women's roles in that company's productions.

He was, to hear the preachers tell it, a rogue and vagabond and as such could not, with propriety, call at the house of a respectable young gentlewoman. That he was also an intelligencer in the service of the queen's principal secretary, Sir Francis Walsingham, helped his case not at all. That was an equally disreputable vocation. It was also a secret known to only a few. By virtue of having herself been employed, albeit briefly, as another of Walsingham's intelligence gatherers, Rosamond was one of them.

'You are wasting your time and a good deal of face paint if you have come to ask me to work for your master again.' She approached the hearth to peer more closely at the lines Leveson had drawn on his face. He had achieved a most realistic effect.

'He will be pleased to hear it.'

Her attention diverted by her inspection of his costume and cosmetics, Rosamond was slow to comprehend Leveson's meaning. 'What did you say?'

'He sent me here to deliver a warning.'

The fingers Rosamond had lifted to touch the false hump on Leveson's shoulder stilled in midair. Any message from Principal Secretary Walsingham was serious business. He was one of the most powerful men in the kingdom and, although she had defied him once without dire consequences, she had no desire to cross him a second time. 'I am listening.'

'You are not to go near the French embassy.'

'How did he—? Never mind. I can guess. Walsingham has a spy, mayhap more than one, in the household at Salisbury Court. But I cannot see that I have done any harm by going there.' Rosamond disliked following orders without knowing why, no matter who issued them. 'I have the most innocent of reasons to return. I am to take lessons in the Italian tongue from Master John Florio, the foremost teacher of that language in all of England.'

Even beneath the stiff mask of his heavily painted face, Rosamond recognized the pained expression her statement provoked. 'He suspected you would be difficult. There is a second part to the message.'

That would no doubt be the threat to enforce the warning. Rosamond braced herself. Walsingham used both bribery and coercion to ensure cooperation, but he preferred coercion.

'He said to remind you that he has agents at Cambridge.' Leveson busied himself settling the hat with its attached wig back in place on his head.

On a flash of temper, Rosamond silently damned the man. Her voice cold, she gave Leveson a message of her own. 'Tell Sir Francis I wish to speak with him.'

Leveson's lips twitched, although there was no echoing amusement in his eyes. 'He must have guessed you'd make that demand. The third thing I am to say to you is this: under no circumstances are you to visit the house in Seething Lane.'

'As if I should be given answers if I did go there!' The Seething Lane house was the London headquarters of Walsingham's network of spies.

'Will it soften your anger to know that Walsingham has been ill? In mid-August the queen sent him to Scotland, where he sickened. All these weeks later he is still suffering from an ague.'

'Good. Were it in my power, I would curse him with an enormous carbuncle in the middle of his face and a bad case of the piles for good measure.'

In spite of himself, Leveson laughed. 'Rail at him all you like, but you'd be wise to obey his instructions.'

Rosamond fumed for a good hour after Walsingham's messenger left. Then she spent another hour convincing herself that the principal secretary's threat was an idle one. What could he do to harm Rob? Her husband was as law-abiding as any man in England. Not even the queen's spy master could prove otherwise.

Still, Walsingham had given her an order. Even if the threat meant to force her compliance had no teeth, she would have to be careful when she returned to Salisbury Court. That she must go back there was not in question. How else was she to interrogate Tommaso Sassetti?

THIRTEEN

Although Rosamond chafed at the delay, the next day was not a safe choice for a visit to Salisbury Court. It was a Sunday, when Walsingham was sure to have men watching the embassy to see who arrived to hear mass. Suspecting that there might also be someone keeping an eye on Willow House, Rosamond made certain that everyone in her household attended church services at St Olave's, walking there from Willow House in solemn procession.

She spent Sunday afternoon planning a new wardrobe. Alys Greene had enjoyed a bath and had been given garments suitable for a gentlewoman's maidservant, but her obvious happiness caused the greatest change. When they began to examine the wealth of fabrics and trim Rosamond had accumulated without ever taking the time to have them made into clothing, the girl shed the last of her timidity and remembered how to smile.

Impressed by her new servant's eagerness to please, Rosamond took Alys with her to Salisbury Court on Monday. Master Florio looked up from his books in surprise when they were shown into his schoolroom by one of the ambassador's servants.

'Mistress Jaffrey! You are . . . prompt.'

'Did you think I would not come at the appointed time?'

'I believed your only interest here at the embassy was in young Sassetti.'

Rosamond gave the tutor a hard look and reviewed what she knew about him. Could he be Walsingham's spy? He was, now that she thought about it, the only person at Salisbury Court to whom she had given her name. She'd mumbled nonsense when she'd pretended to introduce herself to Francis Throckmorton.

One particular detail from Florio's account of his background came back to her. He'd told her he'd been employed by an Anglican bishop to tutor his son. Such a post was unlikely to have been given to a papist.

Had he pretended to change his faith when he came to Salisbury House? If he had not, then it was doubtful the French ambassador would be so foolish as to speak of sensitive issues in Florio's hearing. What good was a spy if he could not gather information? But if he *had* converted, then how could Walsingham trust him?

With these questions whirling around in her mind, she found it difficult to concentrate on her first language lesson. Italian was easy enough to learn, since she was already familiar with both Latin and French, but Master Florio was a hard taskmaster and made her feel a great fool when she stumbled over words or failed to differentiate between the feminine and the masculine.

'You do not have an aptitude for languages,' Florio said at the end of her allotted hour. 'Mayhap you should consider abandoning your quest to learn Italian.'

Stung, Rosamond retorted with words meant to hurt him in return: 'Mayhap you are not as adept at teaching as I was led to believe.'

Florio reared back as if he'd been slapped. He took pride in his work, which made it all the more remarkable that he'd be so quick to dismiss Rosamond's potential. Constant fault-finding was no way to teach a novice, and she was sure he knew that. She'd gleaned some small insight into his usual teaching technique during her last visit. She felt certain he exhibited endless patience when it came to instructing the ambassador's young daughter.

Rosamond's conviction that John Florio was Walsingham's man grew stronger. She wanted to ask him outright if he'd been ordered to discourage her from further visits to the embassy, but she repressed the impulse. He'd only lie. No one lasted long as an intelligencer if he admitted the truth the moment he was challenged.

In a way, she admired Florio for his dedication to duty. As she well knew, it was no easy task to betray the people you lived with. She supposed he'd report anything said in his hearing by the French ambassador and his staff. Would he also provide Walsingham with the names of those English men and

women who came to the embassy to worship? Rosamond
hoped he would not. She did not understand why recusants
were so stubborn about converting, but she did pity them for
the persecution they endured. In Florio's place, she'd keep
silent rather than hand them over to a zealot like Walsingham.
The principal secretary liked nothing better than to accuse
papists of treason. For that, they were imprisoned and sometimes executed.

Rosamond paid Master Florio for her lesson, agreeing
through clenched teeth that it would not be worthwhile for
her to continue. She did not bother to ask about Tommaso. If
Florio obliged her and sent for Lina's beloved, he'd insist upon
playing duenna while they talked. She resolved to find another
way to locate the Florentine.

She left the house but lingered in the gardens, trying to
decide how to proceed. As if in answer to her prayers, she
came upon the very man she had been seeking. Tommaso
Sassetti sat slumped on a bench beneath an arbor. He stared
in a disconsolate manner down the steep slope toward a row
of riverside houses and the Thames beyond, unaware of
Rosamond's approach.

It was a picturesque pose. The short length of his dusky
orange doublet showed his long, lean limbs to advantage.
Rosamond frowned. Had he somehow learned she'd be
looking for him? At least one embassy servant was aware
she'd asked for him on her first visit to Salisbury Court.

Deciding that it scarce mattered, she continued in his direction. This was the opportunity she'd hoped for, and she was
determined to take full advantage of it. With Alys trailing after
her, she marched up to the entrance to the arbor and stopped
there, blocking Tommaso's view.

'Good day to you, Master Sassetti,' she said. 'I am Rosamond
Jaffrey, one of Lina Walkenden's friends.'

Dark, languid eyes studied her from beneath half closed
eyelids. '*Innamorata* – so fierce!'

'Sirrah! So over-familiar! I am not your sweetheart. Another
woman has that . . . honor. I have seen the ring you gave her.'

At once he abandoned his languid pose. He was effusive,
if insincere, in his apologies, mixing English words with Italian

so freely that Rosamond had difficulty making sense of either. She granted him good looks. She could understand why Lina fancied herself in love with the fellow. But in spite of his fine physique and sculpted facial features and courtly manner, Rosamond found him unappealing.

'I wish to help Li—'

Rising with unexpected speed, he pressed two fingers to her lips. 'Shhh. We must not speak further of her here. Even the rose bushes have ears.'

Rosamond could move swiftly as well. She stepped back out of his reach, fighting an urge to scrub her knuckles over the place he'd touched. 'Where?'

He was taller than she'd realized. For just a moment, he'd loomed over her and he still stood too close. Despite her desire to question Tommaso in private, Rosamond was not comfortable with the idea of being alone with him.

'Tell me where you dwell,' he whispered. 'I will come to you there.'

Rosamond hesitated. She had not ruled out the possibility that he had stabbed Isolde's husband to death, thinking that Hugo stood in the way of his marriage to Lina. There was motive. But where, she reasoned, would she be safer than in her own house, surrounded by her loyal servants? Despite the risk, she told Tommaso Sassetti how to find Willow House.

'I will come to you soon,' he promised, seizing her hand and kissing it. 'You are the dearest friend of my beloved. She has told me all about you. Together we will find a way to save her.'

That Tommasso's command of the English language improved markedly from one sentence to the next made Rosamond wary. So did the way he kept inching closer to her, but she was careful not to let her instinctive dislike of him show. If he knew anything that would help clear Lina's name, she was determined to discover what it was.

Reclaiming her hand, she put a little distance between them. 'I must go.'

'Before we are seen together.' He sent her what he seemed to assume was a smoldering look.

Unmoved, Rosamond turned her back on him and walked away.

FOURTEEN

Rosamond expected Tommaso to appear at Willow House within an hour or two of their meeting in the garden at Salisbury Court, but there was no sign of him that day. The following morning, she sent the ever-faithful Charles out to locate Alessandro Portinari and track his movements. She knew she would have to contrive a meeting with Portinari soon but was in no hurry to arrange what was certain to be an unpleasant encounter. She passed an hour questioning Alys again. In the guise of casual conversation, she elicited the names of many of Hugo Hackett's regular customers. After she dismissed the girl, she wrote them down.

By mid-afternoon, Rosamond was heartily sick of being cooped up inside. She wanted to go forth and talk to people – Hugo Hackett's neighbors in Soper Lane, merchants who had loaned him money, rival silkwomen who might know something detrimental about Isolde. Instead, afraid she would miss Tommaso's arrival if she left, she stayed at home, waiting upon the young Florentine's convenience.

She compromised with a walk in her own garden. Located behind Willow House, it was a pleasant place, private and quiet. A light breeze stirred leaves and made the last flowers of the season bob their heads. Rosamond followed the meandering gravel paths through raised beds and topiary work, reviewing everything she knew about Hugo Hackett's murder and making mental lists of lines of inquiry to pursue.

She believed Lina innocent because Lina had been her friend in childhood. She suspected Alessandro Portinari, even though she had never met the man, because Lina despised him. Isolde was a suspect because she stood to gain by Hugo's death. And Tommaso? There was a puzzle. Did he truly care for Lina or only for the wealth that would come to him as Lina's husband when they wed? Either way, Rosamond had assumed he'd be anxious to talk with her. Where *was* the blasted man?

At the bottom of the garden, a tall stone wall rose up between Willow House and the adjoining property. Intending to walk the length of this boundary before returning to the house, Rosamond made a sharp turn to the right. Her steps faltered. She had supposed herself to be alone, but there was Tommaso, one shoulder artfully propped against the wall, his dark, curly hair mussed and his eyes half closed, as if he'd just tumbled out of a lover's bed. His lambent gaze traveled over Rosamond in a way that was both compliment and insult. When he finished his survey of her features, his lips curved into a smile that was perilous close to being a smirk.

'*Padrona*,' he said.

Mistress, she translated, in the sense of mistress of the house. If he'd meant the other kind of mistress he'd have addressed her as *amante*. Then she'd have had to break his head for him.

Her own smile grim, Rosamond glared at him. 'How did you get in here?'

He laughed and gestured toward a section of wall some distance beyond the spot where he stood. 'An easy climb there, where it is lower. It is good to keep our meeting secret, *si*?'

'There is no need for *that* much secrecy. Come inside. We will talk in—'

'We will talk here.' His indolent pose had been deceptive, leaving her unprepared for how swiftly he could move. He prevented her retreat by blocking her way back to Willow House.

His size alone caused Rosamond to feel a prickle of anxiety, but she knew better than to show fear. 'As you wish,' she said. 'Shall we walk?'

She indicated the direction that would take her closer to safety. Her servants were indoors but not so very far away. If she screamed, someone would be sure to hear her.

Instead, Tommaso herded her toward the most secluded spot in the garden, a turf-topped bench half-hidden by shrubbery. Rosamond allowed him to seat her in this small pocket of privacy, but when she adjusted her cloak, she felt for her second knife, the one concealed in the lining, and took a firm grip on its handle. At once she felt more in control.

The bench, like the window seats in the gallery, curved in

a half circle that allowed two people to sit close to each other and yet be face-to-face. Rosamond studied Tommaso's features, hoping to find a clue to his intentions. He had long, curling eyelashes and big, soulful brown eyes. His demeanor told her that he knew the effect these had on most women.

'My Lina,' he whispered. 'Where is she?'

'I cannot tell you that.'

'*Padrona*, I beg you – I must see for myself that she is well.' This plea was accompanied by passionate gestures. One fist pounded the area above his heart while the back of the other hand smacked against his brow. He closed his eyes, no doubt hoping to give the impression that he was suffering the torments of the damned because he did not know where Lina had gone.

Rosamond was not convinced of his sincerity, but it would have made no difference if she had believed him. She was determined to protect her friend, and that meant she must keep Lina's whereabouts secret from everyone.

'Be sensible, Tommaso. If you attempt to go to her you might be followed.'

'You are cruel to keep us apart. Lina – *è innamorata persa*—'

'*Sei innamorato di lei?*' Rosamond cut him off when he tried to tell her Lina was madly in love with him. The question she posed in Italian asked Tommaso if he loved *her*. Rosamond had not had much time to study the language, but she had insisted that Master Florio teach her a few specific phrases.

The Florentine mimed stabbing a dagger into his own heart. 'You wound me to ask such a thing. How can you doubt me, *madonna*?'

Such posturing put her in mind of a player declaiming upon a stage, except that she found Tommaso's histrionics far less convincing than one of Henry Leveson's portrayals of a comely young heroine. She had to force herself to smile at him as she lied through her teeth.

'I believe you, Tommaso, but let us continue our conversation in English, if you please. I wish to avoid any misunderstanding between us.'

He was not as easily cozened as she'd hoped. 'I do not

misunderstand. You do not trust me enough to tell me where my little love has gone.'

The handsome features turned sulky, putting Rosamond in mind of a small boy denied a treat. She tamped down her impatience and bit back a scathing retort that would doubtless insult him. If she wanted answers, she had to pretend to sympathize with his plight.

She reached out with the hand that was not resting on the hilt of her dagger and gave his forearm a comforting squeeze. 'If you love my friend Lina, you must content yourself with the knowledge that she is safe, and you must help me find the real killer by telling me everything you know about Hugo Hackett's death.'

Tommaso shrugged. 'I know nothing.'

'You must have some thoughts about who might have killed him.'

He sighed deeply. Rosamond started to remove her hand, but he caught hold of it, trapping it against his brocaded sleeve. Rosamond wanted to pull away, but she wanted information more. It was not as if they were touching skin to skin, she assured herself. They both wore gloves.

Then Tommaso began to stroke her palm with his thumb. He gazed at her with his big, beautiful, long-lashed eyes, as if he thought such tricks would work with her. Rosamond jerked her fingers free of his and sat up straighter. She glared at him.

'Where were you the night Hugo Hackett was murdered?'

Tommaso's dark eyes widened, then narrowed almost to slits. 'I was sound asleep in my uncle's house.'

'And yet, immediately after the murder, you left there to lodge at the French embassy. Why?'

The curl of his lip and the way his hand, now resting on the turf between them, clenched into a fist, made it evident that he did not like her question. Rosamond's fingers tightened on the handle of her concealed knife.

'Did you quarrel with your uncle?'

He hesitated, then gave a curt nod.

'Why? Did you accuse him of murder? Or did he accuse you?'

Tommaso moved with lightning swiftness, seizing her upper arms. She did not lose her grip on the dagger, but neither could she use it. Her own cloak held her prisoner as Tommaso bent closer.

'You wound me, *bella donna*, with your suspicions. Are you so stupid that you cannot see the truth when it is right in front of you? It was my beloved who killed Hugo Hackett. She is a passionate woman. She wanted us to be together.'

'Nonsense.'

They were nose-to-nose and eye-to-eye. In a breath, his voice went from seductive to threatening. 'Tell me where she is.'

'Never!' Despite knowing he had greater physical strength than she, Rosamond was more angry than afraid. Tommaso had deceived Lina, and now he was trying to cozen her. 'All you want is the reward Isolde is offering for Lina's capture!'

'I deserve to have the money. I would have been a wealthy man if I'd married her. Tell me where she is!' He stood, hauling Rosamond up with him, and shook her until her teeth rattled.

A red haze formed before her eyes – pure outrage at such treatment. Drawing back one foot, she kicked him as hard as she could.

Her soft leather shoe did no damage to his shin but he retaliated by tightening his grip on her arms. The look in his eyes promised retribution.

Rosamond opened her mouth to scream, but Tommaso guessed her intention. He dragged her closer, covering her lips with his in a brutal kiss that effectively cut off any sound.

Prevented from calling for help, Rosamond squirmed in his grasp, trying desperately to free herself. One of his hands moved upward to grip the back of her head and hold her still for his marauding mouth but the other slid down her arm and caught hold of her elbow. Her dagger was on that side. She was unable to maneuver it out of its scabbard.

Rosamond attempted to lift her knee and slam it into his privates. Uttering a low growl, Tommaso evaded the blow and thrust her against the garden wall. Of a sudden, his bigger body held her in place from chest to knees. She could scarce move, let alone escape.

His first kiss had been hard and angry. Now that he had immobilized her, his manner underwent a sea change. He nipped at the corner of her mouth. '*Amante,*' he murmured against her lips. 'You are worth ten of Lina. Tell me where she is and I will make you glad you did.'

Rosamond could scarce believe what she was hearing. How stupid did he think she was? And what kind of fool thought so highly of himself that he believed he could win a woman's heart . . . and her body . . . by betraying her friend?

She could not avoid the kisses that followed, but the slobber that went with them disgusted her. When he tried to thrust his tongue into her mouth, Rosamond had had enough.

She let him in. Then she bit down as hard as she could.

Tommaso yelped and stumbled away from her.

Rosamond spat out blood and scrubbed at her mouth with one hand while she raised the other. The knife blade gleamed in the sunlight.

A shout from the direction of the house froze them in tableau. They had been seen. Rescuers were on their way.

'Stay where you are, Tommaso.' She brandished her weapon. He would answer her questions now. She'd hold him prisoner until he did.

He had the audacity to laugh.

A dagger was excellent for defense but no use at all when it came to enforcing an order. Tommaso turned his back on her and set off at a trot for the place where he'd come over the wall. To prevent his escape, Rosamond had two choices. She could throw the knife or throw her arms around him and hold on until help arrived. She chose the second option.

With a violent shove, he freed himself. Rosamond landed hard, tumbling to the ground in a welter of skirts. She struggled to stand up, at the same time twisting so she could look toward the house and judge whether the approaching reinforcements would arrive in time to stop the fleeing Florentine.

She opened her mouth to order her servants to pursue him but the command died unspoken. One man racing toward her was far ahead of the rest. Recognizing him, she swayed and nearly lost her balance a second time. A curious mixture of confusion, embarrassment and joy washed over her, a wave of emotion so powerful that she forgot all about trying to capture Tommaso Sassetti.

FIFTEEN

The last thing Rob Jaffrey expected to see when he arrived at Willow House was his wife in the arms of another man. Blinded by a jealous rage, he hurled himself toward the man who had been embracing Rosamond in a sheltered corner of the garden. He was fully prepared to throttle the fellow.

The cowardly cur sprinted toward the lowest section of the garden wall. While Rob was still too far away to stop him, he slithered up the stones like the snake he was. At the top of the wall, he paused to look back, devilish glee lighting his eyes.

'*Salutami* Lina,' he called in Rosamond's direction. A moment later, he had dropped down on the other side and disappeared.

Rob skidded to a halt. As much as he'd have liked to pursue the rogue and thrash him within an inch of his life, he knew his limitations. The injuries he'd suffered the previous summer had been severe. The worst of them had healed, and he walked without a limp, but sprinting across the garden had already left him winded. He'd never be able to get over the wall, let alone run down Rosamond's escaping lover.

Andrew Needham, who had accompanied Rob from Cambridge, was in no better shape. Huffing and puffing, he trotted up to his friend. His pale yellow hair stood up in tufts, looking white in the bright sunlight. He had lost his bonnet in their rush to apprehend the miscreant.

'What did he say?' Needham asked.

Rob shook his head. 'His words made no sense to me. Shall we ask my wife?' He braced himself. This would not be a pleasant interview.

Needham stepped in front of him, blocking the path. He was not a big man, no taller than Rob himself, but it was impossible to move past him. 'Curb your temper, Rob,' Needham warned. 'There's more to this than meets the eye. She marked the man who just went over the wall. There was blood on his face.'

Rob's memory of what he had seen shifted and reformed. A sick horror replaced his anger. If that devil had hurt her—

'Rosamond!'

Pushing past Needham, Rob pelted toward his wife. She had collapsed onto a turf-topped bench and was scrubbing vigorously at her lips with a handkerchief. Just as he reached her, she turned aside to retch into the bushes.

There was nothing Rob could do to help her until the spasms passed but when she sat upright again, he pressed the handkerchief she'd dropped into her hand. She glanced at him, then away.

He had never felt so useless or so much in the wrong. He had misjudged what he'd seen. He should have known that Rosamond, for all her flaws, was not the sort of woman who would betray her marriage vows. He was ashamed of himself for doubting her for even an instant and appalled at what might have happened to her if he had not arrived when he did.

Rosamond took several deep breaths. Her fingers curled into fists in her lap, crushing the handkerchief. 'I could not free my knife hand.' She sounded more aggrieved than frightened. 'The wretched man had my arms pinned to my sides.'

'Did he hurt you?'

'Only my pride.' Her chin came up. 'I did more damage to him.'

Rob was not sure he wanted to know the answer but he asked his question anyway, 'How? Why was he bleeding?'

'I bit his tongue. He should not have tried to stick it into my mouth.' For a moment she looked as if she might be ill again.

Rob drew her into his arms and, for a wonder, she did not resist. 'Shall I hunt him down and kill him for you?'

'I would rather kill him myself but that would not be a good idea.' Her voice hitched, as if she might be trying to fight off tears.

He held her close, stroking her back with one hand. In time with the slow, soothing motion, he rocked back and forth, treasuring these tender moments. It would not be long before she pulled free of his embrace. Rosamond despised any show of weakness, especially in herself.

He was dimly aware that Needham stood guard a few feet away. Rosamond's servants had come out of the house, drawn by the shouting, but once they realized who Rob was, none of them intruded, not even the formidable Melka.

As Rob expected, Rosamond soon freed herself and put a little distance between them on the turf-covered bench. Although she was now able to look at him, there was no welcome in her gaze. Rather, her eyes narrowed with suspicion.

'What are you doing here, Rob?'

'That is a long story.'

She glanced around the garden, caught sight of Needham, and frowned. 'Why did you bring Andrew with you?'

'That, too, is complicated, and a tale best told when we are in private together.'

Her half smile was rueful. 'This is the most secluded spot in the garden. Tell me now.'

Rob shook his head. 'This bench is hard by a wall. Do you know what is on the other side?'

Startled by the question, she turned to stare at the high, brick barrier. 'A neighbor's garden backs up to this one.'

'Thus anyone might be listening, even that man who just tried to rape you.'

Her face flamed. 'Rape was not his intent. At least, I do not believe it was. He was acting under the misapprehension that he could render any woman amenable to his wishes by the application of kisses and the promise of passion. Those blandishments were a clumsy attempt to trick me into telling him something I do not want him to know.'

'The more fool he,' Rob muttered. 'What information was he after?'

'I cannot tell you that, either.'

'What can you tell me?'

'What can you tell *me*?' she countered. 'Or shall I ask Andrew?'

'Andrew does not know.'

'Then why did you bring him with you?'

'He insisted upon coming.' Rob shook his head. 'No more questions, I beg you. Not now. Ho! Needham. It is safe to approach.'

Given no other choice, Rosamond made an effort to be pleasant to Rob's friend, but it was abundantly clear that she was not pleased at being kept in the dark. Nor was he.

Needham was quick to excuse himself, claiming to be passing hungry after the long ride from Cambridge. He expressed the hope that he could coax Rosamond's cook into giving him a bite to eat. With more speed than grace, he fled toward the house.

Rosamond crossed her arms in front of her chest and glared at her husband. 'What was so important that you left your studies? You have already missed more than your fair share of lectures as it is.'

'And I do not need another one from you. Do you know that some husbands would feel justified in beating their wives if they'd come upon a scene such as the one I just encountered?'

'I'd like to see you try!' Her eyes blazed with indignation.

Rob sighed. This was not going well. He did not know why he'd thought it would. He intended to tell her the whole story, but he still thought it would be best to do so in her privy chamber with the door barred.

'I am permitted annual leave of up to four weeks,' he reminded his wife.

'Not when the term has scarce begun. And not when you have just been absent for an entire year. You have an obligation to finish your studies.'

'And so I shall, but first it was necessary that I come here. I had to be certain you were safe.'

'Safe?' she echoed. 'You know as well as anyone that I am capable of looking after myself.'

'Oh, yes. So I saw.'

She glared at him. 'I am grateful for your help, but I had the situation well in hand.'

She had bitten him. Repressing a groan, Rob put his elbows

on his knees and supported his head with his hands. If he and Needham had not appeared on the scene when they did, the fellow would likely have met violence with violence. At the least, he'd have struck the woman who'd wounded him. Deflecting her dagger would have been child's play.

'Please tell me you intended to run away.'

'If you had not come to my rescue, I'd have been inside the house before he had time to staunch the flow of blood.'

Rob did not believe a word of it, not when he'd seen with his own eyes how she'd tried to restrain the villain. It shamed him that he'd been fool enough to mistake that for love-play but difficulty in thinking clearly was often a problem when his wife was involved.

He wanted to ask for her promise that she would be more careful in the days to come, but he knew her too well. Whatever she was up to, she'd continue to go her own way until she was satisfied with the result. In the heat of the moment, she'd rush in where angels feared to tread.

'You are resourceful, Rosamond. I will give you that much.'

'How long do you plan to stay?'

'A question to warm any husband's heart.'

'You need not be sarcastic.' Avoiding his eyes, she toyed with the handkerchief in her lap. 'I have missed you, Rob. I grew quite . . . accustomed to being with you on the ship.'

He stared at her, surprised but pleased by her admission. 'I have missed you, too, Ros.'

Nearly a year and a half ago, he'd taken time away from his studies to travel, ending up in Moscow and in trouble. Because of that, back in England, Rosamond had become embroiled in difficulties of her own. She'd even followed him to Muscovy, although by the time she arrived he'd no longer needed rescuing. Afterward, they'd shared a long sea journey home, during which they'd had time to become reacquainted with one another. For part of the voyage, Rob had been recovering from grievous wounds, but during that last week he'd been able to be a true husband to her. He smiled at the memories.

'I would like to stay here for a day or two.'

He'd have preferred to remain longer but, sadly, she'd been correct in saying he had a responsibility to finish what he'd started at Cambridge. He owed that much to himself and to his parents and to Lady Appleton, as well.

Once, he'd have done anything to stay at Christ's College. Before his marriage, he'd been a sizar, the lowest form of scholar. Although some of his expenses had been paid by Lady Appleton, he'd been happy to perform the most menial of tasks in return for rations in the college buttery and the odd farthing tossed his way for services rendered. He'd roused fellow students in time for chapel, made beds, swept chambers, emptied chamber pots, cleaned boots, carried water, run miscellaneous errands and served at table. It had not been an easy life. He'd still been required to be on time for morning prayers and to attend three lectures every day. Even on the Sabbath, he'd not been able to rest, not when so much of every Sunday was spent in church.

It had only been in the last year that he'd come to realize that some things were more important than earning his degree. His wife's well-being was chief among them.

'It will be . . . pleasant to have your company.' Rosamond took his hand in hers. Her lips curved into a teasing smile that caused his heart to race and blood to rush into other parts of his body. 'Does a visit of a day or two mean you will be with me for one night or two?'

She slid her free hand up the front of his doublet and began to toy with the laces that held his collar in place. Rob caught her fingers and kissed them, unable to keep the foolish grin off his face.

'Two,' he said. 'Most assuredly two nights.'

SIXTEEN

R osamond was in a quandary. As much as she wanted to know why Rob had come to Bermondsey and why he was so leery of being overheard when he explained, she was loath to share her secrets with him. Her plans would worry him. His studies would suffer. More to the point, he'd want to know where Lina was hiding.

Andrew Needham's presence delayed the reckoning. So did Watling's. The cat adored Rob and demanded to be made much of. Normal household routine took them through supper. Afterward, Rosamond and Rob retired to Rosamond's tower bedchamber, where she was able to distract her husband in a most pleasurable manner. Only when they were both pleasantly exhausted and lying side-by-side in bed did she give in to the inevitable.

'We can talk in private now, unless you would rather sleep.' She cuddled closer. 'You first.'

It took Rob a moment to grasp her meaning. With a groan, he sat up, pulling her with him. He rearranged the pillows behind them, slid an arm around her shoulders and cleared his throat. 'A few days ago, a man tried to recruit me to spy on other students at Christ's College.'

Rosamond went still, suspending the idle movements of her hand on his bare chest. 'Why you?'

'I cannot say for certain, but he took pains to remind me that you were once willing to do something similar.'

Rosamond pulled away from him so fast that her long, unbound hair flew in all directions. 'Hypocrite!'

Beside her, she felt Rob tense. A glance at his face, what she could see of it when the chamber was lit only by the fire in the hearth, told her that he thought she had flung the accusation at him.

'Not you. Never you. I meant Sir Francis Walsingham. Three days ago, the queen's principal secretary sent me a warning, forbidding me to visit his headquarters in Seething Lane, even though I never had any intention of going there in the first place.'

'Mayhap we should start again.'

'Agreed. Describe your encounter with Walsingham's man.'

Rob settled her against him once more and tugged the blanket up to their chins. Then he recounted, in minute detail, his meeting with the stranger at Cambridge. Rosamond welcomed his warmth at her side, but his words alarmed her.

'A tall, thin man of some forty years, you say, spindle-shanked and with knobby knees? Did he have a prominent Adam's apple?'

Rob thought a moment. 'It seems to me that he did.'

'Pale blue eyes?'

'Like blue ice.'

She made an impatient huffing sound.

'Who is he?'

'I do not know his name, but I feel certain I have met him. He is one of Walsingham's Seething Lane minions. This does not bode well.'

'No, it does not. That is why I came here. He threatened you, Rosamond.'

She shook her head. 'Needham, mayhap. You. Not me.'

'He suggested that my refusal to spy for him could lead to retribution. It is far too easy to kill someone, Ros. If you were to die, I do not know how I could go on living.'

'I promise I will not allow myself to be shot, stabbed, or poisoned. I can look after myself.'

'You believe that, I know. That is what terrifies me.'

She punched him, gently, in the ribs. Under her fingers, even all these months later, she could feel the difference in the texture of his skin in the places where he had been burnt. Face, chest and arms had all suffered damage. His broken wrist had healed faster than the scars.

Rob caught her wandering hands. 'Stop trying to distract me. Why does Walsingham want you to keep away from his headquarters?'

When she did not answer at once, he tucked her beneath him and planted a gentle kiss on her brow. 'Talk to me, Rosamond.'

She reached up to caress his face and would have pulled him closer if he'd allowed it.

'Is there some connection between Walsingham and the man in the garden?'

'If there is one, I am not aware of it. I do not know what prompted Sir Francis to start issuing orders. As for Tommaso, do you remember Godlina Walkenden?'

'Your schoolfellow, Lina.' There was just enough light for Rosamond to see Rob's features slide into a frown. 'Was it her name that man called out just before he leapt from the top of the wall?'

'It was. He said "Give my love to Lina" in Italian. His name is Tommaso Sassetti and he is a most annoying fellow. First he wanted to marry Lina for her dowry. Now he's after the reward her sister is offering for her capture.'

'Wait,' Rob interrupted. 'Her *capture*?'

'Lina is accused of murdering the sister's husband. Since she is innocent, I have undertaken to do everything in my power to discover the identity of the real killer.'

'Where is Lina in the meantime?'

'Somewhere safe.'

'Ros—'

'She is a fugitive, Rob. An outlaw. The fewer people who know where to look for her, the safer she will be.'

His reluctance was palpable, but after a moment he urged her to go on with her story. Securely nestled in her husband's arms, secretly delighted to have someone with whom to share her thoughts, Rosamond summarized everything she had done so far on Lina's behalf. She ended with a succinct and emotionless account of Tommaso Sassetti's visit to Willow House.

'You need a keeper,' Rob muttered. 'What were you thinking of to invite him here?'

'That I would have loyal servants surrounding me to keep me safe. I did not expect him to arrive as he did. What does it matter now? He did me no harm.'

Rob mulled over what she had told him and, after a short silence, asked, 'Why are you so convinced that Lina is incapable of murder?'

'She was my friend. She *is* my friend.' But there was more to it than that, Rosamond realized. Forced to examine her own motives, she came to a startling conclusion. 'It is because Mama believes in her and expects me to do everything in my power to right a wrong.'

'Lady Appleton would not want you to put yourself in danger.'

Lost in her own thoughts, Rosamond was no longer listening as Rob continued to express concern for her safety. That she had failed to live up to her foster mother's expectations during the past few years was something she regretted most deeply. As a result, she was determined to do the right thing now, in all ways. That included making amends to everyone she had wronged, especially her husband.

When he had been in danger the previous year, she had realized how much he meant to her. The bond between them had been strengthened during the long weeks at sea. And yet, although they had talked of many things aboard the *Winifred*, she had still held a part of herself separate.

'I fought hard to be free of obligations to anyone but myself,' she whispered, speaking more to herself than to Rob.

He answered her anyway. 'I know.' The arm around her bare shoulders tightened.

'I never realized how lonely my new life would be.'

'You can change that, Rosamond. You need lose nothing of yourself to invite others in.'

'Sometimes I want that,' she admitted. 'I even think about children – having a family with you. But women die in childbirth, too, Rob. You worry that I put myself in danger by trying to help a friend, but the threat of sudden death is all around us all the time.'

She felt him nod but could no longer see him. The fire had burned so low that they were no more than shadows to each other.

'True,' he said. 'And we might have been shipwrecked and drowned on our journey home from Muscovy. But we survived. Some risks are worth taking, Ros.' He hesitated, then spoke with an earnestness she could not fail to recognize for what it was. 'After I am awarded my degree, I want to come here and live with you. Will I be welcome?'

Rosamond turned in his arms and showed him, without words, just how welcome he would be. Afterward, her heart full of love for her husband, she slept deep and dreamlessly.

SEVENTEEN

Shouts and alarums roused them at dawn.
Rob tumbled out of bed, scrambling to find his clothing by what little early morning sunlight seeped through the shuttered windows. Rosamond struggled into her shift, still sitting atop the wool-stuffed mattress. Her head had barely

emerged from the soft folds of finest cambric when Alys burst into the bedchamber.

'The constables are at the gate, madam!' she cried. 'They have come to search the house!'

'What have you done now?' Rob assumed the rest of his clothing with impressive rapidity and turned to help Rosamond with her laces.

Alys had collapsed in a corner, sobbing.

'Nothing!'

Melka was nowhere to be seen. Rosamond hoped she had not gone haring off in search of help again. This invasion was unexpected, but Rosamond felt well able to deal with the crisis. After all, she was not hiding Lina at Willow House.

'Are you certain you have broken no laws? You have not been going about in boys' clothing again, have you?'

Although Rosamond knew Rob was teasing her, his words earned him a ferocious scowl. She bit back the reminder that she could do as she pleased. In that instant, it occurred to her that she might be able to use the expectations men had of women to her advantage.

'Husband,' she said, her voice overly sweet, 'is it not your sworn duty to defend hearth and home?' She sent him a coy look over one shoulder as she moved toward the door.

'Alys, you are a witness. My lady has need of me.'

'Do not let it go to your head!'

When she glanced behind her a second time, he was not quick enough to hide the look in his eyes. Her careless words had hurt him. Guilt swamped her, along with regret. She was about to take outrageous advantage of Rob's good nature, just as she always did. It was a failing in her, one she meant to remedy, but just at present she had no choice but to go on as she had begun.

'Come along,' she called, 'We must stop them before they wreck the place.'

A mighty crash from the direction of the gatehouse under-scored her words.

Together they raced through Rosamond's privy chamber and out into the gallery that adjoined the tower. She had not had time to finish dressing. Her hair still flowed down her back in dark brown waves, and her feet were bare.

Andrew Needham bounded up the stairs from the hall to meet them on the landing. He'd been given a chamber near the gatehouse and must have been among the first to be roused by the clamor without. One of the buttons on the front of his doublet had gone through the wrong hole, leaving the entire garment to hang askew, and his fair hair stood straight up for want of combing.

'What have you done to provoke the villagers?' Despite the worried look on his face, his tone was lighthearted, as if he looked forward to the coming confrontation. 'Are we to fight sword against pitchforks to defend the castle?'

'Weapons will not come into it.' Rob sent him a severe look. 'The girl said they are constables. If they have a warrant, we will have to let them search the house.'

As yet, Andrew knew nothing about Lina Walkenden's troubles. It was not surprising that he looked so baffled. 'Never tell me you have been harboring priests!' He grinned to show he meant the suggestion in jest.

Rosamond's breath caught.

Rob sent his friend a sharp look. 'It is unwise to joke about such things. We are not hiding anyone, but the promise of a reward may be what has persuaded the constables of Cheap Ward to suborn their counterpart in Bermondsey into coming here to harass my wife.'

Rosamond's steps faltered halfway down the stairs. Although Rob's conclusion was logical, she had to wonder how constables from London had discovered where she lived. When asked by Clem Dodge, she'd admitted to no more than that she resided in Surrey. She had said nothing that would lead him to look for Lina in Bermondsey.

Tommaso, she thought. Tommaso must have told Isolde where to find her.

Rosamond found flaws in this explanation almost as soon as it crossed her mind. Even if Tommaso had gone straight to Lina's sister after Rob chased him away from Willow House, she could not imagine how Isolde would have been able to organize an invasion of this magnitude so quickly.

That Tommaso might have told Isolde where Rosamond lived before his visit to Willow House made even less sense. He had been quarreling with her the one time Rosamond had seen them together.

A tiny sound from the top of the stair made her turn and look upward. Alys stood there, her terrified gaze fixed on the hall below. Rob and Andrew had already reached the entrance and were arguing about whether or not to lift the heavy bar and open the door. The moment they did, the men on the other side would pour through. If they delayed too long, someone on the other side would likely give the order to break it down.

'Alys!' Rosamond's sharp tone of voice made the girl jump. 'Did you return to Soper Lane?'

She was answered with a vigorous negative head-shaking, but Alys avoided meeting her eyes.

'The truth, Alys. How did the constables find me?'

With another piteous wail, the girl threw herself to her knees, hands lifted toward Rosamond in supplication. 'You have been so generous, madam. I did not mean to betray you. But I did leave something behind, under a floorboard in the chamber where I slept. I did not think anyone would see me if I fetched it while they were all at work.'

'You were wrong. You were followed back here.'

Rosamond ran up the last few steps to the landing and hauled the girl to her feet. She caught sight of Melka watching them from the shadows of the gallery and was relieved to know that her tiring maid was still on the premises, but she kept the focus of her attention on Alys, who was sniffing and sniveling and stammering as her eyes overflowed with tears.

'I did not see anyone, madam.'

'When did you go?' Rosamond gave her a shake when she did not answer promptly enough.

'The day after you brought me here. Forgive me, madam. I never meant to cause you harm. You have been nothing but good to me.'

The timing made sense. Isolde could have sent one of the apprentices after Alys. Once she'd discovered where Rosamond lived, she'd turned informer. Somehow, likely with bribes, she had persuaded the authorities to venture into another jurisdiction.

Furious banging on the door between the courtyard and hall prevented Rosamond from slapping the silly baggage – not as a punishment but to ward off hysterics. She released Alys just as Rob opened the door.

Angry, agitated voices drifted up from the hall below.

Rosamond fought the urge to race down the stairs and confront the intruders. Instead, she descended at a slow, dignified pace, resolved to play the role of dutiful wife and pretend that she was dependent upon her husband for protection and to tell her how to behave.

Engaged in elaborate playacting of his own, Rob greeted her effusively. 'Ah, my dear, there you are. Do you know this gentleman? He is Lawrence Walkenden, your old friend Lina's brother.'

Rosamond leveled a cold stare at the heavy-set man standing beside her husband, noting as she did so that his eyes were the same hazelnut-shell color as Lina's. 'You have arrived passing early for a visit.'

Her gaze roved over the men clustered just inside the door. She expected to see Clement Dodge, the constable from Cheapside Ward. He was not among them, but she did recognize two others. Reynold Iden was Bermondsey's petty constable, elected by his fellow householders in the village for a term of one year. He was a well-meaning but bumbling sort whose father had taken his turn as constable a dozen years before. The other familiar face belonged to Fulke Iden. No doubt he had accompanied his son to offer Reynold the benefit of his experience. Rosamond had heard that the first Constable Iden had arrested a number of felons in his time.

'I have come for my sister,' Lawrence Walkenden announced.

'She is not here nor has she been. I doubt she even knows where I live.'

'You will forgive me, Mistress Jaffrey, if I do not take your word for that.' Walkenden's garments marked him as a man of means. If he was also a man of influence, that went a long way toward explaining why Constable Iden was willing to cooperate with him.

'Have a care how you insult my wife.' The low, threatening rumble of Rob's voice had Rosamond staring at him in amazement. She'd had no idea that her husband could sound so impressive.

Walkenden was unmoved by the implied threat. He offered up a legal document of some sort, claiming it was his authorization to search the premises. Rob made a production of reading every word, but there was never any doubt about the outcome. The house would be searched.

The very idea was offensive to Rosamond, but she took heart from the knowledge that, in the end, the searchers would go away empty-handed. There was nothing for them to find.

As they spread out, putting grubby hands on Rosamond's possessions, carelessly tossing breakable items to the floor, Rob slung an arm around her shoulders. His fingers clenched tight on her flesh – warning, not comfort.

'Not a word, Ros. If you want revenge, you can sue for damages later.'

'I want Isolde Hackett's head on a platter,' she muttered.

'I'll keep an eye on them,' Needham volunteered. 'They are looking for a person. They have no need to go through every drawer and coffer.'

'I fear they do,' Rob said. 'According to that warrant, they are also searching for any letters Lina may have written to Rosamond.'

They were mad if they thought Lina would be fool enough to confess to murder in writing, but there *was* a letter she'd rather they not find, the one Lady Appleton had written. Was there anything suspicious in it? 'A matter of life and death' sounded dramatic but if it became necessary, Rosamond could provide any number of explanations for that wording. She would not admit to visiting Leigh Abbey. There was no need. If asked, she would tell them that a second message, a verbal one, had arrived a day after the first to tell her that the crisis had passed.

Rosamond fidgeted, unable to stand idly by while her house was ransacked. At the first opportunity, she slipped free of Rob's grasp and scurried back up the staircase.

'Your presence will only make them search with more dili-
gence,' he called after her.

She ignored him. She found Walkenden in the outer room
that led to her bedchamber, the one she referred to as her privy
chamber. It was furnished with a comfortable Glastonbury
chair, a footstool, and a table that held the book she was
currently reading – Thomas Tusser's treatise on good husbandry.
She watched in stoic silence as Walkenden delved into every
nook and cranny.

From the inner chamber, she heard the sound of more
searching. Her cheeks heated as one of the constables remarked
upon the disordered state of the bed. Rob joined her in time
to hear the bawdy exchange that followed. She felt his body
tense, but he had better sense than to express his indignation
aloud.

In the next instant, she heard a hiss followed by a spitting
sound. A man yelped in pain. In a gruff voice, he roundly
cursed all cats and the inconsiderate fools who kept them for
pets but failed to exact punishment for his injury. Watling
emerged from the bedchamber at full speed, his tail puffed up
to twice its normal size, and swarmed up the spiral staircase
that led to the upper regions of the tower.

'Good boy,' Rob said under his breath.

On the next level was Rosamond's study, similar in many
ways to Lady Appleton's but lacking a hiding place behind
a *mappa mundi*. *Just as well*, she decided. If the searchers
found such a thing, they would be convinced she was up to
no good.

The top floor of the tower was given over to a large
bedchamber, one in which Rosamond stored clothing,
including the disguises she was wont to employ when
she did not want to be recognized. This highest point in the
house looked out over the rooftops of London. On a clear
day, she could see all the way to Shoreditch, where a fellow
named James Burbage had built a permanent playhouse called
the Theatre.

Following the cat, Lawrence Walkenden entered the study.
Rosamond and Rob went up after him. He made a meticulous
search of Rosamond's books and papers, opened every chest

and inspected every coffer and box, but it did not occur to him to look behind the hangings that decorated the walls. *Careless of him*, Rosamond thought.

All the same, Walkenden's search was thorough enough to unearth the letter from Lady Appleton. Rosamond took an involuntary step toward Lina's brother when he found it, causing Rob to send her a questioning look. She had told him everything about her investigation on Lina's behalf except for *how* she had learned that her friend was in trouble. She had not dared mention Lady Appleton's name. The moment she did so, Rob would have been sure to guess where Lina was hiding.

He caught hold of her forearm and gave it a warning squeeze. Rosamond glared at him. She had no intention of making a fuss that would betray the significance of the message.

Walkenden read what Lady Appleton had written and then replaced her letter where he had found it before moving on to the rest of Rosamond's correspondence. Some of those missives were from Rob. Rosamond disliked having a stranger read words intended for her eyes alone, but there was no help for it. She felt a little better when she realized that Walkenden first checked each one for the date. He did not continue reading if he saw that a letter had been written before Hugo Hackett's murder.

A quarter of an hour later, everyone had returned to the ground floor. Fulke Iden, well past his prime and disinclined to do more than snoop and supervise, sidled up to Rosamond when she reached the foot of the stairs. 'I told them they'd find naught here, Mistress Jaffrey. Clumsy oafs,' he added at the sound of something heavy crashing to the floor in the parlor.

Still puzzled by the absence of Constable Dodge, Rosamond asked, 'Are all these men constables?'

The old man chuckled and stroked his beard. 'Lord love you, no. My boy's the only official present, Mistress Jaffrey. The rest are hired henchmen.'

Rosamond did not know whether this news made her feel better or worse. She supposed that it scarce mattered who the men were. So long as they had that warrant, she could do nothing to stop them from searching her house.

Lawrence Walkenden did not apologize for the intrusion. On his way out with his men, he leveled a threatening look at Rosamond. 'Should you hear any word of my sister, Mistress Jaffrey, you would be well advised to report her whereabouts to the nearest justice of the peace.'

So much for her attempt to convince him she was an ordinary, well-bred gentlewoman in thrall to her husband! Irritated by Walkenden's attitude, she spoke her mind. 'We would both be better employed in discovering who really killed Hugo Hackett.'

Lina's brother gave a start of surprise. 'Surely there can be no doubt as to that.'

'No? You knew Hackett, Master Walkenden. Despite his wife's claim that he was a paragon of virtue, people other than your sister had cause to wish him ill.'

'That he had enemies I will admit, but none who would want him dead.'

'Are you certain of that?'

Like most men, Lawrence Walkenden did not like being challenged by a woman. He turned his back on her and headed for the door.

Rob held it open for him, a broad grin on his face. 'Good day to you, Master Walkenden.'

Walkenden took his amusement amiss, stopping in his tracks to offer unsolicited advice in an aggrieved tone of voice. 'You would do well, young sir, to keep your wife at home. Meddling women are the very devil.'

EIGHTEEN

Rob had never lived in Willow House with his wife, but he shared her anger at the invasion of her home. His heart ached for her as he watched her stop in the doorway of her privy chamber to survey the chaos the searchers had left behind.

'It is a good thing Lina did not go to her half brother for

help when Isolde accused her of murder,' she muttered after roundly cursing Lawrence Walkenden. 'He'd have had her in gaol before she could blink.'

Rob spared a moment's sympathy for the other man, despite his high-handed behavior. It was a difficult situation for a brother to be in when one sister turned against the other. He had two sisters himself and wondered which one he would believe, Susan or Kate, if one swore that the other had committed some heinous crime.

Rosamond paused in the act of retrieving scattered papers from the floor to scowl at him. 'Keep your wife at home? You had best not follow such addlepated advice!'

He held up both hands, palms toward her. 'Pax, Rosamond. I am here to help you restore order to your belongings.'

Rosamond huffed out an exasperated breath. She looked delectable. Her disheveled hair hung long, loose, and tangled and – he glanced down – her feet were still bare. To his chagrin, instead of turning to him for comfort, she scooped Watling out of the Glastonbury chair and clasped him tight against her breasts.

'Rosamond, I—'

'Go away. You will only get in my way. And here.' She thrust Watling at him. 'Take him, too.'

Rob retreated into the gallery. Uncertain whether it was safe to enter the tower when Rosamond's temper was so volatile, Needham had chosen to wait for him there. He lounged on one of the semi-circular window seats, his right foot up on the cushion and his right hand draped loosely over his bent knee. The back of his hatless head rested against the window-pane. Rob was not fooled by the casual pose. He saw the look of deep concern that lurked in his friend's eyes.

Still holding the cat, Rob seated himself on the opposite side of the window seat. The gallery overlooked Rosamond's walled garden, triggering a vivid memory – his wife struggling with Tommaso Sassetti. The anger he'd felt then returned in a rush, along with a strong desire to seek retribution. Without realizing what he was doing, he tightened his grip on Watling.

Pain shot through his arm as Rosamond's pet dug in with

all four sets of claws. Rob released him at once, then grunted
when the furious feline landed a hard kick in his midsection.
Retreating a safe distance, he glared at Rob before sitting
down to begin a vigorous grooming.

'We have all had a difficult morning,' Rob told the cat.
Shifting his attention to Needham, he said, 'I suppose you are
wondering what all the to-do was about.'

'You will tell me when you are ready. Or I will prize it out
of you by cunning, mayhap over a cup of aqua vitae.'

Rob studied his friend. Part of the reason he liked Needham
was the other man's cheerful outlook on life, but there was
such a thing as being too optimistic. Rob had not told Needham
about the accusation Walsingham's minion had made against
him. Now, faced with the need to decide how many of
Rosamond's confidences to share, he thought it best to first
confide what he himself had held back.

'I would have honesty between us,' he began. 'I know you
are not a recusant. You go to church and chapel as often as I
do. But there are many at Cambridge who are clandestine
papists. Are you one of them?'

Needham's thunderstruck expression told him nothing. It
could mean he'd never dreamed of such a thing or, just as
easily, that he was astonished that Rob should have discovered
his secret.

When Rob, following the interview with Walsingham's
minion, had considered what he knew of his friend's history,
the idea that Needham was a secret Catholic had seemed
preposterous. Andrew Needham was a second son sent to
Christ's College by his father in the hope he would one day
become a doctor of divinity. He was no great scholar, but he
tried hard, spending more time than Rob did with his books.
He often read far into the night, then rose at four in the
morning to study the texts again. It was a mark of their friendship that he had been willing to miss several days of lectures
to accompany Rob to Willow House. Needham had reminded
him that it was never wise to travel England's roads alone.
A solitary horseman made a tempting target for vagabonds
and masterless men.

Needham's mouth opened and closed several times before

he finally managed to get a word out and then it was to ask a question of his own. 'Do you take me for a fool?'

'If you damn yourself to a life of fines and imprisonment and mayhap worse, then yes.' Rob did not bother to mention the oath of allegiance Needham would have to take in order to be granted his degree.

In one slow, deliberate movement, Needham sat up straight. Once both feet were on the floor, he stood, towering over his still-seated friend. He was not a big man, but he was a solid presence and Rob could tell by the color rising in his face that he was exceeding angry.

'This is a monstrous accusation.' Needham's voice was low and choked with barely suppressed rage. 'Who dares slander me with such a lie?'

'The better question is why? Sit down, Needham. I am not the one who has doubts about your loyalty.'

When the other man resumed his seat, sitting stiffly this time, jaw set and eyes cold, Rob told him everything Walsingham's man had said, including his reference to Rosamond's employment as an intelligence gatherer. 'That is why I had to come here. I had to make certain she would not become embroiled a second time in the spy master's schemes.'

Needham shook his head, as if to clear his mind. 'I do not know what question to ask first,' he admitted. '*Has* Walsingham solicited her help in some new endeavor?'

'On the contrary. He sent word that she should bide at home and mind her own business. You can imagine how well she took that advice.' Rob's lips twisted into a brief, rueful smile. 'What she *has* embroiled herself in is something that has naught to do with spies. I will tell you the whole story anon, but first I would know how anyone could think you a likely recruit to the papist cause.'

'I cannot imagine.'

'It would not take much to make Walsingham suspicious. The man sees papists hiding beneath every bush. Are there any recusants in your family, no matter how distantly related?'

'None, unless. . . .' Of a sudden, Needham looked stricken. 'There is my godmother's daughter. She is a nun in one of those convents founded by English women on the continent after all the religious houses in England were dissolved. You do not suppose . . .?'

Rob did not like the sound of this. 'Have you had any correspondence with her?'

'None. I swear it. My godmother died soon after I was baptized. Her husband remarried, taking as his second wife a woman who is a devout Catholic. She raised the girl and a few years later the entire family fled abroad to avoid being persecuted for their religious beliefs. I was still a child at the time. I only know about the nunnery because my mother hears news of her from time to time and passes it on to me in her letters.'

'That is not enough to condemn you,' Rob said, hoping it was true, 'but I would not speak of this distant connection to anyone again, not even to me.'

'It is forgotten.' True to his character, the worry lines in Needham's brow smoothed out as if they had never been.

Watling hopped up on the window seat. After circling once, he stretched out full length, his front paws in Rob's lap, and sent an expectant look his way.

Just like his mistress, Rob thought, *alternating between demands to be set free and wanting my undivided attention.* Obediently, he stroked the feline and was at once rewarded with a deep, rumbling purr.

'You have his wholehearted affection,' Needham remarked.

'Only for the moment.'

'You were going to tell me why your wife's house was searched.'

'So I was.' Rob launched into an abridged account of the story Rosamond had told him. 'She will not say where Lina is now,' he added, 'but I think I can guess.'

Godlina Walkenden had to be at Leigh Abbey. That was the only place that made sense, especially when he remembered how tense Rosamond had become when Lina's brother found a letter from Lady Appleton among her possessions. Rob had not been able to see what that gentlewoman had written to her foster daughter, but he had caught a glimpse of her familiar signature. Walkenden would have seized on it had there been anything blatantly incriminating in the missive, but there was something about it that worried Rosamond. When Walkenden had set the letter aside, showing no further curiosity about its contents, she had all but sagged against Rob in relief.

'I do not suppose you can dissuade her from searching for the real killer.' As Rob had, Needham accepted Rosamond's belief that Lina was innocent of the crime.

'She will not stop until she uncovers the truth.'

Needham nodded. 'Well, then, we should stay and help her.'

'We can offer,' Rob said. 'Whether or not she will accept is beyond my ability to predict.'

NINETEEN

B y the time Rosamond had set her house to rights, there was little left of the day. She resented the waste of time and blamed Lawrence Walkenden. She'd had plans to return to Soper Lane and to Lime Street to ask more questions. She'd hoped to have Rob's company while she did so.

To herself, if to no one else, she could admit how much she had missed him since he'd returned to his studies at Cambridge. They'd spent nearly two months living in each other's pockets on the voyage home from Muscovy. The journey had not been without its dark moments. More than once they'd feared the ship would sink, so fierce were the storms it sailed through. And they'd quarreled, sometimes over inconsequential things, other times because they saw the world around them from different points of view. But they had always reconciled again. They were still, as they had always been, the best of friends. If Rob was not as easy to influence as he had been during their childhood, Rosamond could only admire him for standing up to her. At least he did not simply issue orders and expect her to follow them, the way most men did when they dealt with rebellious wives. He presented a reasoned argument and left her to make the right choice on her own.

She went in search of him and found him playing chess

with Andrew Needham in Needham's chamber off the retainers' court.

'I have been a most neglectful hostess, Andrew. I ask your forgiveness.'

He rose and made her a courtly bow. 'I have been most royally entertained,' he assured her. 'And Rob has told me how your friend was unjustly accused. If I can be of any assistance, I am at your command.'

She could not hold back a smile at this gallant speech. She suspected he'd been practicing it all day. 'I am most grateful for the offer, but as you and Rob must return to Cambridge on the morrow, there is little you can do to help.'

'And if we stay another day?'

Rosamond glanced at Rob. 'Did you put him up to this?'

'Indeed I did not. He's a generous fellow, Needham is.'

'Let me think about it,' Rosamond told them. 'There is naught to be done today. It is nearly time to sup.'

They talked of other things over the meal. Andrew told amusing stories about life at Christ's College. Rob said little, content to listen to the other two and enjoy their company.

'How I wish women were allowed to pursue an education,' Rosamond said. 'Why should men be the only ones allowed to study and attend interesting lectures and have access to hundreds of books and manuscripts?' Archbishop Parker had donated over one thousand printed volumes and nearly five hundred manuscripts to Corpus Christi, another of the colleges at Cambridge.

'You would be bored to tears within a fortnight,' Rob said. 'It is a challenge to stay awake to the end of most of the lectures.'

'And it is not as if undergraduates are allowed a choice in what to read,' Andrew chimed in. 'The curriculum is set by the master. Morning prayer between five and six, then an hour-long lecture on Aristotle's natural philosophy, then two lectures in Greek, and at three in the afternoon yet another lecture on Cicero. Worse, we may speak only Latin in our daily life, except in the privacy of our rooms or on holidays.'

'I read both Latin and Greek.' Speaking those languages was another matter, but Rosamond assumed she could learn.

'My wife is far more clever than I will ever be,' Rob advised his friend. 'She absorbs knowledge like a sponge sops up water while I plod along, slow as a snail, stuffing ideas into my head and holding them there by brute force. Only in the study of languages have I ever come close to sharing her skill, and even there she surpasses me for fluency. My Russian is better only because I spent so many months living in Muscovy.'

Surprised by his praise, Rosamond smiled at her husband before turning back to their guest. 'You must study more than Aristotle and Cicero. What else are you taught?'

'Divinity, civil law, physics, Hebrew, Greek, philosophy, logic, and rhetoric,' Andrew answered.

'Do not forget the quadrivials. They are arithmetic, music, geometry, and astronomy,' Rob explained for Rosamond's benefit.

She made a face at him. 'Could I share your tutors if I visited you at Christ's College?'

Andrew looked shocked by the very suggestion, but it was regret she heard in Rob's voice when he answered. 'Women are not permitted to reside in College, and only a few females may enter the grounds for any reason.'

'Who are the exceptions?'

'Nurses in time of sickness. Laundresses.'

'What about the master? Has he a wife? And has she daughters? An enterprising mother might establish a school for girls in her house and take advantage of all the learned men at her husband's disposal to instruct them.'

'No wife,' Rob said, 'and I am not certain he would be allowed to keep her in College even if he had one. But here is an even more compelling reason why you would not be happy as a scholar at Cambridge, Ros. Attending plays, other than those acted in Latin in the hall at Christmas and in the Lent term, is forbidden.'

'How barbaric!'

'No dice or cards or drinking parties, either,' Andrew said, 'and meals are far less congenial than this one. We eat in the hall at three tables, one for Fellows, one for those who already have their degrees, and the last for the rest of us. Boiled beef with pottage and bread is what we are fed at a typical meal, together with a halfpenny worth of beer. We eat in silence save for one student who reads aloud from the Bible. After grace, we are expected to retire to our chambers.'

'I should not care for such a regimen,' Rosamond admitted, 'although if Rob and I shared a chamber, an early night might be quite pleasant.'

'I,' Rob said, 'would prefer to be done with schooling altogether and live here with you.'

'This is a fine house.' Andrew drained the last of the wine in his goblet and stood. He stretched and pretended to yawn. 'It will be an excellent place to raise a family. But now, if you will excuse me, I believe I am the one ready to retire early. It has been an exhausting day.'

Rosamond watched him go, lips twitching with the urge to smile. 'Did you pay him to say that?'

'No need. He knows as well as I do that we *will* live together one day.'

'But not just yet.' She faced him across the table. 'First you must return to Cambridge and remain there until spring. Did you not tell me that you are permitted only twenty days' absence from your studies in any given year?'

'I will take good care not to exceed that allotment.'

'Rob—'

'You must not think my coming here shows any lack of faith in your abilities, Ros, or that I am meddling by staying on an extra day. I cannot help but be concerned about your safety. I am glad you will have naught to do with Walsingham's schemes, but the longer you persist in trying to help Lina, the more you put yourself at risk. If you come too close to discovering the truth, the real murderer will take steps to stop you.'

'I am aware of the danger, but I have sturdy henchmen in my employ. I can secure the house. I will not walk alone in the garden again until Hugo Hackett's killer has been apprehended and locked up.' She took a last sip of wine and met his eyes. 'I have been thinking about Tommaso Sassetti. I do not believe he is the murderer.'

'Why not? He is a seducer and betrayer of women, mayhap

worse. What if all his mouthing and pawing in the garden had led to—'

'He is driven by greed, not lust.'

Rob snorted. 'That would not have stopped him.'

'Then I would have.' Her lips quirked as she once again fought a smile. 'Do you suppose his tongue is still swollen?'

He choked back a laugh. 'I'd not be surprised. Your teeth are passing sharp, as I have reason to know.'

'I hope he can talk. I still want answers from him.'

'Ros—'

'He is driven by greed,' she repeated. 'He wanted to marry Lina for her dowry, but if he took it into his head to kill for financial gain, his victim would not have been Hugo Hackett. He'd have slain his uncle, eliminating his rival and no doubt coming into a goodly inheritance at the same time.'

'Tommaso might have thought it to his advantage to do away with Hackett first,' Rob argued. 'A new guardian might have been persuaded to permit their marriage. He could not have guessed that Lina would be blamed. If she had not had the bad luck to be the one to find him, the coroner would doubtless have declared that the murder was committed by person or persons unknown.'

'But why would Tommaso go to the mercery on that night of all nights?' Rosamond countered.

Having finished his wine, Rob reached for a bowl full of walnuts and the nutcracker. Considering what she'd said, he made two neat little piles, one of empty shells and the other of meats. 'I yield to your logic. What of your other suspects? Last night you said you had both Isolde and Alessandro Portinari on your list.'

'I have spoken to Isolde Hackett twice. I do not like her any better than I like Tommaso, but I can think of no good reason why she should have killed her husband.' She reached across the table, filched one of the shelled walnut meats and popped it into her mouth.

'And Portinari?' Rob pushed half of the pile of shelled walnuts closer to his wife.

Rosamond sketched out the theory she'd devised when she'd first heard about the wealthy Italian – that Hackett had notified him of Lina's change of heart and Portinari had paid a late-night visit to the mercery that had ended in violence. 'I have had Charles watching the Florentine,' she added. 'I have not yet decided how best to approach him.'

'Let me question him for you.'

'What excuse have you to visit a silk merchant?'

'To buy a gift for my wife? That is as good a reason as any you might devise. Or did you think to persuade Master Baldwin to approach him?'

'Master Baldwin is not in London.'

'A pity but all the more reason to assign this task to me.'

Rosamond shook her head and helped herself to more walnuts. Rob did the same. They sat in silence while they nibbled. After a moment, a thought occurred to her. 'There is one thing you can do to help me find Hugo Hackett's killer, something I cannot do for myself.'

'I am at your command.' Only the faintest trace of sarcasm tinged Rob's words.

'Do you recall that I told you that Alessandro Portinari, in company with Hugo Hackett, visited a woman named Black Luce? She has a house in Clerkenwell. I do not imagine it will be difficult to locate.'

'You want me to visit a brothel?'

Rosamond sent him her sweetest smile. 'If you do not, I will have to.'

'And just what do you think I will be able to discover? Bawds do not tell tales about the men who use their services.'

'One might, if you offer her a generous bribe.'

He rolled his eyes. 'Very well. I will go to Clerkenwell for you, if only to prevent you from setting foot in such a place yourself, but I am taking Needham with me.'

'I will make the sacrifice worth your while,' Rosamond promised.

'Do you intend to bribe me, too?'

'In a manner of speaking.' Rising from the table, she held out a hand. 'Let us adjourn to the bedchamber and I will show you what I have in mind.'

TWENTY

Delighted to be of service, intrigued by their mission, Needham's face flushed with pleasure as he and Rob set out the following morning. 'I have a cousin studying at Gray's Inn,' he announced, 'and Gray's Inn is located hard by Clerkenwell. If there is anyone who can tell us how to find a nearby bawdy house, it is a student of the law.'

Rob saw no harm in starting their quest at one of the Inns of Court. He was less enthusiastic about visiting the establishment run by Black Luce. A few hours after leaving Bermondsey, when he and his friend stood in St John Street looking up at an ordinary but commodious dwelling, he was even less inclined to carry out Rosamond's plan.

Needham cleared his throat. 'Have you ever visited a trugging house before?' Now that they had arrived at their destination, he no longer looked so eager for the adventure. Beads of sweat dotted his forehead.

'I married at sixteen. When did I have the chance? Have you?'

'I was never tempted, not after my father took me aside at a tender age and explained, in graphic detail, what diseases like gonorrhea and syphilis can do to a man. He said a man was sure to catch one or the other if he was foolish enough to lie with a whore.'

'We are not here to sample the wares,' Rob reminded him, 'only to buy information.'

'I hope you brought enough money. Remember what my cousin said. These are not the kind of doxies an apprentice can buy for sixpence.'

Needham's cousin had reckoned that the women who lived in this house – as many as a dozen of them at any given time – each earned as much as ten pounds a month. Of that, they received only a portion. The rest went to their bawd, who provided them with protection and luxurious surroundings, the better to attract wealthy customers who could afford to pay their fees.

Rob had started toward the house when Needham caught his arm. 'Do you suppose she is a Moor?'

'Black Luce?' Rob had not given the matter any thought. Most whores, or so he'd heard, had professional names, everything from Long Meg and Little Nell to Petronella and Ambrosia. According to Needham's knowledgeable cousin, this bawd's proper name was Lucy Baynham. 'More likely she earned the name through dark deeds and a black heart. Come on. We cannot stand outside all day.'

The door to the brothel opened into a screens passage similar to that in most houses, but the servant who admitted them was a giant of a man dressed all in black. He did not need the sword, dagger, and cudgel conveniently at hand to be intimidating. His size alone would keep most customers on their best behavior.

'Good day to you, young gentlemen.' Despite the polite tone of voice, the guard had a calculating look in his eyes. 'How may we serve you?'

When neither Rob nor Needham, intimidated by his appearance, rushed into speech, he stepped aside to reveal a row of portraits on the wall behind him. 'We cater to every taste here, as you can see.'

Each full-length, nearly life-sized painting showed an individual woman. All of them were richly dressed, but every bodice was low-cut and showed a great deal of flesh. Each skirt was arranged in such a way as to give a glimpse of bare ankle and, in one case, the suggestion of a naked thigh. All their faces had been executed in exquisite detail. Rob could not help himself. He stepped closer to study one of the portraits, in which an otherwise demure expression had been turned into something quite different by the lustful look in the sitter's eyes.

Taking note of Rob's interest, the giant chuckled. 'It's early in the day yet for that one, but if you have money enough, even she will make herself available to you. La Fleur is a popular choice, most skilled at what she does.'

'Oh, er, no. We are not here to . . . I have no interest in . . .

that is to say we've come to speak with Mistress Baynham. It is a matter of business.'

The giant scratched the end of his bulbous, red-veined nose as he considered Rob's statement. 'Mistress Baynham is most particular about the clients she agrees to entertain. One of the others—'

'We want to talk to her, not, er, the other.' To his chagrin, Rob felt the rims of his ears, his most prominent facial feature, grow warmer with every word he spoke. He had not been this embarrassed since the time he'd been caught stealing apples as a schoolboy prank.

'It will cost you a half crown just for an audience,' said Mistress Baynham's doorkeeper.

After a moment's fumbling in the money pouch Rosamond had supplied, Rob handed over two shillings and a testoon. The giant pocketed the coins and led the way into a small anteroom that was all smooth woods and sweet smells – costmary strewn in the rushes and lingering scents of a half dozen different perfumes and body powders.

A second servant, this one an old woman, appeared to offer them food and drink while they waited. She rattled off prices five times as steep as what they would be charged for the same items in a tavern. A cup of ale would have been welcome, dry as Rob's throat was, but he declined to waste his wife's money. When the giant left to fetch his mistress, the woman servant remained, keeping a sharp eye on them lest they try to sample something without paying.

Nearly an hour passed before Black Luce appeared. A tall, stately woman, she had skin several shades darker than the pink and white complexion most English women enjoyed. Her hair was ebony and her eyes the color of jet. She was of Spanish or Italian descent, Rob decided, before her low-cut bodice drew his gaze to the lushness beneath her face and his thoughts scrambled.

With an effort, Rob jerked his head up to meet eyes that sparkled with laughter. Black Luce was younger than he'd expected, no more than a few years older than he was. For one disconcerting moment, she reminded him of the

Englishwoman with whom he had become entangled while in Moscow.

Rob was uncertain how much Rosamond knew about his folly, but the mere memory of how foolish he had been strengthened his resolve not to let this woman – this *bawd*, he reminded himself – take advantage of him.

Black Luce studied him in return. Her intense, assessing gaze made his skin crawl. When she turned her attention to Needham, Rob's friend had much the same reaction. His face became flushed, like that of a man with a fever.

'It is expensive to buy my time,' the brothel-keeper said in a low, husky voice, 'and two at once costs even more.'

Rob had to clear his throat before he could speak. 'What price do you charge to answer questions?'

She frowned, causing a crease to appear in the smoothness of her high forehead. 'What kind of questions?'

'There is a man, an Italian silk merchant, among your regular customers. He—'

'Get out.' The dark eyes were no longer amused.

'But—'

'Rafe! To me!'

'Please! A woman's life may depend upon what you know.'

'What woman?'

'The one accused of killing Hugo Hackett.'

The bawd's sharply indrawn breath told Rob that she recognized the name. That meant she could guess that the Italian he was interested in was Alessandro Portinari. But whatever she knew about those two men, Black Luce was not about to share it with Rob. 'Toss them into the street,' she ordered when her giant doorkeeper reappeared.

Rafe grinned, showing off gaping holes where there had once been teeth.

Needham fled.

Rob was too slow. Halfway to the exit he was seized from behind. With one hand twisted in his collar and the other grasping the back of his doublet, Rafe lifted him off his feet and sent him flying through the door Needham had left open. He heard it slam shut behind him as he landed face down on the hard, unforgiving surface of St John Street. He sprawled there, half bereft of his wits, the sound of feminine laughter washing over him.

Rob rolled over under the watchful eyes of a half dozen women hanging out of the upstairs windows of the bawdy house. He wiped blood from his face with one gloved hand. A stone had bitten into his cheek when he landed. As far as he could tell, nothing was broken. He had suffered only bruises and deep humiliation.

'That went well,' Needham said in a dry voice as he helped Rob to his feet.

'It could have gone worse.' Rob dusted himself off. 'Rafe could have come after us with that cudgel.'

'Or the sword.' Needham glanced over his shoulder as he tugged Rob away from Black Luce's house.

Limping a little, Rob went, but he could not stop himself from looking back when they reached the corner. By then, only one face remained at the window, watching their retreat with an intensity that was almost palpable.

'Rosamond is not going to be pleased,' Rob muttered as they continued on. Worse, she would likely fall back on her original plan and find a way to visit Clerkenwell herself.

'She would be less happy had we shared that woman's favors and used her money to pay for it. Short of such a sacrifice, I cannot think how we'd have had any greater luck prying information out of her.'

'She is paid well to keep her clients' secrets,' Rob agreed, 'as well as to provide them with anything they desire in the way of female companionship.'

Needham chuckled. 'Such a delicate way of putting it! You should not have been worried about me joining the papists, my friend. After today's debacle we are neither of us fit to be anything but Puritans.'

They had walked a considerable distance and had nearly reached Smithfield before Rob realized they were being followed.

TWENTY-ONE

'I must go,' Lina insisted. 'I could not live with myself if anything happened to Rosamond because of me.'

'What do you think you can do in London besides put yourself in danger?' Susanna asked. 'I can assure you that if you are arrested for a crime, innocent or not, your life will be a misery, what little is left of it.' She had once been put on trial for murder herself. But for the grace of God and the efforts of good friends, she would have been executed. 'Your guilt will be assumed, your trial will be swift, and you will not be granted the mercy of hanging. The man you killed was your guardian and the head of your household. That makes your offense petty treason. You will be tied to a stake and burnt alive.'

Susanna hoped her blunt words would convince Lina to change her mind and remain in hiding at Leigh Abbey. Instead, although the young woman's face lost every trace of color, her resolve hardened. Chin thrust out at a stubborn angle in a fair imitation of Rosamond at her most provoking, Lina stood her ground.

'I will leave on the morrow, Lady Appleton. I am most grateful for your hospitality, but you need feel no further obligation toward me. I made my way here on my own and now that I know Rosamond has a house in Bermondsey, I can find my own way there.'

'That is the last place you should go if you truly care about her safety.'

The mulish look remained in place, although Lina would not meet Susanna's eyes. 'There is something I must tell her.'

'Send a message.'

'I dare not put this in writing.'

'I have a code you can use. Rosamond knows it but no one else will be able to interpret what you write.'

Lina shook her head. 'I needs must go myself.'

In the days since Rosamond's return to London, Lina had sunk ever more deeply into melancholy. She slept away half of every morning and retired as soon as she had supped. She took no interest in needlework or reading or even games of chance. Brooding, Susanna had surmised, and who could blame her, but leaving the safety of Leigh Abbey would be a terrible mistake.

'Think, Lina. It will only make matters worse for both of you if you are captured. If Rosamond is suspected of helping you, she will be arrested, too.'

'It that happens, I will swear she knew nothing of my whereabouts.'

'She will not let you disavow her. I may not know everything about my foster daughter's life during the last few years, but nothing can have altered Rosamond's stubborn nature. Once she has set a course, she continues on until she has reached her goal.'

'I will tell her to stop.'

'It will do no good.'

'But there is information I did not share with her.' Lina sounded close to tears. 'It is something she needs to know, and I must confess it to her in person. That is the only way I can make her understand.'

'It is not necessary for you to risk yourself,' Susanna argued. 'If only you will trust me, I will make certain that she receives your message.'

Lina dabbed at her eyes, sniffling.

'If you can tell Rosamond, surely you can confide in me.'

'Noooo,' Lina wailed. In a flurry of carnation-colored skirts, she turned and fled from the small parlor.

Susanna called to a passing servant. 'Go after her. Make sure she does not leave her bedchamber again once she's gone inside.'

'Best set a guard outside her window to make certain of it,' said Jennet from a nearby alcove.

She had been there all along, seated on the padded bench beside the casement. As a young tiring maid, she had mastered the art of fading into the woodwork. In that way, she'd overheard many a conversation she should never have been privy to. More than once, Susanna had found her servant's invisibility useful. On this occasion, despite her anxiety, she laughed.

'I am no better than Hugo Hackett if I confine her to her chamber.'

'Let us hope she does not repay you as she did him.'

'She is no murderess, Jennet.' Susanna settled into her comfortable Glastonbury chair, glad she did not have the bother of repeating the argument with Lina for Jennet's benefit before asking her old friend's opinion. 'I do not know what to do about that young woman. She seems to have no idea of the risk she'll be taking if she returns to London.'

'If this secret matter of hers is so urgent, she should have shared it with Rosamond when she was here.'

'Mayhap it is something that did not seem so important then. Lina has had a good deal of time to think about what happened since Rosamond returned to London.'

Jennet snorted. 'That girl is a great doddypoll and always was. She wants Rosamond to do her thinking for her. I remember what she was like when she lived here. Rosamond led her around like a mother goose with a gosling.'

'Lina was not the only one Rosamond dominated. She was a natural leader, and the other children followed her willingly.'

'Usually into trouble.'

'Nevertheless, I can scarce keep Lina prisoner here, not even for her own safety. She is a grown woman, albeit one who refuses to listen to common sense. As for the information she is so anxious to convey to Rosamond, for all we know it may be as crucial as she believes.' Susanna sighed. 'I do not see that I have much choice. If she is determined to go to London, she cannot make the journey alone,'

'You mean to go with her.' It was not a question.

'I think I had better.'

Jennet set aside her embroidery and stood, smoothing out the plain blue wool of her kirtle as she rose. 'I will see to the packing and find suitable garments for Lina to wear. If she is to have any hope of avoiding arrest, she must travel in disguise.'

Susanna considered the notion and found it good. 'Yes. Select clothing that will allow her to fade into the background so that no one notices her.'

'Shall we dress her as our servant?' Jennet asked.

Our servant? Inwardly, Susanna groaned. When they'd both been much younger, Jennet had often been her companion in danger, but they *had* been much younger then. 'Rosamond has my coach,' she said aloud. 'We will have to travel on horseback.'

Jennet had never been fond of that means of transport. Now that she was older, such a journey would be even more difficult for her, but Susanna did not hold out much hope that this would deter her faithful companion.

'If you accompany Lina, madam, I will be at your side.' Jennet's smile told Susanna that if she thought Jennet would balk at the prospect of a little discomfort, she was much mistaken. 'We can use the horse litter stored in the stables.'

'That old thing? It dates from my grandmother's day.'

'It is in good repair nonetheless, and there is ample room inside for three people.'

Susanna winced at the thought of spending two full days jounced about while confined in a cramped space but she could think of no better alternative. They would stop for the night in Rochester, as she always did when she visited London. The rooms at the Crown were large and sumptuous and would, at least in part, mitigate the discomfort of the first leg of their journey.

'Do you mean to take her to Bermondsey?' Jennet asked. 'It will be safer to lodge elsewhere.'

'Agreed. We must avoid being seen at Willow House, but an inn is too public for safety.'

'A pity you do not own a house in London.'

Of a sudden, Susanna found herself grinning. 'On the other hand, I am well acquainted with two gentlemen who do. It only remains to decide which location will best suit our purpose.'

TWENTY-TWO

The area was crowded with pedestrians and men on horseback, but Rob swore he could feel a particular pair of eyes boring into the back of his head. Moving one hand to the knife at his belt, he slowed his steps. The sensation grew stronger. He was certain he heard light, running footsteps on the cobblestones. Expecting an attack, he spun around, drawing his dagger from its sheath.

Squealing like a stuck pig, although the knife did not come within a foot of nicking her, a young woman jumped back. For a long moment she stared at the blade, eyes wide. By the time she gathered her wits and tried to flee, Rob had seized her upper arm and hauled her into the nearest shelter, a narrow alley between two tenements.

A bemused look on his face, Needham followed them as far as the entrance. His bulk blocked them from view, should there be any interested observers passing by on the street.

Rob already knew whence she'd come. He remembered her portrait from the wall at Black Luce's. La Fleur, Rafe had called her. Clothed as she was, her face devoid of cosmetics, she might have been taken for a maiden had that painted likeness not revealed that she was much less innocent than she now appeared.

'Why did you follow us?' Rob sheathed his blade but kept hold of her arm. 'What do you want?'

'Why do you think? You have ready money. I will answer any question you put to me if you pay me enough.'

'You would betray your bawd?' This was a dangerous game and made Rob mistrust his captive even more.

'Do you want information about a certain wealthy Italian silk merchant or not? I am the only one who can give it to you. I am the one he asks for when he visits Clerkenwell.'

'How do you know of our interest in him?'

Having recovered from her fright, the doxy turned saucy.

'Take me to a tavern for a set meal and I'll tell you that much without payment. For more you will have to hand over coin of the realm.'

'A tavern? You dare be seen with us in public when word of it might get back to Mistress Baynham?'

She scoffed, missing the sarcasm in Rob's question. 'No need to worry about that.' She gestured toward a decrepit sign that depicted a sack with a piglet peeking out of the top. It creaked loudly as a gust of wind set it swaying. 'The sort of man who'd eat in a low place like that one is never likely to cross the threshold of Black Luce's house.'

Rob hesitated only a moment, even knowing that this enter-prising young whore would likely cost him every penny in his purse and might still tell him nothing that would help Rosamond save Lina. Releasing her, he executed a small bow and offered her his arm. 'I pray thee, mistress, will you do us the honor of dining with my friend and me?'

She laughed. 'A real gentleman, you are! I accept with pleasure.' Tucking one hand into the crook of Rob's arm and seizing Needham's elbow with the other as they left the alley, she towed them toward the disreputable-looking tavern known as the Pig in the Poke.

Inside it was dark, noisy, and noisome. A fiddler played for pennies while patrons crowding around six of the eight trestle tables devoured meat pies, washing them down with small beer or cheap wine. At the seventh, three men were gaming, tossing dice while drinking the smoke of the Indian herb called tobacco.

Rob stared. This was the first time he'd seen anyone indulge in that newfangled pastime. It was an expensive amusement. A quarter ounce of the stuff cost ten pence, which was no doubt why the three men were sharing an instrument that looked like a little ladle, each inhaling the smoke in turn to take it into their mouths, their heads and their stomachs. Tobacco was supposed to be good for rheums and diseases of the lungs and inward parts.

When they had settled on stools drawn up to the remaining table, Rob let the girl order food and drink. Each mutton pie cost him three pennies. A quart of sweetened Spanish wine set him back a shilling. He'd have preferred ale but one of the few rules observed by London drinking houses was that taverns sold no ale and alehouses did not offer wine.

Despite the outward appearance of the place, the meal was both savory and filling. Rob ate with good appetite while the girl from the bawdy house explained how she knew their business with Black Luce.

'There are passages within the walls,' she confided. 'One runs behind the room where you met with her. It is no feat at all to hear what is said on the other side of the paneling.'

'Does she know her girls spy on her?' Needham asked.

'She'd not like it if she caught us at it, but she's quick to make use of those passages herself.' She drained the last of the wine from a plain glass beaker, set it aside and propped her elbows on the table. 'That's the last question I answer for free. I want a gold angel for each one.'

Rob's eyebrows shot up. Most people did not earn that much for a whole year's hard labor. 'What makes you think your information is worth more than a shilling?'

'You came looking for answers. I have them. A crown, then.'

'Still too dear. A half crown is as high as I'll go.' At a value of two shillings and sixpence, she could scarce think herself underpaid.

'Show me the money.'

He meant to dole out the coins one at a time, but the moment his purse was on the table she had it in her grasp. With swift, precise movements she opened it and counted what she found within. 'You've enough here for five answers.'

There was more money than that in the little leather bag but Rob decided against arguing with her. 'Give me back enough for the reckoning.'

With obvious reluctance, she handed over what he already owed for their food and drink. In the next instant, the purse disappeared beneath the edge of the table. When her hands reappeared, they were empty. If he wanted his money back, he'd have to search her skirts and petticoats for a hidden pocket.

'The Italian silk merchant,' Rob said. 'What is his name?'

She laughed. 'You would waste one of my answers on such a trifle?'

'It would be trifling if I wasted it asking for *your* name. My question stands. I wish to be certain we are talking about the same man. There may be more than one wealthy Italian who frequents Black Luce's house.'

'Very well. His name is Alessandro Portinari. Is that what you wanted to hear?'

'What can you tell us about him?' Needham interrupted.

'Second question.'

Rob suppressed a groan at the gleeful look in the woman's eyes. Needham had been too vague. She could say anything or nothing in response.

She lowered her voice and leaned toward them across the tabletop, as if she was about to impart some great secret. 'He is most vigorous for his years and passing kind and considerate. If I had a dozen clients like him, in a year's time I could retire and open my own house.'

'Let us move on to the most important concern.' Rob had no inclination to waste time on the Florentine's virtues. 'Is he infected with the French pox?'

The whore sprang to her feet, body rigid. 'He never is! Do you think me such a fool as to risk my own life by catering to such a one?'

'We mean no insult,' Needham said.

She was too angry to listen. Turning on her heel, she stalked out of the tavern, taking Rob's purse with her.

By the time Rob and Needham scrambled after her, she had a considerable lead. Rob spotted her moving in the direction of Clerkenwell, weaving her way through the crowds at a dead run.

'It's no use,' he said, wanting to go after her but recognizing the futility of such an effort. 'Clever as she is, even if we manage to catch her she'll find a way to escape. I would not put it past her to claim we're assaulting her.'

'You could accuse her of stealing your purse.'

'I'd just as soon avoid involving a constable.'

'At least we know where she is going,' Needham said.

'But it is the one place we cannot enter without risking life and limb. I, for one, have no desire for a second encounter with that gigantic doorman.'

By mutual consent, they turned their steps southward, away from St John Street.

'We did learn something,' Needham said. 'At least one of the charges against Alessandro Portinari is false. He does not suffer from the pox.'

Rob was not as much of an optimist as his friend. 'You are assuming,' he pointed out, 'that what that woman told us was the truth.'

TWENTY-THREE

As soon as Rob and Andrew left for Cambridge on Friday morning, Rosamond set off in the direction of the French embassy in Lady Appleton's coach, the ever-vigilant Melka at her side. She was in need of more information about Alessandro Portinari if she was to clear Lina's name.

Rosamond neither liked nor trusted Tommaso Sassetti, but she did have the wherewithal to bribe him. She felt certain that if she offered him enough money, he would answer her questions about his uncle. With luck, he would be able to tell her something that would lead to proof that Portinari was guilty of murder.

She had ample time to review what she already knew during the long, slow journey across London Bridge, through the city and out onto Fleet Street by way of Ludgate. It would have been faster to take a wherry and walk the rest of the way, but she wanted Melka and Charles and her two henchmen with her. The latter were less conspicuous as running footmen than as bodyguards.

Rosamond smiled to herself as she remembered how Andrew Needham had turned bright red all the way to his hairline and left Rob to report on their visit to Black Luce's house. Rob, who had always had the ability to laugh at himself, had regaled her with a merry account of their adventures. The whore who'd enticed them into the Pig in the Poke had confirmed that Alessandro Portinari was a regular client but denied he was diseased. That he was most vigorous for a man of his years and considerate, too, was irrelevant, although Rosamond supposed these attributes would have counted for something had Lina married him.

Lina had believed what Widow Kendall told her because the widow believed it. Rosamond found herself more inclined to take the word of a whore. After all, Black Luce's employee had observed Alessandro Portinari's health and behavior from a much closer vantage point than that of a respectable matron catching glimpses of her neighbor through his windows and listening to serving maids' tittle-tattle.

The manservant who admitted Rosamond and Melka to Salisbury Court, this time through the front entrance, seemed taken aback by her haughty demand, in English, to speak with Tommaso Sassetti. He showed them into a small antechamber and told them to wait. A short time later, Tommaso swept into the room.

He stopped at the sight of Rosamond. If she chose to bring charges against him, she could cause him a good deal of trouble. She half expected him to turn tail and run. Instead he chose to feign delight at seeing her again.

'*Padrona!*' he exclaimed, just the slightest lisp betraying that his tongue was still swollen from her bite. 'I pray you have come to forgive me.'

'I have not,' Rosamond said. 'You behaved like a boor.'

His face fell. 'I am but a weak and foolish man, driven to overreach myself by your beauty.'

Did he think she was so susceptible to flattery that she would forget the details of their last encounter? She longed to take him to task and give him a good clout or two to the head, but she wanted information more.

She produced the purse she had brought with her and jiggled it to make the coins inside clink together. 'Answer my questions honestly and this will be yours.'

Tommaso's dark, expressive eyes fixed on the leather bag, then shifted to her face. 'That might contain naught but groats.'

Rosamond opened the bag, reached inside, and pulled out a ryal. 'There are ten of these in all.' Each gold coin was worth fifteen shillings. She was offering him a princely sum in return for information.

He kissed the backs of his fingers and made as if to send the affectionate gesture in her direction. '*Padrona, ti amo.*'

Melka stepped up beside her mistress when Tommaso tried to move closer. He scowled at the servant but took the hint and backed away. Rosamond passed the money to her maid for safekeeping.

'I will tell you whatever you wish to know,' Tommaso promised, 'but not here where anyone might disturb us.'

'Where, then?' Rosamond shared the Italian's desire for privacy, but she was wary of his intentions.

'I know a privy chamber off a passage on the floor above us. Your maid can stand guard outside while we talk. She can warn us if anyone approaches.'

As if to reinforce the necessity of talking elsewhere, the same servant who had admitted Rosamond reappeared to show an elderly man into the antechamber. The newcomer sent their little party a curious look before seating himself on a bench to wait for whatever person he had come to visit.

Tommaso led Rosamond and Melka toward a staircase. They had almost reached it when he stopped short and shooed them back the way they'd come. He herded both women behind a tapestry that covered a window embrasure, holding one finger to his lips to warn them to keep silent.

Rosamond did not care for being crushed between Tommaso and her maid, but she stayed still. Through a small gap in the hanging, she watched a man in a dark green doublet stride past their hiding place. Once he was out of sight, Tommaso once again set off toward the stairs.

'Who was that?' Anyone who caused Lina's lover such concern interested Rosamond.

'Monsieur de Courcelles, the ambassador's secretary. He does not know I have moved into the embassy. He has only just returned from France.' Tommaso all but ran up the stairs and along the passage at the top.

'He would not approve?' Rosamond tried to keep the amusement out of her voice. Poor Tommaso. No one wanted him.

'He finds fault with my translations. He is the one who

told the ambassador to inquire at Oxford for an Italian tutor for his daughter when I should have had that post.' He stopped beside a small door set in the paneling on one side of the passage. 'Here.'

Rosamond peered into a space not much bigger than the interior of a standing wardrobe. Before she could object, Tommaso gave her a little shove and followed her inside, shutting Melka out.

There was scarce room for two people to stand bolt upright in the cramped space. Had it not been for Rosamond's wide skirts and the cloak that covered her completely, the full length of Tommaso's body would have been pressed tight against her own.

Her hand went at once to the dagger sheathed in its purpose-sewn pocket in the cloak's lining and closed on the handle. With the ease of long practice, she drew the blade, thrust it through the opening at the front of her cloak, and maneuvered it so that the point pressed against a particularly tender area of Tommaso's body. At the first prick, he went still as a statue.

'I left you with your tongue in one piece,' Rosamond said in her sweetest voice. 'It would be a shame to cut off any other . . . parts.'

At once the Florentine flattened himself against the far wall, leaving a small but significant space between them. Knife at the ready, Rosamond considered whether to go or stay. 'What is this room?'

'You English call it a squint.'

A glance at the wall opposite the door revealed a grille. Light filtered through it from the open air beyond.

'Do not move,' she warned him as she shifted her position until she could peer through the peephole. It gave her a bird's-eye view of the hall below. Curiosity satisfied, she returned to her former position and addressed Tommaso. 'Tell me about the night Hugo Hackett was murdered. You were still living with your uncle in his house in Lime Street, were you not?'

'*Sì.*'

'Were you at home that night?'

He nodded.

'Was your uncle at home that night? *All* that night?'

Tommaso hesitated.

'The truth, if you please.'

With a shrug, he obliged. 'Someone sent him a message. After he read it, he was angry. He left the house soon after.'

As she had theorized. Pleased, Rosamond pursued this line of questioning. 'How long was he gone?'

'I did not pay attention to the time, *padrona*.'

'Was it long enough for him to go to Soper Lane, quarrel with Hugo Hackett, stab him and come back?'

'You accuse my uncle of murder?' He sounded more intrigued than offended.

'I think it a possibility that he killed Hugo Hackett. How is it that *you* do not sound surprised by this suggestion, Tommaso? *Was* he gone long enough to kill Hackett?'

'He was away for more than two hours, but he might have gone anywhere. He could have been visiting a woman. He is most fond of women, my uncle.'

'So I have heard.' And it was true that Portinari's absence from home was not proof that he had killed Lina's brother-in-law. She would have to question Hackett's neighbors. Mayhap one of them had seen a man of Alessandro Portinari's description that night. It would only take one such sighting to make the constables take notice. Although Rosamond ordinarily despised the insular Londoner's mistrust of strangers, she was willing to take full advantage of the prejudice against foreign-born merchants if it led to Portinari's arrest and Lina's exoneration.

'My uncle was great friends with Hackett,' Tommaso volunteered, 'both in business and in pleasure. Why would he kill him?'

'So you know about your uncle's visits to a certain house in Clerkenwell. Why, I wonder, were *you* not the one to mention them to Lina.'

'I do not comprehend, *padrona*. What a man does in private is his own concern.'

Do not trouble the wife, or the intended bride, with such trifles? Rosamond had to fight a strong temptation to give Tommaso a little jab with her knife. 'Why did you move out of Alessandro's house if it was not because you suspected him of murder?'

Silence greeted her question. Even in the dimly lit squint, Rosamond could see enough of his face to tell he was sulking.

'If you want the money in my purse, you must answer *all* of my questions.'

Tommaso heaved a deep sigh. 'We quarreled when he refused to pay my gambling debts. I did not want to leave. He threw me out. That is why I sought employment here at Salisbury Court, where I can live as well as work.'

'And no doubt that is why you are avoiding that man, de Courcelles. You are afraid he will convince the ambassador to dismiss you.'

Tommaso grinned. 'Thanks to you, *padrona*, I will not be destitute if I am forced to leave here. Have I earned my pay, or is there something more you wish from me before we part?'

Hearing the suggestive undertone in his words, she clutched the knife more tightly. The fellow was incorrigible! 'You have done enough.'

'Then I will leave first. It is best we are not seen together. For your reputation, *padrona*.' He added the last as an after-thought, just before he opened the door a crack and peered out.

'Give him the money, Melka,' Rosamond said.

Tommaso slipped into the passage, closing the door behind him with a soft thunk. Left alone with her thoughts, Rosamond wondered if he had told her the truth. She thought he had but there was no way to be certain without talking to Alessandro Portinari himself.

Would Tommaso flee the country, now that he had money? She hoped he would. Lina would be better off without him.

Rosamond felt sorry for her friend. She had believed this shallow fellow was in love with her. She was glad that Lina was safely hidden away in Kent. It would be time enough for Rosamond to break her heart when she could also tell her that she had been cleared of the charge of murder.

Twisting around in the confines of the tiny room to replace her knife in its sheath, Rosamond found herself once again looking at the grillwork. Without thinking, she leaned closer and peered through the slats.

The hall below was no longer empty. She recognized its occupant as de Courcelles, the man in the dark green doublet

Tommaso had been so desperate to avoid. He had a look of impatience about him, as if he'd expected to meet someone and they were keeping him waiting.

Even as Rosamond thought this, a second man hurried into the hall, begging de Courcelles' pardon for being late. Rosamond recognized him as Francis Throckmorton, the man she'd last seen when he mistook her for an English recusant and showed her the way to Salisbury Court's chapel.

Unaware of being watched, de Courcelles handed Throckmorton a packet. By some trick of the acoustics in the hall, his words carried clearly up to Rosamond's aerie: 'Put these letters into the queen's code.'

'At once,' Throckmorton replied, and hurried away again.

De Courcelles crossed the hall and left by another door.

Rosamond's hands were shaking as she let herself out of the squint. In an instant, her priorities had undergone a sea change. She knew now why Sir Francis Walsingham had warned her away from the French embassy. He must suspect there were treasonous plots being laid at Salisbury Court.

She had no doubt about the identity of the queen de Courcelles had referred to. He could only mean Mary, Queen of Scots, a woman who was presently a prisoner in England, a woman who had a strong claim to the English throne as well as to that of Scotland. For years, Mary's supporters had schemed to overthrow her cousin, Queen Elizabeth.

Rosamond knew her duty. Before she confronted Portinari, before she took any further steps to clear Lina's name, she had to get word of what she'd just witnessed to the Queen of England's spy master.

TWENTY-FOUR

Certain she'd be turned away without a hearing if she went to Sir Francis Walsingham's headquarters in Seething Lane on her own, Rosamond considered how else she could deliver a message. Walsingham lived somewhere in the city with his family, but she did not know if it was at the house in Seething Lane or elsewhere. He had a country house at Barn Elms near Richmond, but there was no guarantee that he would be there. He was most likely at court and the royal court could be anywhere. The queen moved about as the whim struck her . . . or whenever the palace privies needed to be cleaned.

Rosamond could see only one reasonable course of action – locate Henry Leveson and persuade him to take her to Seething Lane. Since he was a member of the Earl of Leicester's Men, the logical place to find him was James Burbage's Theatre in Shoreditch, where Leicester's company of players had been performing for some weeks.

The French embassy was outside the old city wall and so was Shoreditch. Rosamond reckoned her coach could make better speed by circling this ancient fortification than by taking a more direct route through the heart of London. She was delayed instead by the poor quality of the roads and arrived just in time for the start of that afternoon's production.

When she'd attended plays in the past, Rosamond had always sent Charles ahead to pay their admission fee. This time she was the one who put two pennies, one for herself and one for Melka, into the slot in the gatherer's money box. Momentarily distracted, she stared at it. Made of clay and fired with a bright green glaze, it would have to be broken to secure the company's profits in a proper cash box at the end of the day. Clever, she thought. So long as the gatherer kept a tight hold on it, the design was proof against pilfering by pickpockets.

The purpose-built playhouse known as the Theatre was crowded with playgoers. Rosamond looked around in dismay. At the Horse's Head, she always reserved one of the inn's rooms. Its balcony, overlooking the temporary stage set up in the inn-yard, served as a private box. Here all the seats were already occupied. She would have to stand amid the rabble in front of the stage, jostled on every side and assaulted by a multitude of smells both foul and sweet.

No one paid any attention to Rosamond or Melka, for which Rosamond was grateful. Slipping between larger, predominantly male persons, she claimed a spot with a clear view of the stage, as much so that Henry Leveson could see her as so that she could watch the players. Only after she had established her claim did she begin to listen to the chatter around her.

The cries of sellers of food and drink were loudest. 'Bottle ale here!' one called out. An odd hissing sound escaped every time one of these was opened.

Playgoers were urged to buy pippins and plums, pears, cherries and figs and it was not just fruit on offer to eat. Shellfish were for sale, too – mussels, periwinkles, whelks, and oysters – as well as nuts in a multitude of varieties. Discarded shells crunched underfoot.

Here and there, bits of conversation filtered through the noise and what she heard made Rosamond's heart sink. The players about to take the stage were not members of Lord Leicester's company. The Queen's Men, just back from touring in the countryside, had taken over the venue.

Rosamond wriggled through the crowd, dragging Melka after her. The gatherer, still at his post, gawked at her. He was just a lad, no doubt one of the players' apprentices tasked with collecting admission as part of his training.

'No refunds!' he yelped as Rosamond bore down on him.

'I do not want money. I want information. Do you know a player named Henry Leveson?'

A head topped with shaggy ginger curls bobbed up and down, but Rosamond saw the alarm in his eyes.

'I mean him no harm.'

Hearing the impatience in her words, the gatherer was not convinced. He had to swallow before he could speak. 'Try the Bell in Gracious Street, mistress. That is an inn much favored by Leicester's Men.'

Traveling in the cumbersome coach, it took Rosamond more than an hour to reach the Bell, a large establishment with a roofed-over yard big enough to serve as a playhouse during the winter months. Once inside, she had no difficulty locating Leveson. He was in the common room, drinking with his fellow players and lamenting their loss of the Theatre to a rival company.

On the journey from Shoreditch, Rosamond had devised a plan to cull her quarry from the herd. Knowing her maidservant would not approve of the methods she intended to use, she had left Melka in the coach.

Rosamond removed her cloak, to better show off both her costly attire and her woman's curves. Then she walked boldly up to the table occupied by Leicester's Men. She put a little extra sway into her hips and fixed a pout on her face.

She had caught the attention of two of the players by the time she reached them, but Leveson was expounding on some point or other to the man seated across the table from him and did not look up.

'Naughty boy, Henry,' she said in a throaty purr.

Startled, he swung around on his stool until he was facing her. Recognition flared in his eyes, followed at once by dismay. To prevent him from speaking her name or demanding to know why she had come, Rosamond plunked herself down in his lap, twined her arms around his neck and leaned in close enough to nuzzle his ear.

'Take your cue from me,' she whispered. In a louder voice she scolded him. 'You promised you would visit me this afternoon yet I find you here, wasting your time with other men.'

Before Leveson could make a sound more coherent than 'urg,' she planted a smacking kiss full on his mouth. While it was not uncommon for English women to greet men with kisses, this went far beyond what was acceptable in public. Cheers and whistles erupted all around them. Someone made a ribald remark. Rosamond ignored it and kept her eyes locked on Leveson's.

He stood so abruptly that she fell to the floor, landing hard on her rump. She glared up at Walsingham's player-spy, waiting for him to help her to her feet, but he had not yet regained the power of speech, let alone the ability to offer her his hand. It was left to one of his less addled companions to grab her around the waist and stand her upright. The fellow managed a not-very-surreptitious caress of her right breast in the process of letting go. She kicked him in the shin for his trouble, then concentrated on Leveson once more.

'I would speak with you, my love. *Alone.*'

Belatedly, Henry Leveson collected himself and embraced

the part she had assigned to him. He managed a credible bow.
'I am yours to command, my lady.'

Arm in arm, they left the inn.

Leveson waited until they climbed into the coach before he
exploded. 'What the devil are you playing at? You could have
been recognized.'

'No one was looking at my face. Oh, do close your mouth,
Henry. It was necessary that we talk in private.' The coach
was already moving. Before entering the Bell, Rosamond had
told Charles where she wished to go next.

Leveson rolled his eyes heavenward, then gave an awkward
chuckle. 'Well, if nothing else, you have raised my credit with
my fellows. You may have behaved like a strumpet but they
could tell you were no common drab.'

'I should hope not,' Rosamond said.

At her side, Melka went stiff with outrage. Rosamond put
a restraining hand on her maidservant's plain wool sleeve. Far
from being insulted by Leveson's comment, she was rather
pleased with the success of her performance.

'I modeled my character after the very finest courtesans,'
she informed him, 'the ones I've seen in the audience at the
Horse's Head.'

Leveson made a choked sound before giving in to laughter.
Uncontrolled mirth consumed him until tears streamed from
his eyes.

Rosamond passed him a handkerchief. While she waited for
him to recover, she moved aside the leather curtain and saw
that they were already in Tower Street. She did not have much
time to explain what she wanted.

'Leveson, pay attention. I learned something of great importance at the French embassy this morning, something Sir Francis
needs to know.'

Her words sobered him as quickly as if she had dashed cold
water into his face. 'Walsingham forbade you to return there!'

'He is not my father or my guardian or my husband and
even if he were, I would not have obeyed him.' She gave a
careless wave of one hand. 'That scarce matters now. He will
want to hear my report.'

'I would not be so certain of that. The great man has

been in a foul mood for weeks. Being ill has made him intolerant.'

'He has always been intolerant.'

The coach stopped.

'We have arrived in Seething Lane,' Rosamond said. 'I need you to vouch for me. Walsingham's men will not admit me otherwise.'

'It will do you no good to get into Walsingham's head-quarters if you must speak to the great man himself. He is not there. He is with the queen at St James. And before you suggest I take you to the palace, consider that it is likely he will refuse to see either one of us. I am under orders to make my reports to a contact. Walsingham's secretaries receive initial reports. Otherwise the queen's principal secretary would be inundated with trivia. Besides, it is best if his intelligence gatherers are never seen in his company. If our identities became known, it would destroy our usefulness.'

St James was located in Westminster, an easy journey by water even if the tide was against them, but Rosamond saw the sense in Leveson's arguments. She would have to settle for telling her tale to one of the spy master's senior agents.

'Who is in charge in Seething Lane?'

'Walter Williams.'

'Can he be trusted?'

'Walsingham thinks so.'

'Then delivering this intelligence to him will have to suffice.'

Rosamond allowed Leveson to help her out of the coach and lead the way to the same entrance she'd used several months earlier. On that occasion, she had been equally unwelcome at Walsingham's headquarters . . . until she had convinced the spy master that she'd uncovered the identity of a murderer.

With Leveson to provide surety for her good behavior, Rosamond was admitted, albeit grudgingly. They were escorted to a smaller version of Sir Francis Walsingham's study, the chamber in which she had spoken to the principal secretary on her last visit. Instead of being dominated by Walsingham's enormous desk, this office made do with a long table, its surface littered with papers, both loose and in boxes. Behind it sat the same officious minion who had once tried to bar

Rosamond from entering the house in Seething Lane. Without a doubt, he was also the man who had tried to recruit Rob at Cambridge, prominent Adam's apple, ice-blue eyes and all.

'Master Williams,' Leveson greeted him. 'You will remember Mistress Jaffrey.'

He was no happier to see her again than she was to recognize him. 'You were told to stay away from here, Mistress Jaffrey.'

She rushed into speech before he could have her thrown into the street. 'A man named Francis Throckmorton was given a packet of letters to translate into the queen's code. I saw this with my own eyes and heard this with my own ears at Salisbury Court this morning. I believe Sir Francis Walsingham would like to have this information.'

'Sir Francis is not here.'

'So I understand. That is the only reason I am talking to you.' You *toad*, she added to herself.

They glared at each other in mutual dislike until Williams reached for a quill and dipped it into his inkwell. 'Sit down, Mistress Jaffrey. I will make a record of your report.'

Rosamond remained standing and enjoyed a brief, pleasant fantasy of leaning forward, swinging hard, and striking the side of his head with her open hand. It would make a satisfying smack, she thought, although it would doubtless also leave her with a bruised palm.

Pen poised to write, Williams continued to address her in condescending tone of voice. 'I do not suppose you know the name of the man who gave Throckmorton this packet of letters.'

'As it happens, I do.' Rosamond reminded herself that the important thing was to report what she knew to the proper authorities, even if that meant catering to an officious underling. 'It was de Courcelles, the French ambassador's secretary.'

'Claude de Courcelles? Did he see you?'

'I was not visible to either Master Throckmorton or Monsieur de Courcelles.'

'How is that possible?' A sneer accompanied the question. 'You claim you overheard a private conversation between de Courcelles and Throckmorton and yet neither of them knew you were there?'

'I was in the squint that looks down upon the hall. It was pure happenstance that I peered through it at that particular moment, but when I heard the words "the queen's code" I could not help but understand their importance. Even as a girl living in Derbyshire, I knew that it was treason to send coded messages to Mary of Scotland. There was an attempt back then to free her from her prison. It failed.'

'Such attempts will always fail. How is it that you knew the identities of these two men?'

'I met Master Throckmorton on my first visit to the embassy. He took me for a fellow recusant and, albeit reluctantly, gave me his name.' She smiled at Williams across the cluttered table. 'I, on the other hand, avoided telling him mine.'

'You should not have been there at all.'

'I go where I please.'

'How do you know that the man he met with was de Courcelles?'

Rosamond had no qualms about betraying Tommaso. She thought it likely that John Florio, if he was Walsingham's spy at Salisbury Court as she suspected, had already reported that she'd gone to the embassy in search of the other Italian. 'Tommaso Sassetti identified Monsieur de Courcelles.'

'Sassetti?' Williams wrinkled his nose, as if he smelled something foul. 'What did you want with Sassetti?'

'I approached him on a . . . domestic matter. It has naught to do with any plot against the queen.'

Williams was at his most officious when he responded. 'It is up to those who know more than you of plots afoot in England to decide whether something is of interest or not.' He waited with ill-disguised impatience for her answer.

Rosamond did not suppose there was any point in refusing to tell him what he wanted to know. With an army of spies at his disposal, it would be the work of an hour to uncover the whole story for himself. It only surprised her that the man she still thought of as Walsingham's minion did not have that answer already, especially when he clearly knew enough about Tommaso Sassetti to have formed a negative opinion of the Florentine.

'A friend of mine has been falsely accused of murdering her sister's husband. I believed that this Sassetti, who is known to her, had information that would help me find the real killer. Just at present, Sassetti lives at Salisbury Court. I went there in search of him.'

This succinct summary seemed to satisfy Williams. Head down, he scribbled a note to himself. 'Is there anything else you wish to add?'

She could think of several things she wished she could say to him but deemed it wiser to hold her tongue. 'I think not.'

Williams let a small silence descend before fixing Rosamond with a hard stare. She was tempted to try to make him blink first but once again thought better of the impulse.

Instead, Rosamond affected a meek demeanor that would have fooled no one who knew her. 'If I have answered all your questions, I will go now, Master Williams. You need not be concerned that I will interfere in any way with whatever you mean to do about the matter of Francis Throckmorton and the queen's letters. And I feel certain,' she added, choosing her words with care, 'that you mean to have nothing further to do with me or mine.'

Before he could respond, she turned her back on him and, head held high, swept out of the room.

TWENTY-FIVE

Even before Rob Jaffrey visited Black Luce's house in Clerkenwell, he had been concerned about Rosamond's safety. Afterward, he came to a decision. He would postpone his return to Cambridge until he had traveled to Leigh Abbey. He wanted to hear Lina Walkenden's story first hand. Only then could he determine the seriousness of the risk his wife was taking as she investigated Hugo Hackett's death.

Rob had not told Rosamond of his change in plans but he did confide in Andrew Needham. He was not surprised when his friend insisted upon accompanying him. They made good time from Bermondsey to Rochester. There they stopped at the Crown, the inn Lady Appleton always stayed in to break her journey when she traveled between Leigh Abbey and London.

Rob had just dismounted and turned his hired bay over to an ostler when he heard a familiar voice call his name. He turned slowly, certain he must be mistaken, and was confronted by a daunting sight. His mother advanced on him with a speed that belied her years.

'By all that's sacred, it *is* you Rob! But what are you doing in Rochester?'

'Good day to you, Mother,' he said, embracing her.

She held him tight against her for a long moment before stepping back. 'You are *supposed* to be at Cambridge.' Her welcoming smile faded, replaced by a look of concern. 'Are you ill?'

'I am quite well, Mother. You will remember my good friend Needham?'

Jennet Jaffrey spared Andrew Needham the merest of glances before she poked one finger into her son's chest. 'If you are not ailing, what are you doing on the road to Leigh Abbey?'

'We . . . er . . . that is . . . I was coming to see you.' He managed a weak smile. He might be a man grown, but fear of his mother's disapproval could still make him squirm.

Unconvinced, Jennet sent him a dubious look. 'Why?' Before he could answer, she glanced over her shoulder and up at the windows of one of the inn chambers. 'Never mind! I can guess. That girl has cozened you into helping her.'

Needham's eyebrows shot up. 'That girl?' he mouthed.

'If you are speaking of *my wife*,' Rob said, 'she believes I am on my way back to Christ's College.'

'And just where is it you have been? Bermondsey, I'll wager! Well, you had best come with me to Lady Appleton. You can explain yourself while we sup.' With that, Rob's mother turned on her heel and marched back toward the inn, leaving her son and his friend to follow.

Had he got it wrong? Rob wondered as he trailed after her. Surely Lady Appleton would not be going to London if she was hiding Lina Walkenden at Leigh Abbey.

Jennet did not stand on ceremony. She led the two young

men straight into her mistress's chamber. Lady Appleton's lack of surprise at seeing them told Rob she'd been watching from the window overlooking the inn-yard.

'Come in, my dears,' she greeted them. 'I have already dispatched my new maidservant to request additional food.'

Rob saw the twinkle in her eyes and wondered what had amused her. He did not think she was laughing at him, although he could not be certain. He supposed there was a certain amount of humor to be gleaned from watching a mother reprimand her errant schoolboy of a son, even when that son was no longer a boy.

The inn chamber was large and well appointed, the best the Crown had to offer. Lady Appleton urged them to sit, taking the bobbin-frame chair for herself and leaving them a choice of Turkey-work stools. The embroidery on the cushions matched the hangings on the bed, an immense piece of furniture with a tester resting on posts and a headboard elaborately carved with flowers and birds.

'Rob *claims* he was on his way to visit me,' his mother announced as soon as she was settled.

'And you doubt him? This is a logical place to stop for the night if he crossed the Thames at Horndon.'

She assumed he came from Cambridge. Once at Gravesend, on the Kent side of the river, it would have been but another five miles to Rochester. Rob corrected her before his mother could do so. 'We rode here from Bermondsey.'

That distance, some twenty-three miles, was near the limit of what a man on horseback could travel in a day unless he had a change of horses. Rob had heard that messengers who could commandeer fresh horses every thirty miles might cover as much as a hundred and fifty miles in a day, but he did not believe it.

Lady Appleton's hands, which had been loosely clasped in her lap, abruptly clenched. 'Have you been with Rosamond?' At his nod, she asked, 'How much did she tell you about Lina's troubles?'

So he had been right, after all.

'Almost everything. That is why I wished to consult with you. I am . . . concerned for Rosamond's safety.'

'Has something happened? Is she in danger?'

'She is trying to find a murderer! The very attempt puts her at risk.'

Lady Appleton leaned forward, her expression troubled, and placed one hand on his arm. 'You would risk as much if it were your friend Needham here who had been falsely accused.'

'I would,' Rob agreed, 'but I hope I would have the good sense to accept help in my quest.'

'I see,' said Lady Appleton. 'She sent you away, and you think that a husband belongs at his wife's side, even if that wife does not want him there.'

'Not if he has an obligation to finish what he began at Cambridge,' Jennet muttered.

Hearing the bitterness in his mother's voice, Rob winced. She'd been disappointed in him the previous year when he'd abandoned his studies to travel to Muscovy. He did not want to let her down again and yet how could he abandon Rosamond if she needed him?

He kept his eyes on Lady Appleton, the one person in his life who always seemed to know the right thing to do. That gentlewoman patted his arm and started to speak, then cocked her head at the sound of approaching footsteps.

'Open the door, if you please, Master Needham. I believe that our supper has arrived.'

A procession of servants trooped in carrying platters and pottles and made short work of setting up portable tables to hold the bounty. There was cold ham and beef, bread and ale, and a bowl of apples from this year's harvest – Kent was famous for its apples. Bowls of stew, thick with beef and pot herbs, steamed in invitation.

When everything was in place, those who had brought the food and drink withdrew, all but one. For the first time, Rob took a close look at a young woman wearing the plain blue wool garments of a maidservant. She bore little resemblance to the wealthy merchant's daughter he had known during the years Lina had lived at Leigh Abbey but he had no difficulty identifying her as Godlina Walkenden, the very person he had been traveling to Leigh Abbey to question.

Alarm flashed in her eyes when she realized she'd been

recognized. She began to back away, although where she
thought she could flee to he could not imagine.

'I mean you no harm, Lina.'

Needham turned his head to look first at his friend and then
at Godlina Walkenden. He smiled at her in a reassuring manner.
'You need not be afraid. He is telling you the truth. He is just
concerned about Rosamond.'

'Has something happened to her?'

Rob heard the panic in Lina's voice and wondered what she
supposed had gone wrong. Before he could ask, Lady Appleton
summoned them all to the table.

'Sit and eat while it is hot.' She suited action to words by
dipping her spoon into one of the bowls.

Rob meant to seat himself next to Lina, but Needham was
there ahead of him. Rob had to circle the small table and take
the empty stool across from them. As he began to eat, he
watched his friend with growing concern. Needham was
showing all the signs of a man who had been struck by Cupid's
arrow. How that could be when Needham knew who Lina was
and what she had been accused of doing, Rob could not fathom,
but he had no choice but to believe the evidence in front of
him. As the meal progressed, Needham offered Lina the
choicest morsel from the platter of meat. When she spoke, he
hung on her every word.

Lady Appleton observed this doting behavior as well but
chose not to comment upon it. Neither would she allow Rob
to interrogate Lina while they ate. Instead, she asked him for
an account of his visit to Rosamond.

He began with a highly edited version of the scene he'd
witnessed in the garden, watching Lina's face as he described
Tommaso Sassetti's behavior. She kept her head bowed, hiding
her expression. If she was in love with that Florentine lout,
Rob felt sorry for her. He felt even sorrier for Needham.

Next he recounted how Willow House had been searched.
'It seems your sister has offered a reward for your capture,'
he told Lina, 'and managed to convince your brother of your
guilt.'

She did look at him then, her eyes luminous with tears,
but she still did not speak.

'What of Alessandro Portinari?' Lady Appleton asked. 'Rosamond must have talked to him by now.'

'She spoke to Widow Kendall.' Rob summarized what Rosamond had told him about that encounter.

He paused to drink a little more of a fine Canary wine before he broached the subject of his visit to Black Luce's house. He had felt the weight of his mother's disapproving gaze throughout his recital of events. She would be livid when she heard him confess that he'd gone to a bawdy house. It would not matter that his intentions had been pure.

He cleared his throat and plunged into the tale. Jennet Jaffrey's face turned an interesting shade of purple but, to his great relief, she said not a word. Neither did Lina, although she started and stared when he reported that Widow Kendall had likely been mistaken when it came to Portinari and the pox.

Lady Appleton, looking thoughtful, reached for an apple. 'Why were you on your way to Leigh Abbey? Other than to visit your parents, that is.' She took a bite as she waited for Rob's reply.

Rob avoided looking at his mother. 'I wanted to hear for myself what Lina could tell me about the night of the murder. If she did not kill Hugo Hackett, then the person who did must have been delighted when she was blamed. No one has more to lose than the real killer if Rosamond's questions cast suspicion elsewhere.'

'You are afraid that your wife has already placed herself in mortal danger.'

'Having killed once, it is easier to kill again.'

Lady Appleton nodded as she chewed and swallowed. 'That is a consideration, but Rosamond is not as vulnerable as you suppose. Do you think I would have encouraged her to pursue this investigation if I thought she would come to harm?'

'Begging your pardon, madam,' Rob said, 'but none of us can predict violence. Anyone can kill if given sufficient provocation.'

Lady Appleton sent him a sharp look. 'As you will have guessed, we are on our way to London. Lina has additional information to relay to Rosamond, after which I mean to take a hand in the investigation myself. I trust that eases your mind.'

Rob finished the last morsel of meat on his plate and washed it down with the wine, reluctant to contradict her but in no way reassured. No female of Lady Appleton's years, no matter how sharp her mind, could do much to protect another from a determined assassin.

Having settled matters to her own satisfaction, Lady Appleton rose from the table. 'I have arranged for a room for the two of you for the night. Sleep well. You have a long ride on the morrow if you expect to reach Cambridge by nightfall. Will you go by way of Horndon, Chelmsford, Dunmow and Thaxted?'

Rob nodded. 'After Thaxted we can rejoin the main road we traveled on our way to Bermondsey, the one that passes through Saffron Walden to reach Cambridge.'

'We could accompany you to London first,' Needham offered. 'It would be no trouble.' Although he spoke to Lady Appleton, his gaze remained on Lina.

'That will not be necessary.' Lady Appleton shooed them out of her chamber, depriving Rob of the opportunity to question Lina and Needham of any opportunity to pursue what appeared to be the beginning of a courtship.

Rob's mother followed them out to seek a word in private with her son. To his great relief, she did not mention either Bermondsey or Clerkenwell. Her only concern was that he promise her he would return to Cambridge. Since she did not specify when, he gave her his word and sent her back to Lady Appleton in a happier frame of mind.

His own mood remained unrelentingly somber. Lady Appleton might love Rosamond like a daughter but Jennet Jaffrey did not. She would be delighted if something happened to her unwanted daughter-in-law.

'I do not like letting them go to London on their own,' Needham said when Rob joined him in their chamber.

'Nor do I. Besides that, how can adding three more females to the one already looking into Hackett's murder do anything to help keep my wife safe if the real murderer decides to eliminate her?'

'Three,' Needham opened the bottle of wine their host had provided along with a warm fire, candles, and a bed.

'I *said* three.'

'I mean there are already three women involved in the investigation – Rosamond, Melka, and young Alys.'

'I do not believe that mere numbers signify.' Rob accepted a portion of the wine from his friend and drank deeply. 'I am the first to admit that Rosamond is a force to be reckoned with all by herself, but that will avail her nothing if she is set upon by hired henchmen.'

'You might hire henchmen of your own to protect her.'

'She would only send them away. No, there is only one answer.'

Needham saluted him with his wine. 'Then let us drink to our safe and swift journey back to Bermondsey on the morrow.'

TWENTY-SIX

The day after her visit to Seething Lane, Rosamond once again set off in Lady Appleton's coach. This time she was bound for the Royal Exchange. In common with anyone in London who could afford the prices, she often visited the shops housed there, particularly the milliners on the first floor and the glass-sellers on the level above that. Over one hundred shops offered every luxury imaginable, all under one roof.

Rosamond sailed past the women who sold apples and oranges outside the Exchange gate in Cornhill with her entourage – Melka, Charles, and the two burly henchmen. She was not so foolish as to face Alessandro Portinari on her own. One woman shouted insults when they failed to stop and buy. Since fruit sellers were little better than beggars and as likely to pick a pocket as to deal honestly with a customer, Rosamond paid no attention. She had bought an apple from one of them when she was new to London. It had been full of worms.

A spacious, stone-paved quadrangle graced the center of

the enormous brick building. Galleries rose up on every side. From above Rosamond's head, the shouts of apprentices drew her wistful gaze toward open doorways but she did not have time to buy, let alone to browse. Moreover, her business was at ground level.

Children played in the quadrangle, running and shouting while their mothers or nurses made purchases and visited with one another. The arcades beneath the lower galleries served as general meeting places for merchants of all nationalities. The Flemings had their favorite spot and so did the Florentines. Charles, who had spent the better part of two days following Alessandro Portinari everywhere he went, had drawn a map to show Rosamond where to look for the silk merchant.

'Follow me,' she ordered her entourage, 'but at a distance.'

In among the marble pillars, along what might have been called a cloister walk had it been planted with herbs and flowers, Rosamond strolled with seeming casualness, alert for the sound of anyone speaking the Italian tongue. She passed closed doors sealing off spaces that had originally been intended for shops. When their interiors had proven too dark, they had been converted into storage vaults, but excessive dampness made them unsuitable for even that purpose.

Just where Charles had said the Florentines would be, Rosamond came upon three prosperous-looking men standing close together and gesticulating in a manner that reminded her of the way Tommaso waved his hands when he spoke. She wondered if this was a peculiarly Italian habit.

One of the men was thin to the point of emaciation. The second was no more than a decade older than Rosamond herself. She pinned her hopes on the third, who was old enough, at least three score years, to be Alessandro Portinari. He had a look of dissipation about him, too, for all his velvet and jewels. She shifted her gaze to his hands. Among the many rings on his fat fingers, most of them gold, was a large cameo of a death's head, the exact piece of jewelry Lina had described.

Rosamond took a step closer, alert for over-strong scent. Her next inhalation brought with it the pungent smell of civet. It was an expensive perfume that many people found appealing, but Rosamond shared Lina's opinion. Given a choice, she'd never come within a foot of any man who stank of it.

A casual glance reassured Rosamond that Melka and Charles were nearby. A nod from Charles confirmed the identification of Portinari. The two henchmen kept their distance but they were close enough to come to Rosamond's aid if she called for them. Secure in the knowledge that no harm would come to her in such a public place, taking a deep breath to quiet the sudden onset of nervousness, she launched herself at her prey.

'Master Portinari!' she called out in a high, shrill, carrying voice. 'Where is your nephew?'

The fat Florentine turned, a look of astonishment on his jowly face. His dark eyes narrowed as they settled on her. A few gruff words in Italian served to send his two companions scurrying away.

'Who are you?' he demanded in English as excellent as Tommaso's. He had been in England for a long time.

'A woman wronged.'

His derisive snort dented Rosamond's self-confidence. She had accounted herself as good as any player when it came to portraying a woman seduced and abandoned by a heartless young man. Too late, she wondered if she should have chosen another approach.

'What do you want?' Portinari asked.

No going back now, Rosamond thought. She struck a pose. 'Revenge.'

He laughed, a full-bodied roar that had heads turning to stare at them.

Rosamond sighed. This was not going the way she had hoped, but she made one more attempt to establish a common bond and provoke him into betraying a violent nature. 'Did you know that Tommaso tried to steal your intended bride?'

Portinari's amusement vanished. The sudden coldness that came into his eyes put Rosamond in mind of a snake. When he looked her up and down with an assessing gaze, she felt a shiver of apprehension course through her and had to fight the urge to turn and run.

He held her gaze with an unblinking stare. 'Who are you? The truth. I will know if you lie.'

She believed him. 'Master Portinari, Godlina Walkenden is my friend. She did not kill Hugo Hackett, and I will not allow her to be blamed for his murder.'

He rubbed his clean-shaven chins – there were three of them – and regarded her with greater interest and less hostility. 'You are Mistress Jaffrey.'

'How—?'

He cut her off with a wave of one hand. 'You and I have something in common, Mistress Jaffrey. I am as certain as you are of Lina's innocence.'

Because you killed Hugo Hackett? Rosamond was not quite brave enough to ask that question aloud.

'I will not allow her to be tried for murder.' Portinari's manner changed in a heartbeat from threatening to avuncular.

'Why should you care what happens to her? She refused to marry you.'

'Ah. I see. You labor under a misapprehension.' He spoke softly, his voice pleasant, his tone confiding.

'What misapprehension?' Although she was still wary of him, Rosamond's antipathy toward the silk merchant had lessened to a marked degree.

'You believe your friend and I were merely betrothed. In fact, our marriage contract, signed and witnessed well before Hugo Hackett's unfortunate demise, was worded *per verba de presenti*. Under your English law, Godlina Walkenden and I are already bound by the unbreakable ties of matrimony and, as her husband, I am compelled to protect and defend my lawfully wedded wife.'

TWENTY-SEVEN

The afternoon was well advanced by the time Susanna, Jennet, Lina and their hired escort rode through Bermondsey on their way to London. They did not go near Willow House. Susanna reckoned that if Rob's fears for his wife were not exaggerated, and she did not believe they were, it would be exceeding unwise for Lina to be seen there, even in disguise. Instead, they continued on along the old Roman road they'd been following since Canterbury, five miles north of Leigh Abbey. Watling Street ran almost straight and was much traveled. It rose sharply as it passed the church of St Olave to enter Long Southwark.

Once across London Bridge, they still had some distance to travel to reach Blackfriars, where Sir Walter Pendennis, Rosamond's stepfather, kept lodgings. A friary in the days before King Henry broke with Rome, the precinct retained one important feature claimed by religious houses – it was free from the jurisdiction of city authorities. Lina should be safe from arrest once they were inside the walls of this nine-acre enclave.

Their party entered from Carter Lane through what was known as the New Gate, passing the parish church of St Anne with its small, detached burial ground. Blackfriars was home to people of the highest rank and the artisans who served them, including a fencing master and a printer. Amid the houses, gardens, and tenements there was even an indoor playhouse where the Children of the Chapel, a company of boy players, performed. The wealthiest residents of the precinct were Lord Hunsdon and Lord Cobham, who had fine, fair houses with private gardens and wood yards. Walter's two comfortably appointed chambers were located above what had once been the monks' buttery.

After Susanna dispatched their hired escort to see to the horses, she led Jennet and Lina toward a door near the north end of the former cloister. Lina drew back, unnerved by the sight of a gallery built over the Fleet River to connect the building they were about to enter to the imposing structure on the opposite bank.

'That is Bridewell Prison,' she whispered.

'It is,' Susanna agreed, 'but it was once a royal residence, and access to a religious house was thought to be convenient.'

These days, Bridewell housed vagrants and bawds instead of royalty, but Susanna felt certain they had nothing to fear from its proximity. Still, it would be foolish to dawdle in the open. 'Come along, Lina. The sooner you are inside and out of sight the better.'

By the time Susanna reached the top of the narrow flight
of stairs leading to Walter's rooms, she was a trifle out of
breath. She had avoided long journeys for the last two or three
years. After this jaunt, she felt the effects of their long hours
on the road in every muscle and joint. When she could speak
without wheezing, she rapped on the door.

'Jacob Littleton! Are you there?' Littleton was Sir Walter's
man and looked after these lodgings in his master's absence.

'Who is it?' a voice called back from the other side – a
feminine voice.

'I am Lady Appleton, a good friend to Sir Walter and his
wife.'

The door opened to reveal a sturdy female holding a broom,
although whether for defense or because she had been sweeping
was not immediately clear. Rheumy eyes full of trepidation
looked their little party up and down. She hesitated a moment
longer and then stepped back to allow them to enter. She was
the housekeeper, Susanna surmised, and tried to remember if
either Walter or Eleanor had ever mentioned her name. If they
had, she could not recall it.

'Where is Jacob Littleton?' she asked

'Gone to Westmorland, madam, on business for Sir Walter.
I am Molly.' Belatedly, she bobbed a curtsey. 'I look after Sir
Walter's rooms when his man's away.'

'We will be staying here for a few days, Molly,' Susanna
told her. 'You need not trouble yourself about us, other than
to buy food, and I will give you money for that.'

'Yes, madam.' Molly glanced out the window at the
gathering dusk. 'If you want aught to eat this night, I'd best go
now.'

Susanna handed over a few coins and sent her off on her
errand.

Jennet and Lina had already gone ahead into the bedchamber,
leaving Susanna to examine the front room. It had changed
little since the first time she'd seen it. It still smelled of
marjoram, strewn in the rushes on the floor, and the space was
still dominated by a large writing table. A second smaller table
and a chair were in their accustomed places beside the window.
The chair's blue velvet upholstery was faded now, the gilt trim

a little tarnished, and it was missing the bright yellow cushion Walter had liked to tuck into the small of his back.

Lina returned from the inner chamber. 'There is only one bed and it is passing narrow.'

Unless Walter had replaced it, he had a boarded bed on four short legs with a shelf at the head to hold books and candles. Susanna was not best pleased herself at the prospect of sharing a bed with both Jennet and Lina. The younger woman was a restless sleeper and Jennet had a tendency to kick. She told herself they could do far worse.

'Think of the poor women in Bridewell,' she advised Lina. 'Those fortunate enough to have a bed at all sleep on pallets of straw on the cold stone floor.'

'I do not see why we cannot stay in Bermondsey.'

'You know why, Lina. Willow House has already been searched once. They were looking for you. Do you think they have given up?'

Lina sulked. 'That was Lawrence. My brother. Why should he bother to return?'

'Because Isolde believes with all her heart that you killed her husband. I would not put it past her to have someone watching Rosamond's house. Surely you do not want to be arrested.'

Lina scraped the toe of her boot through the rushes, intensifying the smell of marjoram in the air. 'I need to talk to Rosamond. That is why I came back to London.' Her lip trembled, a sure sign she was on the verge of tears.

Another bout of crying was more than Susanna could tolerate. Lina's complaints had begun to try her patience, especially when they were coupled with her insistence that she could only confide her great secret to Rosamond.

Before the first tear could make its way down Lina's cheek, Susanna seized her by the arm, hauled her over to a box-seated chair and pushed her into it. She dragged the other, more comfortable chair away from the window for herself and sat facing the young woman while Jennet took up a position by the door, ready to sound the alarm when Molly returned.

'This has gone on long enough. Whatever you have been holding back cannot be so very terrible. If you are prepared

to share it with Rosamond, then surely you can tell me what
it is.'

'You will not understand.'

'That may be true but it scarce matters. Out of a genuine
desire to help you, I have put Rosamond at risk. I have
every confidence in my foster daughter's ability but now
that it appears you have left out some crucial part of your
story, I am deeply concerned for her safety.'

Susanna blamed herself for not being harder on Lina from
the beginning. She'd been too quick to assume that everything
the young woman told her was true.

'Did you kill Hugo Hackett?'

'No! I did not lie about that!'

'What did you lie about, then? No crying!' she warned when
Lina's face began to work. 'You are going to tell me everything
right now. No excuses. Do you understand?'

Lina managed a nod.

'Good. Just blurt it out, Lina. You will feel better once
you've confessed.'

'I married him!' She buried her head in her hands.

Jennet gasped. Susanna frowned. 'Married who? Tommaso?'

Lina's voice was barely audible. 'Alessandro. We were
betrothed *per verba de presenti*.'

This unexpected announcement took Susanna aback but not
for long. 'Has the marriage been consummated?'

'No.' Lina sniffled. 'There was to be a wedding in the parish
church and a grand celebration afterward. Alessandro was
going to hire players to entertain the guests with a comedy
and bring in the city waits to provide music for dancing.'

With an effort, since she was not feeling all that charitable
toward Lina, Susanna gentled her voice and leaned closer.
'That is not the whole story, is it? There is still something you
are hiding. You need not fear to confide in me, my dear. I will
not condemn you, no matter what you have done.'

Lina burst into tears.

With a sigh, Susanna waited out the deluge. She provided
a handkerchief, ignored Jennet's muttering, and tried not to
let her imagination run wild. What *had* this foolish young
woman done to cause her such distress?

It took far too long for Lina to regain control of herself, but eventually she managed it. She swallowed convulsively and whispered, 'I suppose I must tell you everything.'

'There is no help for it, Lina, and I do much doubt your sins are as terrible as you imagine.' Susanna hoped her bracing tone and encouraging words would lend the younger woman strength.

'I know the difference between a betrothal *de futuro* and one *de presenti*.' A tiny smile flashed and was gone. 'You took care that all the girls in your care understood England's laws on marriage. I knew what I was doing when I signed the marriage contract with Alessandro Portinari. I read it and I saw it was *de presenti* and I was glad of it, although I did not tell Hugo or Isolde that I was aware of what those Latin phrases meant.'

'Why were you glad?'

'Alessandro is old and far from toothsome but he is rich. When we met, he was kind to me and pleasant to be with – he made me laugh – but I agreed to marry him because he promised me all the things I most wanted. Once we were wed, he was going to set me up as a silkwoman. I would have had my own income then.'

'You would not be the first woman to marry an old man for his money,' Susanna said. 'Nor the first to have second thoughts and cry off.'

Lina drew in a shuddering breath. 'I thought . . . I thought he was too old to demand a husband's rights in the bedchamber. I thought I'd not have to do more than entertain him with conversation and play at cards and dice.'

Enlightenment dawned. 'And then you heard, from his neighbor, that he was in the habit of visiting brothels.'

Her face a mask of misery, Lina nodded. 'And worse than that, she told me he was diseased and that if I married him I would also be infected with the French pox.'

'And that is why you told Hugo you would not marry him?'
Lina nodded.

Susanna sent the younger woman a quizzical look. Nothing she had so far confessed was so very terrible. Then the light dawned. 'How does Tommaso Sassetti fit into this tale, Lina? Why is it his ring and not Alessandro's that you wear?'

Color flooded into Lina's face. She could not meet Susanna's eyes. 'You will despise me when I tell you.'

'I promise I will not think less of you if you will just tell me the whole truth.' Hiding her impatience, Susanna reached across the small distance between them to take Lina's ice-cold hands in her own. 'You have come this far. Finish your tale.'

'I love Tommaso. I knew it the first time I set eyes on him. But it was already too late for us. We did not meet until after the marriage contract was signed.'

Susanna rubbed one finger over Lina's gimmal ring. 'You thought you could have it all,' she murmured. 'A rich, elderly husband and a vigorous young lover.'

'I know it was wrong to want such a thing, but what choice did I have? I could not escape the marriage, and I could not give up my beloved Tommaso.'

'Tommaso himself did not object?'

'He . . . he thought we would be able to marry if only we could convince Hugo to break the contract. Tommaso did not know it was *de presenti*. I thought . . . I thought that after the wedding I could make him see reason. We were meant to be together. I knew it and Tommaso did, too.'

Or said he did, Susanna thought. Lina had been both greedy and stupid and some would say she deserved to be forced into marriage with Portinari.

Susanna felt sorry for her. She understood now why Lina had been so desperate to flee Hugo Hackett's house. To be final and irrevocable, her marriage to Alessandro Portinari had to be consummated. That consummation could have been arranged, with or without Lina's cooperation, so long as Hackett and Portinari were in agreement.

Unfortunately, everything Lina had just confessed to gave her even more reason to kill Hugo Hackett. Rob had said Rosamond suspected Alessandro Portinari of the crime but to Susanna it sounded as if the Florentine silk merchant would have had every reason to keep Hugo alive, *especially* if Hugo had sent word to him of Lina's change of heart.

On the morrow, she decided, they must hold a council of war. Surely if they put all the bits and pieces they knew together, the name of the real murderer would emerge.

TWENTY-EIGHT

Rosamond had returned to Willow House from the Royal Exchange in an agitated state of mind, her faith in Lina shaken by Alessandro Portinari's disclosure. Hours later, she was still trying to come to terms with what he had told her.

Seeing her reluctance to believe him, the Florentine merchant had invited her to dine with him at his house in Lime Street on the morrow. At that time, he'd promised, he would show her proof that what he claimed was true. He would produce a copy of the marriage agreement Lina had signed.

Lina knew better than to agree to such a thing. That was what troubled Rosamond most. At a young age, both girls had learned the difference between a marriage contract *de futuro* and one *de presenti*. The first was a simple promise to wed at some point in the future. It could be broken without much difficulty by either party. The second committed the couple to each other forever, providing there was no legal impediment to their marriage.

By late afternoon, Rosamond was pacing the length of the gallery and back again, unable to remain still. Had it been Lina, not Portinari, who had lied to her? If that was the case, what possible explanation could there be for her behavior?

Watling was asleep on Rosamond's favorite window seat. She flung herself down beside the cat and stared into the walled garden, but all her thoughts were turned inward. She was beset by doubts. If Portinari had told her the truth, that forced her to reexamine everything she thought she knew. If Lina had lied about one thing, then all parts of her story became suspect. It was even possible that she was guilty of Hugo Hackett's murder.

Portinari had not said he believed in her innocence, only that he meant to shield her from the consequences of being accused of that crime. It followed that if the Italian had not stabbed Isolde's husband himself, he might well think Lina had done so.

Lowering her head to her hands, Rosamond closed her eyes. Her thoughts spun madly as she tried to make sense of the conflicting stories she'd been told. Nothing fit together. If Lina had signed that marriage contract, how could she then accept a ring from Tommaso? And Tommaso – what of him? How could he not know that his uncle was, to all intents and purposes, already married to Lina?

What if he had known? She liked that possibility even less. 'And it makes no sense,' she muttered to herself. If Tommaso and Lina had been desperate to be together they'd not have murdered Hugo Hackett. They'd have killed Alessandro Portinari.

When Watling butted her arm, Rosamond opened her eyes and hauled him into her lap. Stroking the cat calmed her. After a time, her thoughts became clearer. What she needed to do was set down on paper the order in which events had occurred. If she did that, she might be able to see where the discrepancies were. Perhaps then she would know who had lied to her and who had told her the truth.

Carrying the cat, Rosamond left the gallery for her study in the tower. Pen in hand, she reviewed what she'd been told, first by Lina, then by Isolde Hackett, Alys Greene, Cecily Kendall, Tommaso Sassetti and Alessandro Portinari.

At the top of the page she wrote: *Lina visits Cecily Kendall.* It had been during one of these visits that Alessandro Portinari first saw her. Rosamond did not know how long ago that had been but she knew that everything else had happened afterward.

On the next line she wrote: *Portinari approaches Hugo Hackett about marrying Lina.*

It seemed likely the two men already knew each other. The mercers were a tight-knit group, one of the twelve great Companies of London, but they also had strong ties to the silkwomen, many of whom were their wives, and to the foreign silk merchants in London, too.

Hugo Hackett either borrows money from Alessandro Portinari or owes him money for silk.

Rosamond frowned, considering this third item. Should it be first on her list? She had no way of knowing when the two merchants had first done business together. Undecided, she circled the sentence, drew an arrow from it to the top of the page and added the symbol to indicate a question.

Hugo tells Lina he has found her a husband.

Lina had said that had occurred some two months past. Rosamond added *(sometime in August).*

Portinari courts Lina.

Her friend had admitted to enjoying his attention . . . and the gifts.

Lina meets Tommaso at Portinari's house.

Rosamond pondered this item. Had they met before or after Lina signed the marriage contract? She still had doubts about Portinari's claim that they were already wed but there had likely been a betrothal of some sort. When had it taken place? *Before* Lina met Tommaso, she decided. It must have been earlier. Lina would have refused Portinari outright if she was already in love with another man.

Tommaso gives Lina a ring.

Portinari takes Hugo with him to Black Luce's house (three weeks before the murder).

Cecily Kendall tells Lina that Portinari has the pox.

Lina and Hugo quarrel.

Portinari receives a message and leaves his house for several hours.

Someone stabs Hugo to death.

Lina finds Hugo's body and rouses the household.

Isolde accuses Lina of murder.

Rosamond stopped writing. Profound discouragement changed rapidly into frustration, causing her to throw down her pen, heedless of the spatter of ink it left on the page. This list was useless as long as she did not know exactly when and in what order the events took place. All she'd proven with this futile exercise was that she scarce knew more now than she had when she began her quest to prove Lina innocent.

TWENTY-NINE

Rob Jaffrey and Andrew Needham arrived back in Bermondsey just at dusk. Leaving Needham scrounging for food in the kitchen, Rob went in search of his wife. He found her in her gallery, scowling down at the paper she held in one hand.

The expression on her face would have frightened away a horde of attacking barbarians. He kissed the look away, laughing when the enthusiasm with which she kissed him back proved that she was glad to see him. He paid no mind to the disgruntled comment that followed, but when she asked why he'd returned, he sobered at once. She was not going to like what he had to tell her.

'By now, Lady Appleton, my mother and Lina are already settled in your stepfather's lodgings in Blackfriars. We met them on the road.'

'They were wise not to come to Willow House,' Rosamond murmured.

'I told them everything that happened after you left Leigh Abbey.'

A frown put creases in Rosamond's forehead. 'Then why did they continue on to London? Lina was safe in Kent.'

'She says she has something to tell you, something she refuses to share with anyone else.'

Rosamond glared at the paper in her hand. 'I can guess what that is.'

When she offered it to him, Rob scanned only the first few items before his head jerked up and his eyes met Rosamond's. 'She *married* him?'

'So Portinari claims.'

He gave a low whistle. 'And then she was told he had the pox.'

In her usual concise manner, Rosamond recounted her meeting with Alessandro Portinari and the story he had told her. 'I need to talk to Lina. Portinari may have lied to me.'

'But you do not think he did, do you? You think this marriage is what Lina wants to confess to you.' The greater implications were impossible to miss. 'Her belief in his illness gave her a most excellent reason to think Hugo Hackett deceived her when he arranged the match – reason to kill him in the heat of anger.'

Rosamond shook her head, although doubt clouded her eyes. 'If she'd killed him in the heat of anger, it would have been during their quarrel. He survived that and locked her in her bedchamber. What am I missing, Rob? What am I not seeing?'

He took her in his arms. 'You will make sense of it. I have faith in you.' He nuzzled her neck. 'In the meantime, I recommend another early night.'

'A good night's sleep?' she said in a teasing voice.

'Not necessarily.'

They grinned at each other, but Rosamond was not so easily distracted. 'Did Andrew return with you?'

'He did.'

'Then I want to hear his impressions of Lina.'

She started toward the door but came to an abrupt halt when Rob spoke. 'Needham is not an unbiased witness. He has been behaving like a lovesick fool ever since he first set eyes on her.'

'Andrew and Lina? As if things were not complicated enough!'

'It could work out for them. Prove Portinari the murderer and he'll be executed, freeing Lina to marry elsewhere. Convincing her of Sassetti's shortcomings may be more difficult. While she listened to what I told Lady Appleton, she hid her reaction. She did not speak up to defend him, but I fear that was because she did not believe me.'

'And with your mother there, you did not fill in all the details for fear of blackening my name as well as his.'

In some ways, Rosamond knew him far too well! 'As to that, I may also have led Mother to believe that I would return at once to Cambridge.'

'You did not accompany them to London?'

Rob shook his head. 'We saw them off, then waited a

quarter of an hour before setting out after them. We were delayed the more when Needham's horse came up lame near Greenwich.'

Rosamond began to pace. 'Mama must plan to send me a message once she has arranged a safe place for us to meet. Or mayhap she will simply tell me to come to them in Blackfriars.'

'She could send Jacob.'

'However it is accomplished, I should speak with Lina as soon as possible.' She fussed with the gold chain she wore around her waist, fingering the pomander ball that hung from it. 'There is one difficulty. I have already agreed to dine with Alessandro Portinari on the morrow. He has promised to show me this marriage contract he claims to possess. Mayhap we should go to Blackfriars first, without waiting for Mama to send for me.'

'Tomorrow is Sunday,' Rob reminded her.

Rosamond swore. 'That means we will have to attend church. I do not mind paying the fine, but my absence would be noticed. I do not think it would be wise just now to call attention to myself.'

'You will have to leave for Portinari's house right after the service if you mean to arrive in good time. Will you permit me to accompany you?'

Rosamond hesitated only an instant. 'It will be a relief to have you with me.'

'As for Lady Appleton, I suggest that you dispatch Needham to Blackfriars first thing in the morning. He can tell her that we will join them there as soon as we leave Portinari. If for some reason she does not think that is a good idea, she can send him to intercept us and tell us where to go instead.'

'An excellent plan.'

'I have another.' Well pleased to find that they were of one mind, Rob's thoughts leapt to the hours ahead. 'Let us sup together, mayhap engage in a game of chess and then to bed, to sleep, perchance . . . or not.'

'If not, we'd best build up our strength,' she said with a delightfully wicked chuckle. 'Shall we go down to supper?'

Rob offered her his arm and together they descended the

stairs to the parlor on the ground floor. He could, he thought, become quite accustomed to this business of living with his wife.

THIRTY

As Rosamond and Rob entered Alessandro Portinari's house in Lime Street, she glanced at the upper window of the house next door. Was Cecily Kendall there, watching? What would she make of seeing Rosamond arrive?

Then she remembered. Widow Kendall had not met Mistress Jaffrey. It had been Mistress Flackley with whom she'd discussed her unsatisfactory Florentine neighbor.

They dined well in sumptuous surroundings. Beneath a pristine white tablecloth that hung to the floor, the dining table was solid oak as were the chairs and benches drawn up to it. Despite the fact that there were no other guests, a full complement of spice boxes – mace, cloves, cinnamon, and ginger – were lined up for their use. As the day was overcast, beeswax candles had been lit in iron supports suspended from the ceiling beams. To keep the light strong, a servant appeared after the first half hour to lower the pulley and trim the wicks. By then the three of them were nearly finished with their meal. The plate arranged on a cupboard against one wall winked at them as the candles descended in an impressive display of wealth. Rosamond could understand why Lina had been dazzled.

Her nerves too jangled to allow her to enjoy the delicacies offered by Portinari's cook, Rosamond only nibbled the food and sipped a little of her wine. She felt nothing but relief when their host rose and invited them to follow him into his study, a room that was no less ostentatious than the one they had just left. Its ceiling was decorated with the signs of the zodiac. Italian stucco in brilliant colors graced the walls.

From a locked coffer, Portinari produced a document written in Latin. Since Rosamond could read that language without difficulty, it did not take her long to realize that Portinari had told her the truth. He and Lina, before witnesses, had agreed to marry, making the promise *de presenti*. The contract could still be broken. Lina could refuse to take matters further. But should she wish to marry someone else while Portinari lived, he could thwart her plans by producing this pre-contract.

Seated on a settle with Rob beside her, Rosamond studied the Florentine merchant. He had exerted himself throughout the meal to appear genial. He insisted that he wanted to help Lina, if only because he already considered her to be his wife and therefore his responsibility. If he had claimed to be in love with her friend, she'd have been more suspicious of him, but several matters remained in need of clarification.

'I will concede that Lina intended to marry you,' she began, 'but when she learned something to your detriment, she told Hugo Hackett that she would not honor her commitment.'

From his ornately carved coffer-seat chair, Portinari favored her with an avuncular smile. 'You are direct, Mistress Jaffrey. I will return the favor. Widow Kendall was wrong on several points, having leapt to unwarranted conclusions based on insufficient facts.'

'How do you know it was Cecily Kendall who talked to Lina?'

'Hackett sent for me in the evening of the night he was murdered. Over a very fine Rhenish wine and one of your excellent English cheeses, he informed me that Lina had changed her mind.' Portinari patted his belly. 'Say what you will about Hackett's faults, he kept a good supply of food and drink in his counting house.'

For a moment, Rosamond was distracted. 'A cheese, you say? And mayhap a knife with which to cut it?'

Chuckling, Portinari nodded. 'A large, sharp knife. After Hackett enumerated Lina's reasons for rejecting the marriage, I proposed we give her time to calm herself before attempting to explain the old woman's mistake.'

'You cannot deny that you visited the bawd known as Black Luce. We know that you did.'

'How . . . enterprising of you.' Portinari's thick lips quirked in amusement. 'No, I do not deny going there. As an unmarried man, I had no reason not to frequent such an establishment.'

'Did you kill Hugo Hackett?'

If she hoped to rattle him, the ploy failed. His calm was unshaken. 'No, Mistress Jaffrey, I did not. He was in good health and good cheer when I left him. He saw me out through his shop, made certain I found a link boy to light my way home, and sent me on my way back here with a wave and a smile.'

'If you would, sir,' Rob said, 'could you recount your entire conversation with Hackett? It is possible there was something in what he said that could lead us to his murderer.'

'There was not. He told me of Lina's accusation. I explained that Widow Kendall had been misled by a malicious rumor repeated by a disgruntled former servant.'

'It would be helpful if you could be more specific,' Rob persisted.

Portinari leaned toward him. He lowered his voice, but there was no disguising his amusement. 'Are you certain you want your wife to hear this, lad?'

Annoyed, Rosamond answered before her husband had time to open his mouth. 'His wife can speak for herself. You will not shock me, Master Portinari. I have already heard what Widow Kendall believes to be true.'

Now openly laughing at them, Portinari shrugged. 'As you wish. The widow thinks I suffer from the French pox. I do not. Nor am I ill from any other cause. Furthermore, as I reminded Hackett that night, the visit we paid to Black Luce together was intended to be the last time I went there. Anticipating that I would soon have a wife at my disposal, I fully intended to teach her how to pleasure me. I envisioned no further need to pay to couple with a woman.'

'And you think this reasoning will *please* Lina?' Rosamond did not trouble to hide her disgust.

'I was prepared to be loyal to my marriage vows. What more could any wife ask for than a reformed libertine?'

Rob touched Rosamond's arm, a timely reminder that they had come to question the man, not revile him. She did not reply directly to Portinari's taunt. Instead she shifted the focus of her interrogation to Hugo Hackett.

'You may have had good intentions, but what of your companion?' Rosamond wished she'd asked Widow Kendall how long the two men had remained at Black Luce's house. Portinari had not yet had a wife to go home to but that was not true of the mercer.

Portinari's deep, booming laugh made the buttons on his doublet shake. 'I will not try to claim that Hackett was there merely to witness my farewell to my favorite among the girls or that it was the first time he had visited a bawdy house. He often made use of whores, but his usual haunts were not so . . . exclusive as Black Luce's. I took him with me as a reward for convincing his wife that the match with Lina was a good one.'

'I would have thought that Hackett himself might need convincing.' Rosamond said. 'I intend no insult, but there are many Londoners who would balk at marrying a kinswomen to a stranger.'

Once again Portinari answered with a shrug, as if such things were but trifling inconveniences to him. Mayhap they were. 'Hackett owed me money. That was sufficient incentive to deal with me. His wife knew nothing of his debts, but she liked the idea that some of my wealth might come her way. As for Lina, she was more than willing to marry a rich and influential merchant.'

Rosamond considered all Portinari had told her, searching for inconsistencies, before she asked her next question. 'I suppose you could find a physician to swear to your health, but it seems to me that when you visited Hackett that night you expected him to convince Lina that you had sworn off whores. How was he supposed to do so without revealing that he'd gone to a bawdy house in your company? I do not believe his wife would have been pleased by such an admission.'

'She was not to know of it.' Another shrug expressed his disinterest in Isolde's feelings. 'Even if she found out, all he'd have been required to say was that he went there to bear witness. He saw me give Luce and one of her whores generous bonuses for past service.' Portinari smirked. 'Who is to say that we did not leave at once when that transaction was complete, innocent as two little lambs?'

'Any woman with the sense she was born with,' Rosamond shot back.

She did not understand how Alessandro Portinari could think that taking a married man to visit a bawdy house was an appropriate reward. The Florentine was naught but a dissipated old lecher and a pander besides, a vile scoundrel who had aided and abetted another man's adultery.

Despite this reprehensible behavior, Rosamond did not think Portinari was lying about the sequence of events on the night of the murder. She ran through them in her mind. After locking Lina in her bedchamber, Hugo Hackett had sent for Portinari. There was a separate door to the counting house by which to admit him so no one else in the house would know he was there. Hackett told Portinari of Lina's change of heart and then showed him out through the front door and helped him find a link boy. If that part of the Italian's story was true, then the boy must have seen Hackett, alive and well, at the time Portinari left the mercery.

Tracking down a link boy would be a daunting task. There were hundreds of them in the city, out and about every night with their torches – horrible-smelling smoky things, cheaply made of the dried pith of the rush plant dipped in grease. These enterprising lads hired themselves out for a farthing to light the way home for anyone out after dark. A good many of their clients were drunken revelers staggering out of alehouses. Honest link boys kept them safe from harm. Dishonest ones led their victims into dark alleys, there to be set upon and robbed.

Rosamond considered what else she could do to confirm Portinari's story. There were Hackett's neighbors to be questioned. Mayhap one of them had seen Portinari leave the shop. It had been night but not so late that no one was abroad. The watch patrolled the streets. Had the watchman assigned to Soper Lane seen anything? She wondered, too, about the other occupants of Hackett's house. Where had they been during Portinari's visit? Had no one been awake to see Hugo escort him out? Alys had said she'd gone early to bed. Rosamond supposed the apprentices and servants and even Isolde had already retired. All of them had to rise at an early hour in the morning.

'Have you any further questions?' Portinari sat at ease, apparently unperturbed by Rosamond's disapproving frown. He was either innocent of murder or confident that he had covered his tracks.

'There is just one more matter left to unravel. When did your nephew meet Lina for the first time? Was it before or after the marriage contract was signed?'

Portinari shifted his bulk into the chair, the only sign that he was at all disconcerted by her mention of Tommaso. 'Does it matter?'

'It may. Were you aware that he hoped to marry Lina himself? He gave her a ring and if he did not succeed in tupping her, it was not for lack of trying.'

Rosamond hoped to provoke a reaction from Portinari but neither his expression nor his demeanor gave anything away. When he answered her, he sounded as affable as ever. 'Tommaso always was a headstrong young fool. He did not know of the marriage contract, not unless Lina told him about it. It was, in fact, signed before they met. No doubt my *wife* enjoyed his attentions. It is a very old tradition, is it not, this thing called courtly love? I am convinced there was no more to it than that.'

The more fool you, Rosamond thought. Everything she knew of Tommaso suggested that the younger man would not hesitate to cuckold his own uncle.

'I have answered your questions, Mistress Jaffrey,' Portinari said. 'Now it is my turn. Where is Lina?'

'I do not know,' Rosamond lied.

'I only wish to help her. If she will come here to me, I will protect her.'

If she came to him, he'd force himself on her, consummating and finalizing the marriage. He might be wealthy and influential enough to keep her from being charged with murder but there would be a cost. Once she was his wife, Lina also became his property. She'd have no more rights than his horse or his dog or his slave. That might be preferable to arrest and execution, but if Rosamond could discover who had really killed Hugo Hackett, then Lina would have a third choice.

Rising, she dropped into a formal curtsey. 'If Lina finds a means to send word to me of her whereabouts, I will relay to her everything you have told us. That is all I can promise.'

THIRTY-ONE

'I do not trust him,' Rob said when they had left Portinari's house and were walking briskly toward the river.

'Nor do I. I believed some of what he said but not all.' She gave her husband a sharp look. 'Do all men visit brothels before they marry?'

'Not all men, no.' Attempting humor, he added, 'Some cannot afford the price of a whore.'

After this witticism fell flat, Rob proceeded in silence. He wondered what Rosamond was thinking. She could not be pleased to have confirmation that her old friend Lina, knowingly and willingly, had bound herself to a man like Alessandro Portinari. He supposed that Lina must have had her reasons. Marriage to a doting old man would seem a better fate than unending servitude to the Hacketts. In the days of their youth at Leigh Abbey, Lina had been a follower who had never shown any inclination to think for herself. She'd slip easily into the traditional role of 'wife.'

At Old Swan Stairs, Rob hailed a wherry. They had passed the Vintry and were approaching Queenhithe and the Salt Wharf, huddled in their cloaks against a heavy mist, before Rosamond spoke again.

'Mayhap Lina was badgered into signing. Threats. Even beatings.'

'We will discover the truth soon enough.' Blackfriars was not much farther upriver.

'If Lina intends to tell us the truth.'

'Do you question her honesty?'

'I question her common sense.' Rosamond rubbed her hands together against the chill. 'If she lies to me, I will know. Her left eye twitches.'

'She lied to you at Leigh Abbey.'

'She . . . avoided telling me the whole story. That is not quite the same thing.' Rosamond heaved a deep sigh. 'She also burst into tears with the slightest cause, a most useful ploy.'

'One you despise and therefore never use yourself, for which I am most grateful.' Rob slid one arm around her shoulders. Without hesitation, she leaned against him. In companionable silence, they watched the houses and wharves pass by. The tide was in their favor. They were almost at Paul's Wharf. Baynard's Castle loomed up just beyond. From there it was only a short distance to Blackfriars Stairs.

With an abruptness that startled Rob, Rosamond sat up straight. Shading her eyes with one hand, she peered toward the shore. He saw nothing out of the ordinary, but Rosamond vibrated like a hound on the scent.

'What is it?'

'Look there. See the man just entering that house near Paul's Wharf? The tall fellow in the gray cloak?'

Rob shifted on the embroidered cushion that served as a seat, but he was too late to glimpse anything but a door closing. Wisps of fog further obscured his view.

The waterman rowed on, sending the wherry skimming over the surface of the water. They were rapidly carried away from whatever person Rosamond thought she'd recognized.

'What man did you see?' Rob asked.

She shook her head. 'There is no time now to explain. I will tell you later.'

'A clue, if you please.' The boat was already turning toward shore. The buildings of Blackfriars rose up out of the gloom.

She spoke in a rapid whisper. 'The day before I visited the Royal Exchange, I went back to Salisbury Court. I wanted to talk to Tommaso again. Do not lecture me, I beg you.'

The wherry bumped gently against the bottom of the water stairs. 'Go on.'

'I saw something suspicious while I was there and took that intelligence to our friend with the Adam's apple. No more for now. I will tell you the rest when we are alone. I promise.'

Although her confession disturbed him, Rob held his

tongue. She was safe. Whatever her dealings had been with Walsingham's minion, he had not detained her.

Rob helped his wife out of the small boat and paid the waterman, then escorted her through the Blackfriars precinct and into the building where Sir Walter Pendennis lodged. 'Does it occur to you,' he said as they mounted the narrow staircase that led to Sir Walter's rooms, 'that you and Lina are both guilty of the same sin?'

She bristled. 'What sin?'

'Omission. You are exceeding careful about how much you share. I suppose I cannot blame you for that, but it makes it damnably difficult for me to be of help to you. Furthermore, what you withhold could well put us at cross-purposes.'

The look she sent him was an odd combination of guilt and resentment, but before she could speak, Rob's mother opened the door to Sir Walter's lodgings. She did not look pleased to see them.

'Why are you here instead of at Cambridge?' Jennet Jaffrey asked.

Rob bent down to kiss her cheek. 'I will soon return there, never fear.'

His gaze shifted to the interior of the room as he and Rosamond entered. Lina sat on the window seat, head bowed, shoulders shaking. Although he heard no sobbing, he assumed she was crying . . . again.

Needham stood nearby, body hunched forward at an awkward angle. The way he was twisting the cap in his hands told Rob he wanted to offer comfort but feared rejection.

Seated a short distance away in a chair upholstered in faded blue velvet, Lady Appleton watched the two of them with a resigned expression on her face.

Rosamond lacked her foster mother's patience. She strode purposefully across the room, shoved Needham out of her way and seized Lina by the shoulders to give her a good shake. 'Stop it this instant. Your tears do not fool anyone.'

Lina blinked up at her old friend, eyes awash. Her mouth opened and closed. Little mewling sounds emerged instead of coherent speech.

'Rosamond!' Lady Appleton spoke sharply.

'If she was brave enough to climb out a window, break into her sister's house, and flee all the way to Kent with the constables after her, she can face a few simple questions.' With a sound of disgust, Rosamond let go and stepped back.

Lina wiped her nose on her sleeve and glared. 'You are not the one in danger of arrest.'

'If that worries you so much, you should have stayed at Leigh Abbey.'

'There is something you should know,' Lady Appleton said. 'A difficulty arose this morning when we attended services at St Anne's.'

'Why did you bother going to church?' Rosamond asked in surprise. 'No one knows you are here. No one is likely to fine you for non-attendance.'

'I wanted to go,' Lina said in a small voice. 'I find myself in need of God's forgiveness.'

'You are in more need of mine.' Rosamond's hands curled into fists at her sides. 'What happened at church?'

'I saw someone I know. I feel certain she recognized me and fear she will go straight to Isolde with that news.'

'It seems unlikely anyone can find you in a precinct as large as this one, even if they do come looking,' Rosamond said.

'Just what I've said all along.' Rob's mother muttered the words under her breath, She'd set about serving wine and an assortment of sweets, nuts, and cheese. By the time everyone held one of Sir Walter's large brown earthenware cups in hand, the mood in the chamber had eased, but it was still far from convivial.

'I chose to come here rather than to hide Lina in Master Baldwin's warehouse in Billingsgate,' Lady Appleton said, 'because I believe that the old laws of sanctuary still apply in Blackfriars.'

'You believe? You are not certain?' Rosamond was still on her feet, too agitated to settle anywhere. She even refused the offer of a piece of marchpane.

'There is no guarantee of Lina's safety anywhere,' Lady Appleton said, 'but as long as she does not set foot outside the old friary walls, she does not fall under the jurisdiction of the city of London.'

'Portinari has offered Lina his protection,' Rob reminded them, mindful that it appeared the merchant was, in fact, Lina's husband.

'She is safer here,' Lady Appleton said.

'Let her speak for herself,' Needham suggested, giving Lina an encouraging smile.

She burst into tears.

'I should say she has already done so, by agreeing to marry for money.' Hands fisted on her hips, Rosamond glared down at the sobbing woman. 'Why did you try to deceive me, Lina? You should have told me everything when I came to you in Kent.'

Rob heard the hurt in his wife's voice. He was not sure anyone else did.

'I feared you would think me a fool for agreeing to the marriage.'

'And so I do. All the same, it would have been convenient had I known about it before I started asking questions.'

'Why do you think I came to London? I wanted to explain the circumstances in person, so that you would understand. I wanted to make things right and now, because I went to church, I am in t-t-terrible danger.'

Lady Appleton cut in before Rosamond could make a rude remark. 'Sit down, Rosamond. Stop looming over her. Andrew told us what Portinari said about the nature of the marriage contract. Lina had already confided as much to me. Did you see the document in question?'

'I did. It is as he said.' Rosamond lifted the seat of the box chair, no doubt to see if it contained any interesting documents, before settling herself atop the cushion that padded it. As was her habit, she curled both legs beneath her.

'Well, then, there is no point in badgering Lina over what cannot be undone. We must fix our attention where it belongs, on exonerating her of the charge of murdering Hugo Hackett.'

'Portinari claims that his nephew did not know about the formal betrothal. Is that true, Lina? Did Tommaso believe you were free to marry him?'

Rob's gaze shifted to the window seat just as Needham at

last gathered enough courage to sit down beside the beleaguered bride. The bleak look on Lina's face did not change, but she seemed to take comfort from his nearness.

She nodded in answer to Rosamond's question. 'I deceived him, too. I let him think we had a chance at happiness.'

'I cannot think what possessed you to knowingly and willingly sell yourself to one such as Alessandro Portinari.'

With the first sign of spirit Rob had seen from her, Lina sent Rosamond a defiant look. 'At the time, I *wanted* to marry him. I signed those papers because I did not want *him* to be able to back out of the arrangement. There is nothing wrong with that! I was looking out for myself.'

'Old, fat, and smells bad – were those not the words you used to describe him to me?'

'But wealthy, Ros. Do not discount how much more appealing money can make a man. So long as I remained in Hugo Hackett's house, I had nothing I could call my own.'

Rob expected Needham to be appalled by Lina's admission. Instead, his friend placed a comforting hand on the young woman's forearm. Sheer folly, Rob thought, but he said nothing aloud. He remained as he was, his back propped against the linenfold paneling, watching a dramatic scene unfold before his eyes like a spectator at a play.

'You might have told me all this when we were still at Leigh Abbey,' Rosamond complained.

'I was afraid you would be shocked and disgusted by my willingness to marry an old man for his wealth. As you are. And I was ashamed too. I was so quick to accept him that I did not stop to think of the consequences. I was horrified when I learned he'd been keeping secrets from me. That he visited whores was bad enough, but when Cecily Kendall told me that he suffered from the pox, I realized that Alessandro did not care for me at all. He'd not have had a single qualm about infecting me with that terrible disease after we wed!'

Rosamond listened to this outburst with a thoughtful expression on her face. 'As it turns out, he is not diseased at all. Furthermore, although he does not deny that he was accustomed to visiting one of the women at Black Luce's house, he claims that his intent was to be faithful to you once your marriage was consummated.'

'Are you *certain* he is not diseased?'

The expression on Lina's face caught Rob's attention. Was that skepticism . . . or hope?

Rosamond glanced at Lady Appleton. 'Is there any sure way to tell if a man has the pox?'

'I will consult my herbals, but it seems to me that Rob and Andrew have already obtained the testimony of the one person in the best position to know.'

'Black Luce's girl?'

'Even she.'

Lady Appleton's answer told Rob that while he and Rosamond had been dining with Portinari, she had persuaded Needham to tell her everything he knew, even the details Rob had omitted from the story, in deference to his mother's presence, when they were in Rochester.

'Your commitment to marry Portinari appears to be irrevocable.' Rosamond sent Lina a hard look. 'That reduces the likelihood that he killed Hugo Hackett. At the same time, the fact that Tommaso Sassetti was deceived about your commitment to his uncle gives him a powerful reason to want to do away with your guardian.'

Lina's lower lip trembled. Not unexpectedly, tears welled up in her eyes. Rosamond ignored both reactions.

'As I feel certain you have been told by now, I experienced Tommaso's idea of courtship for myself. I was not interested, but it is plain that you were swayed by his attentions. Are you still a virgin?'

Lina's face flamed. 'What difference does that make?'

When Lady Appleton cleared her throat, everyone in the room looked her way. 'It could make quite a lot of difference. In some few cases, if a woman is married but untouched and a panel of midwives can affirm that she is still a virgin, then the marriage can be annulled. An annulment permits both parties to marry elsewhere, should they choose to. If, however, the marriage appears to have been consummated, then both parties are bound to each other for life. Even if they never live together as man and wife, even if it was not the husband who was responsible for his wife's loss of virginity, neither can marry elsewhere until the other one dies.'

'Oh,' Lina said in a small voice. She neither admitted to losing her innocence nor denied it.

Rob did not much care what the truth of the matter was, although he could see that Needham did. His friend's despair was palpable.

In the somber silence that followed Lady Appleton's explanation, Rob's thoughts drifted back in time. Vivid memories filled his mind, as fresh as if only days instead of years had passed since the night that had irrevocably changed his life.

Rosamond, sixteen years old and determined to marry, had crept into his bedchamber at Leigh Abbey. She'd flung off her nightgown, revealing her nakedness. She was the most desirable woman he had ever seen, and he had loved her for as long as he could remember.

Only two months older than Rosamond, Rob had been as inexperienced as she was. They'd fumbled a bit and laughed a great deal. In the end, they accomplished what they'd set out to do, consummating marriage vows made in private and without witnesses that were nevertheless as binding as a church wedding. Rosamond had taken great care to make sure that their union could never be dissolved.

THIRTY-TWO

B ack at Willow House that evening, Rosamond was restless. She did not believe Lina was in any immediate danger of arrest, but if she had been recognized in church then Rosamond needed to solve Hugo Hackett's murder in a timely manner. More than that, she had to discover proof that someone besides Lina could have stabbed Isolde's husband to death.

Rob found her in her study, pacing and planning. She heard him come in and close the door behind him, but she did not acknowledge his presence until he spoke.

'Who was it you saw at Paul's Wharf?'

His question surprised her. It seemed to her that they had many more important matters to discuss and this was a subject sure to distract them. Nevertheless, she answered. 'It was a man named Francis Throckmorton.'

'Who is he?'

'A recusant.'

Rob's lips curved into a wry smile as he came closer. 'Shall I keep asking questions or will you tell me the whole story at once?' Her hesitation had him shaking his head. 'Mayhap it will encourage you to confide in me if I tell you that Melka has already let slip that you set out for Salisbury Court within a quarter hour of the time Needham and I left here on Friday. I assume you went looking for Sassetti. Did you also meet with this Throckmorton at the French embassy?'

'Melka should mind her own business.'

'You *are* her business and she is worried about you. She worries even more when you disappear for hours and no one knows where you have gone or in what guise.'

Mere annoyance flared into a spurt of anger. 'I did not go to Salisbury Court in disguise and if you intend to lecture me, *husband*, you can—'

'I thought we were past that particular debate. I have no desire to control your actions. I simply want to share your burden, share your life. We were best of friends once, Ros. Companions. That was, as I recall, why you wanted me as a husband instead of some fortune-hunting jackanapes selected for you by your mother.'

Rosamond's temper cooled under the balm of his words. She, too, missed the closeness they'd shared as children. To recapture it would be heaven, but they had both changed in the years since. It was impossible to go back to the way they had been. Still, she did trust him more than any other person living. There had been times when her actions had left him frustrated, even appalled, but he never stayed angry. She did not believe he knew how to hold a grudge.

'Come and sit with me,' she invited, indicating the padded bench beneath the window, 'and I will tell you about my visit to the embassy.'

When they were settled side by side, she recounted the details of her interrogation of Sassetti and the circumstances that had led her to overhear the exchange between de Courcelles and Throckmorton. 'What choice did I have then but to report what I'd seen to Walsingham?'

'None, I suppose. How did you get in to see the great man?'

'I did not.' Glossing over the details, Rosamond described how she'd gone first to the Theatre and then to an inn in search of Henry Leveson. 'I have told you about him. Leveson was the one who escorted me to the house in Seething Lane when I last had need to speak with Sir Francis Walsingham.'

'I do not suppose you bothered to take Charles or one of your henchmen into that common room with you?'

'There was no need. If anyone had threatened me, I was prepared to use my knives.'

'Oh, that makes me feel so much better!' Rob's wry smile did not do much to soften the sarcasm in his voice.

'I was never in any danger.'

Although Rob did not contradict her, his eyebrows shot up nearly as far as his hairline.

Ignoring this expression of incredulity, she continued her narrative. 'I met with Walsingham's minion. It was the same man who approached you at Cambridge, the one with the prominent Adam's apple. His name is Walter Williams, but I think "minion" suits him better. He is a most annoying fellow.' She frowned at the memory of Williams's condescending attitude.

'I can think of other things to call him,' Rob muttered.

'Thick-skinned turnip eater?' Rosamond suggested.

He laughed. 'Go on with your story.'

'There is not much left to tell. It was obvious that the information I brought was important and that I had placed the correct interpretation on what I'd seen – that Throckmorton had been entrusted with treasonous letters to Mary, Queen of Scots. That is why I was so surprised to see him at Paul's Wharf. Throckmorton's instructions were to put the contents of those letters into code so that they could be sent on to the Scots queen by some clandestine means. Walsingham should have ordered his immediate arrest, and yet there he was, walking free.'

'No doubt Walsingham's men are keeping watch on him.'

'I hope they are. Do you think Throckmorton lives in that house at Paul's Wharf? He had the look of a man entering his own home. I feel certain his demeanor would have been different had he been calling on a friend or meeting a confederate.'

When Rob did not respond, she cocked her head to study his expression. His face was creased with concern.

'Is there something you have not told me?' Rosamond asked.

'As we were returning from Blackfriars, Needham caught sight of a man behaving in a suspicious manner. Later, looking out an upper window, he caught sight of the fellow again, this time lurking outside the gatehouse. An hour ago, he was replaced by a second man. That one is still out there and appears to be keeping a close eye on Willow House.'

Rosamond scoffed. 'A single watcher at a time? And only spying on my gatehouse? It will be child's play to elude such a one.'

'That is true enough, now that we know someone is there. But Ros – who sent them? I do not think Needham would have spotted them if they were Walsingham's men.'

Rosamond toyed with the pomander ball attached to her belt. It was filled with lavender, rosemary and powdered myrtle leaves, but for once the pleasing combination of scents failed to soothe her. Rob had the right of it. Walsingham's spies knew how to make themselves invisible.

'Isolde Hackett must have sent them. She is convinced I can lead her to her sister.'

'Does she truly believe Lina killed her husband?'

'I think she does. I would feel sorry for her if she was not such a mean-spirited creature. She was most unkind to poor Alys.'

'Then we must make certain to leave her watcher behind when we return to Blackfriars.'

Rosamond smiled. 'Shall we walk straight past him in disguise or would you prefer to creep out of Willow House by another route?'

'Are we to slither over the garden wall as Tommaso did?'

She reached behind her to rap her knuckles against the closed shutters. 'It is a great pity it is a moonless night. Otherwise you would see that this east-facing window overlooks the ell that is the kitchen. Beyond that is the cook's herb garden. It is surrounded by a high wall, and in that wall there is a well-hidden gate. I keep it locked and barred besides, but it exists should I ever have need of it. You and Andrew may wish to make use of that means of leaving the property on the morrow.'

'We are not going back to—'

She put her fingers to his lips to stop his protest. 'I have no intention of sending you back to Cambridge. Not yet. On the contrary, I want you to go to Soper Lane to ask questions of the neighbors and, if you can do so without arousing Isolde's suspicions, talk to Hackett's apprentices about what they remember of the night their master was murdered.'

Rob was eager to be of use, as Rosamond had known he would be. Because she was deceiving him, she felt a tiny prickle of guilt, but not enough to confess that she had plans of her own for the next day. In a disguise guaranteed to deceive any watcher, she intended to visit a certain house in Clerkenwell.

THIRTY-THREE

At mid-morning the following day, in the privacy of her bedchamber, Rosamond assumed her favorite disguise. It did not take long to change into the male garments but twisting, pinning and flattening her long thick hair in order to hide it under a wig was time consuming. She studied the result in her looking glass, well satisfied. Her narrow face and high forehead had come to her from her father. When they were not surrounded by masses of dark curls or by one of the elaborate headdresses women were wont to wear, she could easily be taken for someone of the opposite sex. A plain black cap completed the effect.

She left Willow House through the kitchen court and the hidden gate Rob and Andrew had used a few hours earlier. Her servants were too busy to notice her passing, except for Alys. The girl looked startled at the sight of a stranger in the house but did not challenge her. Rosamond resolved to speak to her when she returned home. Although it served her purpose to be ignored, Alys *should* have sounded the alarm.

In the guise of a beardless youth, Rosamond made her way from Bermondsey to Clerkenwell. She had been told enough about Black Luce's house in St John Street to locate it without difficulty. She strode boldly up to the door and demanded to see Mistress Baynham, for such, Rob had told her, was Black Luce's proper name.

'I have a letter to deliver to her,' Rosamond added.

Her normal speaking voice was low-pitched, and she could extend its range even lower if she concentrated. In this disguise, it was her custom to speak as little as possible.

The burly fellow employed to break up fights and expel unruly customers from the premises extended a hand the size of a meat platter. 'I will take that.'

'I have been instructed to deliver it myself and wait for an answer.' To keep him sweet, Rosamond dropped a coin into his outstretched palm.

She half expected the giant to slam the door in her face. Instead he gestured for her to follow him. He led her swiftly through the house, giving her little time to take note of her surroundings and none at all to study the portraits Rob had described. She was most curious about those but even more intrigued by the notion of meeting the notorious bawd known as Black Luce of Clerkenwell.

The goodly room into which Rosamond was shown was like nothing she had ever seen before. Half of it appeared to function as a counting house but the rest was a workroom of another sort. One entire wall was taken up by a huge, open clothes press. The variety of women's clothing stored there had Rosamond's eyes popping. She saw everything from nearly transparent night rails to what looked to be the sort of garments nuns wore in the old days when there *were* nuns in England.

An olive-skinned, lushly-endowed, dark-haired woman sat

at a long table near the hearth where a cheery fire burned to ward off the November chill. Surrounded by ledgers, she was dressed as any goodwife might be, with modest simplicity, and wore a pair of spectacles perched on the end of her nose. She did not look pleased by the interruption, and the explanation offered by her doorkeeper did not improve her mood.

'I am Mistress Baynham. Give me the letter you have brought.'

Rosamond produced a carefully worded document, one she had composed only a few hours earlier. Her palms grew damp as she watched Black Luce break the seal and begin to read. She was not surprised that a bawd would possess that ability. Anyone in trade found reading, writing, and ciphering to be useful skills and what was running a brothel but a business?

Luce's eyebrows lifted as she perused the text. What it said was simple enough: *This is to present to you Mistress Rosamond Jaffrey, lifelong friend to Godlina Walkenden, wrongfully accused of the murder of Hugo Hackett. She requests your assistance in clearing her friend's name.*

'What trick is this?' the bawd demanded, peering at Rosamond through the two round glass pieces of her spectacles. Behind them, Luce's black eyes were rife with suspicion.

'Send your man away and I will explain.' This time, Rosamond did not trouble to deepen her voice.

Luce's gaze sharpened. It dropped to Rosamond's chest, where the rigid doublet, stuffed with bombast to preserve its shape, both flattened and concealed the female breasts beneath. The same garment, shaped something like a pea-pod, also extended well below Rosamond's hips, masking another area of the body that might otherwise have given away her gender.

Time seemed to stretch while the two women stared at each other. Expecting to be thrown into the street at any moment by Luce's brute of a henchman, Rosamond forgot to take in air.

'Go back to your post, Rafe,' Luce ordered.

Rosamond took deep, even breaths and willed herself to be calm. Everything depended upon what she said and did in the next quarter hour. As soon as the door closed behind the giant, she removed her boy's cap. Then she removed her wig.

Luce Baynham burst into peals of delighted laughter.

Mirth took years off her appearance. Rosamond stared, struck by the realization that the other woman could be no more than a few years older than she was. Luce was still chuckling when she waved Rosamond onto the stool opposite her own seat at the work table.

'Well met, Mistress Jaffrey. I will hear you out but I can make no promise to assist you. You are, I presume, the one who sent those two young men to visit me?'

'I did. That was a mistake.'

'They were . . . entertaining.'

'You thwarted their efforts.'

'On the contrary. I sent someone after them to answer their questions. They paid her well and she gave me a portion of what she collected. Everyone profited from the exchange.'

'She ran off before they had all the answers they sought. And, in truth, they did not then know all the questions they needed to ask.'

Rosamond had chosen to pay her own visit to Clerkenwell for two reasons. The first was simple curiosity. The second, doubtless more important, was to seek confirmation of what Alessandro Portinari had told her about his last visit to this place. His only other witness, Hugo Hackett, was not in a position to confirm or deny Portinari's story.

'What do you want to know?' asked Black Luce.

'Alessandro Portinari claims that the evening he brought Hugo Hackett here was Hackett's first visit to this establishment and intended to be his, Portinari's, last.'

'Both things are true.'

'He says he told you that he plans to be a faithful husband.'

'That, too, is true. I was sorry to lose his business. He paid well for his pleasures.'

'He was not . . . that is . . . was there ever any question about his, er, health?' She felt heat rush into her face and knew her cheeks were flaming.

Amused by her visitor's embarrassment, Luce leaned forward, elbows on the table. 'If you make your question more precise, I will answer it.'

'Does he suffer from the French pox?'

'Ah. I wonder where such a story came from? You have

met the man. I ask you, Mistress Jaffrey – have *you* seen any of the signs? Is his body wasted?'

Rosamond shook her head. Just the opposite, as Luce well knew. She decided not to recite Cecily Kendall's list of symptoms. It was true that Portinari was losing his hair, but so were many other men his age. As for the bad breath, Rosamond had not noticed it herself, only the overwhelming scent of the civet he used to perfume his clothing.

'What about hideous scars? Lesions? A nose most horribly ulcerated?'

Clearing her throat, Rosamond blurted, 'Your . . . employees see parts of the body that I do not.' *And do not wish to!*

Luce laughed. 'That is true. Well, then, set your mind at rest, Mistress Jaffrey. My employees, as you call them, would be of little use to me if they were unclean women who spread disease. If a man's pizzle is covered in sores, let alone about to fall off, they have orders to refuse to lie with him.'

'And if there are no such obvious signs?'

'The women in my house are examined for signs of disease once a fortnight. Moreover, they fumigate themselves and use vinegar to clean their private parts after each customer leaves. If Portinari were infected with *morbus gallicus*, his favorite whore would have shown symptoms by now. He has been a frequent visitor here for several years.'

'I appreciate your honesty.' Prepared to accept Luce's expert opinion, Rosamond started to rise.

'Do you wish to ask me anything about the other man, the one who was murdered?'

'You said he only came here once.'

'That is because he was told never to return. I do not permit men to mistreat my women.' The very thought had anger sparking in her eyes.

'What did he do?'

When Luce told her, Rosamond felt the color drain from her face. She had never imagined such brutality in connection with an act meant to demonstrate love between a man and a woman. 'Why?' she whispered.

'I can only suppose such perversion gave him pleasure, but it rendered Dowsabella unfit to service anyone else for a week.

That meant a considerable loss of income, as she is accustomed to couple with four or five men in each night's work.'

Rosamond swallowed her next question. She did not think it wise to suggest that this might have given Dowsabella, or Luce herself, reason to kill Hugo Hackett, not while she was in Black Luce's house alone and no one knew where she had gone.

Instead she asked, 'Did you complain of Hackett's behavior to Portinari?'

'I would have, had he still been in my house, but once he made his announcement and gifted me with a heavy purse to help make up for the loss of his custom, he left without availing himself of a farewell jostle.'

The reminder prompted Rosamond to extract a purse of her own from inside her doublet. She set it on the table between them. 'For your trouble.'

Black Luce lost no time collecting the offering and depositing it in the large, iron-bound casket on the floor beside her chair. She had just lowered the lid when they heard a great commotion from the front of the house. A moment later, the door opened to reveal a frightened young woman wearing only a night rail.

'Begging your pardon, madam, but there are men at the door who say they have a warrant to search the house.'

'At this time of day?' Luce's astonishment was palpable. 'What do they think they will find?'

'They say they are looking for a woman wearing men's clothing.'

Rosamond and Luce exchanged a startled look. Rosamond knew it was against the law to cross-dress but she had no idea what penalty she would face if she were caught. A fine, at the least. She did not want to think about what the worst might be.

'Keep them busy as long as you can,' Luce ordered.

As the door slammed shut, Rosamond started to replace her wig and cap. 'Is there a back way out? I am certain I can outrun them.' Being fleet of foot had served her well in the past. When they were children, she had often beaten Rob in footraces, much to his chagrin.

'I have a better idea.' Luce seized both cap and wig and

stuffed them into the casket with the money bag, closing the lid. As soon as she had turned the key in the lock, she was up and moving toward the enormous clothes press on the other side of the chamber. 'Stand on that stool,' she ordered, 'and pull all the pins out of your hair.'

Luce selected an elaborate gown and threw it over Rosamond's head, leaving her to poke her arms through the openings left for sleeves. The garment was designed to be worn on top of a kirtle and bodice. Open at the front, it showed off the underskirt. Closed, it displayed the embroidery on the gown itself. The sleeves attached to Rosamond's doublet were not a good match, being a plain dark blue with turned back cuffs, but unless the men sent to arrest her had a knowledge of fashion, that detail would not matter.

'These are not just any garments,' Rosamond exclaimed, enlightened. 'They are costumes.'

'My women dress to please their customers.'

'But a nun's habit?'

Luce chuckled. 'You would be astonished by how many men like to pretend they are swiving a woman sworn to a life of chastity.'

Rosamond had no time to contemplate this extraordinary notion before two men burst into the room. What they saw was a scene most domestic. Rosamond, her long dark hair falling in feminine waves around her face, stood on the stool while Luce, on her knees beside it, pinned up the hem of the gown. With the front closed, no hint of what Rosamond wore beneath was visible.

Luce stood. With a withering glare at the intruders, she held out her hand for their warrant. Still without speaking, she read and returned it. 'I do not recognize this magistrate's name.'

'You have no need to,' said the man who had produced it. 'My men have their orders.'

'It is nothing to me,' Luce said with a shrug. 'Let them look where they will. But if even one tooth cloth is missing, I will report it as theft to the magistrates I do know.'

The second man had already begun to search the room. He sent a speculative look Rosamond's way, undressing her with his eyes, but that was not because he suspected she was wearing a boy's clothing beneath the gown. She managed a saucy wink in return and hid her revulsion. Let this rude fellow imagine she was naked under the rich brocade. That was better than having him guess the truth!

The two women kept up the pretense that Rosamond was just another of Luce's whores until the searchers gave up and left the house. Only then did Rosamond hop down from the stool.

Luce helped her out of the elaborate gown and thrust a plain kirtle at her. 'Put this on over your breeches. And this over all.' She produced an even plainer cloak with a hood to cover Rosamond's loose hair. 'You know that they would have arrested you had they caught you?'

'I know.' Rosamond sighed. 'It is a most nonsensical law. It is all very well for men to dress as women on the stage. Indeed, it is required, since no woman may perform in public. But for a woman to dress as a man under any circumstances is illegal.'

Luce just shook her head. 'You are a most unusual gentle-woman. Now answer me this: how did they know to search this house for a woman in man's clothing? Those were not local men. I am not even certain that was a legal warrant.'

'I must have been followed here, although I do not under-stand how anyone could have recognized me.'

She frowned, remembering that Alys had glimpsed her on her way out of Willow House. Even if the girl had seen through Rosamond's disguise, why would she tell anyone outside the household? *Who* would she tell? Unless she had been deceiving her new mistress all along.

The thought that she might have taken a spy into her home troubled Rosamond. She could envision Isolde Hackett catching Alys when that young woman returned to Soper Lane for her belongings. If she'd forced Alys to tell her where Rosamond lived, that would explain why Lawrence Walkenden had been moved to search Willow House for Lina.

When she was ready to depart, Rosamond remembered her wig and cap and asked for them to be returned.

Black Luce hesitated. 'Are you certain you want them now that your disguise is known?'

'Better for me to take them with me than leave them here. If those men come back, they might be found. I would not want you to suffer for helping me.' A sudden thought made her pause on her way to the door. 'Do you suppose they are lurking outside, watching for me to appear?'

'It will not matter if they are.'

'Because they will not recognize me in these garments?'

'Because you are not going to use the front door or exit through my garden. There is another way out.' Luce touched a rosette in the paneling beside the hearth, and a section of the wall swung open into utter darkness. 'If there had been more time earlier and if I could have been certain that those searchers did not know about the passages in the walls of my house and beneath it, I would have hidden you in here to begin with.' She grinned. 'Are you brave enough to follow me into the bowels of the earth?'

'Without hesitation,' Rosamond said, and suited action to words.

THIRTY-FOUR

In Soper Lane, Rob Jaffrey and Andrew Needham had spent a frustrating morning attempting to gain information by indirect means. They had agreed between them that to ask pointed questions about Hugo Hackett's murder would arouse suspicion. Even innocent men and women had a natural inclination to mistrust outsiders and would therefore tell them nothing.

'We may have approached this the wrong way,' Rob conceded as they left yet another shop without learning anything more than they had known when they went in.

'Are you certain there is a right way?' Needham's usual optimism was conspicuously absent. 'It was the middle of the night. These good people were all asleep in their beds and so were their servants and their apprentices. No one saw anything or heard anything or can tell us anything.'

Rob had been watching the door to Hugo Hackett's mercery. A lad emerged, carrying a parcel. 'Speaking of apprentices, I wonder where that one is bound?'

Without another word, the two young men fell into step behind the boy, keeping him in sight until he reached his destination. By the painted trade sign above the door, this was an apothecary shop. It showed a Turk's head with a gold pill balanced on his extended tongue. They loitered outside this establishment, located in Bucklersbury, enjoying the mingled scents of exotic spices and waiting for the apprentice to complete his business within. A delivery, Rob surmised, mayhap for the apothecary's wife. The family doubtless lived above the shop.

As soon as the boy reappeared, Rob pounced. 'A moment of your time, lad?' He held up a silver penny as incentive to stop.

The apprentice, no more than fourteen, had narrow shoulders, a splotchy complexion, and a negligible chin. His eyes lit up at the sight of the coin. 'At your service, gentles. And if you require to be privy with me, I know where there is a room.'

Rob felt his eyebrows shoot up. Just what did the young apprentice think they wanted him to do? 'You need only walk with us awhile. We have questions about your late master.'

Thin lips twisted into a sneer. 'Not much to tell. He's dead.'

'Did you kill him?' Needham asked in a conversational tone.

'Me? He'd not let the likes of me near him with a knife! He was loath to trust me with a pair of scissors, even when I needed them to cut cloth.'

With the lad between them, the two young men continued on toward Soper Lane. They aroused no unwanted interest. A lad in apprentice's blue was anonymous by definition, and Rob and Needham looked like any of a thousand others of moderate means abroad in the city for the day. The only thing that set the trio apart was how slowly they walked. They did not have far to travel. Once in sight of the mercery, Rob knew that their opportunity to get answers from Hackett's apprentice would be gone. He met his friend's eyes over the boy's head.

'Ask,' Needham mouthed.

What did they have to lose? Rob hefted the purse attached to his belt so that the coins inside clinked together. 'There's more than a penny in this for you if you tell me true. I want to know what happened the night of the murder.'

The sound of money caused other ears to perk up. Gazes sharpened. Rob steered the lad around a pair of mounted men, using the horses to block the view of potential pickpockets.

'Well? What can you tell me?'

'Someone killed my master. That is all I know.' The lad's gaze fixed on the purse.

'Someone? Do you know who?'

The lad's hesitation was telling. 'The mistress says it was her sister.'

'Do you believe her?'

Of a sudden, the boy looked younger than his years. 'I do not want to. I never saw any harm in her.'

'Godlina Walkenden quarreled with Hugo Hackett earlier that same evening.'

'She did, yes, and he locked her in her room for it. I do not know who let her out.'

Rob did not correct the lad's impression that someone else in the household had set Lina free. 'Tell me what happened after she was imprisoned.'

'Nothing that I know of. I was soon abed and sleeping. We must rise at first cockcrow.'

'Where do you sleep?'

'In the warehouse.'

Rob pictured Hugo Hackett's house in his mind. He had never been inside, but he and Needham had surveyed the exterior from all available angles and he had Rosamond's description of the floor plan as she'd heard it from Lina and from Alys. 'You can see the counting house windows from the warehouse, as well as the outside stair leading to its private entrance.'

The lad goggled at him, disconcerted by this display of knowledge.

Rob gave the money pouch another jiggle. 'Am I correct?'

'We can only see into the kitchen yard and beyond if the

warehouse door is open, and it is supposed to be kept locked as well as closed.'

'Supposed to be? Was it that night? You'll be in no trouble for telling me, lad. I only seek the truth.'

Needham caught hold of the back of the boy's jerkin an instant before he tried to run. 'None of that now.'

Squirming in a futile attempt to break free, the apprentice glared at them both. 'You do not know the mistress. She'll have my hide for spreading tales.'

'She need never know.' Rob lied without a qualm, certain now that the boy knew something of value. 'Just as she need never hear that you earned five silver pennies this day.'

'Five?' The struggling ceased.

'For the truth, mind you.'

At Rob's words, the boy grinned. 'What is it you *want* me to say?'

Rob shook his head and waved an admonishing finger. 'Truth,' he repeated. 'Even if the truth is that you did naught but sleep undisturbed throughout the night.'

They had stopped next to the Great Conduit in Cheapside, where water was piped in for public use from both Tyburn and Paddington. The street was crowded, but for the most part there were only women and boys fetching water in buckets. A few members of the Waterbearers' Company carried tall, conical, three-gallon containers bound in iron. One and all, they were intent upon their own business. No one noticed when Rob dropped the first penny into the lad's hand. Needham shifted his hold so that they could continue walking but did not release his captive.

'The warehouse door is supposed to stay closed and barred, but the privy is in the yard,' the boy said. 'I had the belly gripes.'

'Go on.' They were fast approaching the turn into Soper Lane, and Rob wanted to hear the whole story before there was any chance that Isolde Hackett might catch sight of them.

'I was in the privy a long time. When I came out, I heard voices. I looked up and saw a light in the counting house.'

'Could you tell who was in there?'

'One voice was the master's. That was enough for me. I
went back into the warehouse and barred the door.'

Portinari had said he'd left the premises by way of the shop,
Rob recalled. 'This warehouse – it connects to the workroom?'
At the boy's nod, he continued. 'And on the other side is there
a door that leads into the shop?'

Another nod confirmed this information. At the same time,
a sly look came over the boy's face. 'Ten pennies and I'll tell
you what else I saw.'

'Done. But if I discover that you've fabricated some tale
just to get more money out of me, I will not only complain
of it to Goodwife Hackett, I will take you to court.'

'I have no need for invention, good sir. I saw what I saw
when I cracked open the door to the shop and peered through.
My master had escorted his visitor through the hall and down
the interior stairway and was just letting him out into Soper
Lane. I saw them plain as day as they went past me, each of
them holding a candle. They were talking about finding a link
boy to guide Master Portinari home.'

Rob felt a stab of disappointment. It appeared that Portinari
had told them the truth. A pity, that. The Florentine merchant
would have made an ideal villain. Blaming a stranger for
Hackett's death would have pleased everyone. Better yet, it
would have set Lina free from her unwanted betrothal. Ah,
well – if it was not to be, then he would have to search
elsewhere for Hackett's murderer.

'Did you then return to your bed?' he asked the boy.

'I did, good sir, and so to sleep, but not for long. I do not
know how much time passed, but it was still well before dawn
when the entire household was aroused by the screaming.'

'And you saw no one else while you were in the kitchen
yard. No one . . . lurking?'

The apprentice shook his head.

'Were there any other lights showing within the house?'

'You hesitate,' Needham said, giving the boy a shake as
they stopped just at the top of Soper Lane. Pedestrians flowed
around them, oblivious.

'I am trying to remember.' The boy's forehead creased in
thought. 'There *was* another window lit, but I am not sure

which chamber it was in. The mistress was still awake. I do know that. She never sleeps but a few hours a night.'

Had Isolde Hackett known Portinari was there, or that Hugo was still alive when he left? Rob wished he could confirm the apprentice's story with the victim's widow, but that course of action was out of the question.

The lad showed signs of agitation, his gaze darting this way and that. 'The mistress will be wroth with me if I delay any longer. She knows it should not take me this long to deliver silk buttons to the apothecary's wife.'

'One more thing – at what hour of the clock did Master Portinari leave?'

'Just past ten.' At Rob's skeptical look, the boy laughed. 'I heard the church bells ringing and then the watchman passed by. My master and his guest were still descending the stairs when he called out the hour loud and clear.'

'The watch,' Needham repeated, shaking his head as they watched the lad scamper away, his reward tucked into his codpiece for safekeeping.

'Ten o'clock, look well to your lock, your fire, and your light, and so good night,' Rob recited. Once the city gates were closed at dusk, the watch made regular rounds throughout London, armed with lantern, bell, and pike.

'Do you think the watchman saw anything?' Needham asked.

'It is possible. It is also possible the lad invented everything he told us.'

Needham frowned. 'He did not mention seeing a light in Lina's chamber.'

'Her window would not have been visible from the kitchen yard. She told Rosamond that she escaped into the small garden at the back of the house. She picked the lock on the garden door, not the one from the kitchen yard into the warehouse.'

She had also told his wife that she had gone into the counting house by way of an inside door and found that chamber in darkness. It had been the candle she'd carried that revealed the presence of Hugo Hackett's body.

'I wonder if Lina heard the watchman on any of his rounds?' Needham asked. 'Mayhap she was too distraught, but I believe it would be worthwhile to ask her.'

Rob shot his friend a pitying look. Needham had heard Lina admit that she'd planned to marry for money and then take a lover. Even so, his infatuation with her had diminished not one whit. Did he imagine himself a knight in shining armor pursuing a quest to rescue a fair lady?

Once upon a time, Rob had deluded himself in a similar fashion. He knew, to his sorrow, that such naive self-deception never turned out well for the poor besotted devil who indulged in it. He was also aware, based upon that same experience, that it would be useless to try to warn Needham away from the object of his devotion. Rob resigned himself to the inevitable. Needham was looking for an excuse, any excuse, to return to his beloved.

'I see no need for us both to talk to the watchman. While I do so, you may as well go ahead to Blackfriars and report what we learned from the apprentice to Lady Appleton.' Rob meant to search for the link boy, too, but there were so many of them in London that he doubted he would have any success.

Needham did not need to be told twice. 'I will meet you anon at Willow House,' he called over his shoulder. Then he was off at a trot, nearly bowling over a passing pedestrian in his haste.

THIRTY-FIVE

Lina Walkenden welcomed the arrival of Andrew Needham at Sir Walter Pendennis's lodgings in Blackfriars not so much because she liked her friend's husband's friend but because her companions were slowly driving her mad. Jennet Jaffrey, always forward even for an upper servant, let her disapproval show in every comment she made, every look she sent in Lina's direction. Lady Appleton, although she tried to hide it, was deeply disappointed in her former charge. Lina had disregarded all those lectures she'd given the girls in her household, the ones about thinking through the consequences before taking action.

It was not my fault, Lina thought. *I knew what I wanted and went after it.*

She had miscalculated only in thinking that she could put up with Alessandro Portinari's embraces. At his age, she had not expected her marriage to be of long duration. He'd die – of natural causes – and leave her a wealthy widow, the best of all possible conditions a woman could hope for. Then she'd met Tommaso and discovered that physical attraction was a more powerful force than she'd imagined. Tommaso had spoiled her for other men. Even before Cecily Kendall's horrifying revelations, Lina had been dreading the nights she would have to spend in her elderly husband's bed.

'And so,' Andrew was saying when she began to listen again, 'it seems that Master Portinari is not the murderer. Rob sent me to tell you this while he searches for the watchman who passed by that night.' He considered the expression on Lina's face, his own most solemn. 'I thought this news would please you. We have made progress.'

'You have eliminated as a suspect the person I would most like to see blamed.' She spoke slowly, half convinced Needham was a lack-wit.

'But if the apprentice saw that much, someone else may have seen more, if not the watch, then the link boy Portinari hired.'

Lina did not hold out much hope. She cursed the inconvenient feelings of guilt that had driven her to return to London just to tell Rosamond something she had already discovered on her own. It would have been better to remain in Kent and even more prudent to have stayed locked in her chamber on that fateful night when murder had been done. That way, no suspicion would have fallen on her, and someone else would have discovered Hugo's body.

A sob escaped her. Had she done *anything* right?

She gave a start when Andrew Needham's arm came around her shoulders and he drew her to him, cradling her head against his chest. 'No tears, I beg you. I cannot stand to see you so unhappy.'

Lina might have appreciated the gesture and the sentiment more if the braiding on his doublet had not bitten painfully into her cheek. She pushed him away, words of rejection trembling on her lips. They never made it out of her mouth. At that moment, the door to Sir Walter's lodgings flew open and a half dozen armed men burst into the outer chamber.

Jennet screamed.

Lady Appleton cursed.

Lina stumbled to her feet, backing away from the intruders. She held her hands up in front of her as if to ward off a blow.

Needham stepped in to shield her with his own body. 'Who are you? What do you want?'

Lina heard the sneer in the officious voice of the man who answered. 'We have come to arrest a fugitive. Give us Godlina Walkenden.'

Lady Appleton swept forward. 'I am Lady Appleton of Leigh Abbey in Kent. What authority do you have to take my young friend?'

'She is accused of murder, madam. What more reason do I need to arrest her?'

Lina mustered sufficient courage to peer out from behind Andrew Needham's bulk. The speaker was no one she had ever seen before. He towered over Lady Appleton, tall and skeletal. Even from the side, she could see that his lips were thin and lightly pursed. Then he turned his head to stare at her and she gasped. The cold, merciless expression on his face struck terror into her heart.

'The right of sanctuary still exists in Blackfriars precinct,' Lady Appleton announced. 'No London authority has jurisdiction here.'

'The queen's writ runs everywhere. Stand aside.' He directed this last command to Needham.

'I will not.'

A scuffle ensued. Lina covered her eyes and kept them closed even when she heard her protector cry out in pain and exclamations of distress from Lady Appleton and Jennet. By then brutal hands had hold of her and she was being hauled out of Sir Walter's lodgings by two great hulking brutes in leather jerkins. The others of the company formed a circle around them, making it impossible for Lina to see anything but large male bodies.

Lina's two captors grasped her by the elbows and lifted her right off the ground. Moving at a fast trot through the precinct, they carried her in this manner all the way to Blackfriars Stairs and onto a small row barge. She was deposited on a bench and told to remain there by the leader of the ruffians. Since the vessel was already moving away from shore, she had little choice but to obey. She was not so desperate as to throw herself into the Thames in an effort to escape.

They did not travel far by water. Lina recognized the large landing place as Paul's Wharf. She was taken ashore by way of the common stair at the bottom of Paul's Wharf Hill and marched east for a short distance before the party turned north and went up a steep, hilly lane. Their destination was a large and ancient house currently undergoing renovations. She was escorted straight into a small room and there left alone with the leader of her captors. Eyes of such a pale blue that they were almost colorless regarded her with distaste.

'Sit down.' His imperious manner set her teeth on edge, but she obeyed as he seated himself on the other side of a small table.

An unobtrusive clerk slipped into the room to sit in a corner, ready to take notes. The inquisition began not with a question about Hugo Hackett's murder but with an inquiry into her betrothal to Alessandro Portinari.

'Why did you agree to marry someone who is not a native-born Englishman?'

'I did not have any choice,' Lina lied. 'The decision was made by my sister's husband.'

Her captor did not seem interested in Hugo. His next questions concerned her loyalty to queen and country and her willingness to, as he put it, 'do a small service to earn your freedom.'

'What service?'

'It is a secret matter. I must be certain we can trust your discretion.'

Hugger-mugger, she thought. That could not be good. 'I wish to clear my name,' she said aloud.

'If you do as you are told, you will be assured of a pardon, even if you are charged with so heinous a crime as murder.'

That was not quite the same thing, but given that no one knew where she had been taken, Lina feared she could be made to disappear forever if she refused to cooperate. 'What is it you want me to do?'

'Nothing so very onerous. You must contrive to befriend a man who will shortly be brought to this house under guard. Report everything he says to you, most especially if he requests that you take a message to his friends.'

The task sounded simple enough. 'What do you hope I will learn from this man? And who is he?'

'You need know nothing more at present.'

With that, he had her escorted to a bedchamber where food and drink had already been set out for her. It was a large, comfortable room . . . with bars on the windows.

Just before the door closed, Lina heard raised voices. One of them sounded familiar, but she told herself she must be mistaken. What possible dealings could Tommaso Sassetti have with the men who were holding her prisoner?

THIRTY-SIX

R ob finished recounting his day's progress to Rosamond with the comment that he'd wasted far too much time tracking down the watchman. He'd found him in an alehouse.

'The fellow may be a respectable householder in the parish, but he is also a doddering old fool. He says he remembers nothing of the night in question. They are all of a piece, or so he claims, one running into the next with nary a ripple. To listen to him, no one living in Soper Lane has ever been robbed, let alone become the victim of murder.'

Rosamond was distracted by the sound of horses' hooves on cobblestones. Someone had been allowed to pass the gatehouse and enter the courtyard. 'Any luck with the link boys?' she asked as she made her way to the window. One end of the parlor had a good view of the entrance to the house.

'None are about during the day. I can go back tonight if—'

'Something is wrong,' Rosamond interrupted. 'Mama and your mother have just arrived but Lina is not with them.'

'Needham?'

'No.'

Rob pressed close against her side in order to peer into the gathering dusk. 'He left for Blackfriars hours ago. If there was trouble there, he should have been the one to bring word of it.'

Together they waited for Charles to show the two women in. Trepidation had Rosamond's heart racing. Her palms were moist, her throat uncommon dry. She reached for the pitcher of barley water set out on a sideboard, then changed her mind and poured out four cups of Xeres sack. Something bad had happened. She knew it even before her foster mother entered and Rosamond got her first good look at the stricken expression on Lady Appleton's face.

Jennet Jaffrey marched straight up to her son. 'I feared for you!' It sounded like an accusation but was accompanied by a fierce hug.

'Mama?' Rosamond's whisper came out as a hoarse croak.

'It appears that someone followed Andrew Needham to Sir Walter's lodgings, then sent for henchmen. They showed no warrant, only forced their way in and took Lina away with them. When Andrew tried to stop them, he was most grievously wounded. After he was struck down, he was borne away unconscious by the intruders. I do not know where they took either Lina or Andrew. We followed them as far as the water stairs and were in time to see Lina placed aboard a small row barge. Four of the men went with her. Andrew was bundled into a wherry by two other men. Seeing us in pursuit, the leader of the raiding party sent one man back to delay us. By the time we were free to hire a boat of our own, both craft had vanished into the crush of water traffic on the Thames. They set off downriver but they could have put ashore anywhere from Puddleduck to the Tower.'

Rosamond had not yet shared her day's adventures with Rob. In this company, she decided against recounting her visit to Black Luce's house and her own near brush with arrest.

While Lady Appleton and Jennet answered the questions Rob put to them, Rosamond considered what it might mean that Andrew had been taken. What did they want with him? Was there, she wondered, a connection between someone following her to Black Luce's and someone else trailing Andrew to Blackfriars?

She began to rethink her suspicion that Alys had betrayed her. She had not had an opportunity to ask the girl if she had recognized her mistress as the 'boy' she'd seen that morning. Perhaps it was as well that she had not.

Who, she asked herself, aside from the present company, knew that she sometimes wore boys' clothing? Leveson, she thought. Walsingham's minion, Walter Williams. No doubt Sir Francis Walsingham himself. But what would the queen's spy master want with either Andrew or Lina?

'We will visit every gaol and prison in the city until we find them,' Rob said.

'What if she was taken to a private house?' Rosamond asked. On at least one occasion, Sir Francis Walsingham had questioned a prisoner in his house in Seething Lane rather than send him directly to the Tower.

Three pairs of eyes fixed on her. Rob regarded her with a puzzled frown. Lady Appleton looked intrigued.

'Why would she be anywhere but Newgate?' Jennet sounded skeptical. 'That is where they lock up accused murderers.'

'Not all murderers.' Rosamond shifted her focus from her mother-in-law to her foster mother. 'If the men who took Lina and Andrew did not show you a warrant for Lina's arrest, then it is possible they acted without authority. Can you describe the leader of the raiding party?'

'I fear I did not pay proper attention to his appearance. Everything happened much too fast.' Lady Appleton considered the question. 'He was passing thin.'

'With a cold, calculating look in his eyes,' Jennet added.

'Did he, by any chance, have a prominent Adam's apple?' Rob made a strangled sound but did not speak.

'He wore a high, full ruff that covered his throat.' Jennet spread her hands to approximate its size.

'Do you know such a man?' Lady Appleton asked.

'I do, but I cannot for the life of me think what he would want with Lina.'

Rob shook his head, unwilling to believe what they were both thinking. 'Surely this raid was prompted by the reward Isolde Hackett offered.'

A little silence fell. It was broken after a few minutes by Lady Appleton's sigh. 'There was a time,' she lamented, 'when I had many influential friends. These days, most of them are dead . . . or else rusticating in the country.'

'Some might say that is the same thing,' Rosamond quipped.

Jennet shot her a quelling look.

'We do need help,' Rosamond admitted.

'Do you have someone in mind?' Rob asked.

'I do,' Rosamond said. 'Alessandro Portinari.'

A chorus of protest greeted this suggestion. Rosamond admitted to herself that the Florentine would be of no use if the queen's principal secretary *was* behind the abductions but he did have influence with Isolde. She owed him money, thanks to her late husband's debt. Better yet, Portinari had a compelling reason of his own to want to find and rescue Lina Walkenden.

THIRTY-SEVEN

Dark water lapped at the side of the wherry. The vile things floating in the Thames were blessedly hidden from view. It was late to be traveling from Southwark to London by boat, but the city gates were already closed and locked and would remain so until dawn. The ferry that carried passengers and horses from Pickleherring Stairs to Tower Wharf had made its last crossing hours earlier.

With Rob beside her to provide both protection and comfort, Rosamond stepped ashore. As they turned their steps westward, she glanced toward Billingsgate, where Nick Baldwin had his warehouse. She had changed her mind and now thought it a great pity that Master Baldwin was not in

London. If they had his help, they might not have to deal with Alessandro Portinari.

A brisk walk brought them to Lime Street. A servant, recognizing them from their earlier visit, did not hesitate to admit them to Portinari's house. The Florentine kept merchant's hours, dining at noon and supping at seven, and had just settled in at table. He ate steadily while he listened to what they had to say, consuming remarkable quantities of meat, poultry, and pastries and washing them down with a generous amount of wine.

'You have no idea who ordered Lina's arrest?' he asked Rosamond.

'The men did not identify themselves. They may have been constables, but they are just as likely to have been hired ruffians.' She had no intention of mentioning any other theory. Portinari did not need to know that she had ties to Sir Francis Walsingham and his network of spies.

The merchant shifted his gaze to Rob. 'And you – you believe your friend was followed to Blackfriars from Soper Lane?'

'I do.'

'Wait here.' Portinari heaved himself out of his chair and left the room.

There followed sounds of men coming and going, doors opening and closing and shouted orders. When Portinari returned a short time later, he was dressed to go out.

'I have sent messages to others who may know something of this matter, but by far the most likely person to have hired henchmen to do her bidding is Isolde Hackett. I believe I have some small influence with her. Shall we find out?'

Rosamond expected they would walk to the mercery. Instead, three Italian chairs, each carried on poles by two men, awaited them in the street outside Portinari's house. She had seen quite a few of these newfangled conveyances in the last year or two. Where once they had been used primarily to transport invalids from place to place, of late they had surged in popularity among the wealthier merchants of the city, serving as an alternative to a litter or a coach.

'I find a chair convenient when I travel London's narrow streets,' Portinari explained.

Rosamond backed into one of the vehicles and seated herself in the cramped space. The urgency of their mission prevented her from pointing out that she could walk to Soper Lane as quickly as she could be carried there. An argument would only waste time.

In truth, the chair was naught but a wooden box with a semicircular roof and a door with a window cut into one side. She felt a jolt as the carriers hoisted it off the ground and set off at a trot. At first she was afraid of being dropped, especially when they picked up speed, but she reminded herself that the poles passing through the front and back of the box were securely attached by straps to the shoulders of the bearers. To her surprise, the ride was smoother than traveling in a coach.

With time alone to think, Rosamond wondered why Portinari had not availed himself of this method of transport on the night Hugo Hackett was murdered. It could not have been for any lack of servants. In addition to the six bearers, several more men accompanied their little party for no other purpose than to carry lanterns to light their way. It appeared that Portinari could command a small army at short notice.

She was curious about the messages Portinari had sent. How many had he dispatched and to whom? What other persons besides Isolde did he suspect might have abducted his betrothed? It occurred to Rosamond that the Florentine might have a goodly number of enemies about whom she knew nothing.

At this point in her speculations, their party arrived in Soper Lane. The apprentice who admitted them to the mercery took one look at Rob and turned pale as death. No doubt he was the lad who'd reported seeing Portinari on the night of the murder. Rosamond would have taken time to reassure him that they had no intention of betraying him to his mistress had Isolde Hackett herself not chosen that moment to storm into the shop.

'Who have you allowed in at such a late hour, you useless lackwit?' She lifted one hand as if to strike the boy but was forestalled when she recognized Alessandro Portinari. 'You! What do you want here?' Her gaze swept past him to pass

over Rosamond and Rob. Only by the narrowing of her eyes
did she show that she recognized Rosamond. Her attention
focused on the wealthy Italian merchant.

'I seek my betrothed,' Portinari informed her.

'If I knew where she was, I would be a happy woman.'

'She has been taken into custody.'

'Excellent news!' Isolde's countenance brightened for an
instant before dissolving into a frown. 'How is it that you do
not know where she has been taken? And why has no one
come to me to claim the reward?'

'Ah, yes. The reward. You would do well to rescind that
offer, Widow Hackett. You can ill afford it, given the debts
your husband owed at the time of his death.'

'You dare threaten me?' Her attempt to sound haughty did
not quite succeed. Underneath her bravado, Lina's sister was
frightened. The beads of sweat breaking out on her forehead
betrayed her.

'Shall I try bribery instead?' Portinari oozed false sincerity.
'I am prepared to forgive all the debts Hugo Hackett owed
me when he died if you cease persecuting your sister. It does
you no credit to defame an innocent woman.'

'Innocent?' Isolde's voice rose to a screech. 'Do not talk
to me of innocence. She is an ungrateful, vindictive vixen. I
saw her standing over my dead husband with my own eyes.
The murder weapon was still in her hand. I will not rest until
I witness her execution. She must be burnt at the stake for
what she has done.'

'What happened to the knife?' Rosamond asked.

Blinking in confusion, Isolde turned her way. 'What?'

'The knife. The murder weapon. Lina did not take it with
her. What did you do with it?'

'You have no business here, Mistress Jaffrey. I do not have
to answer your questions.'

'Yes, you do,' Portinari said.

Isolde looked as if she wanted to protest but thought better
of it. 'I do not know where the knife is. I did not want it
anywhere near me.'

'Where did it come from?' Rosamond asked.

'It was a kitchen knife. Hugo had used it to cut cheese.'

'Then anyone might have picked it up and stabbed him with it – a stranger who chose that night to break into the mercery as easily as someone living in this house.'

'Lina killed him,' Isolde insisted. 'The coroner's jury came to that decision.'

'Only because you convinced them it was so,' Rosamond reminded her. 'Do you still claim you do not already know where your sister has been taken?'

'By all that is holy, I do not. If I did, I would be with her, doing all I could to persuade her to confess.'

A sudden vision blossomed in Rosamond's mind – Isolde turning the handle of the rack while Lina writhed in torment on that most terrible of torture devices. Even as she blinked to dispel the disturbing image, she accepted that Hugo's widow was telling them the truth. Isolde did not know where Lina was.

When Rosamond climbed back into the carrying chair to return to Lime Street, her thoughts were far from pleasant. It appeared that Isolde had not been the one who had set a watch on Willow House or had Andrew followed to Blackfriars or dispatched men to take Lina prisoner. That left her with a much more unpalatable theory. Although she could not imagine why Sir Francis Walsingham would involve himself in a crime with no political overtones, let alone arrest Lina, she could think of no one else who would be ruthless enough to send men to violate sanctuary.

They arrived at Portinari's house all too soon. She had no idea what to do next.

'We had best go inside,' Rob said as he helped her out of the chair. 'There may have been some reply to the messages our new ally sent out before we left for Soper Lane.'

'You are worried about Andrew,' she murmured. In her concern for Lina, she had all but forgotten that Rob's closest friend – aside from herself – had been injured and was now missing.

'How can I not be?'

'He will be cared for, surely, by the men who took him. If it did not trouble them whether he lived or died, they would have left him in Blackfriars.'

'Will he?' Rob's eyes narrowed as he slanted a suspicious

look at her face. 'You think the leader of those men was Walter Williams. I'd not trust him with the care of my worst enemy.'

'From the description, it could be Williams, but I cannot fathom what Walsingham would want with Lina. Mayhap I am wrong. There must be more than one tall, thin, cold-eyed man in London.'

Before Rob could reply, they reached Portinari's parlor. The man waiting within turned toward them and Rosamond gasped.

'Sassetti!' Rob took a threatening step toward Portinari's nephew.

'Wait!' Rosamond put a restraining hand on her husband's arm. 'If he is here, it means he knows something about Lina.'

'I do!' Tommaso bleated, his wary gaze traveling from Rob to his uncle and back again as if he did not know which of them to fear most. 'I know where she is.'

It was Portinari who seized his nephew by the front of his doublet and lifted him until only his toes still touched the floor. Speaking in Italian too rapid for Rosamond to follow, he berated the younger man. She thought she understood the gist of it. Tommaso's uncle did not intend to put up with any more dissembling.

'He cannot answer if you are choking him,' she warned.

Portinari abruptly let go. Tommaso staggered back and had to cough a few times before he could speak. 'Lina was taken to Thomas Randolph's house on St Peter's Hill.'

'I know that name,' Rosamond murmured. 'He is a diplomat of some renown. He has served as Queen Elizabeth's ambassador to both France and Scotland.'

'Have you met him?' Rob asked.

'No, but Mama has.'

Portinari took a threatening step toward his nephew. 'What is this man's interest in my Lina?'

'I do not know. I swear it.'

'Then how do you know she is in that house?' Rosamond asked.

'I-I was passing. I saw men take her inside.'

Although Rosamond felt certain he was lying, she saw no advantage in saying so. She could not, however, keep the sarcasm out of her response. 'Do you mean to say you stood by and did nothing to help her? And here I thought Lina was the love of your life.'

After a nervous glance in his uncle's direction, Tommaso decided it would be safest not to reply.

'Oh, yes,' Rosamond continued. 'I had forgotten. You were only interested in Lina's dowry and did not care at all for the woman. What a pity you did not know that she was already betrothed to your uncle. You might have saved yourself a good deal of trouble and spared Lina's feelings into the bargain.'

'We waste time,' Portinari interrupted. 'We must go at once to St Peter's Hill and rescue Lina.'

Rosamond glanced at Rob. He returned a questioning look. She gave a slight shake of her head.

'I beg you to think this through, good sir,' Rob said. 'We do not know how many men were left on guard.' He shifted his attention from Portinari to Tommaso. 'How many did you see?'

'A dozen at the least.'

'And Andrew Needham?' Rob asked. 'Is he also being held there?'

Tommaso looked shifty. 'I know no one by that name.'

'But no doubt you saw him. He would be difficult to mistake. He was injured at the same time Lina was taken prisoner. Did you see a wounded man brought into Thomas Randolph's house?'

Tommaso shook his head, denying any knowledge of Andrew, but once again Rosamond doubted he was telling them the truth. Equally skeptical, Rob directed a murderous glare at the Italian.

Tommaso did not notice. He straightened his doublet and squared his shoulders, preparatory to addressing Portinari. 'I have told you where to find her, uncle. You promised a reward for that information.'

'You cannot pay him,' Rosamond objected. 'For one thing, I do not think he has told us everything he knows. Moreover, he does not deserve a reward. He tried to steal your bride.'

Portinari chuckled. 'I was fully aware of their courtship and prepared to step in if matters went too far. Until then, it amused me to watch Tommaso's efforts and know they were doomed to fail.'

'You might have warned Lina,' Rosamond muttered. *Before she fell in love with the wastrel.*

Portinari shrugged and turned back to his nephew. 'Listen well, Tommaso. You will have the reward only if your information proves reliable. Describe this house, that I may recognize it.'

When the younger man had done so, Portinari addressed Rob.

'You urge caution, but if we are not to attack in force tonight, what alternative do you suggest?'

Despite his concern for Needham, Rob understood the value of planning ahead. Rosamond knew what he would say before he spoke, just as she knew that Portinari would be more likely to agree to the plan if it was proposed by another man. Hands clenched into fists, she held her tongue and put her faith in her husband's good sense.

'Let us try calm reason before we resort to violence,' Rob said. 'On the morrow, my wife and Lady Appleton, who is known to the owner, will pay a visit to the house on St Peter's Hill.'

THIRTY-EIGHT

As soon as Rosamond and Rob returned to Willow House, she reported their progress to Lady Appleton and Jennet. Even though she had no proof to support her theory, she also shared her belief that it was not Thomas Randolph but rather Sir Francis Walsingham they were dealing with.

'It is still Randolph's house,' her foster mother reminded her. 'I met him some five years past, at a time when I was recovering from injuries sustained on a visit to Scotland. He was about to take up his duties as English ambassador in that country. He struck me as a reasonable man. If he is at home, I feel certain he will agree to meet with me. It is a good plan, Rob. The last thing we want is more violence.'

Early the next morning, leaving Rob's mother behind, they took a wherry to Paul's Wharf, the closest landing place to St

Peter's Hill. They were drawing close to the water stairs when the glint of sun on steel caught Rosamond's eye. She clamped one hand on Rob's forearm and jerked her head in that direction.

Moving in a stealthy manner, several men – more than one of them familiar to her – crept toward a house hard by the wharf. Rosamond recognized it as the dwelling she had seen Francis Throckmorton enter two days earlier, when she and Rob had been on their way to Blackfriars.

Their boat bumped against the dock. Rob flipped a coin to the waterman and helped the two women disembark. 'What is Tommaso Sassetti doing there?'

'Which one is he?' Lady Appleton asked.

'The dark-haired fellow.' Rosamond drew the hood of her cloak over her head, turning herself into just one more anonymous woman out and about in London. 'It is not his presence that alarms me so much as the company he is keeping. Is that tall, scrawny man the one who took Lina?'

Lady Appleton had to squint to see against the glare of the sun. 'It may be. We are too far away for me to be certain.'

Rosamond's eyesight was better than her foster mother's and she'd spent more time in the fellow's company. She had no difficulty identifying him. 'That is Walter Williams, one of Walsingham's agents.'

'It seems your suspicions were correct,' Rob said. 'Do you recognize any of the others?'

Rosamond would have preferred to be proven wrong, even if that delayed their recovery of Lina and Andrew. 'The man just behind Sassetti is Henry Leveson.'

'Ah,' said Rob.

'Who is he?' Lady Appleton urged them into motion. To remain where they were would attract unwanted attention.

'A player. A friend of sorts but, first and foremost, another of Walsingham's intelligencers. It would be best if they took no notice of us.'

Rosamond could guess why they were surrounding that particular house. Belatedly, Williams was going to arrest Francis Throckmorton for treason.

Only Leveson looked their way as they walked on. A slight widening of his eyes told Rosamond that he was surprised to see her, but he said nothing to give away her presence. Unchallenged, she continued into Thames Street. Just short of St Peter's church, she turned into a narrow lane and began to walk uphill. To the north, on the highest ground in the city, St Paul's cathedral dominated the skyline.

The house Tommaso had described was on the east side of St Peter's Hill Lane. It looked quiet, serene and passing well fortified. A number of the windows were barred.

'A convenient prison.' Rosamond's heart was beating too fast. She took deep breaths to calm herself.

Lady Appleton approached the entrance, leaving Rosamond and Rob to follow after her. When a servant appeared, she asked to see Thomas Randolph.

'He is not in London at present, madam.' He started to close the door in her face.

'Wait!' Rosamand called out. 'Is Sir Francis Walsingham within?'

'Sir Francis is at court.' The door slammed shut.

'If he knows that much, then this house is indeed being used by Walsingham's network of spies.'

'Is it time to loose Portinari on them?' Rob asked.

Rosamond shook her head. 'We are not far from Paul's Wharf. Unless I miss my guess, Walter Williams will bring Throckmorton here, too. We will wait and watch awhile.'

Slowly, the pieces of the puzzle had begun to fall into place. Rosamond continued on up the hill, leaving the others to follow. She stopped when they reached Knightrider Street, pretending an interest in the wares on display in front of a glovemaker's shop. Speaking rapidly and in a low voice, she told her foster mother what must have brought Tommaso Sassetti, Francis Throckmorton, Walter Williams, and Henry Leveson together. Then she gave her a brief account of her past history with Leveson.

'He mentioned that Sir Francis has been ill. I suspect that is why Williams is in charge.'

'A reasonable assumption,' Rob agreed. 'One way or another, Williams has been involved in everything that has happened during the last two weeks. The only thing we can acquit him of is Hugo Hackett's murder.'

'You say that Henry Leveson has helped you before,' Lady Appleton mused. 'Is he likely to come to your aid again?'

'I have no way of knowing. He would obey Walsingham without question, but I cannot say how loyal he is to Williams.'

'I once knew something of the world of intelligence gatherers,' Lady Appleton said.

'That was before Sir Francis Walsingham became the queen's spy master.'

'Some things never change. There are always connections within connections.' She considered for a moment. 'If I am not mistaken, Thomas Randolph's late wife was a Walsingham. That would explain how his house came to be used as a prison.'

'That and its location close to Paul's Wharf.'

Even as she spoke, Rosamond caught sight of a party of men just starting up the hill. Throckmorton slumped as he walked between two others, as if he had taken a beating and needed the support they lent as they gripped his arms. They marched him straight into Thomas Randolph's house. Williams, Sassetti, and Leveson also went inside.

'Now what?' Rob asked.

'Now we continue to wait,' Rosamond said. 'If either Sassetti or Leveson comes out, we accost him and demand answers. If Williams appears first, we follow him.' She was hoping the first to appear would be Henry Leveson.

It was not long before a lone man did emerge from the house. Lost in his own thoughts, Walter Williams walked right past three people he should have recognized and took not the least notice of any of them. Rosamond allowed him to establish a healthy lead before she set off in pursuit.

THIRTY-NINE

Lina Walkenden perched on the edge of the bed in the chamber in which she'd been imprisoned since the previous day. A short time ago she had heard a commotion below stairs. She felt certain she knew what it meant. The man her captor had spoken of had been brought in for questioning. Soon they would come for her. She was supposed to take the poor man food and drink and pretend to be sympathetic to his cause. To aid in her deceit, she had been supplied with his name – Francis Throckmorton – and the fact that he was a recusant.

Why me? she thought, feeling desperate. It was Rosamond who was good at pretending to be someone she was not. 'I am no Rosamond,' she whispered aloud.

Was she supposed to pass herself off as a Catholic? Lina had no idea how to do that. She'd never had anything to do with papists. Their faith was outlawed in England. Even the strangers she knew in London – Italians, Flemings, Frenchmen, and Spaniards among them – had fled their respective homelands to escape persecution for their *Protestant* beliefs.

Without warning, the chamber door opened. Lina sprang to her feet, stumbling a little as she rose. Strong arms caught her by the shoulders, and she found herself staring into the familiar deep brown eyes of Tommaso Sassetti.

Her heart filled with gladness. Tommaso had found her. He had come to rescue her.

'*Cara,*' he whispered.

Then he spoiled everything by backing her toward the bed while trying to kiss her.

Lina shoved him away, a feat she'd not have been able to accomplish if he'd expected her to object to his lovemaking. At once a hurt expression appeared on his beautifully sculpted face, but Lina also caught a glimpse of something else. Behind Tommaso's long, curling lashes and half-lowered eyelids lurked a gleam that could only be avarice. His languid, amorous façade hid a vain, conceited popinjay who had always been more interested in her dowry than in her.

'What are you doing here, Tommaso?'

'*Innamorata*, are you not glad to see me?'

When he tried again to embrace her, Lina evaded his grasping hands. He had left the door open behind him, but she doubted she'd get far if she tried to escape, not without help. It was her turn, she thought, to bedazzle Tommaso.

She fabricated a slow, seductive smile. 'I will show you just how glad I am as soon as we are safely away from this place.'

'Dear one, you gladden my heart. I adore you.'

'I love you, too,' she lied. 'Now let us leave in all haste, before we are discovered.'

He did not move.

'Tommaso?'

'We cannot go.'

'Why not?'

'Because these men . . . they are . . . I am. . . .' As his words trailed off, he shrugged.

'They are, you are *what*?'

'Intelligencers,' said Tommaso. At her blank look, he added, 'Spies. Paid informers.'

Tommaso was a spy? She could scarce credit it. Then a most disconcerting thought occurred to her. 'Were you the one who suggested I be brought into this?'

'No! *Innamorata,* I would never place you in danger.'

'*Am* I in danger?' She had been treated well enough, and she had been promised she would not be charged with Hugo's murder if she cooperated. When she stopped and thought about it, she supposed she might be better off if she did not try to escape from this house.

'I feared for you when I heard what happened to the man.'

'Man? What man?'

'The one who tried to stop them taking you.' Tommaso's dark, expressive eyes narrowed in what might have been jealousy but more likely counterfeited that emotion. 'What is he to you, this man who was grievous injured for your sake?'

'Grievous—? Tommaso, what are you talking about? Who was injured? And how do you know how serious his condition is?'

'I have seen him. He is here, locked in the cellar. A callow, pale-haired fellow,' he added with a disdainful twist of his lips. 'I do not know what you would want with such a one when you have me.'

Andrew Needham? It had to be. She had heard him cry out when he'd tried to prevent those ruffians from carrying her off, but she hadn't realized he'd been badly hurt. 'Take me to him at once.'

'*Cara*, you cut me to the quick. How can you prefer—?'

'How can you let an injured man suffer? Take me to him, Tommaso. Now.'

A most peculiar change came over him at her demand. The way he looked over his shoulder toward the open door made it appear he was afraid of something . . . or someone. Lina touched his sleeve.

'Who is the man who brought me here?'

'I cannot talk about him.'

He *was* afraid. Remembering the cold, cruel eyes of her captor, Lina felt a reluctant twinge of sympathy, but it was not strong enough to deter her from her purpose. She steered Tommaso toward the bed and made him sit. Then she hopped up beside him so that they could watch the door and listen for approaching footsteps while they talked.

'You are so brave to come to me!' Lina clung to his arm, pressing herself against his side, letting him think she meant what she said. 'I know there is a way out for both of us and that poor wounded boy, too. We have only to find it. Tell me about this spying. Tell me everything you know.'

She was not surprised when he obliged, only sad that she had not realized sooner what a self-centered braggart he was.

'I work for the French ambassador,' he told her. 'I hear secrets there and I tell them to the English and they give me gold coins.' He elaborated upon this theme at length, but Lina had no interest in spies in the French embassy.

'What brought you to this house?' she asked when he paused for breath. 'Does it have aught to do with Francis Throckmorton?'

Tommaso shrugged. He darted a wary glance at the open door.

'Did you take part in his arrest?'

'I helped gather proof of his treason from his house. There were maps showing landing places all along the coast and listing the houses near each one of them where secret Catholics live. It is said that the French duc de Guise is gathering troops on the Continent for a great invasion and waits only for word from his English allies that the way is clear.'

'Clear to make Mary Stewart queen?'

Tommaso nodded. 'There is no chance of that now, even without a confession from Throckmorton.'

Lina was glad to hear it and relieved to know that the task she'd been assigned would not make matters worse for the prisoner. Nothing she discovered would either save or condemn him. He was already a dead man.

But there was one who was not yet dead.

'What of Andrew Needham, the man in the cellar? Why hold him prisoner? He is no recusant.'

'The man who ordered him brought here thinks otherwise. He is convinced that this Needham is a secret Catholic. That is why he will not let anyone tend his injuries. He wants the fellow's wounds to fester so he will be in great pain. That way, when he questions him, he will more readily confess.'

The very thought made Lina's stomach clench. 'We must help him, Tommaso.'

'*Cara*, would you have me accused of treason, too?'

In the distance, a door opened and closed. Footsteps came toward them. Lina spoke rapidly. 'If you do not take me away from here and you will not assist a wounded man, then at least send someone who will. Go to Rosamond Jaffrey for help. I know you know where she lives. Tell her where I am and what has become of her husband's friend. If you ever loved me at all, Tommaso, promise me you will do this. I cannot bear the thought of that young man losing his life for my sake.'

'I would die for you, *madonna*!' With one of his over-dramatic gestures, Tommaso clasped her hand in his and held both against his heart. 'I swear on my honor that I will do as you wish.'

Lina would have found the oath more believable if he'd sworn it on his greed, but she thought he would keep his promise. By now, Lady Appleton would have joined forces with Rosamond. Lina did not know how the two of them might contrive to rescue Andrew Needham but they were the most resourceful women she knew. Together, they were certain to find a way.

FORTY

L ondon's streets were always crowded, especially around
Paul's Churchyard. There Rosamond, Rob, and Lady
Appleton might have lost sight of Walter Williams had
his tall black hat not added to his unusual height and given
them something to look for. They were only a few yards behind
him when he passed through Ludgate.

Impatient, Rosamond scurried ahead, attempting to shorten
the distance between them. Her mind seethed with unanswered
questions. Why hold Throckmorton at Randolph's house? Why
not take him to Seething Lane or direct to the Tower? And
why was Lina also being held there, assuming she *was* there
in truth? They had only Tommaso's word for that. She had
expected him, or Leveson, to appear before Williams did. Why
had the chief minion not stayed to supervise Throckmorton's
interrogation?

Preoccupied with such thoughts and intent upon keeping
Williams in sight, Rosamond took little note of her surroundings until she was almost run over by a boy with a hoop. They
had already entered Fleet Street. Was Williams going to the
French embassy? She had that answer when he passed the
entrance to Salisbury Court without so much as a glance in
that direction and continued on past Whitefriars. Beyond
Temple Gate lay the Strand, that great, wide highway that
connected London to Westminster.

'He's stopping.' Rob hauled his wife into the recessed
doorway of a shop. Lady Appleton turned aside to pretend
interest in the meat pies offered by a street vendor.

Rosamond peered around her husband's shoulder and was
in time to see Williams enter a tavern. The painted sign showed
the head of a bull. Above the door were branches and leaves,
indicating that wine as well as beer was sold at the Bull's
Head. 'Should we go in after him?'

'I think you must,' Lady Appleton said. 'Otherwise he may slip out by a back way while you watch the front.'

Rosamond's head snapped around. '*We* must? Where will you be?'

'I have had a little idea. I will meet you at Willow House anon.' Before Rosamond could ask what she intended to do, Lady Appleton was walking briskly westward along the Strand.

'Trust her,' Rob advised, and escorted Rosamond into the tavern.

The interior of the Bull's Head smelled of sweat, spilled beer and spices. Rosamond detected cinnamon, resin, gentian and juniper, all of which could be used to flavor spiced beer. Although the room they entered was poorly lit, she had no difficulty spotting Walter Williams. He was seated on a bench drawn up to one of the trestle tables, deep in conversation with a man she had never seen before.

'One of his spies, I warrant,' Rob murmured. 'No doubt they had arranged to meet here at this hour. That explains why Williams left Randolph's house. He was obliged to keep the appointment. He'd not want to risk missing a report from one of his intelligencers.'

'One of *Walsingham's* intelligencers,' Rosamond corrected him.

'Williams must be a handler, one who collects information and passes it on.'

'But *does* he?' She had her doubts about how much Walsingham was being told. Was Williams taking advantage of the spy master's illness to advance himself? She'd not put it past him.

Ignoring a group of men engaged in dicing and an old woman asleep in the chimney corner, Rosamond and Rob seated themselves at one of the other tables. Rosamond sensed that her husband did not like exposing her to a place like this but their surroundings did not alarm her in the least. She had her knives in boot and cloak and Rob was similarly armed. Besides, it seemed unlikely anyone would attack them inside the tavern.

A lad in a blue coat appeared to recite the offerings. It was a surprisingly long list. There was beer – strong, small, or spiced – as well as cider and a variety of wines that even included clary, a drink made by mixing clarified honey, pepper and ginger with the fruit of the grape.

'We've Rhenish, Gascon, and Malmsey,' the boy boasted, 'and beer that is as clear in color as wine from Alsace.'

They ordered Malmsey and were served in plain glass beakers of generous size. These were nearly empty by the time the man reporting to Williams took his leave.

Rosamond moved quickly, leaving her own table to slide in beside Williams on his bench, cutting off his escape. Following her lead, Rob settled himself on the freshly vacated stool opposite.

'Well met, Master Williams,' Rosamond said. 'We have much to discuss with you.'

'I have no time for idle chatter.' When Williams tried to rise, Rob clamped one hand over his forearm to keep him in place.

Rosamond shifted closer and let Williams feel the tip of the knife she'd extracted from the sheath inside her boot. It pricked him just above the waist and was hidden from sight by the thick planks of the tabletop. The other patrons of the Bull's Head had no suspicion that anything was amiss.

Red in the face, Williams glared at them but made no further attempt to leave. His Adam's apple worked furiously when he swallowed. Like most bullies, the man was a coward at heart.

'What do you want?'

'Answers. Tell us what we want to know and you'll come to no harm.'

For a beat, Rosamond feared he would call her bluff. His ice-blue eyes bored into her, testing her resolve, but he blinked first. 'If I tell you what you want to know, you will be in my debt.'

'No,' Rob said before Rosamond could speak. 'We are not here to negotiate. You have imprisoned two people dear to us. We want them back. You will explain why you took Lina Walkenden and Andrew Needham from Blackfriars and then you will return with us to Thomas Randolph's house and authorize their release.'

The sneer on Williams's face vanished when he realized how much they already knew. Rosamond gave him another little jab with her knife to reinforce her sincerity.

'We have no interest in the man you just arrested,' Rob added.

'Did you mean to turn Lina in for the reward?' Rosamond asked.

That surprised a laugh out of their captive. 'Just the opposite.' The temptation to boast of his own cleverness overcame his usual disinclination to share information. 'You know how we work. On occasion, bribery is more effective than threats. I offered Lina Walkenden a way out of her . . . difficulties. In return for a small favor, I will arrange a pardon for her.'

'But she is not guilty of anything.'

'It scarce matters if she killed Hugo Hackett or not, and it is your own fault that I was obliged to involve your friend.'

Rosamond felt her eyes widen. 'So you were the one who tried to have me arrested for dressing as a man!'

She was aware of Rob's questioning look but he did not interrupt.

'I was.' Williams preened a little.

'You failed,' she reminded him. 'And how galling it must have been when I stumbled upon the very information you had sent Tommaso Sassetti to Salisbury Court to discover.'

Williams glowered but said nothing.

'Spies seeking to thwart treasonous plots are of little importance to us compared to the well-being of our friends,' Rob said. 'It is time to undo what you have done. Together, we three will return to St Peter's Hill. Once there, you will order the release of Lina Walkenden and Andrew Needham. In their company, we will leave you to deal as you wish with the traitor you arrested this morning.'

Although his annoyance was palpable, Williams gave a curt nod of agreement. Rob released his arm. Rosamond slid out of the intelligencer's way to allow him to stand.

She should have felt triumphant. Instead a deep sense of unease came over her. Williams had given in too easily.

FORTY-ONE

Since it would have taken Susanna far too long to return to Willow House, change into 'court dress' and collect Jennet to serve as her attendant, she went alone and on foot. She walked so rapidly along the Strand from Temple Bar to Westminster that her bad leg ached and her heart thundered from the exertion by the time she reached St James's Palace. She told herself to be grateful that the royal court resided there, just west of the queen's larger and more grandiose palace of Whitehall, rather than rusticating on one of Her Grace's many rural estates.

Susanna was accustomed to walk a mile and a half each way to attend church in Eastwold every Sunday, and the distance she'd just covered was only a little more than two miles. She told herself that it was just the speed with which she had accomplished her journey that left her winded. Accordingly, she gave herself less than a quarter of an hour to recover and tidy her garments. She had no time to waste.

Petitioners were permitted into an antechamber off the first of the four courts around which the palace had been built. It was packed with people in as much or more need of help than Susanna, each of them prepared to wait as long as necessary for Queen Elizabeth or one of her favorites to pass by. Any who did would be accosted and inundated with pleas for everything from clemency to land grants. Bribes would flow almost as freely as requests.

Susanna took the time to listen to the murmur of voices around her. Some of what she heard was pure speculation, some wishful thinking, but she did glean two useful tidbits. Sir Francis Walsingham had been seen only a short time earlier, confirming that he was still at court. Better yet, as she had hoped, among those attending upon the queen was Her Grace's long-time favorite, the Earl of Leicester.

Robert Dudley, Earl of Leicester was, if not precisely

Susanna's friend, then at least a man well known to her. She had spent several years in his father's household as a young woman, before her marriage to Sir Robert Appleton. Lord Robin, as Leicester had been in those days, had given her the first kiss she had ever received from a toothsome young man. That he had later thought her capable of poisoning her husband did not signify. Besides, she did not have a better plan than the one where she sought him out and asked for his help.

Although Susanna had always avoided the royal court, she was not ignorant of the way it worked. The giving of 'tokens' was the accepted means of achieving one's ends. Since she had anticipated needing money to pay off Lina's gaolers, she had with her the wherewithal to achieve her new goal. With a determined gleam in her eyes, she began the long and expensive process of gaining access to the Earl of Leicester.

A little over an hour later, she was shown into the small chamber where Leicester sat writing. Flushed, overweight, his face deeply lined, he did not look well. He was plainly astonished to see her.

'Your presence here does not bode well.' He did not rise from his chair.

'Is that any way to greet an old acquaintance?'

'Those days are long in the past.'

'And therefore all the more cherished. Robin, I need your help.'

'Few approach me who do not want something.' His eyes narrowed. 'Has this aught to do with Robert's daughter?'

Susanna was not surprised that Leicester knew of Rosamond's existence. Like most powerful noblemen, he had a wide circle of correspondents who reported all manner of things that might interest him. One might go so far as to call this a network for gathering intelligence, although it was by no means as organized as the one Sir Francis Walsingham controlled.

'It does concern Rosamond, in a way.' She seated herself, without invitation, on a nearby stool. 'Let me explain.'

He was frowning even before she finished telling him Lina's story. She stopped at the point where Rosamond began to investigate the crime and therefore had no reason to mention Lina's current whereabouts.

'Innocent though she is,' Susanna said, 'if this young woman is tried for murder, only a royal pardon will spare her life.'

'The queen has more important matters to concern her.' Leicester avoided Susanna's eyes by returning his attention to the document he had been reading when she arrived.

'Ah, I see. In other words, you no longer have as much influence as you once did with Her Grace.'

He bristled at that. 'Present me with a formal request for a pardon and I will give it to the queen.'

'I have no petition ready.' She indicated the plain garments she wore. 'As you can see, I did not plan to come to court today. But this is a matter of some urgency. Surely Her Grace will wish to hear what I have to say.'

'You expect me to take you to the queen? You must be mad to think I will agree to that.'

'No doubt I am.' She had spent the last twenty-five years assiduously avoiding a face-to-face encounter with Elizabeth Tudor.

Susanna felt certain that the queen knew of various past activities Sir Robert Appleton's wife had undertaken on behalf of the Crown. Whether Her Grace would be inclined to acknowledge her debt to Susanna was open to question.

Leicester drummed his fingers on the surface of his writing table, his frown deepening into a scowl.

'Men working for the queen's principal secretary have taken Lina into custody. Even now, Rosamond may be placing herself in danger by attempting to help her friend. I—'

'Walsingham?' Leicester interrupted. 'Walsingham is involved in this matter?' The sneer in his voice when he spoke the other man's name made it plain that the two courtiers were bitter rivals.

'Mayhap I should have mentioned that sooner. Yes, Robin. I know not why but, to Lina's detriment, Sir Francis Walsingham has taken an interest in the case. If you will not arrange an audience for me with the queen, can you take me to Sir Francis? I understand that he is here at St James.'

Leicester's expression smoothed out at the thought of causing trouble for his enemy. He rose stiffly from his chair.

Susanna had heard that he had been making frequent visits to the baths at Buxton for his health.

'Never let it be said that I did not do my best to oblige a lady.' He gestured for her to precede him from the chamber.

The earl's influence took them past several levels of underlings and into what Susanna could only surmise were Sir Francis's privy lodgings at court. In the outer room used for business, a minion presided over a table littered with ledgers and papers. Sir Francis himself was nowhere to be seen.

'Sick again, is he?' There was no sympathy in Leicester's voice as he glanced toward the closed door to the inner room that doubtless served as Walsingham's bedchamber.

'The fever has returned, my lord, but that does not prevent Mr Secretary Walsingham from performing his duties.'

'Excellent news. This is Lady Appleton of Kent. She has need of his immediate attention.' With that, the Earl of Leicester made a courtly bow to Susanna and departed.

'Another day would be better,' the underling said.

'No, it would not. Time is of the essence.'

A creak so faint that Walsingham's man did not hear it reached Susanna's ears from the direction of the inner room. That door had opened. They had an audience.

'I am a skilled herbalist,' she announced. 'I can recommend an excellent remedy for a fever if you will allow me to examine the patient.'

'You are an expert on poisonous herbs, Lady Appleton,' Sir Francis Walsingham corrected her. 'I do not believe I would feel quite safe accepting any suggestion you might make.'

'Sir Walter Pendennis will have told you I can be trusted,' Susanna said as she turned to face him.

This was the first time they had met, but she had heard Walsingham described more than once. She had no difficulty discerning signs of illness. His saturnine countenance was flushed. His piercing eyes, unexpectedly blue, were bloodshot. Both his long, narrow face and his closely trimmed beard were damp with perspiration, and his white ruff had wilted despite having been heavily starched.

Brushing past the man at the table, Susanna took the spy master by the arm and steered him back into his bedchamber.

'Lie down, Sir Francis, before you fall down. You are suffering, I believe, from an ague.'

When they were ailing, most men either railed against fate or became docile as lambs. Surprisingly, Walsingham fell into the latter category, although he did insist upon collapsing into a chair rather than taking to his bed.

'How often does the fever recur?'

'Every few days,' he admitted, 'ever since I first fell ill in Scotland back in August. Cursed place!'

'What medicine have you been taking?'

'What else? The Stuff.'

'A most unwise choice,' she chided him. 'The Stuff is naught but opium poppy juice coagulated into pellets. That is all well and good if you wish to sleep until the fever passes but I do much doubt that you want to drift off into oblivion when that means neglecting your duties to the Crown.'

He sent her a malevolent glare. 'What remedy do *you* suggest?'

She drew off her gloves and placed one hand on his forehead. It was hot but not dangerously so. 'Take cinquefoil, powdered and mixed with wine. And I beg you, Sir Francis, do not allow a barber-surgeon to bleed you. Loss of blood will only drain your strength.'

Walsingham bellowed for his servant to fetch cinquefoil and wine. The effort seemed to exhaust him. He closed his eyes, leaning his head against the back of the chair, but he had not forgotten Susanna's presence.

'I perceive that you came here because you want something, Lady Appleton. You may as well tell me what it is.'

FORTY-TWO

Walter Williams claimed he did not know where in Thomas Randolph's house Andrew Needham was being held. To discover his location, he questioned a lad he identified as Randolph's servant, one who had been left behind to take care of the property while the master was away. They engaged in a quiet exchange of words from which Williams emerged looking pleased with himself.

Rosamond's uneasiness increased.

'The cellar,' Williams announced. 'We must go back outside and through the garden to reach the entrance.'

Rosamond did not trust that self-satisfied smile. She insisted that he descend the short flight of steps ahead of her. Rob came last, leaving the heavy wooden door open. They were prepared to make a quick escape if the need arose.

Used as a storeroom, the underground space was packed with barrels and crates. Rosamond expected to find Andrew Needham confined in an inner room used as a cell, door locked and Andrew himself secured inside with shackles or fetters. Instead, he sprawled on the stone floor in plain view.

The sight of his motionless body, his face pale as death, limbs askew and blood staining his doublet, sent a chill straight to the marrow of Rosamond's bones. For one terrible moment, she thought Andrew was dead. Then he groaned, and she heard Rob release the breath he'd been holding.

'Needham? Can you hear me?' Rob knelt at the injured man's side.

Close behind her husband, Rosamond rested one hand on his shoulder. 'How severe are his injuries?'

'He's been badly beaten.' Rob ran shaking hands over Andrew's arms and torso, searching for wounds. 'A broken rib, I think. Cuts. Bruises. A gash on his head.'

Williams glared down at them. 'Did you expect us to coddle him? He is naught but a filthy papist!'

Rosamond felt Rob tense under her fingers, but before he could turn on Walsingham's agent they all heard a faint sound from the darker recesses of the storage area.

Williams gave a start and squinted in that direction. 'Who is there?'

'No doubt another rat,' Rob muttered.

The only light in the cellar, since it was three-quarters under ground, came from a high window in the back wall. It was sufficient to show Rosamond that Andrew was sweating profusely in spite of the chill and damp.

'We need to get him to Mama,' she whispered. 'I do not know what to do for him but she will.'

'Agreed,' Rob said. 'You find Lina. I will—'

'I am here.' Lina emerged from her hiding place in the shadows, careful to keep her distance from Williams. Behind her came a second person – Tommaso Sassetti.

Rob did not look pleased to see the Italian, but he signaled for the other man to help him lift Andrew. 'Between us we can carry Needham as far as the river and hail a row barge.'

Just as Rosamond moved back to give them room, she heard the tromp of heavy boots on the flagstones in the garden. They were fast approaching the stairs to the cellar. If she'd had any doubt about their intent, it vanished when Williams darted out of reach behind a barrel.

The first henchmen hove into view.

'Take them!' Williams shouted.

Lina gave a squeak of alarm. Wild-eyed, she looked around for a new hiding place.

'Stand fast!' Rosamond snapped out the command and at the same time offered Lina one of the two daggers she'd already retrieved from their hidden sheaths.

Lina hesitated, then seized hold of the handle. A fierce and determined look came over her face.

Tommaso was armed with a poniard, Rob with a dagger. The henchmen had halberds, giving them the advantage for reach, but only two of them descended the stairs to the cellar. They outnumbered their enemies. With Rob standing next to her and Lina and Tommaso beside them, Rosamond suddenly felt ten feet tall and strong as an ox. She was confident of success and exhilarated by the thought of defeating the minion's minions.

The first man took one look at their weapons and laughed.

Rosamond's resolved hardened. She would wipe that arrogant grin off the fellow's face.

No sooner had that thought skittered through her mind than the grin in question vanished. It was replaced by an expression of surprise and, an instant later, by a look as blank as a freshly wiped slate. The henchman dropped to his knees before toppling over to land face down on the unforgiving stones at Rosamond's feet.

What had just happened took a moment to sink in. The second henchman had used his halberd to strike the first on the back of the head, knocking him unconscious. As Rosamond watched in astonishment, he turned the bladed end toward Williams, preventing Walsingham's agent from dashing up the steps and escaping.

'A moment, if you please,' said Henry Leveson. 'I believe these good people wish to leave *before* you have the opportunity to sound another alarm.'

Rosamond could have kicked herself. She had been so anxious to find Andrew that she had allowed Williams to speak with that servant. He'd used the brief exchange to order Randolph's man to send armed henchmen to rescue him and capture Rosamond and Rob. She should have realized he'd already know where his prisoner was being kept. He'd have been the one to give the order to confine Andrew in the cellar.

Williams glared at Leveson. 'Sir Francis will hear of this.'

'I intend to tell him myself.'

'Never mind that now,' Rosamond interrupted. 'We have an injured man to care for.'

While Leveson kept Williams at bay, Rob and Tommaso gently lifted Andrew's limp form. Rob grasped him beneath the arms and Tommaso, an expression of distaste distorting his features, took his feet. They carried him up the stairs with Lina at their heels. Rosamond was the last to leave the cellar.

'We are in your debt, Henry,' she said as she went past him.

'If you leave here you will all be outlawed,' Williams shouted. 'You will live out the rest of your days as fugitives, hunted and—'

A thump followed by silence had Rosamond glancing over her shoulder. Williams lay in a crumpled heap on the stone floor next to his unconscious henchman.

'I never did like him.' Leveson flexed his fingers as he emerged into the garden in Rosamond's wake.

The small yard gave onto a narrow passage that led to the street. It was already late afternoon and rapidly growing dark, which would make the way down St Peter's Hill to Paul's Wharf doubly treacherous. Rosamond had other worries, too. Would Willow House be a safe refuge? Williams knew where it was, just as he knew about Sir Walter's lodgings in Blackfriars. As soon as he regained consciousness, he would come looking for them, and he would not be alone.

'We should take Andrew to Billingsgate,' she whispered to Rob. 'Nick Baldwin's servants know me. They will not turn us away. We can send word to Mama and your mother to meet us there.'

'Does Williams know where Master Baldwin lives?'

'He may, but he will hesitate to order a search of the premises, especially if he believes Master Baldwin is in residence. We will have time to get help for Andrew.'

Rosamond darted a glance at the injured man as she slipped past the others to take the lead. Andrew looked half dead already. She could almost see the life slipping away from him. He would surely die if his injuries were not treated soon. She increased her pace, scurrying ahead until she reached the gate that led to the street.

The sight that met her eyes had her skidding to a stop and ducking to one side so that she was shielded by a wall.

'What is wrong?' Leveson called from the rear of the group.

'Walsingham,' she whispered.

As she watched, her heart racing, the queen's principal secretary dismounted at the front of Randolph's house. Only when he turned to help his companion from her horse did Rosamond realize that the spy master's arrival was not the disaster she had feared. With a glad cry, she opened the gate and bolted out of the passage.

'Mama!'

Lady Appleton at once took charge. She ordered Rob and Tommaso to lower Andrew to the ground so that she could examine him.

Walsingham watched, his long, pointed face set in a pained expression. Out of the corner of her eye, Rosamond saw Tommaso Sassetti slip away, anxious to avoid calling attention to himself. A glance at Walsingham assured her that he, too, had noticed the Florentine's precipitous departure.

Henry Leveson had a swagger in his walk as he approached the queen's spy master. Rosamond hid her smile. Underneath that illusion of self-confidence was a player giving a performance.

Even though he'd had just cause, Leveson had struck down two of Walsingham's men, one of them the minion in charge of intelligence-gathering operations at the house in Seething Lane. He had to be trembling in his boots for fear that Walsingham would not approve of his actions.

She was too far away to overhear what the two men said to each other but there was no mistaking Walsingham's reaction. His anger was palpable, but was he wroth with Leveson or with Williams?

'The wounds on Andrew's scalp and arm have been left to fester,' Lady Appleton announced. 'At least two ribs are broken. I cannot tell if he has other injuries within his body.'

'He cannot stay here.' Rosamond cast another wary glance in Walsingham's direction. 'Will the principal secretary allow us to go to Willow House?'

'He will. I have already told him everything, and we are in complete accord. Sir Francis,' Lady Appleton called. 'I need a cart to carry Master Needham as far as the river and if you could dispatch a man to the nearest apothecary to buy bole armeniac, I would be most grateful.'

'Bole armeniac?' Rosamond asked.

'A fine clay imported from Armenia and one of the ingredients I will need in order to distill a medicine to treat Andrew's injuries.'

'Fetch both items, Leveson,' Walsingham ordered. 'Is there anything else you have need of, Lady Appleton?'

'All the rest should be readily available at Willow House – oil of the white of an egg, wheat flour, honey and Venice turpentine.' She looked to Rosamond for confirmation. At her nod, she informed Walsingham that she intended to transport Andrew there as soon as the cart arrived.

'Take Mistress Jaffrey and Mistress Walkenden with you,' Walsingham instructed her, 'but leave young Jaffrey with me. There are one or two questions I would put to him.'

Rosamond caught Rob's eye. She knew he wanted to stay with his friend, but this was important too. Someone had to keep the spy master sweet.

A short time later, as she was about to follow the cart down St Peter's Hill, Walsingham materialized at her side.

'This is the second time you have proven useful to me, Mistress Jaffrey.'

Rosamond did not care for the calculating look in his eyes. She had a feeling he was thinking of other 'uses' she might have. 'An accident, I assure you, Sir Francis.'

To this he made no response other than to bid her good day and turn toward the house. He held himself stiffly, as if it was an effort to walk that far.

Rob took his place. 'What did he want?'

'Nothing. He paid me a compliment.' She pressed a quick kiss to his cheek. 'I must hurry. The others are halfway to Paul's Wharf by now. Go answer Sir Francis's questions. The sooner he is satisfied, the sooner you can rejoin us.'

Leaving him, Rosamond raced down the hill. Twice, she looked back over her shoulder. No physical presence pursued her but she had the strongest feeling that she would have to run much faster and much farther before she could truly escape the sticky strands of the spy master's web.

FORTY-THREE

'Your man Williams made certain promises,' Rob said. 'He never meant to keep them but since you have allowed Mistress Walkenden to leave, Sir Francis, and have not clapped the rest of us in irons, may I hope that you will honor them?'

Lady Appleton had insisted that the queen's principal secretary wanted to help them. Rob was not so sure. Sitting across from the man in a small, square room heated by a charcoal brazier, he could understand why people took one look at Sir Francis Walsingham's dark complexion, pointed beard, and somber black garb and thought him a devil.

At the moment, Walsingham's face had smoothed into a noncommittal blankness. 'What are these promises that Watt Williams made?' He uncorked a drinking flask and took a long swallow of the liquid it contained.

'A pardon, should Godlina Walkenden be found guilty of Hugo Hackett's murder.'

'I have already given Lady Appleton my word that Mistress Walkenden will be pardoned, although I will be most surprised if it becomes necessary. I do not believe she will be charged with any crime, let alone brought to trial.'

Even if she killed him? Rob pictured Lina as he had seen her in the cellar. She had held Rosamond's dagger in a firm grip, fully prepared to use it to kill.

As if he could read minds, Walsingham repeated himself. 'I have given my word, but there are certain conditions. You are not to speak of anything you have seen or heard in this house or elsewhere. To do so might well compromise the security of England.'

'Does this clemency extend to the actions taken here today? To come to our aid, Henry Leveson was obliged to attack two of your agents.'

Walsingham blinked. In another man, Rob thought, that would be a wince, mayhap accompanied by a groan.

'He had good cause,' Rob added.

'I will investigate further. I do not plan to bring charges against anyone involved in the altercation in the cellar.'

'Not even Williams?'

Walsingham allowed himself a small, tight-lipped smile. 'As to that, I would first hear an account of your dealings with him. Leave nothing out.'

Rob was happy to oblige. 'It began at Cambridge. . . .'

An hour later, the inquisition was complete and Walsingham was showing marked signs of fatigue. He drank again from the flask, slopping a little of the liquid into his beard.

'If I may ask, Sir Francis,' Rob ventured, 'how will you deal with Williams?'

'Privately, Master Jaffrey. Watt had been authorized to act as he saw fit. He may have been overzealous in his actions and misguided in his attempt to use a woman to worm secrets out of another prisoner, but he still has his uses.'

In other words, Williams would likely go unpunished for his treatment of Andrew Needham and his attempts to coerce first Rosamond and then Lina into doing his bidding. That angered

Rob, but he thought better of making his feelings known. Walsingham might have been ill – even now sweat beaded his brow – but there was nothing sickly about his penetrating stare. This was a man who would do anything in his power, use any means at his disposal, to protect queen and country.

When he was dismissed, Rob at once set out for Willow House. His mind was sore troubled. Walsingham had commanded them to forget everything they knew about his business, but he clearly forgot nothing he had learned about them. Rosamond in particular had caught the spy master's attention. That alarmed Rob. His wife might swear she wanted nothing more to do with intrigue and danger, but in some ways he knew her better than she knew herself. She would never be content to spend all her time shopping or visiting with her gossips like an ordinary goodwife. This was a woman who delighted in going to plays in disguise. She'd be easy prey for Walsingham if he decided he wanted her to work for him again.

Anxious as he was to speak with Rosamond, when Rob returned to the house in Bermondsey, he went first to Needham's chamber. Lady Appleton and Alys, the girl Rosamond had rescued from Hugo Hackett's shop, were in attendance on his ailing friend. Lady Appleton looked up from the act of applying a cold compress to Needham's forehead to offer Rob a reassuring smile.

'His injuries are not as severe as I first feared. If I can succeed in lowering his fever, he should make a full recovery.'

'Damn fool,' Rob muttered. 'He wanted to be Lina's knight in shining armor, but he forgot to don the armor.'

'He was also mistaken in thinking his valor would win him the heart of the lady fair.'

'Where is she?'

'Gone to reconcile with her betrothed.'

'She went to Portinari? Of her own accord?'

'She meant to marry him from the first, my dear. He is very wealthy. Since he is also an old man, she has hopes that he will die soon after the wedding and leave all he owns to her.'

Rob did not know why he was surprised. Lina had agreed to the betrothal, rejecting it only when she believed Portinari had contracted the French pox. 'Did Rosamond go with her?'

Lady Appleton removed the folded cloth from Needham's

fevered brow and accepted a new one, freshly soaked in cold water and wrung out by Alys. 'Rosamond and Melka both accompanied her. They took my coach. I expect they crossed London Bridge shortly before the city gates closed for the night.'

At hearing this news, a deep sense of dread settled over Rob. Had he returned a quarter of an hour earlier, he would have been in time to . . . what? Prevent them leaving? He'd still have come to Needham's chamber first to check on his friend's condition. And if he had attempted to give unwanted advice to his wife, he'd no doubt have been ignored. If Rosamond thought it important to escort Lina to Lime Street, she'd not have been talked out of going.

'The ferry from Pickleherring Stairs does not run this late,' Lady Appleton said, 'but you should be able to hail a wherry at Sellinger's Wharf to take you straight across the Thames to Billingsgate.'

'Needham—'

'There is nothing you can do to help Andrew heal. Leave him in my care and go after your wife.'

'She will not thank me for trying to protect her.'

'Perhaps not, but that you think she needs your protection speaks volumes.'

'You are worried about her, too. Why?'

'I wish I knew. Still, there are times when we must simply trust our feelings.'

Rob needed no further urging. Delaying only long enough to collect sufficient funds for any emergency, he left Willow House at a run.

FORTY-FOUR

Cecily Kendall watched from the window of her lodgings as Rosamond, Lina, and Melka arrived at Alessandro Portinari's dwelling in Lime Street. The old woman lifted one gnarled hand to her mouth, a gesture visible to Rosamond even in the gathering dusk.

'Are you certain of your decision?' Rosamond asked her friend. 'It is not too late to change your mind.'

'I am already married to Alessandro. There is no decision to make.'

'Nor is there any need to spend your life in misery.'

Lina laughed. 'What makes you think I will be miserable? As his wife, I can persuade him to freshen his breath with sweet-smelling washes and stop perfuming himself with civet. In return, he will shower me with gifts and set me up as a silkwoman. I believe I will find my life most tolerable.'

Rosamond was forced to accept that she could not change Lina's mind. Mayhap her friend *would* find happiness as an old man's plaything. Who was she to say?

'Have you any other questions to ask me that you do not wish my dear husband to hear?' Lina asked. They both knew that Portinari's servants were even now reporting her arrival to their master.

There was only one Rosamond could think of, a minor point but one that had bothered her. 'Why did you omit Alys when you enumerated the members of your sister's household?'

'Alys?' For a moment, Lina looked as if she did not recognize the name. Then recognition dawned. 'Do you mean that mousy little creature Isolde took in to do piecework? She never even crossed my mind, for you only asked me about servants and apprentices and she is neither.' She frowned. 'What will happen to her, I wonder, now that Hugo is dead?'

'You need not trouble yourself about her,' Rosamond said. 'Someone has already taken her in.'

Before she could say more, Alessandro Portinari came out of his house to greet his wife. Rosamond studied him closely. His joy at seeing Lina appeared genuine. Mayhap he would be a good husband to her, after all.

She glanced again at the window of the house next door and sighed. Whatever her faults, Goody Kendall's concern for Lina had been sincere.

'I had best go reassure the widow that all is well,' she said, inclining her head in the direction of the neighboring house. 'Believing what she does about your betrothed, she is doubtless most upset at seeing you reconciled.'

'That is kind of you.' Portinari started to lead his bride inside.
'You need not waste much time with her,' Lina said over
her shoulder. 'She is naught but a meddling old busybody. Had
she not interfered, I'd never have quarreled with Hugo and no
one would have thought to blame me when he was killed.'

Would Hugo Hackett have been murdered at all without
Widow Kendall's interference? Rosamond wished she knew
the answer to that question. Aloud, she said only, 'She meant
well.'

On the way up the stairs leading to Widow Kendall's lodgings,
Rosamond thought back to her previous visit. At the time, she
had been seeking information about Alessandro Portinari and
his nephew and confirmation of the story Lina had told her.
She had thought some of the widow's behavior odd but since
her prejudices had provided useful information, she had not
delved too deeply into their origins. Now she realized that
there was a contradiction between Cecily Kendall's fondness
for Lina and her apparent belief that her young friend was
guilty of Hugo's murder.

The widow greeted the arrival of Rosamond and her maid
with outright suspicion. 'Who are you and what do you want?'
She did not rise from her post by the window. The servant
who had admitted Rosamond and Melka hovered in the background, prepared to sound the alarm should anyone threaten
her mistress.

Rosamond was taken aback by the old woman's ferocity.
She needed a moment to remember that she had been in disguise
when last they met. Widow Kendall did not recognize her.

In the time it took to cross the room, Rosamond had to
decide what approach to take. Admit to being Mistress
Flackley? No. Claim to be a friend of Mistress Flackley's and
therefore the recipient of her confidences? No, not that either.
A mixture of truth and lies would have to serve, substantiated
by the fact that Cecily Kendall had just witnessed her arrival
at Portinari's house in Lina's company.

'I am Mistress Jaffrey. I am Lina Walkenden's friend and
in her confidence. She bade me come and assure you that she
knows what she is doing.'

'By giving herself into the keeping of that vile old lecher?'

'Even so. It seems that you were mistaken in your assessment of Master Portinari's, er, health.'

The old woman muttered something under her breath. Her gnarled hands twisted in her lap.

'You acted out of kindness, madam, in repeating what young Roeloff saw, but he did not follow Portinari inside the . . . establishment. He could not possibly know what went on there.'

The widow gave a derisive snort and used the end of her walking stick to smack the stool pulled up close to her chair, the one upon which her bad leg had rested during Rosamond's previous visit. 'Sit down and explain yourself, Mistress Jaffrey, for I am far from convinced.'

Rosamond obliged and found herself at eye level with the old woman. The look Cecily Kendall sent her was rife with skepticism.

'Suffice it to say that Lina wanted to marry Portinari from the first. I do not see his appeal myself, but for her his wealth alone is sufficient to blind her to any disadvantages in the match.'

The widow scowled. 'I do not understand how any good Englishwoman could willingly tie herself to an Italian!'

'He is a denizen of England.'

'That makes no difference.'

Widow Kendall's vehemence confirmed Rosamond's earlier conclusion that her antipathy toward Portinari, at least in part, was because he was foreign-born. Or mayhap she thought he was a papist.

'How can she ignore his visits to that bawdy house?' the widow demanded.

'He has promised he will never go there again. He means to be a faithful husband. As for your claim that he is infected with the French pox, he denies that utterly.'

'And so he would, whether he has it or not!'

'Someone familiar with the symptoms has confirmed that he is free of them.'

'A physician? A barber-surgeon? A cunning woman?'

'Black Luce herself, if you must know.'

Widow Kendall's eyebrows shot up. 'Do you expect me to take the word of a whore?'

'It makes no sense for her to lie,' Rosamond pointed out, 'and as I feel certain young Roeloff must have told you, she runs an exclusive establishment. It would be exceeding bad for business if one of her girls caught the pox or any other disease from a customer.'

The widow snorted.

'Her care for the reputation of her house is supported by her actions with regard to Hugo Hackett,' Rosamond continued, warming to her topic. 'As you know, he was with Master Portinari when Roeloff followed them to Black Luce's. Hackett—'

'How do you know that?' Cecily Kendall interrupted. 'I did not tell Lina about her brother-in-law. My only concern was to warn her away from the Florentine.'

'Are you certain?'

Offended, the widow very nearly snarled at her. 'I may be old but I have not yet lost my wits.'

Thinking back on what Cecily Kendall had confided to her when she had been Mistress Flackley, Rosamond realized the widow had not said she'd told *Lina* about Hugo Hackett's visit to Black Luce. She'd said she'd told 'her' and Rosamond had assumed she meant Lina. She had also assumed that Widow Kendall believed Lina had killed her brother-in-law.

'Who? Who did you tell?'

The old woman toyed with the lace at her wrists and did not answer.

'You believe Hugo Hackett was stabbed to death because of the information you supplied. Do you believe Lina murdered him?'

'I never thought that. Not for an instant. That girl would not harm a fly.'

'But she is the one who has been accused of the crime. Even now, constables seek to arrest her and put her on trial. If she is convicted, she will be burnt at the stake.'

Cecily Kendall's eyes brimmed with tears. 'God forgive me. I meant no harm.'

'You did nothing wrong.' Rosamond leaned forward to take

both of the old woman's hands in hers. They were ice cold to the touch. 'Who did you tell about Hugo Hackett's visit to Black Luce?'

'Isolde. I told Lina's sister that her husband visited a bawdy house in Portinari's company.'

'When? When did you tell her?' Rosamond hardly dared breathe as she waited for the answer.

'The evening of the same day I warned Lina of her danger. I was *certain* she would be risking her life if she married him.' The look of despair on Widow Kendall's face wrenched at Rosamond's heart.

'You spoke up out of kindness. No one can fault you for that. But now you must tell me the rest. How did you come to confide in Isolde?'

'She came here, furious with me for interfering in matters that she said were none of my concern. Her accusations were hurtful, and I lost my temper. Before I thought better of it, I gave in to the desire to prick her pride and told her what I had not shared with her sister, that her husband had not only gone to Black Luce's brothel with Alessandro Portinari but that he had stayed on after Portinari left.'

'Whereupon Isolde Hackett went home and confronted her wayward husband.'

Widow Kendall began to weep in earnest. 'I fear she did more than confront him.'

FORTY-FIVE

By the time Rosamond took her leave of Widow Kendall, it was full dark. The streets of London were poorly lit. Only a few lanterns had been hung outside their doors by conscientious householders. If she were a sensible woman, Rosamond thought, she and Melka would at once rejoin Lina in Alessandro Portinari's house, where they had planned to spend the night. Tomorrow would be time enough to confront Isolde Hackett.

Her own impatient nature drove her to make a different decision. She told herself she had nothing to fear. She and Melka would travel by coach, amply protected by Charles and the two burly henchmen she employed as grooms. At the mercery, although the shop would be closed to business for the day, the apprentices and servants would still be much in evidence. None of them seemed overburdened with loyalty to their mistress. They obeyed her out of fear.

'I should have seen it sooner,' Rosamond said aloud as the coach lumbered past the Royal Exchange and on into the Stocks Market.

Even this part of the city was quiet at such a late hour. In the Poultry they passed the Counter, where Isolde had wanted Constable Dodge to imprison Rosamond. Now it would be Isolde who languished there . . . until she could be tried, convicted, and burnt.

Melka's head bobbed up and down. 'Always the wife,' she said with a conviction that made Rosamond cringe.

'Not always.' She sighed. 'I did consider Isolde, back at Leigh Abbey, but Lina insisted that her sister loved Hugo and persuaded me to look elsewhere for his killer.'

Isolde's devotion to her late spouse had seemed genuine when Rosamond met her in person. It was Cecily Kendall's revelation that changed everything. Rosamond could think of no more powerful motive for a wife to kill her husband than learning that what she believed to be an idyllic marriage was, in truth, a lie. Disillusioned, angry, hurt – what woman would not strike out at the cause of her pain?

It was Isolde herself who answered Rosamond's determined knocking at the door of the mercer's shop. In the short time since Rosamond had last seen her, she seemed to have aged. There were deep shadows around her eyes and her shoulders slumped. Her movements were listless . . . until she belatedly recognized her visitor.

'You!' Isolde's eyes flashed with pure hatred. 'What have you done?'

'The real question is what have *you* done?' Rosamond pushed past her into the shop, closely followed by Melka, Charles and the two henchmen.

From one moment to the next, Isolde's fury turned into alarm. Her hands trembled as if she was afflicted by a palsy. 'I do not know what you mean,' she whispered.

'Yes, you do.'

Taking the other woman's bony arm with one hand and carrying a lantern in the other, Rosamond drew her out of the shop through the workshop and warehouse beyond and out into the kitchen yard. Together they mounted the outer stair that led to Hugo's counting house. On the landing, a small square space enclosed by decorative railing, Isolde attempted to break free, but she was no match for Rosamond. Determined to force her prisoner to return to the scene of the crime, Rosamond tightened her grip and hustled Isolde inside.

A quick but thorough survey of her surroundings assured her that no potential weapons were near at hand. 'We will talk here, in private.' To emphasize that point, she closed the outer door. Her escort remained on the other side, having followed only as far as the small, cobblestone-paved kitchen yard. They were obeying her orders. She wished to question Isolde without witnesses in the hope that would make the other woman less reluctant to confess. She gave Lina's sister a none-too-gentle push toward the window seat and released her.

Rosamond settled into what must have been Hugo's chair. The cushion was deeply indented. 'Let me make this easier for you, Isolde. You confronted your husband in this very room right after you returned from speaking with Cecily Kendall.'

The silkwoman sent Rosamond a narrow-eyed look. 'You are mistaken. I did not believe a word that old witch said.'

'But you did go and talk to her. You went to Lime Street right after you overheard Lina tell your husband what Widow Kendall knew about Alessandro Portinari. You had to discover for yourself whether or not it was true. Mayhap you even felt some belated compulsion to protect your sister.'

Isolde glowered but said nothing.

'Your manner provoked the widow. She told you why she believed Alessandro Portinari to be diseased. Then she revealed that your own husband went with the Florentine to a notorious bawdy house in Clerkenwell and remained behind after Portinari left.'

'Lies. All lies. She is a vicious old beldam.'

'Misguided, mayhap, but the boy she sent to follow Portinari saw what he saw. It is not difficult to work out what happened next. You came home and accused your husband of being unfaithful to you.' Rosamond frowned, remembering something else she knew about the night Hugo Hackett had been murdered. 'Portinari was still with Hugo when you returned.'

Isolde kept her lips firmly pressed together, but the twitch of a facial muscle gave her away.

'If not for that, Hugo might have convinced you that he only went to Black Luce's because Alessandro Portinari insisted upon bringing him along as a witness. He might have claimed that he never availed himself of the services offered there. But you would have known he lied if you overheard what Portinari discussed with him. What the Florentine said must have confirmed what Widow Kendall told you.'

Rosamond glanced toward the door that led to the rest of the house. It was easy to imagine Isolde standing on the other side with her ear pressed against the wooden panels.

'It is no good denying it. I know that your husband sent word to Portinari after he locked Lina in her bedchamber. He told Portinari about Cecily Kendall's claims and how Lina reacted. Portinari rushed here at once, determined to assure Hugo that the old woman was mistaken. What more natural than for him to remind Hugo that he already knew this, having been with Portinari at Black Luce's house? Did Portinari also remind Hugo that he had stayed on after Portinari left? Mayhap Portinari even made mention of paying for the whore Hugo was to mistreat that night. Did he let on that he knew Hugo was a frequent patron of other, less expensive stews? Your husband, Isolde, was the sort who'd hire a poxy whore for fourpence if she'd let him do what he liked to her.'

'Stop!' Isolde clapped her hands over her ears and squeezed her eyes shut.

'Whatever you heard that night made it impossible for you to deceive yourself any longer. Your husband had been betraying you for years, regularly going from a whore's bed to yours.'

Isolde came up off the window seat in a rush and threw herself at Rosamond with such force that the chair she was sitting in toppled backward. Rosamond's head hit the floor with a thump, momentarily stunning her. She barely had time to raise her arms to protect her face before blows began to rain down on her. Isolde might be all skin and bones, but there was strength behind the fists she used to pummel her adversary.

Encumbered by her cloak, her skirts, the chair, and the furious woman on top of her, Rosamond was unable to roll aside. She bucked, attempting to throw off her attacker, but Isolde tightened her knees to hold Rosamond's legs immobile and continued her assault. One blow slipped through Rosamond's guard and left her with a split lip. She tasted blood.

'I'll kill you before I'll let you spread such lies,' Isolde shrieked.

'They are not lies!' Rosamond's words came out in short, breathless bursts as she struggled to dislodge the maddened woman. Her strength ebbed as the throbbing in her head increased. 'You killed your husband. You seized the knife he'd been using to slice cheese, and you stabbed him to death.'

Another blow landed, this one squarely on Rosamond's nose. Blood spurted. Some of it spattered Isolde.

She reared back, a look of horror on her face. 'Blood,' she said in a hoarse whisper. 'There was so much blood.'

She staggered to her feet but seemed unable to remain upright. In a welter of billowing skirts, she sank to the floor. As suddenly as her assault on Rosamond had been launched, it came to an end.

Fumbling with one hand for a handkerchief to hold to her nose, fighting dizziness, swaying a little, Rosamond shifted so that she could roll onto her knees. She kept a close watch on Isolde, but all the fight seemed to have gone out of the other woman. She sat bolt upright, her eyes glassy and her expression devoid of emotion.

'Isolde?' Rosamond crawled toward her until she could place one hand on her arm. If Isolde felt the touch, she gave no sign of it.

Was this how she had been after she killed Hugo? Rosamond imagined Isolde retreating to her bedchamber, leaving her husband's body here in the counting house. Had there been blood on her hands or on her cuffs? That would have been easy enough to explain away if she touched the body after Lina sounded the alarm. Isolde had been the first to respond to her sister's screams.

Rosamond could almost sympathize. Enraged by Hugo's betrayal, Isolde had struck out. Then, shocked and horrified by what she had done, dazed and confused, she would have been incapable of rational thought. Rosamond could picture her sitting like this, alone in the dark in her chamber until she was jerked back to reality by Lina's terrified cries.

It was what Isolde had done next that Rosamond could not forgive. She had seized the opportunity to blame her own sister for Hugo's death.

Rosamond got slowly to her feet, hauling Isolde up after her. It was time to send for Constable Dodge. Even if she could not prove that Isolde had killed her husband, she could bring charges of assault against her. Bright drops of blood still dripped from her nose.

Just as they reached the door that led into the house, it was flung open from the other side. Rob's broad shoulders filled the frame. His jaw dropped when he saw the ravages to his wife's face but it was relief that showed most plainly in his eyes. 'Thank God you are safe.'

Rosamond let go of Isolde's arm and lifted her fingers to Rob's lips before he could say another word. 'I know I should have waited for you, but it is over now. Lina did not kill Hugo Hackett. Isolde did.'

The sudden dilation of Rob's pupils was the only warning Rosamond had. She whirled around, expecting another attack, but Isolde was moving away from her. She opened the outer door just as Rosamond started in pursuit

Isolde halted on the landing. There was no escape that way. Charles and the henchmen guarded the foot of the stairs. Eyes, wide and terrified, met Rosamond's as Isolde looked over her shoulder. Then she was swarming up the railing.

'I won't let them burn me!'

Rosamond made a grab for the back of Isolde's skirt. She caught hold of it. For a moment, she thought she might be able to prevent the silkwoman from taking her own life.

In the next instant, the smooth fabric slipped through her fingers.

Isolde plummeted to the unforgiving cobblestones that paved the kitchen yard. By the time Rosamond reached her side, she was unconscious from a grievous wound to the head. Within the hour, she was dead.

FORTY-SIX

When the city gates opened at dawn, Lady Appleton's coach crossed London Bridge and returned its occupants to Willow House. There Rosamond surrendered herself to her foster mother's care, accepting possets and poultices and worried frowns and the necessity of recounting everything that had transpired in Lime Street and Soper Lane. It was some time before she could escape to the sanctuary of her bedchamber.

She'd thought she wanted to be alone . . . until she found Rob waiting for her.

He had been her strength throughout the long hours following Isolde Hackett's self-murder. The ordeal had left them both exhausted.

'Did you see Andrew?' She settled deeper into the soft down mattress at his side. Rob had gone to his friend's chamber while Rosamond reported to Lady Appleton.

She felt him nod. 'Needham was awake and appears to be on the mend. My heart is much lighter for knowing that, but I am even more relieved that you are safe.'

'I did not intend to put myself in danger.'

'You never do.'

Rosamond bit back a sharp retort and instead said, 'It was well done of you to discover where I'd gone and come to my rescue.'

'If Isolde Hackett had been armed, I'd have arrived too late to save you.'

Rosamond said nothing. He was right. She had not had time to reach for her knives. She was not certain she would have used them even if they had been within reach. The taking of a life left scars, even when it was done in self-defense.

'I think . . . I think I should like to try living a more conventional life.'

She heard Rob's breath catch. 'Does that mean you will give up wearing disguises?'

Rosamond started to laugh and winced when that made both her nose and her lip sting most abominably. 'I will consider putting aside the boys' clothing.'

'I have an idea. Let us henceforth face the world together. I will have your back, and you will have mine.'

She snuggled closer, ignoring the numerous aches and pains now making themselves felt. Even Mama's nostrums were not strong enough to quell them all. 'I like this plan, but we must also promise never to keep secrets from one another.'

She felt him tense.

'It was the pain of disillusionment that drove Isolde Hackett to kill.' Rosamond lifted one hand to stroke Rob's smooth-shaven cheek. 'If you have been in the habit of visiting whores, you had best tell me now.'

'You know I have not.' He caught her fingers and brought them to his lips. 'Rosamond, when I was in Muscovy—'

'Oh, I know about that.' She interrupted before he could confess details she had no desire to hear. 'That is in the past. It is the present that matters.'

'The present and the future. I wish I did not have to return to Cambridge.'

'It is a necessary separation but blessedly brief, and you will return to me by Easter.'

'That is time enough for Walsingham to approach you. What if he tries to recruit you again?'

'You worry too much. That possibility may never come to pass. Even if it does, I know how to say no.' She trailed her fingers over the coverlet and then beneath, until she could tug at his nightshirt. 'Surely we have much more pleasurable ways to occupy ourselves until you have to leave.'

In some matters, they were indeed of one mind. They passed what time remained before Rob's departure in a most satisfactory manner.